with the

# Winds

catching

# Sunlight

# Winds with the catching Sunlight

## NELLY ALIKYAN

*For my future husband.*
*May I always feel at home with you.*

# ALSO BY NELLY ALIKYAN

*Catchers Series*

With the Flames Catching Midnight

With the Rains Catching Dawn

With the Ice Catching Twilight

With the Storms Catching Dusk

With the Winds Catching Sunlight

With the Ashes Catching Daybreak

*Whittle Magic Series*

Alluring Darkness

Beholding Darkness

Claiming Darkness

Desiring Darkness

# ALSO BY N. ALIKYAN

Buttercup Baby

Promise of A Lifetime

# SOUNDTRACK

1. Give Me Love by Ed Sheehan

2. Once in a Lifetime by Landon Austin

3. All For You by Dean Lewis

4. Minefields by Faouzia & John Legend

5. By Your Side by Tenth Avenue North

6. Obsessed by Dan + Shay

7. Can't Take My Eyes Off You by Frankie Valli

8. Beautiful As U by All-4-One

9. Give You Love by Forest Blakk

# PROLOGUE

## ASHTYN

Every tendon of muscle within the older woman's body was visible behind Ashtyn's closed eyes. She saw every healthy bit and guided a specimen from each of those to the wound in Lori's side. The woman shouldn't have a stab wound, but she'd been attacked by a group of men trying to take advantage of women and children and fought to give the Master Assassin enough time to catch up to them.

She was truly the hero here. It wasn't her job to fight off attackers like it was the Assassin's, yet she'd done it. Selflessly.

Ashtyn felt the specs of healthy tissue moving through Lori's system as if they were beneath Ashtyn's own hands, soft as they brushed beneath her palms.

She stopped the movement once the tissues reached Lori's open wound and settled them there as if tucking each bit into bed. They snuggled in together and slowly began closing the wound, blood clotting to refrain her from bleeding out.

As Ashtyn's eyes fluttered open, she caught the ashen whiteness of Lori's face but ignored it to place her full attention on the wound. It was drying up slowly and would give

Ashtyn time to sew it together to heal properly. She didn't waste any more time and turned for her washing materials and thread and needle.

Ashtyn dipped her hands, which were dirty from all that she'd already worked on and the blood from this wound, into the water to clean before she carefully took the washcloth and tapped away at Lori's side in order to prevent it from infection and make it presentable for a proper suture. Then she rewashed her hands and picked up her final pieces, eyes dropping in desperation to be done here and head to bed.

She fought the need and smacked herself in the face a moment to keep awake.

Her abilities made her feel like a magician sometimes, that control over muscle and tissue she shouldn't have, but she wasn't one. If she were, she'd be able to help Lori through this next part. She didn't even have a remedy for Lori to drink to wash away the pain.

Ashtyn brushed at the dirty sweat on her forehead with her arm as she steadied her hands and pinched the two sides of the wound together. She hardly allowed herself to blink as she began closing the wound, piercing one end then the other until the thing was pinched together. Lori groaned the entire time, but Ashtyn ignored it. The woman could handle a bit of pain if it was going to save her life.

After tying off the string and finalizing her inspection of the wound, Ashtyn stood on wobbly legs and called to no one in particular, "She's done. She needs her rest and good taking care of!"

Ashtyn didn't stick around to see which one of them came to Lori's help. Instead, she moved through the wide tent until she dropped before another woman.

"What's your name?" She'd tried at the beginning to make her voice sweet, but it was nearly thirty-six hours later, and she couldn't be bothered any longer. The kids had come first, and she'd been soft enough with them.

"Pina," this woman groaned.

"We've cleaned it and tried to piece it together, but it keeps bleeding out," a man double Ashtyn's age said with wide eyes and a croak of hysteria about him.

Ashtyn sighed. She knew the others within this village had attempted to help the wounded in the time Ashtyn took with the others, but sometimes their help only meant more work for her.

Ashtyn sanitized her hands once more, then grabbed the small dagger to cut the sutures that were made on the woman's torso. "Can you tell me what happened?"

Pina cried. "They cut my baby out. My baby... my ba—"

"Shh," the man cooed at her, rubbing her hair back. "Your baby is safe and with the women of our village. She will be here and healthy for you when you are better."

Pina gave a grateful sigh and a single glance in the man's direction told Ashtyn he'd had to remind her of this fact a dozen times already. She wouldn't fault the woman though. To go through such trauma was one thing. To have her baby in danger along the way was a whole other form of torture.

Ashtyn fought her eyelids as they closed, then shook herself to force some adrenaline to pump. Being that she was brought in only a little while ago, Ashtyn had only just noticed Pina.

The Master Assassin must've been finding these women and children little by little as he made his way through the group he'd stopped this time because they kept coming in. It'd been quiet for a few hours now though, Pina and her baby having been the last to come, so Ashtyn reminded herself that after this one, she could sleep.

With the wound opened, Ashtyn settled her hands above

it, and closed her eyes, focusing on the tendons within Pina rather than the tug for rest her mind was begging her for.

There was a tear inside from the improper removal of the placenta. She assumed that was done by the savage men and not by this man trying to help her now. Ashtyn then traveled through Pina's body, finding areas of pure health, and spoke to those sections. *Come*, she whispered to them. *Come and help Pina live.*

She took a large inhalation as the healthy muscles moved through the woman's body, all twirling around the wound before finding their resting spot. Then they landed and closed their eyes, allowing their health to aid in Pina's recovery.

Ashtyn felt them tingling her palms and knew Pina was on her way to recovery when the attention to her palms stopped.

When Ashtyn opened her eyes, Pina's eyes were closed, but her heart had felt fine. The woman needed sleep and hopefully was in less pain now.

Ashtyn quickly cleaned her hands and finalized the last suture for the day.

She quickly and steadily closed the wound on Pina's stomach, then met the man's eyes. "You will stay with her?"

"Yes." He gave a thankful smile. "Thank you dearly."

Ashtyn forced her lips to lift but wasn't sure how convincing of a smile came out. She then rose to unstable legs and turned for the end of the tent they were in to go find the small tent the village had set aside for her.

It wasn't too often she got to use her special abilities on helping people. She helped whenever she was around and the need was there, but Ashtyn spent most of her time going over medical texts and making sure she understood other ways of healing. Ways that didn't include her special talent. She made sure she understood which remedies to give for which illnesses and what types of salves to use for which burns. Everything there was to know. She was determined to make something of her life. And she'd decided only a while back that her life would be that of a medic's. A healer's.

She knew she wasn't a good person, so hopefully this would balance out her life.

As she got closer to the exit of this 'infirmary,' the tent folds opened with two teenage boys with gashes and blood about them, so Ashtyn snapped herself awake. "You're hurt!"

"They'll be fine," a rough voice said from her side. "You need to rest."

Ashtyn turned her head to catch the speaker and felt like the world was slowing down and speeding up all at once. When she caught back up with it all, her gaze flickered up the form of a big man with dark hair and dark eyes. He was covered in blood but didn't look hurt in the slightest. "Master Assassin?"

"Yes." His tone was clipped, demanding. "The village can take care of them. They only have small gashes. You need to sleep."

Ashtyn shook her head and turned back for the boys who were now seated by the opening to the tent. She would heal them. She would be a good person.

Ashtyn moved for them, legs unstable and vision blurring. "I can heal them. A couple more minutes won't hurt m—"

She crumpled into a large body.

He lifted her into his arms, and Ashtyn's head lolled back as her gaze barely picked up the Master Assassin. "You need to rest."

"I don't ne—" Could he hear her? Was she speaking aloud or in her thoughts? Were her eyes open? She saw the swings blowing in the cool winds as a little blonde girl ran about laughing. She saw the girl squeal as her name was screamed and a hand reached for her. She saw...

# CHAPTER 1
# ASHTYN

Ashtyn was in an unfavorable mood.

But was she ever in a favorable mood for this to be considered unfavorable?

Yes.

Yes, when she was trying on gowns, she was in the most favorable of moods. Ashtyn loved gowns, and especially those made by the magical hands of Atiana St Bonémore.

She turned, her strides forceful and ruthless, toward the dining hall where she would be meeting with the Posse, the King's most inner circle, to discuss matters of the plague in the north of the lands and the possibility of her becoming a Master. The latter was the part that scared her more than anything. She'd always been aware, quite incessantly and annoyingly, that she was probably a Master Healer, and she'd never been a fan of the idea because apart from the Master Magician who had been able to conceal her identity, Masters lost much of their privacy. Once it was made aware that a Master was in the vicinity, said Master had eyes on him the entire time. She knew Sparrow, the Master Assassin, only got away with it because he was also a spy thus able to conceal his identity better than most.

Plus, she was nervous. She was a healer, through and through, but part of her was afraid to admit that she felt like a magician sometimes. Like a fraud of a magician. A magician unable to do much else but heal.

When she arrived, everyone was there and chatting among themselves. It was a sight Ashtyn assumed might be quite overwhelming for most. The King, his twin daughters with their men, the Master Assassin and an Island barbarian; their closest friends and spies Miels and Tristan with their women, the Remedies Expert and an Island barbarianette, and the two warrior best friends, Gemma and James.

It was a lot of eyes on one person.

A lot of powerful eyes.

Ashtyn closed the dining hall doors behind her, then took her seat beside Gemma in their unassigned assigned seats. She appreciated having the women about in case she needed them to advocate for her against their men.

Seated at the full table, Ashtyn remembered only a year ago when the King's entourage was smaller leaving chairs empty with only five members to the Posse. Back when he hadn't known of his second daughter.

"How was the dress fitting?" Rosaelia opened. "Atiana showed me the gown she designed for you. It was beautiful."

Ashtyn felt her insides flutter with excitement. "Atiana and I planned for it after this meeting."

Rosaelia's eyes sparked with mischief which made Ashtyn wary. What did the Princess have up her sleeve? She was normally the kinder, more reserved princess.

Ashtyn didn't question her, and Rosaelia didn't say any more as the King picked up conversation. "You know why you are here, Miss Dubois?"

Ashtyn swallowed. "I do."

"We've tried alternatives," Miels started. "Had Etel make vials for them. Started to teach the apothecaries other remedies they could use. None of it is helping with this specific plague. We've helped with other ailments but for this sickness in particular, it isn't working."

"We also can't know for sure your skill will work," Tristan picked up. "From the books we've read, plagues as hard as this one has been cured only by Masters—Healer or Sorcerer. As the Sorcerer is now dead, we need to rely on the former. This is, unless a magician is needed for anything airborne."

Ashtyn remembered the sight of the Master Sorcerer. Sparrow's mother. A Master who had given birth to a Master. It didn't happen often, if ever.

She'd died protecting Princess Rosaelia in the Island Nation, and though it was upsetting considering she had been an ally for a short period of time, Sparrow wasn't particularly saddened by the fact. The man hadn't known her and all he did know was that she'd left him and his father, then his father had been killed.

Ashtyn really couldn't blame him. She'd been the lousiest of mothers.

"But we're not sure if I am a Master." *I'm almost certain I am.* The thought scared Ashtyn more than she cared to admit.

"We know," Sparrow answered. "And I know you don't necessarily want to find out because you don't want the attention, like Evony doesn't. The problem being, Evony can work without others knowing, you need to be active and present. There will be no way to definitively hide your identity."

Ashtyn sighed. She almost wanted to throw her hands up and say she wouldn't be doing anything that might catch people's attentions of her especially unique abilities.

But she couldn't do that.

If there was a chance of her healing all these people from this plague, she wanted to do it. To be helpful in those people's lives in a way she couldn't always be here because she wasn't 'a true medic.'

"We'll test you before, of course," Evony added.

"Tristan and Norya will be taking you soon to meet with a couple of people with the plague that he knows," Sparrow informed her. "You will test your abilities on them. Whether or not it works, they will keep it a secret. It is only when it works and you truly begin healing—or more importantly, when we find the source of the problem and you heal that, that you'll truly be talked about. Which takes us to our next topic— finding this source. We are not yet sure what the plague is coming from, but we're almost certain it can be stopped by a Master Healer. In the event of an airborne sickness, a magician will be required and in that case, we will call for the South's help." He placed his hand on Evony's belly as if reminding himself that she would not be participating, away from the dangers of this plague, with him by her side the entire time.

The Northern and Southern Lands were open borders.

Except when it came to magicians.

They'd been outlawed in the North before the princesses had been born and had all congregated in the South.

Evony, being the Master Magician, was an exception for magicians in the Northern Lands. Because of her particularly amazing abilities, she was able to keep herself concealed, but most wouldn't risk that. Now with King Edmund trying to reverse the ruling of his father, there was a chance for magicians to move freely throughout both lands. With time.

Evony only smiled at her husband before meeting Ashtyn's gaze again, speaking of herself in the third person. "Unfortunately, though we have a Master Magician, she will not be able to help."

*Good.* Ashtyn thought. The very last thing she wanted was for Evony to put herself and her baby in danger for this. The girl had a tough life and she deserved to be happy now.

Ashtyn internally cringed. She sounded like a sap.

These were all things Ashtyn thought but never said. She didn't need the Magician thinking she actually cared for them. Still, she didn't like sounding like a sap even to herself.

"Okay," Ashtyn finally said. "And if we find that I don't need a magician?"

"If we find out you can heal the plague from bodies, then we'll be taking you around the towns to begin the process while we look into the source of the problem," Tristan answered.

"It will not be long after that begins that I will begin to receive missives from the South for you to present yourself to the council to be questioned and named a Master as we all know how quickly gossip spreads," the King continued. "It will be your decision whether you would like to attend or not, but it will become public knowledge."

"You'll already begin receiving attention, male attention specifically, when the gossip spreads that you can heal the plague," Sparrow added the part she'd been dreading the most. "It will be desired—a possible Master, even if you do not end up being named a Master, as a wife."

"There's no way to hide my abilities from running through the gossip mills or for the South to find out," Ashtyn relented the fact. "But will there be any way to stop those men from trying with me? Didn't you guys stop them with Emerald?"

"It took years of threats and slight shows of aggression since I couldn't actually kill them for it to get it in their thick skulls that Ro was off limits," Sparrow answered. "We can always do the same for you, but you would still draw the attention from all those men, especially those in power, and have a line waiting behind you. Ro can hide herself in plain sight when we're in villages and towns who do not recognize her, but you will be working. They will know who you are."

"The only real way to stop them," the King spoke up, "will be if you are already spoken for the way Evony was when Lord Alexei came for a visit."

The original Posse and the Southern couple smirked at one another at the memory.

"I need to be betrothed?" she exclaimed. Much of this conversation she'd been aware of and was simply hearing confirmation for. This little tidbit she'd never guessed.

"Technically," Sparrow answered. "It would only stop them for a bout of time, it may not even stop all of them. Betrothed means you're not yet tied to your man so there will be a chance that you could be theirs. I do not think you understand how desirable a possible Master will be, especially one tied to the crown. Some men would respect a betrothal, but others will allow their greed to dictate their actions. They'll attempt seductions in order to win you from your betrothed. Lords especially will be in that latter category. The only thing that will truly push them off is marriage. Then you will already be fully taken, and you could never become their wife, unless they tried to make you a widow, I suppose."

"So we let everyone believe her married," Norya concluded.

James laughed across the table. "I don't think lying will work."

"Why not?" Ashtyn asked.

"You know how strong the gossip mills are," Rosaelia spoke up. "Once your talent is known, it will run through the North. You'll be spoken of nearly as much as we are. They will find out the marriage never took place and the race to have you will escalate. Nothing short of a husband beside you will stop it."

"So they will only respect my boundaries if a man is around?" Ashtyn growled.

And people questioned why she hated them so much.

"Technically no," Miels answered. When all the women around the table, who looked equally as annoyed as Ashtyn, quirked their brows in his direction, he smirked. "Years ago, women used to throw themselves at Sparrow for a chance to be the Master's wife. They knew he wasn't married and weren't fooled by any mentions of betrothals. They made it clear that if he wasn't bound, then he was free rein."

Evony's brows furrowed at her husband. "Really? And how many of these women did you have fun with?"

Sparrow ground his jaw as he glared at Miels. His glance dipped to the army knife he had lying on the table, then back at his best friend.

"Don't glare at him," Evony moved into his line of sight. "How many, Sparrow?"

Poor Assassin. His wife was hormonal with pregnancy. Ashtyn couldn't imagine getting a *Master* magician jealous while her body was raging was such a smart idea. She'd likely kill everyone in this room to get her answers.

"I didn't do anything with any of them, love." Sparrow took her face in his large hands and leaned his forehead against hers. "*They* threw themselves at me. I pushed them away."

"And what made them finally stop?" She glared.

He cleared his throat. "I was staying at an inn and one of the women thought she'd sneak into my rooms." His wife stiffened and the room tingled with her magic. "She thought if she could seduce me into bed, maybe have a child to trap me, then she would become my wife. Not only a Master's wife, but the King's second too." He said that final bit with some vile.

Ashtyn could imagine he was just as used as she was. When these extraordinary abilities were made public, the public forget they were human still. Regular people, just like them.

"And?" Evony seethed, the magic in the air becoming stifling as everyone shuffled in their seats.

He swallowed. "There's a reason there're rumors of the things I might do to people if they don't follow the laws. I was so angry, I killed her. The entire suite was covered in blood. Women knew to stay away from me from then on. It's why everyone believed our betrothal immediately—because there was no reason for me to lie about it."

Ashtyn scoffed to herself. That wasn't why. It was because everyone in the palace could see how smitten the two were with one another from the first day. And what the palace knew, the gossip ran with.

Evony eased into his touch. "Good."

He finally broke into a chuckle as he kissed her.

The King cleared his throat as the magic receded and allowed them to breathe freely once more. "So, you see, it is not respecting only a man. A woman would've respected only another woman in Sparrow's case. It is needing to showcase that you are truly bound."

"You'll have time to think it through," Rosaelia added. "You will be going out for the test rounds in a couple of days. If your abilities do not work, then there will be no need to do any of this to begin with."

Norya leaned back in her chair. "Though we all know who she wants stuck by her side anyway."

Everyone laughed, even quiet little Etel, and Ashtyn had to stop herself from raging at them. This was still the King and his Posse.

She pushed out of her chair. "Let me know when we'll be heading out."

"Aye aye, Mrs. Stablehand." Evony's laughs followed her out of the room.

# CHAPTER 2
# GABRIEL

The corridors were alive with servants running about to get the day's work done. Gabriel smiled as he passed two who were on the older side, then chucked to himself as one blushed and twiddled her thumbs. He knew some of the servants thought he was cute, and he hoped they thought him a nice guy as well. He wanted to be remembered as good, not handsome or powerful. Just plain good.

Papa Iskan, the Southern man who had come to the North in search of Evony, always said he was as good a man as anyone could ask for. Papa Iskan wasn't shy about stating his opinion on matters, so Gabriel was especially comforted hearing it from him.

And though all that mattered to him, really the only opinion he truly cared for, was Ashtyn's. At the end of the day, if all else were happy with him and Ashtyn wasn't, none of it mattered. It was dangerous the amount of control that one woman had over him.

It was especially dangerous since Ashtyn did everything in her power to act as if she wasn't affected by whatever was growing between them. Part of Gabriel figured he should give up, but an even bigger—and very nagging—part of him knew that he couldn't do so. Nothing mattered to him as much as she did.

And everyone knew it.

Maybe while he was at the tailors, he could get her a gift. He knew how infatuated she'd become with many of the gowns Atiana made.

He was on his way over there anyway since Princess Rosaelia—who insisted Gabriel call her Rosaelia or the much less formal Ro—instructed him to do so in order to receive a surprise, so it wouldn't hurt to look. This was the second time today he was being sent for a 'surprise.' The first time, nothing had been there, but the Princess insisted it would be there now.

Gabriel wasn't sure what to expect when he arrived at the suite, but he hoped Princess Rosaelia wasn't trying to set something up between him and any other member at the palace. It had happened a couple of times in the past where someone tried to set him up with a beautiful woman, but he'd never felt inclined to be with any of them.

Gabriel turned the corner to the tailors suite which was a large space with multiple areas for all the tailors to work when they weren't working in their private suites. It was oddly quiet at the moment. "Atiana, excuse me, but the Princess asked me to—"

Gabriel's mouth ran dry.

Standing before him on a slight pedestal in the most beautiful gown Gabriel had ever seen was Ashtyn. His healer.

The gown fit all of her curves and was ivory with delicate butternut designs adorning the lower the dress went. It was sleeveless leaving her shoulders and collarbones completely barred, stunning.

Her gaze met his in the mirror. "What're you doing here?"

He cleared his throat. "The Princess told me there was something for me here. With Atiana." He tried to meet Atiana's gaze for longer than a glance, but he couldn't do so. Ashtyn as too hypnotizing.

Atiana's laugh was such a stark contrast to Ashtyn's grimace.

"I'm sorry, Gabriel. I do not have anything for you. Do you think the Princess was trying to be cheeky? Our healer here is my only appointment of the day."

Gabriel's eyes shined as he took his time trailing down Ashtyn's curves in that dress. "She's the best surprise of my life."

Atiana's own grin was wicked. "Yes. She fills the dress perfectly, doesn't she. I cannot imagine a better woman for it."

"She's incomparable, At. There is no better woman."

"She's right here!" Ashtyn barked as her cheeks began to heat.

Gabriel's gaze shot back up to meet hers through the mirror. "And do you not think yourself incomparable in that dress? You're a beauty."

"You need to stop," she seethed through gritted teeth.

Atiana giggled, pinning the final part of Ashtyn's dress. "Oh, stop it, Ashtyn. You know you like his attentions the way all the other women do."

Ashtyn's orbs darkened, then she grumbled, "I'm taking this off now."

Gabriel was stuck watching her hop off the pedestal and move for the back where she could get changed in the privacy the screens provided. Her hips swayed the entire way, and it took everything within Gabriel not to follow after her.

When she disappeared, and he knew she was stripping naked, Gabriel lost his inner battle, close to moving for her, when Atiana cleared her throat and brought him back to the present.

"You look like you've seen better days, Gabriel," she joked as she eyed his clothes. They were stained from all the time he spent in the stables, and there was a rip from where Bella, one of the horses, tried to get treats from his trousers.

He chuckled. "I'm slowly running out. Eventually I'll have to start working naked."

A barely hidden choke came from the back telling him that Ashtyn was intently listening in. She always was, even when she pretended she couldn't care less.

"Oh, I was going to offer you new clothes in exchange for riding lessons, but I don't think I can deprive the entire palace from such views."

Gabriel smirked. "Don't be a tease, At. Lessons for clothes would be an easy trade, and I can use them dearly."

Atiana smiled. "It is quite a bit colder now that it is nearing winter, so it may not be the best time to take lessons, but I'm not sure I want to wait any longer."

"No waiting needed," Gabriel insisted. "I'll call for you when the weather permits it. It is not always so bad in the autumns and winters."

Atiana was smiling when Ashtyn walked out in her normal baby blue dress with a frown about her stunning features.

"Why so glum, beautiful?"

"Don't call me that." She wouldn't meet his gaze.

"Is it because you had to remove the gown?" Atiana joked. "Don't worry. It'll be finished soon, and you can wear it as often as you'd like."

"Great." Ashtyn gave her a smile that wasn't convincing in the slightest, then turned for the door. "I need to get back now."

Gabriel allowed the healer to pass him and took a large

inhalation of her scent. Butterscotch, vanilla, and a bit of citrus. When his gaze met Atiana's, hers were glittering with a tease. "Shut up," he muttered, then turned for his girl.

"What do you want?" Ashtyn barked when he caught up with her.

"To walk you."

"I think I am going to walk to the edge of the Southern Lands. Truly get away from you."

Gabriel laughed. "I can saddle horses to make the trip easier. Or one if you'd like to share." He wiggled his eyebrows which seemed to deepen that frown on her face but made his smile wider.

"I'd rather walk." She sped up.

"Then I'll walk to the South with you. To the edge of the lands. Into the water if you'd like."

She didn't turn for him or say anything more, but her ears pinked. They only did that when she was forcing herself not to smile. It'd taken him the year of watching her intently to learn as much as he could about her, and that much he was very aware of.

He wanted to take her hand, place his hand at the small of her back or the nape of her neck, have her hold him the way Evony did Sparrow, but he knew none of that would be happening. At least not yet.

Soon though, soon. That's what he'd been telling himself all year.

GABRIEL HAD about an hour before he had to meet the others by the stables. He took the time to rest in the warmth of his cottage.

Seated at the small table, Gabriel bit into an apple as he went over his maps while he worked on his woodcraft. He placed the fruit on the edge of the table and picked up his knife and the piece he was currently working on.

The map before him showed the southeastern side of the Southern Lands. It was a part of the land that held the most magicians. He knew many Northerners and even Islanders had immigrated there when King Edmund's father made them illegal in the lands.

It was near those parts that the Master's council was located, right by where Gabriel had spent much of his youth.

Because of that upbringing, he understood much of the geography, but Gabriel liked to continue his education in case anything new popped into the area. Any new establishments or laws or changes.

It was in that area that Gabriel had learned his woodworking, the one thing he did in this world that offered him the most therapy.

His work with the horses offered him peace, as anyone who spent time with the animals would agree; his time chopping wood allowed his frustrations out, which was much needed now when his desire for Ashtyn felt stifling; his leather working was helpful in taking his focus for a few hours; his work around the grounds were amazing for him, anything from building fences to straightening out nails to creating cabins; but none of it settled him down the way woodworking did.

Gabriel had been nearly eight years old, having lived in the South for about six months, when one of the males in town had come up to ask him about the trees he spent so much time climbing.

*"Boy, I think you stare at trees more than lumberjacks." His growly voice boomed behind Gabriel, nearly frightening him. When*

*Gabriel turned from where he'd been calculating how best to climb this tree, he met the man's eyes as he continued. "And I would know. I do all my work with trees."*

*"I do not know why," Gabriel responded honestly. "I feel drawn to them."*

*"Aren't you the horse boy?"*

*He smiled proudly. "I am. But it is different with the trees. It feels like something to check up on from time to time but not anything I need to base my life around."*

*The man chuckled. "How strange you are, kid."*

*"Thank you." Gabriel had never taken that as an insult.*

*"You ever work with trees, kid?"*

*Gabriel shook his head, back to looking up at the large thing.*

*"Tell you what. How about you come apprentice with me a little? I can teach you to woodwork."*

*Gabriel's head snapped around. "Truly?"*

*The man gave a single nod. "Then you can create beauties out of the wood that comes from these trees." He smirked. "Maybe make your future ladies something."*

*Gabriel's brows furrowed. "Ladies? But I will have one."*

*The man smirked. "Just you wait, kid."*

*Gabriel didn't stay on the topic of girls. Right then, he cared more for the woodworking. "Gabriel. Your new apprentice's name is Gabriel."*

*The man chuckled. "Kody, kid. Your new mentor's name is Kody."*

Kody had been in his early thirties then and one of the best male figure's Gabriel ever had. He'd only been lucky that the man ended up falling for one of the magician's Gabriel lived with. He loved knowing the Southerners he'd left behind still led happy lives.

He stared down at the piece he was carving. Would it be

what he gave to Ashtyn, or would he make her something else? What would best describe his feelings for her?

Gabriel cleared his mind, going back to the map and trying not to think of that vexing woman. Currently he was carving a monument that stood at the edge of the town he'd lived in while in the Southern Lands. He didn't yet know what he would do with it, but he liked to remember the time with mementos like these.

He took another bite of his apple, putting it back down and continuing his shavings as he glanced out the window, knowing soon he'd go out to work but until then, he'd take pleasure in his therapy.

# CHAPTER 3
# ASHTYN

abriel's shining eyes from the dress fitting had her body tingling all night. So distractingly, she'd hardly been able to sleep.

Even now, a whole forty-eight hours later, her body remembered the way his gaze ate her up in that gown. It made her want to kill Atiana for ever creating such a beautiful dress for her and Rosaelia for sending Gabriel to see it. It became so much more difficult to fight any affection for the stable hand in situations like that.

Not to mention, being seen and spoken to in the way Gabriel did made her want to blush and... giggle. The thought of giggling made her sick... but it also made her want to giggle some more. She hated Gabriel even more for it.

As she walked, she made herself forget about that man by remembering another thing that happened forty-eight hours before—the meeting with the Posse. Her only saving grace from turning into a balloon of fire with fury was the reminder that it had happened to the Assassin as well.

His wishes hadn't been respected either.

It had happened to the Assassin as well.

That same reminder ran through Ashtyn's mind time and again to keep from raging at the whole of the male species as she subconsciously made her way to the palace greens. There was a reason Ashtyn hated people.

*But you still desire to heal and protect them.* That annoying part of her brain teased.

"Unfortunately," she whispered to herself.

If it came out she would be heading out to heal the source and the people, she would need to decide what her course of action was going to be. She didn't want to marry. But she certainly didn't want to wait around for men to take the threats from the Assassin seriously—especially because Sparrow wouldn't truly hurt them since that would feed the rumors that the crown used any means necessary for their end goals. Not to add, he was in no rush to leave his wife's side.

She sighed knowing that meant only the assurance that she was a taken woman would hold off attention.

Though she wasn't entirely certain of that matter. They were guessing, based off what had happened to Rosaelia and Sparrow, that she would garner so much attention. Ashtyn had to believe that even if she were to help, the men would recognize how unfavorable of a companion she would make.

She allowed a humorless laugh to pass her lips. Not too long ago—only a few years back—she would've been thrilled for the attention, for the chance to get her pick of any male. The chance to watch men *throw* themselves at her.

She leaned against the palace as her body stopped before the stables, the wind blowing a little stronger than normal as if to clear her mind of every stress she brought upon herself. This, stopping before the horses, had become a habit Ashtyn was trying to get rid of, but she'd only gotten so far as hiding away so she wasn't noticed.

Gabriel was working with the animals, his shirt sweat-ridden even in these winds. Papa Iskan was working with him, and they were laughing, free of all the care in the world. Though older, he was virile the way he worked alongside Gabriel, so Ashtyn wasn't surprised that Iskan pulled his fair share of the work. Mama Beni was a lucky woman to have him.

Watching Iskan work specifically always made Ashtyn smile. He did exactly what Ashtyn always told her patients—he continued moving. It was the best way to remain young. The Southern man was living proof of such a matter.

His dark skin shone under the sun as both men moved the hay for the horses feeding, then began cleaning each stall the animals lived in. Gabriel had that personality about him—one that made everyone comfortable around him. One that made others smile, that made them blush, that brought a lightness to their souls. He was only ever more reserved with the Posse because of their station. The man was the complete opposite of Ashtyn.

She didn't care for being nice to people and she certainly didn't care about making others smile. The Posse she was more careful with, yet still, she didn't particularly watch her tongue as well as she should've around them. Unfortunately that made the Master Magician like her more.

But they also had similarities.

Gabriel cared for living things the way she did. A similarity that put them on opposite sides of the same coin. While he saw the best in people, she wanted them out of her sight the moment they were healed. While he made jokes, she made threats. While he smiled, she grimaced. But they both cared for the living.

He was more than the charming stable hand. He'd shown himself in only the past few months as the protector too, both when they were after Evony and when they'd traveled north to the Island.

Did that mean he'd make a good husband?

Ashtyn snapped herself out of those thoughts the moment they entered her mind. She was being ridiculous. She wasn't going to marry anyone, and most certainly not Gabriel. He was a good man, the best she'd ever met. She most certainly wasn't going to tie him down to her simply to keep others away. She was strong-willed, she could hold off the seductions of those men on her own.

Ashtyn swallowed her irritation and turned away from the stables. The longer she stayed there, the more her thoughts would drift, and that was the very last thing she needed. Gabriel deserved a life of happiness, and she wouldn't steal that from him for her selfish needs.

She successfully made it to the palace steps, one foot inside, when a hand landed on her arm. When it turned her, she came face to chest with a sweaty shirt. She followed that glistering skin up to the charming, bright smile of the stable hand who had a chokehold on her thoughts.

She forced her lips down into a frown as opposed to the water-melting drool her body wanted to allow. "What do you want, Gabriel?"

"You know, if you'd like to watch me work, you can come closer. I'm sure it'd be more comfortable in the stables than standing by the palace."

She huffed to hide that she actually cared that she'd been caught. "I wasn't watching you. I was in my head and happened to stop there." Not entirely a lie.

His lips, still rounded in a grin, twitched like they wanted to laugh but fought against it. He was smart enough to know that would result in unfavorable consequences. "And what were you so deeply in thought about?"

She turned away from that pleasant face. "I need to get back to work."

His hand landed on the small of her back making her body straighten. "I'll walk you, and you can tell me what you were so deep in thought about."

The twinkle in his eyes said he noticed the way her body reacted to his touch and part of him was more than aware that at least part of her earlier thoughts included him. Charming, egotistical ass.

"I was simply thinking of the plague up north. I do not think there is anything amusing about it."

His fingertips lightly grazed her back, up to the middle then back again, causing her to falter her steps. Glancing his way proved he was in thought, unaware that he was even touching her like that.

"Has the Posse figured out if you can help?" He finally broke his concentration.

She swallowed to fight the memory of her meeting. "Most likely. We're going to test it with a few people first before allowing it to become known."

"Will there be any problems? Is that why you're so worried?"

"Other than possibly not being able to help them at all? I don't see why there would be."

His brows furrowed, more serious now. "When do you go?"

"In a few days."

"Do you need me to com—"

"No," she interrupted as they made their way into the corridor that led to the infirmary. "There will be no need.

Norya and Tristan will be with me. In any case, there would be no reason for you to be there."

Silence followed them the rest of the journey, Ashtyn trying her hardest not to notice how close Gabriel was the entire walk.

When they reached the infirmary doors, his hand fisted into the back of her dress as she tried to leave him for her makeshift office. He turned her to face him and caught her stare. "There is always a reason for me to be there when you're involved."

Her mouth moved to say something, then closed and tried again three times before she finalized, "You won't be needed. You should get back to your day."

She turned away, his hand still fisted in her dress and took a step forward. There was resistance from his hold, so she turned narrowed eyes on him.

She scoffed internally. She should've known that wouldn't push him away.

So she deepened the look, eyes darkening as if disgusted by him.

His darkened too.

But there was no disgust there.

Her body tingled more than it had at the dress fitting, sparks flying under her skin. And though his hold was on the back of her dress, Ashtyn gasped as his look turned darker and made her feel as if his hands were running up her skirts. Fingertips brushing her skin and making her want to clench her thighs together while he chuckled, spreading them even wider for his liking. From just that simple look, she could feel his tongue slithering up her thigh, and her pleasure dripping down her legs.

She didn't realize she was breathing hard until his attention jumped to her mouth.

Mortified, she turned back and tried for another step. When he didn't release her, she paused and waited, refusing to turn back.

After a minute, where she could feel the stares of two of the medics in the infirmary on them, he mercifully released her.

Her office was a space in the back that had two foldable walls put up to give the semblance of privacy. There was a curtain that acted as the door between the two walls, but it was still a haven for Ashtyn. None of the other medics ever bothered her in there, as if it were the Rivorbant Waters, the filthiest river in the world, at the very tip of the Island Nation.

Safe with her curtain closed behind her, Ashtyn finally allowed herself to take a deep breath in. She had work to focus on.

*THE BLONDE LOCKS of a six-year-old girl flowed in the winds as she chased her imagination in the gardens. Her squeals were loud and full of life. Her smile made everyone want to befriend her.*

*Yet she was alone.*

*The air wasn't filled with pollen. If it were pollen, she'd be sneezing wildly. But it looked like pollen. Like streaks of the tiniest pink balls dancing around her.*

*They were asking her to play, and she loved playing with them even though nobody else believed her when she spoke of them.*

*"What pinks balls?" She would be asked. "Pollen is yellow." The elderlies would smile at her lovingly.*

*She concluded them a part of her imagination and played with them still.*

*They liked taking her to the flowers. Fields and fields of wild-flowers, all blowing the same pink balls into the air. Such a heavenly smell and so... enticing. If only she could reach her hand out and grab them, she could bask in the euphoria of it all.*

*"Ashtyn!" Calls came for her, but she was too enraptured to turn away from these fields. They were leading her somewhere. Every time she ran after the pink balls, nostalgia hit as if the route she was headed on was one she knew, but at six years old, she didn't know very many routes at all.*

*"Ashtyn!" Another called for her as she stepped over cracks and twigs, feeling airborne as she flew through the fields, the grass tickling her feet.*

*The loudest call came again, and her head snapped back.*

Ashtyn's eyes popped open, body springing from where she'd slumped over her desk in her makeshift office. There was a bit of sweat running down the back of her neck and she felt discombobulated, taking longer than she would've liked to remember where she was.

She didn't normally fall asleep in her office.

Ashtyn fell back in her chair and sighed. That vision of the six-year-old girl didn't come to her often, but she knew there was meaning behind it. She'd seen it at the beginning of this year. She'd seen it when Sparrow had found her and brought her to the palace. She'd seen it when she'd washed her past away and decided to become a healer.

And again now.

She still hadn't figured out the meaning behind it, but as her gaze traveled to the window in her little office, Ashtyn swore she saw the tiny pink balls of not pollen calling for her.

She shook her head as a call for her name roared through the infirmary. "Ashtyn!"

Ashtyn grumbled under her breath as she rose from her comfortable chair and yanked the curtain to her office open, the head medic standing before her. "You could've simply come in, you know."

That probably wouldn't have been a good idea. Had Old Lady Arba found her sleeping, she would've thrown the largest hissy fit.

Arba grimaced, looking past Ashtyn's shoulder to the small space like she'd catch an infection simply by stepping in it. "I could also simply let go of you."

Ashtyn made herself smirk even though she wasn't in the mood to play games with the woman. "We've spoken of this before, Arba. Go ahead. Let's see what the Assassin thinks about that."

Arba ground her jaw, eyes flashing with hatred, right before she turned for her office. "Come here."

Ashtyn's smirk felt authentic now as she followed the woman. The best part about being hired by the Master Assassin himself, and in turn being the Posse's go to medic, was that none of the other medics, no matter their station, could fire her. None of them could do a thing about her in any capacity, and Old Lady Arba hated that fact more than any of the other medics in the infirmary.

When they reached the head office and Arba moved for her desk, Ashtyn paused by the door. "What may I do for you, Your Highness?"

Arba's eyes narrowed. "You may begin with showing me some respect."

"I do for you as you do for me."

Her fists landed on the table and held her as she leaned over it, eyes darkening. "You will not last long here, charlatan."

"Name calling. That's mature."

"Very much so when it is the truth."

Ashtyn crossed her arms before her chest. "What do you want, Arba?"

Her eyes darkened as if she were going to come up with more fun names but decided against it at the last moment and nodded for the corner of her office. "Those boxes were just brought up. I need each one filed in sickness, then alphabetical order."

Ashtyn scoffed. "That's busy work."

"Given to those without the talent or skill to do real work. Now get to it."

"No."

Arba quirked a brow, demeanor darkening even still. "Excuse me, girl?"

"You heard me. No. If you have a problem with that, have a talk with the Assassin. Actually, have a talk with the King. He has another project for me and the very last thing I'm going to do as I prepare for it is sit around and file for you."

"I am your superior!" she roared, indignant.

Ashtyn fought from rolling her eyes. "You are many peoples superior, but mine you are not."

"Excuse me?" she seethed.

Ashtyn stepped into the room and didn't stop until she was right before the desk. "I am the Posse's medic, Arba. I know how much that eats away at you." She gave a mocking laugh and right before she turned to leave, smirked. "All those others you're superior too, though, I'm sure they'd do splendidly at filing. Arron especially."

Ashtyn left without waiting for more insults, though she heard the ends of some. She was back in her little office enjoying the memory of Arba's red angered face. Sure, insisting she should have her son do the work because he was good for nothing else was probably a low blow, but she deserved it.

And he did too. The man only worked in the infirmary because of his mother. He was awful with injuries.

Ashtyn stopped by the window she had fought for in her office. Arba had wanted her two foldable walls to be placed in front of a stark wall, but Ashtyn had put her foot down.

Sparrow had been entirely on her side, shocked enough that she'd relented to the two walls instead of a real office to begin with.

Staring out at the beauty of the day, Ashtyn focused on the winds blowing at the little cottage at the end of palace grounds and swore she saw those little pink balls.

She breathed slowly.

# CHAPTER 4
# GABRIEL

The set of clothes Atiana sent to his cabin the night before had been a lifesaver. He'd sweated through his last remaining good shirt the day before and though he'd washed it and hung it to dry, Gabriel hadn't wanted to wear the old thing for a third day in a row.

This new set of trousers and shirts were clean, made with materials he'd never felt before, and fit him perfectly. This material felt thicker and like a richer fabric, so he hoped these clothes would last him longer.

Atop his trouser and shirt, Atiana also added a jacket to pair with the fits. He was grateful for it given the chill outside and the fact that his own was weathered down a bit more than he'd realized.

Though he was aware that riding would make his body warm enough to not need it, Gabriel put the jacket on as he began to leave his cottage to meet with the tailors assistant by the stables for her first lesson. It still shocked him that with all her years at the palace, this would be her first lesson. He supposed he never really thought about if any of the palace help knew how to ride, but it was something he would begin to question more and more now.

She was waiting outside the stables when he got there, her body stiff and expression tight.

He gave her a warm smile in hopes of making her more comfortable. "You could've gone in to the horses. You didn't have to wait out here for me."

She cleared her throat. "I've never really been this close to the horses before. I didn't want to… upset them."

He chuckled, then nodded for her to follow him inside. "You will not upset them."

Half of the animals inside had their heads out like they wanted to be pet or chosen for a ride. As Gabriel pet Arcana, Sparrow's horse, he turned to find Atiana in the middle of the stables, too far away from any of them to touch.

"Are you all right, Atiana?"

She nodded, her gaze latched onto each animal.

"Are you afraid?"

She gave a slight chuckle and looked so stunning as her embarrassed eyes met his. "Pathetic, I know. Everyone in the nation is around horses at some point or another. I just… always stayed away from them."

"What made you change your mind now?"

She shrugged. "We are in the palace. Even as help, we are given privileges others do not have. I plan on staying here the rest of my life if I can help it. I think after six years, it's about time I do this. And I trust you not to make too much fun of me."

He bit the inside of his cheek to hide his amusement. "Of course. How about we spend today getting comfortable around the animals, then next time we can get atop?" It made wearing this jacket an even better idea now that he wouldn't be sweating while riding.

Her shoulders deflated. "That would be lovely."

"Come on." He motioned for her to follow him to the first animal. "I'm right here. They won't hurt you."

When she finally moved for his side, he slowly got her to pet the horses, then gave her sugar cubes to get her comfortable around their mouths. He moved her from Bella, who was Princess Rosaelia's horse, to Arcana and Barclay and London and down each animal.

It was astonishing. Her outward nature was the complete opposite to Ashtyn's, yet the horses seemed to take to them both easily. Inwardly though, Gabriel thought them the same and that was what the horses were picking up. Both Atiana and Ashtyn were soft on the inside. Ashtyn simply had something holding her back from allowing others to see it.

The horses didn't seem to care. They knew the real her.

Gabriel knew the real her.

When they finished through each horse, one in particular neighed for more attention. It stopped Gabriel in his spot when Atiana smiled and moved for it with such ease. While Bella was the best-trained horse, thus the reason behind being the Princess's, Absko was the largest. Gabriel would've guessed Atiana would be most frightened by him, but the two seemed to gravitate toward one another.

"He normally doesn't like people much." Gabriel stopped behind her as she brushed his mane. "It is difficult even for me to get him to like me at times."

Atiana laughed. "He's my favorite. He's so large, but so gentle."

Gabriel scoffed. "Maybe with you." Absko was the reason behind half of his ripped clothes.

The horse huffed at Gabriel as if telling him to shut up before he made Absko look bad in front of the pretty girl. It made Atiana laugh which got a delighted neigh out of the animal.

"If you're so comfortable, we could always move your riding lesson back to today." Gabriel smiled at the way the two were together. He loved when people grew relationships with his horses. They were like babies to him, and he wanted everyone to love them as much as he did.

"That would be lo—"

"Gabriel." The King's voice boomed through the stables as he made his way inside, looking down at his hands as he fixed his shirt. "Get Absko ready, please. I am goin—"

As he looked up, his gaze landed on Atiana next to his horse, then to Gabriel, darkening in a frightfully dangerous way.

"Right away, sir." Gabriel turned sorry eyes on Atiana. "Turns out the ride will be postponed after all."

She nodded as she swallowed back her nervousness, but her beautiful brown orbs never left the King's. The two stared at one another and neither moved.

Gabriel felt tension fill the air around him and as he tried to figure out what had happened, he found himself narrowing his gaze at the tailor then the King then back again. He cleared his throat. "Atiana, if I could get to—"

"Absko is your horse?" she asked the King. "I thought yours was Lorenth."

Edmund's jaw hardened and his gaze was less than forgiving. "Lorenth died last week. I got Absko in Lorenth's declining health."

"I'm sorry." She remained by Absko's side, letting him nuzzle at her for comfort.

Edmund only gave a nod of acknowledgment, never breaking his stare.

Gabriel cleared his throat once more, needing to get to the horse to prepare him for the King.

Atiana jumped this time, finally peeling herself away and

dropping her eyes. "I'm sorry," she apologized to Gabriel this time, then made a bow of the head to the King without meeting his gaze. "Have a nice trip."

Gabriel wanted to step out with Absko to give them the privacy they so desperately needed, but she was running off before he could do so. The tension didn't die out with her departure, but it wasn't as heavy any longer.

He couldn't believe there weren't rumors around the palace about the two of them if that's how it felt when they were in the same space. He most certainly wouldn't send them around, especially considering he had no idea what exactly was going on between them, but it felt impossible that he hadn't already heard of it.

"What?" Edmund barked when his gaze finally peeled away from the direction she'd gone.

Gabriel should've focused on getting Absko ready, but instead, he said, "You watch her like I watch Ashtyn, sir."

The King didn't acknowledge the comment. "Just prepare Absko, please, Gabriel."

"Right away, sir," Gabriel basically whispered after witnessing the desire and defeat in the King's eyes.

GABRIEL DIDN'T NORMALLY GET visitors to his cottage. It was closer to the woods than the palace, with the expanse of greens separating the two, and the perfect reprieve from a long day outdoors. He didn't mind being the one to prepare everything himself and enjoyed that he had a place that belonged solely to him. He could be offered a suite with the Posse—beautiful living spaces cleaned regularly, hot food prepared and ready when mealtime came, all of it included—and he still wouldn't take it.

He enjoyed the peace in his space. Enjoyed the privacy. Without so many people about, he could do whatever he pleased. The only thing that would make this perfect was convincing Ashtyn to join him in his cottage, making it a true home.

That peace he loved in his space, the one that allowed him to think of his healer while he worked on his carved wood pieces, came to an abrupt halt when there came a knock to his door.

Gabriel huffed knowing unless something had dramatically gone wrong with the horses, there should be no reason to disrupt him tonight. He grabbed a shirt to put on and was glad he'd done so when he opened the door to find Sparrow standing there.

The Master Assassin didn't make it a habit to visit him so late.

Gabriel instinctively stood a little taller. "Master. What can I do for you?"

He huffed. "Just call me Sparrow, Gabriel. We've been on enough trips for you to be trusted and part of my confidants."

Gabriel moved to give the man space to come in as his insufferable cheeks pinked, only ever happening in front of his superiors. "All right then. Sparrow. What can I do for you?"

"Do you remember when Evony first got to the palace, how she was bedridden within a couple weeks?" Sparrow asked as he leaned against the wall, respectably not touching any of Gabriel's things.

Gabriel's brows furrowed. "I do."

"It was because she'd expended too much of her magic trying to distribute a powder that could've poisoned the palace. She worked herself too hard, alone as she was."

Evony, along with being Sparrow's wife, was the Master Magician. It was an impressive feat to hear she'd done such an act, but the woman was a forceful being, so it wasn't shocking.

"Okay?"

"We've come up with different theories about this plague. Since we don't know what the cause is yet, we have to assume it all. And for most cases, Ashtyn—a.k.a. a healer with her special tendencies—should be able to help. But in the event it has to do with contamination of the air, a healer will be of no use. We will need a magician."

Gabriel finally caught on. "And Evony is pregnant, so..."

"So she will most definitely not be dealing with any of those problems."

"Why are you telling me this?"

"You knew Evony was the Master Magician."

Gabriel nodded. It wasn't long after they'd returned from getting Evony back from her mother directly after the rebels attacked the palace that Sparrow questioned him about said knowledge. "I did."

"I could have you teach Tristan and Norya since they will already be heading out with Ashtyn, but I think it'd be best with you there. And faster."

Gabriel stood taller at hearing his healer's name. And hearing there were plans for her to go anywhere.

The way the Assassin smirked in his direction, the man knew what was going through his mind that very moment. Gabriel could be annoyed with him, but he was far more thankful to have been informed. Ashtyn sure would've kept it from him.

"Where're we going? What will I need to do?"

"Ashtyn's leaving tomorrow to see if she can heal this sickness. Even if she can't heal the source whenever we find it, if she can help with the people, it'll be a lifesaver. Literally. While she's doing that, Tristan and Norya will be there for her protection, but we're not trying to draw attention until we're aware of her abilities. Once we know she can heal them, Tristan, Norya, and a few guards will be there to protect her but also to figure out what may be the root to this. You will do the same—protect her and figure out if there's a way a magician may be of use."

"What time will we be goi—"

Sparrow chuckled as he interrupted, "You're not going tomorrow."

Gabriel ground his jaw but was respectful as he got out, "If Ashtyn needs protecti—"

"She won't. She's going to heal only a couple people. They won't let the news spread. This is only to test if she can. In the meantime, Evony wants to see you."

That got Gabriel's attention almost as quickly as the fact that he couldn't be there for Ashtyn. "Why?"

His smirk was cocky now. "She wants to test your knowledge, see how useful you'll actually be. She's a bit upset that she can't be of use at the moment."

"Can't be of use or you won't allow her to be?" Gabriel asked before he could control the words from escaping his lips, cheeks pinking even deeper.

Sparrow only chuckled. "Tomato, tomato."

Gabriel sighed back the relief that he hadn't angered the Assassin, then asked the question nagging away at him, "What time will she be leaving tomorrow?"

"You are not going, Gabr—"

"I know. What time?"

Sparrow sighed. "A little after dawn."

He nodded. "And what time will I be needed with Evony?"

The Assassin shrugged. "Around noon."

Gabriel trusted Ashtyn would be okay for the day with the

two warriors by her side—though the thought that it may take more than a single day ate away at him—so he tried to be okay with not joining them.

"I'll be there," he finally informed the man.

Sparrow gave a knowing smile. "After you prepare Ashtyn with the safest horse and wallow after her for a few hours?"

Gabriel ignored the teasing, so used to it when it came to his healer. Most everyone at the palace had thrown a jab at him at least once. "Yes."

Sparrow moved for the door but paused before opening it. "I like you, Gabriel. You're honest, even when it's self-deprecating. I know I can trust you."

Gabriel smiled now. "Thank you, Master."

Sparrow shook his head and left Gabriel's cottage.

All alone once more, Gabriel was now caught with imaginings of traveling around the north of the lands with Ashtyn, about all the possibilities and opportunities to make her fall in love with him.

SOMETIMES, he really didn't understand why he liked her. She never smiled at him the way he wished for, never complimented him, never attempted to touch him no matter how many opportunities he tried to throw at her, never so much as outwardly reacted to his flirtations. He knew she liked him because as much as she tried to hide it, her eyes never lied to him, but it was a strain to never get anything back from his girl.

Even now, as dawn welcomed the day, she scowled in his direction as he secured Bella for her ride. The woman had her arms crossed over her chest as if he were trying to sabotage her safety rather than ensure it.

"Not a morning person, I see, beautiful." Gabriel gave her a warm smile.

"I had a dream that kept me up most of the night."

Gabriel's shoulders stiffened. "Nightmare."

"No." She glanced away. "Not this time."

He narrowed his eyes. "Was it about me?"

Her head snapped for him, and she was close to growling as she voiced, "Why would anything be about you?"

"Don't bite at me, Ashtyn. Something is bothering you."

"And you've decided you're it." She paused, then quirked her brow. "Actually, you're right. You *are* what's bothering me."

He forced a smirk he didn't feel as he stepped closer to her. "I'm going to take that to mean you had a wet dream and are too afraid to tell me, to allow me to ease your desires."

Her nostrils flared. "All the fawning of the women at this palace has gotten to your head, stable hand. I do not desire *you*."

"Oh? Is there another man then?" *I'll kill him.*

She smirked, her eyes sparkling with cruelty. "Oh yes. You should see the things he does to me. Wasn't around last night though. I was so, so frus—"

He slammed her into the wall. "Stop it!"

"You first!"

One hand remained caging her in as the other traveled down her dress, over her plump, heaving breast. "No one's touching you but me, Ashtyn. We both know this." His head fell into her shoulder. "Since we've met, you've been mine, Ashtyn. You know it. Please stop trying to hurt me." His hand wrapped around her waist as he lifted his head to meet her eyes.

There was a softness to them she was trying to hide as she

scowled. "I wouldn't have to make such ludicrousness up if you would stop implying I wanted anything with you!"

Gabriel breathed slowly, taking in this proximity with his girl, memorizing every inch she was allowing him to touch. His lips were so close to her, they brushed softly, but never enough. He needed to taste her, but she wasn't ready for it.

He finally cleared his head enough to say, "Please have a safe trip, beautiful. I'll be waiting for you. Please... please be good for me."

She scoffed. "For yo—"

His hand moved immediately from her waist to cradle her jaw. "For me, beautiful."

"I don't think my lover would appreciate that," she snapped, and though he knew she was lying, it broke a piece of his heart.

He finally stepped back. "Bella is ready for you."

She didn't acknowledge him as she got atop the horse and rode to where Norya and Tristan were already waiting atop their horses.

Gabriel watched the three of them ride off and tried to ease his pained heart. She'd been trying to hurt him, and it'd worked, but hopefully that was only because she was trying extra hard to fight her feelings for him.

As she disappeared into the forests, his chest stung, and he did everything in his power to stop from going after her.

# CHAPTER 5
# ASHTYN

The ride to this village was longer than Ashtyn had anticipated. It was a small place in the middle of the Northern Lands, too far out for gossip to spread immediately, especially if they kept things as well hidden as she was told would happen.

Because it was up north and they didn't want to tire Ashtyn out before she could test if her abilities worked against this plague, Tristan and Norya insisted they stop for the night rather than riding straight through. It made Ashtyn feel antsy to lay the night in bed, so close to her mission yet still so far away. It made her antsy not having that distraction from the events of the morning, made it impossible not to think of the dream that had led to said morning. The dream of a stable hand pushing her against the stable doors, her breasts heaving against the wood as he came in behind her and whispered dirty things into her ear; as his hands traveled down her body; as he slowly made his way down until he was beneath her skirts, kissing up her legs until...

She needed to forget about that dream and about her

morning and most certainly about stable hands. She'd never enjoyed sex in the past. She couldn't fathom why her mind had wandered there.

Listening to Tristan and Norya go at it in the adjoining room didn't exactly help in forgetting any of it though. Ashtyn made do by placing the earmuffs she used to combat the winds over her head and did everything in her power to spend the rest of her night thinking of their departure come morning.

It only lasted a few minutes before she was remembering the morning just past. Gabriel had been at the stables readying their horses and seeing them off. Though she'd expected nothing less, after the night she'd had, it'd been the last thing she'd wanted. He'd watched her so intently that Ashtyn's skin had been alight with goosebumps.

*"You're taking Bella," Gabriel demanded of her, tightening the saddle on the horse.*

*Ashtyn rolled her eyes. "I'm not a newbie here. I don't need the 'safest' one."*

*"You need whichever one I give you," he told her through clenched teeth. He wasn't angry, his eyes said that much, but the way he spoke made him seem upset.*

*Ashtyn wanted to argue but knew this whole exchange would end much sooner if she didn't. "Fine. Thank you."*

*Gabriel didn't look at her for a whole minute as her companions took their horses out of the stables, giving them a bit of privacy. Ashtyn grew antsy at the proximity of the stable hand she wasn't allowed to have.*

*She cleared her throat. "I need to go."*

*Finally, he turned to face her, eyes searching for something. They were soft, pleading almost. They were what happy dreams must've been made of.*

*He shocked her by taking her hands in his, thumbs rubbing*

*soothingly over the tops. "If anything happens, Ashtyn. I can't... I wouldn't be able to live with mys—"*

*"Nothing's going to happen." She wanted to remain by his side, but she pulled her hands away roughly. "You'll see when we get back." Because even if he wasn't waiting for her to return, he'd be waiting for the horses.*

*"Ashtyn."*

*"Gabriel," she said with authority, needing him to stop this infatuation. "I've told you time and again to find another woman to bother."*

*He didn't look hurt in the slightest. It shouldn't have been shocking. He never allowed her words to hurt him. He stepped away to finish preparing Bella for the ride. "I'll be waiting for you, beautiful."*

*Ashtyn convinced herself he was speaking to the horse and scowled so as not to encourage any more talk. Her demeanor darkened as she remembered the dream that had kept her up all night.*

*It got worse when he asked, "Not a morning person, I see, beautiful."*

She awoke with the memory of the previous morning imprinted in her mind like a dream. She readied quickly in order to erase the pictures, then made her way downstairs to await her companions while she had her breakfast. She'd been instructed not to ingest anything in town for precautions sake, so she pulled out the food the three of them had brought on the journey and took a bite.

Said companions came down about ten minutes later with sated grins about them making the grimace on Ashtyn's face deepen. "You two are pigs."

Norya made a mock of an upset face and pet Ashtyn's hair. "We are so very sorry, our grace of a healer."

Ashtyn snapped out of the way. "Just have your meals, so we can get started."

It wasn't long after then that the three were standing before the cottage of the man named Marcanz whose wife Annie was sick for the second time. He was a confidant of Tristan and Miels's and thus trustworthy to keep this secret.

When they entered the space, Ashtyn took in the little shop. It had small jars aplenty with different varieties of jams and spreads. It was a small space but felt homey.

Marcanz stood taller at seeing Tristan enter his shop, the man's eyes widening as if to ask if they were there to help. Ashtyn took him in. He was an old man, shorter with age now, and she was almost certain the wrinkles on his skin had doubled in the past year with his wife's constant sickness.

"Marcanz," Tristan opened. "I told you we'd be back to see if we can be of help. This is Ashtyn. She is not only our healer for the Posse, but we believe her to be one of the best healers of our time. She will be testing whether or not her abilities will work on this plague. This is Norya, the two of us are here for Ashtyn's safety."

Marcanz nodded and pointed an old finger to his front door. "Please lock up and follow me to the back."

Norya followed his instruction as Ashtyn followed Tristan to the back of the space where Marcanz had his living quarters with his wife. She'd been told on the way up here that Marcanz and his wife never wanted for more and any benefits earned from helping the Posse had been distributed to the village rather than kept for themselves. Essentially, they were some of the most selfless people alive.

Ashtyn scoffed to herself. That'll teach them. Selflessness only brought about pain.

The living quarter was made up of a small kitchenette to the corner, another door leading to the bathing chamber, and a foldable wall like the ones that made up her office in the palace to give them the semblance of a bedroom.

Marcanz moved the foldable wall so the bed was visible to all and lying in it was his wife Annie. She looked fragile, so weak, it was likely she'd die from that before any symptoms the plague brought on.

"Annie dear," Marcanz brushed his wife's hair back. "T is back with that healer he mentioned." Then he met Ashtyn's gaze. "Her voice is suffering from all the coughs, so she tries not to talk so much."

"That's all right." Ashtyn moved for the woman, sitting on the edge of her bed and taking her hand. "I work almost like a magician. I can normally sense the wound and help your body fix itself. The problem here will be finding it. I have never had to heal a non-existent wound."

The couple nodded, both wearing hopeful looks though they visibly tried not to put too much pressure on this trial. Ashtyn appreciated them for it, but she knew how disappointed they'd be if she couldn't help.

Annie's veins showed beneath her sweaty skin. She had a dusting of pinkish-lavender freckles marring her skin that didn't look consistent with any normal being.

As she released Annie's hand and moved hers above the woman's body, Ashtyn closed her eyes. It wasn't a necessity, but she always worked best this way.

She was instantly hit with a sickening need to pull away.

She fought against it, but it made her breath stop for a moment. She'd never healed a sickness this way, sticking to dealing with wounds instead, but she remembered being by Evony's bedside when she'd fallen bedridden and receiving a similar feeling. Evony had tired herself out depositing poisons in the winds. Was this the feeling of a poison or of a body too tired to help itself?

Though as Ashtyn tried again, she realized a very different feeling to when she'd been by Evony's side. Evony's body had pushed back, but it had felt light, airy. It was what had made Ashtyn so confident that Evony only needed sleep.

Annie's body wasn't like that.

Hers fought against Ashtyn almost like an army of guards standing at the entrance of Annie's body. Except these knights were trying to keep Ashtyn from the innocents inside. They were the villains.

Ashtyn fought against the overwhelming need to stop, to give up, to throw up, to lie down and sleep for a week. That's what those little knights made her feel, so she couldn't imagine how much stronger it was to have them within a body. Annie was suffering more than Ashtyn had realized, more than any of them at the palace and in the Posse could've realized.

Once past that initial blockade, Ashtyn was in a valley of dark red, black blood gushing past her, lesions growing faces and laughing at her.

She rushed past that area, somewhere in the stomach, and moved south toward her legs, hoping to find a healthy region there.

Ashtyn felt her body sway, but her mind was so lost in the horror-filled images that she didn't pay it any mind. All around the southern regions of Annie's body, there was darkness, despair, so she moved north. Up, up, way up.

She must've been by her arms, her hands. It was a mess of black blood and shaking clots, laughing faces and cruel intentions.

Ashtyn took a large breath in to find another spot when her body hit the floor, pulling her from Annie's.

Her eyes snapped open. "What happened?"

"Are you all right?" Tristan was kneeling beside her, Norya at her other side, brows furrowed.

"Of course. What happened?"

"You were shaking, her body sweating. It was too much, Ashtyn. I needed to—"

"You stopped me?" she interrupted.

"It wasn't working, and you were making yourself sick, healer," Norya stated. "You needed to stop."

"I didn't need to—"

"That's enough," Tristan barked. "You need a break."

Ashtyn ground her jaw and shoved off the ground and through the store, pulling on the lock to allow herself outdoors. It was later in the day than she'd realized. It'd been early morning when they'd entered Marcanz's house and felt like noon now. She must've been locked away in that nightmare of a sickness longer than she'd thought.

She ignored the winds, thankful they were light at the moment, and breathed in slowly.

Her eyes fluttered quickly, the images of black streams all around her, of blobs of faces, of the touch of...

"Are you all right, sweetheart?"

She jumped out of it, snapping her head to look at the man beside her. "What?"

"You look sickly. You okay?" He wore a charming smile, but there was a darkness to his eyes.

Ashtyn's head tilted. That smile was so similar to the charm of so many men. Those eyes so similar to many of them. Was that a coincidence in the way these particular men were made? An accidental charm dropped into the making of a cold-blooded user? Or was that fate? Without the charm, they wouldn't have a way of getting to their end goal.

Were women capable of the same? How was anyone not afraid to trust another soul?

"I'm fine." She turned to stare out at the forests, hoping he'd take the hint.

She shouldn't have been surprised when he didn't. Men

who desired certain things would ignore anything in order to receive them.

"I don't think it'd be very gentlemanly of me to leave you out here by your lonesome, my pretty girl."

*"My pretty girl. Slip that dress off, my pretty girl."*

Bile rose up Ashtyn's throat.

He stepped closer. "Let me take you to sit down somewhere inside." His hand landed on her shoulder.

Her arm moved on its own, elbow flying back and into his gut. She turned to him with death in her eyes. "Ever touch me or any other woman like that again, and I'll send the Master Assassin after you. I can assure you, he'd enjoy the chase."

The man grimaced, a conceited air coming about him. "As if you can scare me with threats of the Assassin. You know how many women 'know the Assassin'?"

Ashtyn growled, but before she could say anything, Tristan's voice interrupted them. "Everything all right out here?"

The man's eyes snapped up and looked about ready to dismiss him when he noticed the palace emblem on Tristan's sword. His eyes widened.

"No, Tris. Just a man trying to take advantage of women out here," Ashtyn said as she strolled away.

She didn't turn to see what happened in her absence, but she had a feeling the man may not be able to walk the same way after tonight. Or maybe he'd end up in those dungeons at the palace. The Posse didn't interfere too much in the public, but they always took predators seriously.

Ashtyn stopped at a tree only a few yards from Marcanz's shop. Their horses were tied in this opening. She climbed it to a low enough branch and rested against the body of the tree.

Up there, she closed her eyes and breathed in slowly.

*"Slip that dress off, my pretty girl."*

*Ashtyn giggled, dancing around the private inn room Baren had gotten them. "You're very convincing, Baren."*

*He'd already taken off his jacket and was working on the buttons to his shirt in the middle of the space. "I don't have to be convincing, my sweet. You know this is right."*

*She giggled some more and began to slip off her dress. He didn't need to know this wouldn't be her first time because to Ashtyn, it felt like it might be. Might be a moment she could actually enjoy. She was no virgin, but maybe after tonight, she would understand the pleasures she'd been told existed.*

*Once she was naked and on the bed, it took him almost no time to join her.*

*Then he was kissing her, but it was sloppy and messy and didn't bring her out of her head at all.*

*As she tried to slow things down so her body could prepare for what came next, his hands fumbled over her skin, then he was inside her.*

*It hurt.*

*There was no lubrication, so it hurt. A lot.*

*But Ashtyn closed her eyes and took the softness that was in her chest and convinced the tissue to go lower, to heal the pain there.*

*"Yes, my pretty girl," Baren groaned above her.*

*"Slow down. It's not great," Ashtyn whispered.*

*"Nonsense," he huffed. "Your pussy is extraordinary."*

*Maybe he was right. Maybe she was extraordinary. Had she created an illusion in her mind of what these events should feel like? Maybe other women enjoyed this pain and that's what kept them going back. That must've been it.*

*Baren grunted and groaned above her, then finally pulled out like the others she'd been with before and finished on her belly. He took a moment to breathe, then fell onto the bed beside her.*

*"Wow." He smiled. "I'm going to sleep, then I'm going to need to use that body once more."*

*Ashtyn smiled at him as he fell asleep. She took him in. He was quite a bit older than her, but she didn't think that was the problem. Their fourteen year age gap should've made this experience better. After all, older men were meant to know what they were doing. So was this the best it got?*

*"Good night, Baren," she whispered.*

*"Good night, my pretty girl."*

*Ashtyn got cleaned up and dressed when he fell asleep, glad he'd only known her as 'pretty girl' and nothing more. They'd been flirting for months now, and she was convinced he'd never taken the moment to learn her name. If he had, he must've hated her name because he never used it.*

*Dressed and stopped before the bed she'd shared with Baren, Ashtyn sighed. She wasn't happy, hadn't been for a while. She was done convincing herself it would happen. She was nineteen and had plenty of capabilities, talents. She needed to start living by those and stop hoping that she may find that man from her dreams. Especially if sex was part of the deal. This needed to be the end of her search. Now it was time to search for a bigger purpose in life.*

*"Goodbye, Baren," she said in the dark of the room.*

*Just before she left, she heard the sleepy mumbles of, "My pretty girl."*

Ashtyn snapped out of the memory, still atop the tree.

It'd been years since Baren, since any of the men she'd been with, and with age, those years of clarity, and the stories from the women of the Posse, Ashtyn was beginning to believe that what she'd experienced hadn't been the norm. What the women of her life described felt wholly other.

Then she smiled to herself, to her strength, to her mind, for getting herself out of that inn years ago and staying away.

As Ashtyn looked over to the shop once more, she sighed. She needed to protect these people. It was the only thing she had left in her life.

She jumped down from her perch and moved inside once more, locking the door behind her.

When she entered the back quarters, Tristan and Norya were speaking to the couple.

"Where's that man?" she asked.

Norya smirked. "Taken care of."

Ashtyn didn't ask for specifics, she didn't necessarily care.

Instead, she moved to sit beside Annie again. "Would you mind if I tried once more?"

"Of course," the woman croaked, hope and understanding in her eyes.

Ashtyn gave a soft lift of her lips and instead of settling her palms above the woman, she took Annie's hands in hers. As she closed her eyes, she focused on making her way north, up Annie's body and to her mind.

It was a journey of darkness and lost hope, but up in her head, surrounded by all that vileness was the clarity of pink. It was the reminder that discipline depended on one's mind's strength, not their body's.

Ashtyn stopped before that softness and spoke to it, *Would you help her? She needs your strength everywhere.*

There were no faces here, but she felt them all around her. She slowly moved them down, the darkness around her lightening. Then they got to the chest, where things lightened some more, then further, through her arms and legs.

Ashtyn moved back up to the clear spot in her mind. *Would you continue to help her? Keep this poison away from manifesting itself once more?*

Again there was no face, but Ashtyn swore she saw a soft smile and a whispered, *Of course. All she needed to do was ask.*

Ashtyn took a large breath in and traveled back down Annie's body. All around her, the black streams were loosening, the laughing faces disappearing. In slight spots around her body, the darkness was gone altogether.

When Ashtyn opened her eyes, she was lightly sweating, but didn't release Annie's hands. "How do you feel?"

Annie cleared her throat, but her eyes were already alight with hope. "Weak still, but so much better."

"You are very weak. It will take some time, weeks if not a few months. But I suspect a full recovery."

Marcanz's hopeful, wide eyes snapped from his wife to Ashtyn and back. "Truly?"

"I will return this night to check on her. Then once more in the morning before our departure. But I suspect she'll be feeling better within a couple days and able to slowly start living a life once more within a week. As time passes, I suspect her body will gain back the strength she once had." She faced Annie. "You'll need to take things slow. Do not allow hubris to deter you."

Annie smiled as she nodded, tears strolling down her cheeks. "Thank you."

Marcanz's tears were coming down faster as he kissed his wife's temple over and over. "Thank you, my dear. Thank you so much. I am forever in your debt."

# CHAPTER 6
# GABRIEL

Watching Ashtyn ride off without looking back at him cracked a little piece of his heart. It wasn't a surprise, but Gabriel's chest still stung at the show of rejection.

He was thankful though that he had that time between watching her ride off with Tristan and Norya and now spending the afternoon with Sparrow and Evony. It'd given him the chance to bring himself out of the wallows of how desperately he wanted her. Gabriel had no doubts his mind would revert straight back to said thoughts the moment he was done with his meeting, but at least he'd have this reprieve.

Though he wasn't sure how much of a reprieve it was. Evony looked like she wanted him to fail her line of questioning.

"Ignore her," Sparrow advised as he noticed Gabriel twitch under Evony's narrowed gaze where they sat at a secluded table in the library, the doors closed letting everyone know not to come in. "She's just trying to come up with a way to have you not be good enough, so she's allowed to help."

She huffed in her seat across from Gabriel. "You guys suck."

Gabriel didn't react but internally, he smiled. Evony was a ray of sunshine in this world, always teasing and laughing, so getting her in unfavorable moods tended to be scary. But today it was amusing.

"How're we going to do this?" Gabriel asked, a bit nervous being alone with two Masters.

"We just need to know that you're knowledgeable about the different aspects that come with magicians," Sparrow answered. "As long as those are clear to you, you should be able to pick out magicians for our uses. And you'd be able to pinpoint anything a magician would be of use for before we even decide whether or not we need one. If you already know all of this—and trust me, the Magician's not gonna give you 'almost got it' points—there's no point in trying to teach Tristan and Norya yet. It'll take too long, and they'll inevitably forget or overlook something. That'll be something you can teach them along the way or after this plague mess is taken care of."

"Okay." Gabriel sat up straighter and met the Magician's eyes. "What would you like me to answer?"

He was almost looking forward to this.

Evony smiled and there was nothing innocent about it. She was starting with a difficult one. "How is Gwendolyn Powder made?"

This was one of the most important questions as the powder was the only way to deem a magician powerless, but also one of the most difficult as only sorcerers could make it and all sorcerers were in the Island Nation.

In any case, magicians were all taught of the ingredients lest they come across anyone with those specifics, anyone who might cause them harm. Gabriel himself had helped teach many magicians in his time in the South.

"It is a mixture of ingredients from the Sacred Garden—rosulthum, endospyne, graratium, and lothomium—mixed slowly in a brew. It is then added with citrus and rosemary, laced with half its weight in sugar, and mixed into finality with the highest quality of alcohol. It's most difficult aspect is turning the liquid then into powder as it is only harmful to a magician in its powder form, though the particles fall into the winds so quickly, it is unseen, leaving only the scent behind."

He'd told them already after their first trip together of getting Evony back from her mother that he knew what Gwendolyn Powder smelled like because they'd gotten some smuggled their way from the Island and he would use it on magicians in an effort to see if there was any way to fight it. There hadn't been.

"It is why we only used to sell those four ingredients from the Sacred Gardens one season at a time. So it would take a full year of saving, and nothing happening to their ingredients, for the powder to be made. But since the decree not allowing magicians on our nation grounds, we've sold them together as well."

Sparrow scoffed. "I've already ordered for the Gardens to go back to one a season."

Good. It was a shame for all those households who truly wanted the ingredients for their uses, but it was safer this way. People had been known to depower a magician to try experiments on them in the past.

Evony eyed Gabriel, impressed.

Gabriel shrugged. "I'm sure it was one of the first things you learned. It is important for magicians, and I lived with and loved magicians."

She gave a small smile before moving to the next question. "And what of the elements?"

"What of them?"

Evony smirked. "How are they controlled, Gabriel?"

"Depends. Are you doing the controlling or a normal magician?"

Narrowed eyes told him not to make jokes though there was an ever-present teasing gleam in her sapphire orbs.

"Even a normal magician, it would depend. If they are more prone to one of the elements than the others and how much study they take into practicing. For instance, one skilled in earth could cause explosions within nature, destroying landscapes. The degree would matter on how skilled and strong their magic is. But those same powers can be put in place to right such a wrong. To fix it. One skilled in water could send ocean waters toward the village while at the same time, she could stop such a destruction. Fire and air all the same. It is then a matter of choosing where they stand in the matter. Destroying life or preserving it?"

"And do you know what such destruction looks like?"

It was a good question. It was one thing to spew that information and another entirely to witness it. "I have been around all the elements, around magicians who held one skilled element and those who held more. I have witnessed them destroy, though far more often, I have witnessed them preserve."

Evony met his gaze and there was understanding there. She knew how beautiful and terrifying such acts could be.

"It is to be noted though," Gabriel continued, "that elemental magic is some of the most regular. Most, even those skilled in other areas, study at least one element."

She nodded. "It will be your job to figure out whether they will use that element to harm or heal."

"I will take my job seriously." He almost finished the statement by calling her Princess. It was what she was, but he knew she hated being called so.

Evony nodded seriously, then brightened as mischief lined her eyes. "And what of traversing through time and space?" Evony quirked her brow like she had him now.

Gabriel fought his amusement, staring down so she wouldn't see it in his eyes, and cleared his throat. "Very possible albeit one of the most difficult to do. I knew a few magicians who attempted it constantly. Only one ever really got it and she didn't get very far. It is said even the Master Magician has only done it a handful of times though she's to have gone great distances." He finally met her gaze again.

Evony looked equal parts annoyed and proud.

Sparrow scoffed. "I remember one of those with great detail."

Gabriel's eyes widened. "You've done so recently?"

Evony shook her head. "It takes far too much energy. When I do it, I feel fine after, not needing to rest, but my magic is completely depleted. I can hardly do even the most basics of magic. I only do it when it is absolutely required and even then, I need to already be strong with magic, no depletion at all for it to truly do anything."

Gabriel eyed the two of them wondering if they'd share the moment they were speaking of.

Evony finally did. "The first time I was on palace grounds was nearly seven years ago. Gemma and I came to see my twin while James was training. Sparrow saw us from his tower and came running after us. I was strong with magic having hardly used any so I was able to get us out to where James was training, but I couldn't really use magic for three days after that. And nothing large for another week after that—though I believe it was an extra strain because I had taken Gemma with me. Anyway, it doesn't feel all that worth it to me."

Gabriel nodded. "That's what I was told in the South too. They tried it merely to see if they could as that would be a great form of protection but when they noticed most couldn't do it and those who could were hardly getting anywhere and depleted, they stopped."

Evony nodded, interrogation mode snapped back into place. "How did you know to trust them? Or did you trust any magician?"

Gabriel chuckled beneath his breath. "I think at seven, I would've trusted any of them at first. But even seven-year-olds have instincts. It was only a month after living with them, for instance, that I came about a magician who I felt uneasy around. When she asked me to show her around to a shop, I ran off and when Lanlik found me later, she said I was right to trust those instincts." He shrugged. "I've been told there's an aura that hovers over magicians. I cannot see it but something in me senses it. It is why I liked you so very quickly."

Sparrow growled, and Gabriel's cheeks pinked. The whole of the palace knew he only had eyes for one woman, but Sparrow didn't seem to care about that little fact.

Evony's hand brushed her husband's, bringing it to her mouth to kiss, before meeting Gabriel's gaze once more. "On a serious note, Gabriel. Do you think you could find magicians not only willing to help with this plague but also willing to be some of the faces of the reintroduction of magicians to the North?"

Gabriel thought back to Lanlik. She was married with a family. He couldn't ask her to leave. But he trusted in her the most, like a son would his mother. "I trust in my instincts above all else." He swallowed, glancing between Sparrow and her before landing back on her sapphire eyes. "I think all men go through life needing to. But I also have a magician I trust more than any other person. She will help me. It will make matters much quicker and simpler."

They both nodded as Sparrow asked. "And who is this woman?"

Gabriel almost laughed. As the head of security for not only the palace but the Posse, Sparrow needed to know everything. Remembering stories Evony had told him while on the boat to the Island Nation earlier in the year about how angry Sparrow had been at the beginning of their relationship because he didn't know everything about her almost made Gabriel's laughter fall out.

"She... raised me in the South. A magician. She's lovely."

Evony gave a warm smile. "Then maybe we'll get to meet her someday."

*I certainly hope so,* Gabriel thought as Evony moved on to the next question.

THE STACKS of hay were heavy but a nice distraction. In the days since she'd left, only the meeting with the Masters and physical work had helped block the healer's control over his whole being.

Though sometimes—like now—she still managed to wiggle her way in there. Specifically in knowing she was somewhere else in some inn for who knew how much longer. He kept wondering if she was all right; if anything happened while she was away; if she needed anything; if anyone was bothering her or tried to get her to do something she wasn't comfortable with. If she needed him.

"You thinkin' about your sunshine healer?" Dale, another of the stable hands, asked him.

It was more a mocking tone, but Gabriel answered as if it

were a real question. "It's growing late. I don't know when they plan on being back."

He smirked. "She's with the barbarian. That woman is scary. Even if the Posse spy can't handle a disturbance, your healer will be fine with that girl."

Gabriel knew Dale had been interested in Norya and had Tristan not been part of the picture, that he would've tried to win the barbarian's affections, but he wasn't entirely sure how deep those feelings had gone. Had he merely had a crush, or had he fallen for the warrior? If it was the latter, Gabriel pitied him even though he tried to stay away from pitying anyone.

"I know." He dropped the hay before London and Arcana as Dale dropped another before Anton and Haven.

"Leave the boy be," Papa Ignatius, the man who had taken Gabriel in when he'd first arrived to the palace over a decade ago, reprimanded. "A man in love is an irrational one."

A third voice joined their laughter. Papa Iskan was a Southern man who had come up to the North with his wife for a change of scenery after Evony had arrived. Apparently they'd met before her arrival, and he'd wanted to check if she'd found her husband yet. Now he spent much of his time at the stables and as much time as possible outdoors while his wife cooked with the chefs inside.

"She will be yours, Gabriel," Papa Iskan declared. "Just be patient."

It was the same thing he'd been saying since he arrived and noticed the way Gabriel and Ashtyn acted toward one another, though the latter would've skewered him alive had he mentioned it. Gabriel knew he'd be with the healer, believed it too much for it not to be absolute, but hearing the man who'd known Evony was going to marry Sparrow thought so too relieved some of the stress of not knowing when.

"I don't remember which part of this conversation

evidenced my not being patient." He grabbed a brush and started with Absko's mane. Though the horse was a grump, he softened to Gabriel in these moments—the boy loved having his hair brushed.

He reminded Gabriel of Ashtyn in these moments. Not that he was comparing his blonde beauty to a horse, but both were grumpy with moments of softness. He wondered if Ashtyn would also like her hair brushed. He'd love to spend hours doing that for her, watching her shoulder relax and her head fall back as he erased all the worries that plagued her.

"Don't be a smartass, boy." Papa Iskan wore a large grin. "Fates make assholes wait longer. Why do you think Sparrow had to wait all that time?"

"Because Evony's six years younger," Gabriel joked.

"He's not wrong," Dale confirmed Gabriel's comment before saying, "Though the healer is Gabe's age."

"She's also an asshole though so—"

"Hey!" Gabriel called with a grin.

"I'm sorry." Papa Iskan raised both hands. "You're right. She's an asshole. You never are. I shouldn't have said you were."

"You shouldn't have said any of it. She isn't an asshole." She was quite literally the definition of asshole sometimes.

He ignored Gabriel. "So because she's an asshole, they may have to wait a few more years than would've been desired. Fates play those mean games."

"Whatever." He scoffed as he turned back to the horses right as the sound of trotting reached him.

He turned for the forests lining the palace grounds, and his heart settled. Riding straight for the stables were Ashtyn and the warrior duo.

Dale's large hand smacked his back. "Ah, now he's relaxed."

"Shove off." Gabriel pushed him away but couldn't fight the large grin he now wore.

Dale tsked. "Fuck off. Come on, you can say it."

Gabriel narrowed his eyes at the man and chuckled anyway. Then he was back to tracking the distance between where he stood and where Ashtyn existed. Twenty yards. Ten. Five. Ten feet. Five. Two.

She jumped off her horse and landed right in front of Gabriel as if trying to torture him with how close their faces were. He wanted to welcome her home with a kiss.

"You're always so happy." She grimaced. "Why?"

"To counter your contempt for everyone and everything."

Her head tilted in thought making those blonde strands whisk in the winds. "The world does need balance."

His smile broadened. Any of these little moments where she wasn't outright denying him were the ones he cherished late at night when hopelessness began to consume him.

"Are you your natural degree of unfavorable or has something happened?" he asked with a smile to keep the conversation light-hearted, but his heart raced with fears that she was upset or hurt.

"The world goes on, people continue to annoy. I think that's cause enough for any unfavorable attitudes."

Tristan and Norya smirked behind her which made Gabriel think half of her remark was made against them. He'd heard they talked a lot, and he knew they were very loud when they got together, so Gabriel could imagine they got a bit of his healer's fire the past few days.

"Things are looking good." Tristan winked, letting him know that was all he'd say before meeting with the Posse, but it was enough.

If things were looking good, then Ashtyn had probably

figured out how to heal this plague. But the scowl on her face would convince anyone otherwise.

Gabriel flicked her chin. "Come, now, beautiful. Lighten up a little."

"Then the world would be off-balance."

He furrowed his brows in mock concentration. "I'll fix it again."

Her eyes lit up, but the spark was gone in half a second before she smirked. "I'm done with this conversation."

He really wasn't but Gabriel found himself lucky enough to have enjoyed this much time with her, so he didn't want to push it. Hopefully she'd be back for more later. She normally came around to watch him. He could wait. After all, he'd much rather have these short bursts constantly than long ones every once in a blue moon. "Shame."

"But before I leave, I need a favor."

He stood straighter. Anything. Always. "At a cost."

"I want lessons on these horses."

He quirked a brow. "You know how to ride, Ash."

She rolled her gorgeous eyes. "Lessons about them, not how to ride."

"Why?" *Because she wants to know more about you.*

"Because I'm going to be riding them around this country. I want to make sure I know what to do if something were to happen. But even if something doesn't happen, I want to know a bit more about my transportation and companionship."

That was sweet enough especially for the woman who hated showing her emotions.

"You can let me know the cost later. I'm sure I'll hate it, whatever it is," she finished.

Gabriel scoffed as he watched her go. She didn't even wait for his answer. Everyone knew it'd be yes, but it was quite presumptuous for her to leave without hearing it. He shook his head watching her hips sway as she walked away from him.

*My beautiful asshole.*

# CHAPTER 7
# ASHTYN

The Posse were all smiles at the news—she could heal people with this plague. People. Plural.

It'd been Ashtyn's biggest fear after seeing Annie's recovery—was this a fluke or was she truly able to do it? But the three other people they found, two within the town and one on the way back to the palace, evidenced what they now knew as fact—Ashtyn could heal this plague, at least, so long as her patients still carried hope within their minds to help the process. It made her hopeful, though afraid, about healing the source if it turned out not to be a person.

With a person, they'd likely have the warriors and guards or any magicians they partnered with take care of the matter, but with any other sort of problem, she'd be needed.

The King's shoulders deflated though he remained silent, taking in the rest of his family. The women didn't hide their smiles while Sparrow, Miels, and James threw their heads back with a unanimously whispered, "Finally."

Considering all they'd likely done behind the scenes to

figure this out before coming to her and all the stress of being responsible for every person in the North, Ashtyn thought their reactions well contained.

"So should I prepare now?" Ashtyn asked. "Are we heading out tomorrow?"

"No," Edmund, Sparrow, and Tristan said at once.

"What do you mean no? We need to help them. I can."

"We also never run into matters underprepared if we can help it," Tristan argued.

"Tristan, Norya, and I will prepare the guards who will be joining your lot," Sparrow said.

"We'll prepare your remedies for the journey," Miels added in regard to him and his wife.

"I'll be preparing for the magician aspect of this mess. I need preparations in place unless a situation presents itself for a magician," Evony added with a look at the rest of the group like there was something about that bit that she was leaving out.

"James and I will work with those in the kitchens for a solvent for your meals and drinks. It will dissolve much of the taste of what you eat but better that than the possibility of you inadvertently catching whatever they have," Gemma added.

"But I can heal us if we do," Ashtyn argued.

"And who will heal you if *you* fall ill and are too weak?" James argued.

Ashtyn grumbled under her breath but succumbed to his annoyingly prevalent point.

"We'll work with Atiana to make sure you are fitted with the safest and best clothing for the trips but also with the best material carriers for anything you take," Rosaelia added, tugging on Killian's arm as he grumbled beside her.

"All in all," Edmund finalized, "it will take a few days. You will head out next week. Until then, you need to think things through."

"Like what?"

He smirked, and Ashtyn found herself lost in the sexiness of it. The King hardly ever gave such a look to those outside the Posse.

"Marriage. Whether you would like it or not. It is unlikely you will harbor any attention this quickly but it is absolute that it will eventually happen. Don't decide now. You can always change your answer to yes if you go on these trips and find the attention too much, but you can't change it to no if you agree now. So think on it."

*I don't need to think on it. Who the hell would I marry?*

*Gabriel,* that annoying voice in her head that sounded surprisingly like the Magician muttered, making Ashtyn grimace. Absolutely not. She was not going to ruin his life like that.

"Okay."

"Good," the King responded. "Well now that we have *some* good news, let's run with it. Everyone knows what they need to do."

Ashtyn didn't smile but she felt a wave of joy that had become foreign years ago. She was going to go out into the lands and perform her calling, it was the best thing that could've happened for her. And at the best time. This would take her away from the palace and the certain people she needed a break from—most prominently, all the medics in the infirmary and a certain stable hand.

"FOR SOMEONE WHO TREATS EVERYONE, you do not do the best job treating yourself," Atiana commented on Ashtyn.

They were out in the greens watching the fields beside the stables where Gabriel was currently on horseback next to the King. They were practicing being on the animals and having a sword fight which Gabriel was surprisingly talented at. Still though, it was as much a lesson with the weapon for Gabriel as it was for the King to become comfortable on his new horse.

It was a nice distraction from the anticipation of waiting days until she was allowed to leave for the north of the lands.

"For someone who doesn't gossip, you cannot stay out of people's business." Ashtyn didn't turn for the girl, but she knew the tailor was laughing under her breath at the comment.

"I do not like to see my friends hurting. Tell me what is wrong."

Ashtyn fought the part of her brain that was demanding she comment 'who said we were friends' and answered because Atiana truly would keep things to herself, and as a healer, Ashtyn knew it was always better to get things off one's chest. "I went into a town with a few sick of the plague. I was able to heal them."

"That is a problem?"

Ashtyn turned to her and found the girl's stare on the two men in the fields. It shouldn't have surprised Ashtyn. She'd been the one to say Gabriel would immediately fall for Atiana and it wasn't shocking in the slightest that Atiana may favor him in return. He was such a good man.

"If it comes out that I can heal that plague, my power so-to-say will be revealed. Right now, I am only a healer. People assume I heal the same way the other medics do and while sometimes I do, other times, I... use different methods. And based on history, no one but a Master is meant to be able to heal the way I do." *Or a magician.*

Atiana didn't say anything for some time which made Ashtyn nervous. Should she not have revealed her possible Masterhood to the girl? Would this be the one thing she would gossip about? The last thing Ashtyn needed was the palace to find out quite yet. Then the news would spread to the South before she could make the journey to help those who needed her.

"Will it truly be so bad to become known as a Master? You'll finally have those in the infirmary respecting you, crawling at your feet for forgiveness. I know you do not like the attention, but I'm sure, with time, you'll become accustomed to the eyes the way the Assassin has."

"It is not only that." The thought of all that attention made her shiver with disgust but that wasn't her main concern. "I've been informed that so long as I'm unmarried, there will be no stop to the *effort* men will apply for my hand. Apparently women used to throw themselves at Sparrow because of his Mastery and males only stopped with Emerald in the last couple years after the scariness the Posse showed them. If I go that route, it could take years before they leave me be and I'm not sure I'd last that long without committing my first murder. Or a whole species wipeout quite frankly."

Atiana laughed. "Ashtyn."

She shrugged. "What? Honestly, I'm quite out of the loop. I mean, even Emerald has killed men."

Atiana breathed in deeply for a minute before the seriousness settled between them. "The Posse is asking you to marry someone?"

Her face was quite serene, as much as her voice, but her eyes narrowed a little where she watched the men. If Ashtyn didn't know better, she'd think the tailor was berating the King with such a glare. In any case, it seemed to work because Edmund stumbled in his training and his eyes shot to where the two women stood. His brows furrowed before he turned back to Gabriel.

The entire scene made Ashtyn want to laugh even though it was clear that wasn't Atiana's intention. Was the girl so bold as to reprimand their King? Even Ashtyn herself wasn't that crazy. How invigorating of a person to be around.

"No," Ashtyn finally answered. "Not at all. They simply let me know that it will be the easier course to keep the men away. Everything, even showing my abilities to help with the plague, have been left to my decision." *Though I have half a mind to believe the King is only allowing that because he knows I'd accept.* Ashtyn scoffed internally. *Tricky, devious King.*

Atiana's demeanor softened. "Well, we all know you will help them, so the question is—will you choose a husband?"

Ashtyn shrugged. "I cannot imagine marrying anyone."

Atiana quirked a brow. "No?"

"What's the supposed to mean? I just said no."

"Ashtyn, be true to yourself."

"Wha—"

"Gabriel."

Ashtyn rolled her eyes. "Do not worry about any relationship with Gabriel. We are... cordial. You are free to pursue him as you wish."

Atiana coughed as she laughed, eyes wide as she met Ashtyn's. "Are you out of your mind?"

"Excuse m—"

"Why would I ever want Gabriel?"

Because he was a good man. Because he was charming. Because he would do anything to protect his wife. Because... she wanted to throw all of those comments at Atiana but settled on, "You are the one watching him. I've seen you two together."

She gave a disheartened close-lipped smile. "Trust me. I have no interest in Gabriel. To me, he truly is a friend. To you, however, things are quite different." When Ashtyn tried to disregard the comment, Atiana added, "Everyone here knows you two are spoken for. Why else do you think none of the men have come for you, other than because of your charming personality, that is?"

"Then why are you—" Ashtyn cut her question off when her gaze landed on the men again, now coming off their horses. She may have caught Atiana out here a few times, but as Ashtyn glanced between the two of them, it was almost never when Gabriel was alone. Matter of fact...

Her gaze rolled to the tailor. "Oh, you're so cliché."

"Me?" Atiana fought. "Gabriel is the charming, sweet stable hand. It doesn't get more cliché than falling for him."

"It doesn't get more cliché than falling for the King? Really? That's your argument?"

"Shut up," she hissed as the men started walking for them.

Ashtyn wanted to suppress her amusement, but it was difficult. Atop the fact that the whole situation was hilarious, it relieved some of the stress in her chest at seeing the beautiful woman always out in these fields. But as she watched the men walk toward them, she wondered if Gabriel would be upset when he found out Atiana's interests lie elsewhere. Was he already falling for the beauty?

"Atiana," he called as if on cue. "Do not be angry with me. The big thing passing off as a horse ripped the shirt, I didn't!"

Atiana laughed. "Hey! Don't be mean to Absko. He's a sweetheart."

Gabriel scoffed. "You only say that because he likes you. You and Ed. That's it."

Ashtyn smirked, then muttered under her breath so the King wouldn't hear, "Yeah because he knows who his owners are."

Atiana's elbow hit her side as she covered Ashtyn's mutterings with, "I think he can tell you have singled him out of all the horses as the one you do not like. You cannot treat poor Absko like that."

Ashtyn took the time to follow the King's hand from where he was holding Absko's reins up his torso to his handsome features. He was in his midforties and the fantasy of just about every woman at this palace. Ashtyn couldn't deny his almost ruggedly clean handsomeness. The specs of salt-and-pepper starting in his beard was a stark contrast to his head full of dark hair, but it all gave him a regal maturity.

But taking the time to inspect the King also revealed another matter—his gaze was glued to the spot by her side.

Ashtyn's smile grew and she unconsciously sought out Gabriel's gaze—a habit she'd started picking up when she felt an inappropriate comment brewing—and found him already watching her. He wiggled his brows at the two.

So he was aware of the whatever was going on with them? Hopefully this meant he wouldn't be too heartbroken when Atiana didn't want him.

"I have not singled anyone out," Gabriel reminded Ashtyn of their conversation. "He singled himself out by being mean to anyone but you two." His smile was so infectious neither woman could help but return it, though Ashtyn made sure hers was as light as possible.

"I'm sure he'll treat you well enough when you're feeding him too many treats," the King interrupted what Atiana was about to say. "I should be heading inside."

"Perfect!" Ashtyn's smile broke before she thought through her next words. "Atiana was just saying she needed to get back to work. Why don't you walk her to her suite?" She placed Atiana's hand in the crook of Edmund's elbow as he moved to pass them by, making everyone freeze.

It could've been a stupid thing to do, but Ashtyn was confident in the King's need for her abilities, so she didn't necessarily care for the consequences.

Atiana's wide eyes seemed to finally take in what was happening and she went to pull her hand back when the King brought his arm in close to his side and nodded, "Very well."

Ashtyn bit back her grin as the two walked off toward the palace, Atiana's free hand jittering at her side.

"Quite the matchmaker, beautiful." Gabriel's breath touched her ear with how close he'd gotten in her distraction.

Ashtyn smirked as she turned for him. "Being a healer comes in many forms, horse boy."

He tsked, a teasing glean in his dark browns. "I think you can call me handsome, Ash. No one is around to hear you going soft. It'll be our little secret."

He was so close, it wouldn't take much effort to lean up and kiss him.

It wouldn't take much effort to confess her feelings; tell him what the whole of the palace already suspected. It wouldn't take much effort to take his hand and follow him to his cabin where he could make her his. It wouldn't take much effort at all to relinquish all of her control into his hands; to trust him with everything she had.

It would be so easy to be so selfish; to allow her desires of being taken care of to win over knowing the stable hands at this palace deserved more, but this stable hand in particular deserved the world.

It would be so easy to lean in and kiss him, but instead, Ashtyn bit her lip to force the pain to keep her sane and stepped back, his gaze tracking her mouth. "We should get back to work as well."

"Come by my cabin tonight. We can share all of our secrets with the guarantee no one will hear them."

Her heart raced and her body shivered. *So, so easy.*

She inhaled deeply to clear her mind and turned for the palace. "Keep dreaming, horse boy."

LYNA WAS Arba's second which basically meant she was an annoying kiss ass. Ashtyn hated all of the medics in the infirmary, but Lyna was right up there beside Arba. Maybe even a little more than Arba because she didn't have a personality of her own.

"Your ticks are adding up, fraud," she said as she stopped by the open curtain of Ashtyn's office.

Ashtyn didn't look up from her journal, unfazed and completely uninterested in whatever she had to say.

"You were supposed to be filing for Arba instead of gallivanting all day. You've missed three days as it is." When she still didn't get a response, Lyna stepped into the office until she was right before Ashtyn's desk, hands crossed before her chest and head high like a superiority master. "You know, it doesn't matter if the Master brought you in. If you're interfering with the way the infirmary works, and we have proof enough, you'll finally be gone."

Ashtyn settled her quill down and leaned back in her chair. "And what good would that do you?"

"You wouldn't be here any longer taking awa—"

"What? I do not take anything away from you," Ashtyn responded stoically. "If anything, I take the patients you lot don't want to see. The only person to truly have a problem with me is Arba because she's afraid I'll take her position. The rest of you don't have brain enough to think for yourselves."

Ashtyn understood to a degree why Arba didn't like her, but she'd never been able to understand the others in the infirmary. It scared her for humanity if those morons blindly stood by Arba's side without another thought. They were great medics for the most part, so Ashtyn would never do anything to jeopardize their positions in helping patients, but it was dangerous to so blindly trust another.

Old Lady Arba didn't like her, but that was mostly because of her own past trauma. Sparrow had explained it to her early on, the only real reason Ashtyn had allowed the woman to lash out—not that it meant Ashtyn wouldn't fight back.

But Old Lady Arba had her reasoning—the last time she'd been the head in an infirmary, she'd been fool enough to hire a medic who didn't have formal training. That mistake caused her the lives of many, especially children, when the untrained medic was the only one available to heal and she hadn't been able to.

Even Sparrow's reassurances hadn't been able to ease Arba's trauma, so Ashtyn allowed the woman to hate her, though she couldn't make herself simply sit back and take it.

The other medics though, they didn't get that leeway.

"Just get to filing," Lyna said after scoffing her displeasure.

Ashtyn closed her journal and placed it in the top drawer of her desk, knocking the key into place to make sure her nosy colleagues didn't go snooping. She dropped the key into the hidden pocket of her dress and got to her feet. "No."

"Excuse me?" Lyna stood taller. "I am Arba's second. You do the tasks I give you."

Ashtyn stepped around her desk. "And I'm the Posse's healer. You do whatever they tell you."

She gave a vindictive laugh. "No wonder Gabriel's attentions has turned to Atiana. He's finally pulled his head out of his arse. Your pretty little face doesn't work on him any longer and it won't work on the Posse much longer either. You come here with no merits and use the Posse to get your way. You're a disgrace to us all."

Ashtyn scowled. "My pretty face had nothing to do with my positions, Lyna, that much we both know. I'm leaving now seeing as you refused to send either of the patients that came in today to me and I can promise you I'm not spending my days doing busy work."

She smirked. "The sooner you realize that is a rule of thumb and not a fluke of the day, the sooner our acquaintance can be over."

Ashtyn gave a fake smile, then walked straight out of her own office. Her journal was safe in that drawer and nothing else in there mattered to her, so she didn't care if Lyna decided to snoop.

Conversations with Lyna weren't fun and tended never to give any useful information, but today's told Ashtyn one thing —she wasn't the only one to notice Gabriel and Atiana recently. Though she knew the idea was ridiculous considering only a few hours before King Edmund had walked Atiana off and Gabriel had been all too giggly about it, Ashtyn couldn't help but feel unsettled at the idea.

It was preposterous.

Lyna had no idea what she was talking about. It was infuriating to even allow that woman's words to get in her head, but Ashtyn couldn't help it, especially considering there was some merit to them—Gabriel wanted her for her pretty face. There had to be merit there because the man hardly knew her, yet he declared himself hers.

She was so lost in thought that she was halfway to his

cabin before she caught herself and stopped. Standing in the middle of the palace corridors, Ashtyn debated what a stupid idea this was. She'd been in hopes for a while that Gabriel's infatuation was ebbing off, so she couldn't go to him now and confuse him. Especially if her *pretty face* was the reason behind his desires.

Ashtyn closed her eyes to beat back the pain that decision caused in her chest, then promptly turned for her suite.

# CHAPTER 8

# GABRIEL

There was no knock on his door. Not that he'd necessarily expected it, but Gabriel was still deflated his girl hadn't come to him as he rode off from the palace, a note already left with Papa Iskan who'd promised to give it to Ashtyn.

Gabriel hadn't been expecting the invitation this morning, but he couldn't give it up. This was his chance to insert himself in whatever was going on, whatever was going to take up Ashtyn's time.

And the invitation had come from guards, those who would be accompanying Ashtyn. It had been Wells who'd smirked when Gabriel had opened his door that morning.

"Get dressed, Gabe."

"Why?"

"We're heading off to check in on a town about a day's ride before we take the healer. You've won me great coin, so I figure the least I can do is offer you to join."

Gabriel's brows lifted. It would do him great help to learn some more before putting his girl in that danger. "Coin?"

Wells smirked. "I knew you'd find a way to join her. We all figured you'd want to, but I knew you'd weasel your way in."

Gabriel shook his head from the memory of that morning, laughing to himself. He loved that everyone knew of his feelings.

The ride wasn't necessarily a full day's ride but with the stops they would need to make in order to make sure Ashtyn was comfortable—because though she could ride through, her health was important to make sure she could do her job— would make it so. For Gabriel and the guards though, it was only a few hours plus a single stop for the horses to rest.

When they got to the edge of town, stopping at an inn and handing over their horses to the stables, Gian turned to the group. "All right. As the first real stop for this journey, wee just need to make sure it'll be safe to start this with the healer. Colt, Wells, check out the inn. We'll be staying here with the healer so we need to make sure the space will be available and that she will be left alone. Make sure the owners understand this is an order from the King. Noah, Ares, talk to the sick. We need them to prepare and for their families to know to keep this to themselves. We cannot truly stop the gossips from running, but we can do everything in our power to stifle it a bit. Let them think if they run their mouths, their sick won't be healed." He finally turned to Gabriel. "You and I are going to talk to some of the others in town."

Gabriel squared his shoulders. "I'm surprised you're having me do the talking. Aren't you lot trained in that?"

Gian smirked. "You'll have a different perspective. Both from living in the South all those years, but also because you're *not* a guard. I'd value your opinions."

Gabriel gave a single nod, but inside, he grinned wide. He knew he liked these guys, but now more than before because they respected him. It wasn't often but once in a while, the guards felt themselves superior to the other help around the palace. These guys weren't like that. That was probably why Sparrow had picked them out to begin.

"Let's go," Gian ordered, and the group broke apart, Gian leading Gabriel as they moved through the town, cobblestones beneath their feet and homey shops along each side. They were in a main part of town and looked to be walking outward toward where more locals would spend their time rather than any tourists passing through.

"You've been here before?" Gabriel asked.

Gian nodded. "Last year I took time off of being a guard. I... needed to be by myself. I knew that meant I'd lose my position, but I needed out. I spent that time traveling from town to town. When I got back, it was only to grab the rest of my things because I figured I was booted, but Sparrow stopped me. Said he needed someone who knew the towns as well as I did that he also trusted."

Gabriel's lips tipped up. "You call him Sparrow?"

He shrugged. "Sometimes Master or Assassin still slips out, but he likes those close to him to call him by his name. Especially around those who do not know who he is."

They walked in comfortable silence from then on until they made it to the other side of town where the locals stayed. A couple of them waved at Gian like they recognized him, and Gabriel realized Gian hadn't been kidding. He knew these towns. Knew them well enough to know people in them. It would be astronomical if he knew people from every town but as a good guard, Gabriel wouldn't doubt it of the man.

Gian nodded ahead toward a group of large males standing around drinking from mugs. Alcohol was scarcely drunk in the North, so Gabriel doubted that's what it was. "Those are the guys I want to talk to. They take control of the protection of this town. At least for the locals. I want your opinion on anything they say. They're not guarding so something about them could get your attention better than mine. Or something you picked up on in the South."

Gabriel caught the twinkle in Gian's eyes and though Sparrow said the guards didn't know of his magician lookout, Gian had figured it out. He was smarter than Gabriel had originally thought and proved once again why Sparrow would've chosen him for this trip.

"Men," Gian joined. "How're you?"

One of them, a huge muscled guy with a scar across his lips, scowled. "What does a palace guard want with us?"

Gian gave a charming smile that Gabriel copied. "We are going town to town, in search of the roots of the problems in the North. We'd like to know of any problems your town may be having. Compiling a list, you see, to see what we can help with most."

Another one, this one with the sides of his hair shaved off and a huge bite mark on his neck. "What could the pretty King sitting up in his high palace help us with?"

Gabriel spoke before Gian had a chance, "Just think, friend. Anything could catch the King's attention. Now if there's a chance to protect your woman, wouldn't you take it? I would."

His nostrils flared but he didn't look angry. The others around him squared their shoulders and crossed their muscled arms before their chests though. Each bicep on these men was the size of Gabriel's head.

"You have a woman?" the mohawked guy asked.

"I do."

"You?" he questioned Gian.

"Not yet."

"Unfortunate. They are a blessing."

Gian gave a soft smile. "I'm sure."

Mohawk nodded to his friend and the smaller of the lot—though still double his or Gian's size—stepped forward. "Our biggest problem is with our apothecaries. They are not very skilled so a lot of the remedies we may need cannot be made or are not as strong."

"For the plague."

"And other things. Fevers. Even headaches. The owners are self-taught and do what they can but it needs help."

Gian nodded. "We can easily arrange for our Remedies Expert and her husband to come down and help you. Or for yours to head to the palace to learn."

That answer seemed to encourage them because the first one with the scar stepped up then. "What of the plague?"

"We're working on it," Gian answered. "That is the biggest problem we're currently handling with all of the North, but I still like to help in other ways if we can."

"Anything else?" Gabriel asked.

They shook their heads, and Gian started thanking them and turned to leave, but something felt off to Gabriel. Mohawk looked like he wanted to say more.

"Even if it's not something that's necessarily problem some," Gabriel insisted, stopping Gian's retreat and getting a look that told him to go ahead. "Even if it's something that makes you feel ridiculous for thinking of it. Our guts tell us things nothing else can detect."

Mohawk met his gaze and held it. "A couple weeks ago, my lady was out by the water. She said a couple guys went out there. They didn't do anything or even get near her, but they were huddled together in front of a clearing that looked to lead a trail into the forests. She said something about their faces looking off, but she couldn't tell from the distance exactly what it was. I haven't let her go alone again, but I went once, and they weren't there but when I tried going in that direction… something felt off. I tried again a week later, and it was fine. I walked it and it led to nothing."

That was curious. It could've been smugglers with a magician to ward off others moving in that direction. In that case, Gabriel only hoped they were smuggling foods and drinks and other contraband and not women and children.

"Thank you," Gabriel nodded.

He shrugged. "To keep our women safe."

Gabriel tipped his head. "To keep our women safe."

THEY'D ONLY BEEN GONE two days. One to ride up to the town, the night to do their work, and the rest of the next day to ride back down. It wasn't much time in the grand scheme of things.

But apparently it'd been enough.

Enough time away for even his grumpy girl to miss him. Gabriel had surely missed her with a passion.

A smirk grew on his lips as Gabriel rode past the stables, right for his cabin where Ashtyn was sitting on a stump in the back as if out of view from the others around the palace. Her blonde hair blew before her face, long and beautiful, as she leaned over her knees. Her skin lighter than his because of all the time she didn't spend under the sun, but it was so stunning against the soft blue of that dress she favored. And even from a distance, Gabriel could pick up the curves of her lips, her slight nose, and perfectly manicured brows. Her lashes were as dark as those brows, and the perfect contrast to her brown eyes, always lighter under the sunlight.

Gabriel almost didn't want to keep riding forward, preferring to witness her as she currently was, playing with one of his carving knives, but he fought against it for the simple selfish need of wanting to be closer to her. Ashtyn gasped when she heard his horse nearing and nearly dropped the thing, cutting herself with it, making Gabriel jump off his horse and run for her.

Ashtyn was already on her feet, the knife on the ground, when Gabriel reached her and took her hand in his, checking for any nicks. "You could've hurt yourself!"

"Hello to you too," she mumbled.

Gabriel couldn't help the small chuckle that left him. He brought her palm to his lips and breathed in her scent before kissing her palm. "Hi, beautiful." He glanced up, his lips still pressed to her palm. "Miss me?"

She narrowed her eyes. She was going to deny it, but Gabriel had learned to read her eyes perfectly. She had missed him.

This short trip had been great for many reasons. It'd given him insights, sure, but it had also given him the evidence that it wasn't only he who could not handle being away from the other.

And... it'd given him some time with the guards with whom they'd be spending an immeasurable amount of time with. Five guards, all of whom showed Gabriel they knew of his relationship and would never try anything with Ashtyn. All of whom had had plenty of fun talking to him about sex.

Gabriel had learned a lot.

Then gone to bed wanting to do all of it to his healer.

Now, standing before her, it was nearly impossible to shake those fantasies.

"What would make you think such a thing?" she snarked.

He kissed her palm again, enjoying the way shivers broke

out on the small bits of exposed skin, then pulled away, still holding her hand for as long as she'd allow it. "Being at my cabin for one. Playing with my things for another."

"Maybe I was snooping."

He smirked. "That's okay with me. Snoop all you'd like, beautiful."

"Stop calling me that."

His thumb brushed her fingers, loving that she had yet to pull away. "You gonna tell me what you're doing here?"

"Snooping."

He chuckled. "For what? Maybe I can help you."

She shrugged. "Doesn't matter."

"It matters to me."

She stared at him. Those beautiful brown eyes not breaking from his and allowing him to read the emotion there. There was much of it for someone who wished to prove to the world that she felt nothing. There was longing and desire, yes, he'd expected that no matter how much she tried pushing, but there was also confusion and fear?

"Ash—"

"What have you been carving?" she interrupted quickly, finally pulling her hand from his and dropping to retrieve the knife she'd dropped.

Gabriel cleared his throat. "The last thing I finished was a monument from the South." Technically that's not what she asked but he didn't want her to know yet he was working on something for her.

"A monument."

He shrugged. "I haven't been back in nearly fifteen years. I have to keep the memories alive somehow."

Her brows furrowed. "Why didn't you go back?"

His eyes saddened. "At first, I was too young. I figured I might go at seventeen or eighteen. Then other responsibilities were presented to me and instead of taking a couple weeks off to head down, I just stayed. Then I made the promise that I would go for my honeymoon. And since that hasn't happened yet..."

Her brows furrowed. "You shouldn't wait for life to give you opportunities, Gabriel. If they're your family and you love them, you should go."

"Would you come with me?"

Her head was already nodding when she said, "That's not a great idea."

"Before the honeymoon even. I simply wish to introduce you."

"Gabriel..." She wanted to say no. That was clear as day. But she nodded. "Not a good idea," she whispered.

He gave her a small smile and grabbed both her hands once more, this time bringing her knuckles to his lips. "I think it's my best idea yet."

A neighing interrupted what she was going to say, and Ashtyn's gaze darted behind him to his horse still waiting to be brushed down and fed like the others.

Ashtyn gave a small smile. "You should probably take care of him before he grows too angry."

Gabriel kissed her knuckles. "Take the knife." He nodded to the knife she still held in her hand. "Don't hurt yourself, healer."

She fought off a smirk. "How would you know if I did? I'd just heal it better before you were any the wiser."

He smirked. "You underestimate how obsessed with you I am."

Her eyes shimmered as she scowled, but his horse interrupted once more.

Gabriel pulled away, walking backward to his animal. "Stay as long as you'd like, beautiful. Move in if you please."

She rolled her eyes, and as Gabriel turned around, his chest hurt knowing she was already rushing off back for the palace. Not that it mattered. She had been there. Waiting for his return.

She'd been waiting for him.

# CHAPTER 9
# GABRIEL

The knock on his door surprised him. Gabriel hadn't truly thought she'd take him up on his offer the other night, but he had mentioned that it was an open invitation. And only a few hours earlier he'd asked her to move in. He wanted for her to take his offers more than he wanted his next breath. Would he be so lucky tonight for Ashtyn not to fight her feelings?

Of course not.

He opened his door to find the Master couple before him.

He gave the same smile he always afforded them when Ashtyn wasn't in a dangerous situation—which tended to be the most times he was in close proximity to them. "Is everything all right?"

He pushed away from his door to allow them entrance knowing especially that Evony may like to sit even though her belly wasn't yet very large. Pregnancy affected all women differently, and Evony had been tired a lot as of late.

His cabin was small, covered in darker red and brown furnishings, from his couch to the rug to the curtains and tables. He'd wondered that whole year if he should start making it more feminine for Ashtyn, but figured she could change anything she didn't like on her own. For now, he had his small, round table with three chairs around it by the window, a couch above a large rug in the middle before the fireplace, and two armchairs on either side with a small table in the middle.

Evony took a seat in on an armchair that had been moved closer to the fire, Sparrow stopping behind her and kneading her shoulders. "We wanted to talk to you about Ashtyn."

He froze. "What about her?"

"You are aware that her travels up north to start healing those with the plague and search for the source will come with the consequences of the South hearing of her and possibly wishing to name her a Master?" Sparrow opened.

He nodded. "I guessed she was one. Or the next possible close thing to one. I figured if she did this then it was unlikely the gossip mills wouldn't take it for a spin. Most won't be like those she tested her abilities on. They won't be able to help themselves. It is human nature."

"Tristan and Norya will be going with her for protection. I have five more men going too. They all, along with you and Ashtyn, will be scouring for the source of the problem along with their responsibility to protect her. Once we find it, Ashtyn's most important job will be to heal the source which we have to be hopeful she'll be able to do, whether natural or a man-made problem. But if not, that brings in the magicians that you're in charge of. But until then, your main job will be looking for holes where a magician may be of use."

"Okay." Gabriel tried to fight the itching need to find out what they were leading to. This was all a breakdown that didn't require a late visit.

"Merely being able to heal all those people will bring on

male attention," Evony finally got to it. "A lot of male attention."

Gabriel's teeth nearly broke with how harshly he ground his jaw. "Mhm." He'd considered that little fact a bit too much for a sane man since finding out about the plan to send Ashtyn out.

"It will then garner attention from the South to possibly name her a Master. Healing the source, if she can, will pretty much guarantee her celebrity if not Masterhood. It will put the attention of every Northern and Southern man on her."

"Why are you telling me this?" His fists were white at his sides. As a man who avoided physical confrontations, he wasn't used to this amount of tension his body was currently holding.

"The only way to stop the attention, which we all know Ashtyn doesn't want, is marriage," Sparrow answered. "Lying won't be of use. Nothing short of an actual marriage, a husband at her side, will stop them. We know that's the route she'd prefer."

"She told you she wants to marry someone?" If anyone else touched her, he would go ballistic.

"Not necessarily." Evony smirked. "But we know she wants you and wouldn't tell you because she won't want to force you into a union, so I thought it'd only be fair to give you the chance to make the decision for yourself."

Gabriel eyed the couple, trying all the while to seem cooler than he felt. Ashtyn was his. It was widely known. He was hers. The final piece of the puzzle had always been waiting for her to accept it.

"If she accepts your proposal," Sparrow started because they all knew he would ask for her hand, "then it will be expected for you to join her, not only to prove she's married but also simply as her husband, her protector. No one will question what a stable hand is doing with them then. Even our guards who we trust fully don't need to know everything yet. The possibility of bringing magicians into this is too large to let slip just yet. Our guards will know once you get the magicians, until then, this is between us. They can believe you convinced me to stay with Ashtyn for your own selfish needs."

Gabriel nodded, not informing him that Gian at the very least had an idea of his true purpose on this trip. "Everyone already knows of my feelings. I'm sure they suspected I would weasel my way into any trip she took." They did. Wells's heavy coffers proved as much.

Sparrow chuckled. "We know but we thought it'd only be fair to let you in on the other option."

Evony's blue orbs gleaned with mischief. "You two have this weekend for the wedding. You leave early next week."

As Gabriel watched Sparrow help his wife to the door, his lips tipped up as he mumbled softly, "Thank you."

Evony's wink was outright dangerous.

GABRIEL WAS STORMING through the corridors on his way to Ashtyn's rooms. She'd been given a small suite like all the other medics, but it was a little farther out than the others'. At the end of the hall, it was colder than the rest of the corridor.

He hated that she lived there. Couldn't wait to bring her to his cottage, make it their cottage. Somewhere warm and inviting. Somewhere private for her to forget how much she hated everyone at the palace.

He almost forgot himself and smiled at the thought before the marriage proposal that was hidden from him came storming back to the forefront of his thoughts.

He banged on the door, uncaring about the noise because they were far enough from the other rooms.

Ashtyn opened it with an annoyed glare. "What?"

He raged into the suite, the fire crackling making the small room warm but not enough to shield from the winds outside creating a chill everywhere. It was far less furnished than he would've thought, more of that stone that made up the palace visible here than any other room he'd been to. It made it feel as if Ashtyn never wanted to settle into this room. Only a small rug, a smaller table, and a couch made up the space. Nothing personal, nothing homey, nothing that screamed Ashtyn.

Gabriel couldn't wait to get her to his cabin, finally give her a home.

He finally turned to her. "Were you ever going to tell me?"

She closed the door after checking if anyone heard his outburst. "What?"

"To keep all the attention off of you from the possibility of becoming a *Master*, you need to be married." He didn't care about the Master part, but it was still an important matter regarding her that she hadn't mentioned. They weren't in a relationship—she made that very clear—but in the past months, she'd been telling him more and more. Why stop now?

She huffed and folded her arms. "I don't *need* to get married."

"To keep the efforts away you do, and you know it."

She grit her teeth. "I didn't tell you because it's none of your business."

"Everything about you is my business!"

"Gabriel. Stop being ridiculous."

"Ashtyn, I'm in love w—"

"No, you're not. You *think* you are. In reality, you don't really know me."

"That's because you don't allow me to know you! Every goddamned day I try, Ashtyn."

The shocking part wasn't the statement. It was the fact that he was yelling. He never yelled. And certainly not at her.

So he calmed back down. "You're not marrying anyone else."

"Excuse me?"

"You're not marrying anyone else, Ashtyn."

She scoffed. "Who, exactly, put you in charge of my life decisions?"

"Ashtyn, you're min—"

"I am not dealing with this. I leave next week to—"

"I know," he interrupted. "I'm coming with you."

She quirked a sexy, sarcastic brow. "How'd you convince the Assassin to do that?"

"I didn't. He asked me."

Her nostrils flared. "What? Like I need a babysitter?"

"You're an asshole, Ashtyn. You may not need a babysitter, but the others will need someone to keep from killing you."

She fluttered her lashes and sent a hand to her chest. "What flattering words. You sure do know how to win me over."

"If the source ends up being airborne, we'll need magicians. Since Evony can't, we'll need the help of multiple magicians," Gabriel explained so she'd stop being so angry. "Other than her and Gemma, who're both pregnant therefore will not be joining, and James who won't leave them, I know the most about magicians. I will be coming to see if there is any other indication to require a magician."

She seemed to ease knowing there was an actual purpose behind his inclusion. "Fine. Whatever. You have a real excuse. I'm still not ma—"

"You're mine, Asht—"

"You're infatuated, Gabriel! It needs to end! I need you to go. Go find someone better. I'm sure Atiana's crush on the King will end soon enough."

"I don't want Atiana!" he yelled, getting in her face. "There is no one better for me. My interests have been you and only you since the day you yelled at me to move so you could heal Papa Ignatius."

"Gabriel, yo—"

"You're marrying me. No one else is touching you."

Her eyes narrowed. "So this is about sex? If you want it so bad, trust me, there are plenty of women here who would gladly bend over for you."

"I do not want any other woman, and if you insinuate it again, I'll bend you over right now." In the back of his mind, he was shocked by his own words. He'd never bent anyone over, yet instinctively, he knew he'd love it, love the feel of how tight she'd be in that position when he slipped inside her.

"Great," she barked. "Another disappointment. Can't wait."

He gave a mocking laugh. "My inexperience will have nothing to do with your satisfaction. Just because I've never touched a woman doesn't mean I won't be able to please my wife."

"You're a virgin?" she whispered, eyes wide.

He grabbed her face between his hands and brought her in close. "All of me, Ashtyn, will be yours and yours alone. You will be my firsts, lasts, and always."

She pushed away though he saw the battle in her eyes. She was beginning to lose her own war. "I am not your wife."

"Come this weekend you will be. I know you feel for me as I do you. I won't let you make us both miserable because you're scared. You have this weekend to go to Atiana for a dress.

Matter of fact, wear that gown she was making for you. You looked stunning in it."

Her mouth opened and closed trying to figure out what to say, so he didn't give her a chance.

He grabbed her again and brought her in for a chaste kiss. "In two days' time, you will be unequivocally mine and I yours."

He walked out before she could try to argue again, laughing to himself because he knew she would make his life miserable for thinking he could boss her around.

Lords, he loved that about her.

# CHAPTER 10
## ASHTYN

Ashtyn couldn't help the little smirk that would pop onto her lips every time Gabriel sent narrowed eyes her way. They'd only been on this trip to the town the Posse believed the first sick came from a couple of hours when they'd stopped for their first break. Only a couple more hours before they stopped for their second break. And between each one, during each one, Gabriel glared at her.

It wasn't her fault technically. She'd told him her love life would be none of his business so he should've expected that she'd hide away all weekend, so they couldn't marry. Though she'd admit, he'd been fucking sexy bossing her around. It'd taken all of her strength not to listen to him.

But she was doing it for him.

Stopping so much wasn't something any of them needed. All of her companions were accustomed to riding a horse uninterrupted for much longer, but it was something they knew Ashtyn required, though she'd never voice it. Other than the time she'd ridden to Sparrow's childhood home looking for

Evony earlier in the year, she'd never ridden such long, uninterrupted hours. Even the race to the top of the lands to get on a ship to the Island Nation had been done in a carriage—which Evony's magic had gotten for them. So though the horses needed breaks, these were done mostly for her.

On the second break, the guards who'd joined them squatted at some trees, throwing dice between them and starting to bet to kill the time. Tristan and Norya took the opportunity to disappear into the woods. They weren't discrete though and everyone knew of their very active relationship, so it was something Ashtyn had been expecting. Lords, she was lucky they'd decided to have the decency to go behind some trees.

But it all left her alone with Gabriel.

She really didn't want to be alone with him.

So she ignored him and paid attention to her horse instead. Technically the Princess's horse since Gabriel had insisted she get the safest one and Rosaelia wouldn't be needing Bella anytime soon. She was brushing the animal's side with her hands when she felt his presence beside her.

His hand gently landed on the small of her back as he whispered by her ear, "Did you think I didn't expect it, beautiful?"

He always called her beautiful. Why? Sure, she was good looking, but not that good looking.

"What exactly?"

"That you'd hide from me all weekend."

"Then why demand it."

She felt his shrug along her back. "I like to throw challenges from time to time. You could always surprise me."

"Maybe one day I will."

He chuckled as his lips touched the back of her head, and she stiffened. "I know you will, beautiful." He kissed her softly then peeled back.

Her heart raced with the memory of his lips on her, even on the back of her head. Goosebumps rose on her skin, and she swore a faint rush of blood swarmed through her body, threatening to reach her cheeks.

"You're doing a great job," he complimented.

Her head swung to the left. "What?"

He nodded forward. "The way you're gentle with her. You're doing great. That is one of the best ways to grow a relationship with them. You need to be gentle."

Her brows furrowed taking him in, but when their eyes met for a second, she realized he wasn't trying anything. He was simply keeping his promise from before.

She nodded. "I figured. I cannot imagine being anything but to such beautiful creatures."

She didn't turn for him, but she knew the comment got a genuine smile out of him. He loved his animals.

"They're prey animals in nature. They're not known to fight. It is why in some stories you will hear of the horses running off and leaving the human behind. They may not want to but like fight or flight is instinct to us, simple flight is instinct to them."

"Smart animals."

"It is why you must be gentle. A soft touch. You are letting her know you are no threat, that there will be no reason to run from you. You want to build that relationship. You want to continue it while riding with gentle touches that allow her to know you are companions."

The corner of Ashtyn's lip upturned. "With the amount of time we're likely to spend out here, I believe we'll become great companions."

"You already know how to ride so you know the pressures put on to get them to maneuver the way you like, you know you never have to hurt the beasts."

Her lips pouted on instinct. "Never."

There was amusement in his voice. "I think you will find great companionship here, Ash, because all she'll be able to do is listen to you."

She turned to meet Gabriel's eyes, questioning.

"You do not open up easily with us. Do so with her. We'll have more breaks, more opportunities. Take the time to talk with her. You want to be aware of your tone, so no harshness to our sweet animals, and no need to raise your voice—"

"Never."

"As prey animals, they have sensitive hearing, but use them. Take your therapy in the horses, Ash, the way you won't with anyone else. They are not only for travel and exercise. They provide great therapy for many people with traumas."

*He's not insinuating you have traumas*, Ash reminded herself. *He's simply teaching you the things you'd wanted to learn about them.*

"Anything else the master may teach me?" Ashtyn mocked.

Gabriel only grinned. "I do not see a reason this would happen, but it is a fun fact I like to let all of my learners know —they can't breathe through their mouths as we can."

Her brows shot up. "Truly?"

"It is normally something taught to the guards in case they take a horse to battle, but I like to think it can come in handy with anyone around their horse. If something blocks their nasal cavities, keep your voice and touch gentle and help them."

Ashtyn's pets continued, her attention holding onto the large animals. "Oh you poor thing. You got lucky with me, I'm a healer. I won't let anything happen to you."

Gabriel scoffed but there was amusement in it. "Oh, beautiful, the things you say sometimes."

Ashtyn smirked, about to make a remark when one of the guards called Gabriel's name.

Gabriel wiggled his brows in her direction, holding her gaze with sparkling ones of his own, then winked before heading off. He was so handsome, she barely reminded herself to stop longing after him.

Her touches continued on the horse as she turned back to the lovely animal. "You know I was joking right. *I'm* lucky to have you."

They'd have one more stop before making it to the inn. And it was coming up soon. Eventually on these trips, there wouldn't be this many stops but for Ashtyn's sake, they'd have one more. She hated to admit she was glad for it. Her ass was sore. Her legs were sore. Her back, shoulders, even her neck.

Ashtyn had spent the whole of the ride since their second stop talking to Bella. The horse was gentle and even seemed to be responding to her with a shake or nod of her head or a sound every now and then. Ashtyn kept her voice low and made sure to ride far enough away so none of the others heard, but she spent hours speaking to Bella until her mouth felt dry. Most of the talk was about a certain stable hand whose team Bella seemed to be on. Not shocking. He was the one who brushed her and gave her treats.

"So you see, Bella, it's better for him," she finally finished.

Bella snorted, pulling on the reins. Ashtyn read that to mean "You're full of it."

"Look, Bella. You're a horse, and he's your caretaker. Do you not want the best for him?"

Bella made a sound that Ashtyn knew was a yes.

"I do too. I know sometimes it does not seem like it, but the best thing for him is to have a woman without... my problems. I was such a dolt only a few years back. Lords, I'm not even sure I'm not now."

Bella made a sound that Ashtyn had learned to mean continue.

"I was a giggling harpy, Bella. I begged for attention, craved it. I was my happiest when men were drooling over me and women hating me. I was such a fucking dumbass." Ashtyn scoffed to herself. "Can you imagine that, Bella? I was mean to other women because I wanted them to hate me, to be jealous of me? I was a fucking twat. So fucking *pretty*."

Bella's head nodded as she spoke, almost like she was trying to comfort her rider.

Ashtyn's lips tipped into a sad smile as she pet the horse's mane. "I like to say I'm not that girl anymore, Bells, but I don't know. I don't like the attention anymore but that's because I've worked so hard to be rid of it, to stay within the shadows. Look at the palace. Most won't speak to me and those who do—aside from those weirdos in the Posse—aren't kind about it. I deserve it, so that's not the point. I just... Bella, what if all of this, healing and Masterhood bring on that attention and I... what if I revert back?" Ashtyn finally stated her biggest fear.

And as if Bella knew it, she made a sound that almost sounded like, "Finally. You've been talking for hours and now you got to the basis of it all."

Ashtyn's head fell, and she felt so ashamed of herself. "I cannot go back to being that girl, Bella. I cannot be the one who loves all that male attention. I can fight it with one or two men but if I get all that attention, handsome attention, will I become that girl again? The one who was such a bitch to other women? Good women? Women who didn't deserve it?" Ashtyn scowled. "I will not, cannot, put Gabriel through that, Bells."

Bella neighed.

Ashtyn pet her some more. "I knew you'd be on my side, girl."

"Final stop," Tristan's voice boomed through her conversation. He met her eyes. "Take full advantage because after this, we're riding until the inn."

That's a few more hours. Fuck.

Ashtyn hopped off her horse, thankful beyond belief as she rubbed out the pains all over her body.

"Need help?" Gabriel's voice was so close to her ear, she jumped.

Turning, they were nose to nose.

He gave a small smile. "I can rub those out for you. It'll take a while longer before you're accustomed to such riding."

He was so close. So handsome. So charming. So... sweet. She wanted to say yes. To allow him to do anything he wished to her. To allow him to be part of her life, tied to her, with her through this jour—

Bella huffed, shaking behind Ashtyn, and brought her out of her thoughts.

*Thank you, girl,* Ashtyn thought as she forced her lips down into a scowl. "Were you dropped as a child, Gabriel? Banged your head? Because something up there obviously isn't working."

His eyes still twinkled. "So sweet as always, Ash. I'm only trying to help."

Fuck. It would take more than some mean words. He was used to her already.

She deepened her scowl. "I don't need your help. I don't need anyone's. But trust you me, if I did, with the five other single men here, why would you ever expect I'd go to you first?"

Everything within him died. All the humor. Everything that made him, him.

"That's not funny, Ash."

Ashtyn squared her shoulders, trying not to wince from all the cracks. "Who's joking? Colt and Gian are some of the most handsome men around the palace. You're cute, Gabriel, but really? Above them? Handsome and fighters, protectors."

Gabriel ground his jaw, nostrils flaring. "Protectors?" He backed her against Bella. "When have I left you unprotected, Ashtyn? On every trip we've been on, *I've* been there. I would never allow anything to happen to you."

She smirked. "And you think they would? Sparrow wouldn't have chosen them if that were the case. Tristan'll kill them right now if it were."

Gabriel's nostrils flared some more as he caged her in. He was so fucking sexy.

"You're trying to hurt me, Ashtyn. It's not going to work."

She lifted her lips in a cruel grin. "Okay." She pushed out from his hold and over to the guards. She made her smile soft, her eyes shimmering, and hated herself for remembering how to do this so well. It turned her stomach, like she was already back to being that girl she'd been a few years back. "Colt, my muscles are tight. Crack them please?"

Colt had his back to Gabriel so he couldn't see the fumes coming off of the stable hand as Colt held her to his chest, curled her arms to her chest, and lifted her, her back cracking in all the right places.

A growl so deep and animalistic came from where Bella stood, Colt dropped Ashtyn and turned right in time to catch Gabriel's look. He backed away instantly, hands held high. "It was a simple crack. I do it to the guys all the time."

Ashtyn moved back for Bella, passing Gabriel and quickly whispering, "You're not man enough for me."

Gabriel didn't stick around this time, strolling out into the forests, and Ashtyn's heart cracked in her chest. Bella nuzzled into her.

Ashtyn softly pet her. "I hate myself, Bells. I hate what I'm doing to him. But it's for him. I apparently still have that woman inside me. The one I hate. I don't want him to come to hate me too."

# CHAPTER II

# GABRIEL

They'd gotten to their inn with great timing, even with all the stops. It'd given them the time to acquaint themselves with where they'd be staying for the next few days and allowed for Ashtyn to take the time she needed to steady her nerves before she began the next morning.

She'd need more of that after getting into it with Gabriel. Although upset to have gotten into any type of row with her, every time they did, Gabriel's heart sparked a little stronger. When Ashtyn fought someone, truly fought them, it was because she cared, and as much as she liked to pain him by saying she didn't, she truly cared for him. And he'd come to learn, as of late, her way of fighting with him was throwing other men at his face. As if she'd truly want them.

Gabriel still stiffened at the thought.

She was already stressed with what would be expected of her here, so Gabriel would try not to be too much of a bother. He scoffed to himself. He could do that as long as she stopped trying to make him jealous.

He stopped by her door at the inn and slid a note under her

door, one that bid her a goodnight since he knew she wouldn't want to see him quite yet, then he moved for his room next door.

The night passed in a blur. He spent the hours before sleep listening for her rooms, making sure there wasn't anything she needed of him. He knew other men wouldn't be a problem, that she only did that to hurt him, to get him to stop wanting her, and hopefully someday soon, he'd find out why. What was it about her that she was so adamant to hide from him?

In the morning, they survived on the nearly tasteless meals the inn had for them. Correction: the meals were probably amazing. They were made nearly tasteless because of the concoctions made for them to make sure none of the food they ate would do them any harm. They got all the nutrients needed of food, but none of the taste that might make them eat more than was required.

Then, when they were all ready, Tristan led them to their first destination—a home with three sick, all cousins. Ashtyn asked to be left alone with them as her task took plenty of her concentration, so they gave it to her.

Tristan and Norya would remain by her side, outside these doors using the time to scope out the area and question passerby, but they would remain with her always. That was their one cardinal rule.

It left Gabriel and the five guards to do their own scouring.

Gabriel felt invigorated knowing his task was of utmost importance. He'd forgotten the last time he'd gone in search specifically for magicians.

The others had taken their own canteens of water and separated for their treks around the lands. Two guards remained together as they traveled deeper within the forests than the rest of them.

Gabriel had seen the three other guards who'd come with

them split up, each taking a different route, so he was the last to choose where to start. He wasn't part of the protection of the palace, so he didn't have their same training. Whatever it was in them that told them where to check didn't reside in him, so he slowly glanced around until he heard the waters and moved in that direction.

On the way over, he couldn't help but catch the eye of a group of men in their thirties. They eyed him with mistrust, but it was something in their eyes that caught Gabriel's attention. They were... almost pretty in color. Yes, pretty felt like the right word. Then one's lips tipped up as he noticed the direction Gabriel was headed, and apprehension settled into him.

He could always turn around but instead, Gabriel continued on, the waters calling for him.

They weren't too close to the beaches, but there was a small alcove where a lake visited the shoreline here. It was a small space, only about thirty yards of water before two cliffs met and disrupted the views to the waters. It was a beautiful spot for the men to get fish for eating in their town.

Gabriel was surprised to find himself alone when he arrived. He'd thought there would surely be men trying to catch a few animals, but there was nothing. Was it because it was coming up on winter or were they now cautious of eating anything from this body of water? Was that why the man had looked at him like that? Like he was stupid for wanting to catch fish here?

The sunlight shone over the water, glittering it like a thousand shards of glass. It was peaceful out here, romantic.

It was the kind of place he imagined his friends from the South would spend their time; one in particular taking precious moments to ruminate all the marvels the elements supplied here. The water, the dirt of the forests mixing with the beach's sand, the breeze cooling the area a little more than inland, and the sun beaming down even now so close to the winter months to keep him warm enough.

As Gabriel took in the landscape, he felt at ease. As if he'd been here before.

He hadn't. He knew that much, but something about it felt so familiar. Maybe that's why he knew his friends in the South would love it. This felt like the South.

The mix of all the elements as he stood off reminded him of a moment from when he was eight years old. It didn't take much magic, once homed in, to play with the elements, and Gabriel had always loved going out with the magicians in his home to watch them do it.

The water in this lake shimmered like it was preparing to grow. The sand shook like it was deciding what to take the shape of. The dirt farther up where Gabriel stood swayed like they were preparing for flight. The air around him tickled his nose and the sun seemed to shine brighter.

Gabriel's eyes bunched.

This felt familiar.

So familiar.

Too famil—

All at once, everything took route. The water grew and shook over to the sands and dirt, flying with the winds and burning under the sun's blaze. It was cold this time of year, cold right outside this clearing, but here, Gabriel felt heat. Heat and dirt and water and suffocating air until all at once, it came together beneath the water's surface and the most exquisite explosion he'd ever seen took place.

It was breathtaking.

Figuratively, but also...

The wind was knocked out of Gabriel as he was shot through the air and smacked back down. As if laughing at him, the sun had those same pretty eyes lined in pinks and lavenders and a bit of ivory.

This was magical...

This was... he couldn't think. He needed sleep.

*GABRIEL WAS seven years old when his group of orphans found themselves in the Southern Lands. They were a ragtag group aged five to fifteen and traveled through the lands, each looking for the spot that felt permanent. Out of the twelve they started with at the beginning of the journey on the east of the Northern Lands, only eight now remained.*

*Gabriel didn't expect to find a home in the Southern Lands. It was a beautiful place, but he thought it a little too warm. The North was a perfect mix of chills and sun for his likings, but the others had all wanted to come to the South, to get a taste of life here.*

*They seemed to love it. Not all seven of them looked ready to settle down in the town they'd stopped at, but they all basked in the heat and the Southern people. It became clear to Gabriel in that moment that he would be the only one of them wanting to travel back up north. He only hoped at least one of them wanted to travel some of the way with him, at least to the border, so he didn't have to do it on his own. He was confident in his abilities, but at only seven, he knew he needed to be cautious.*

*"You're thinking rather hard, my love." A woman with really tanned skin stopped beside him. She wore a beautiful, bright smile.*

*"You only survive by thinking hard." He furrowed his brows because that was how his group of orphans had made it on their travels untouched all this time.*

*The woman, who must've been twenty years his senior, turned that wide smile warm. "Oh, dear child, you are young. Learn to live in that imagination."*

*His brows furrowed even more. "How?"*

*She stuck out her hand for him to take. "Come with me."*

*One of their top rules while traveling was to never go with a stranger. It was how they remained free from the men who wanted to exploit them.*

*But Gabriel felt a profound wave wash through him just by looking up at her, so he took her hand. "What's your name?"*

*"Lanlik." She led him past homes. "Yours, my dear?"*

*"Gabriel."*

*"Gabriel. A beautiful name. Northern?"*

*She must've known he was Northern from his looks, but he nodded anyway. There were Northerners who lived in the Southern Lands, maybe she thought he was born here. "Yes."*

*They stopped at a home between another house and a shop. "This is where I live with my sisters. That shop there is where we sell our services."*

*"Services?"*

*She tugged him to the home and enjoyed the moment Gabriel took it all in. The inside was nothing like what he'd expected. It had curtains and rugs and pillows everywhere. Plush couches and intricate tables and bowls of fruit. There were three women in the common space, two of which sat at the far end weaving a blanket between them. The other was taking laps around the space, the bangles at her wrists clinking together with every sound. And in the far corner sat a box where sounds came from.*

*"Yes, Gabriel. We're magicians. We offer our services in exchange for the things we require," Lanlik answered.*

*Magicians weren't allowed in the North.*

*That's why some Northerners lived in the South.*

*Gabriel's mouth remained open as he floated over to the sound box. "What is this?"*

*"It is a music box. Anvel is the best at making them, and they make great gifts to spouses. Her services are best used for such things."*

*"It's incredible... but how does the music get inside the box? Where does it come from? Does it ever stop? Will your magic be required to keep it going?"*

*She laughed, her tone soft and exuberant. "Oh, you curious, wonderful child. Those are all things magicians take care of when it is requested."*

*"Magicians aren't allowed in the North." His eyes glazed over as he took in the beautiful intricacies of the box itself. The sounds coming from within were incredible, but the box also held a sort of wonder.*

*He hadn't realized he'd reach out for it until Lanlik stopped by his side, dropping so they were face to face. "Would you like to keep it?"*

*The sound box fell back onto the table it'd been on, and Gabriel stepped back quickly. "I'm sorry."*

*"Don't be, child. You're young. Be curious."*

*Gabriel blinked rapidly as he turned back to the rest of the room, to all the color. "Can you show me all your magic?"*

*She snorted. "All of it, child? That'll take a long time. I think your family will be quite worried."*

*He shrugged. "I don't have a family."*

*Her soft hand landed on his shoulder, turning him to face her. "Is that what you're in search of, Gabriel? A family?"*

*He shrugged again, not knowing. "I want to go back to the North." Then he turned back to the room. "But I want to learn about magic first." Magicians weren't allowed in the North.*

*Turning back to Lanlik, Gabriel analyzed her furrowed brows. Was she mad he didn't wish to stay?*

*Then she smiled. "Okay. If you have no one waiting for you, you* can stay here. You learn your fill and when you're ready, I'll take you up north myself."

"But I don't want to take you away from your family."

"You won't, sweet child." She pushed his hair back. "I have a good friend up in the palace. He works with horses. I think he'd love to take you in."

Gabriel's head snapped, eyes widening, and a small smile grew on his lips. "Horses?"

She laughed. "Yes, child, horses. I'm guessing you really like horses?"

He nodded vigorously. "Did you read my mind? Is that how you knew?"

"No. Most magicians cannot enter others' minds. Come." She took his hand and led him past the common spaces and into a large room in the back. "This is where we come to practice our magic."

It was a mostly bare room. There were still rugs everywhere, and pillows piled on the ground for sitting, still curtains hanging on the walls, but no furniture. The dark colors continued into this room, but there wasn't much else. And it was a lot quieter than the other room they'd been in, and not only because there was no sound box here.

"Do you need to be here to practice?" He left her side, hand grazing the curtains as he walked around the space.

She had a bowl when she took a seat on a pillow in the middle of the room. "No. But this room has been silenced so we can have peace. Most magicians need to practice to master the specific sort of magic they're gifted with. Only Masters in the past have been able to do it all without all the practice it requires from us, and we haven't seen a Master in a very long time."

Gabriel took the seat in front of her. "What's your area of magic?"

She grinned, eyes sparkling. "I have a special control of the ground we walk on, the winds that flow around us. My magic has to do with the elements."

His eyes widened, heart hammering with excitement. "How do you practice that?"

"By simply speaking to the elements themselves." She placed the bowl between them and inside was dirt.

"How?" Gabriel stared into the dirt, mesmerized.

She shrugged. "The same way certain things in life will come easier to you, this comes to me. All magicians tend to be able to handle at least one element. I can do them all and with far more ease."

Before Gabriel could ask any more questions, the dirt from the bowl was floating up into the air. Then, in a perfect uniform, it all started swirling in front of him before rushing around him and enveloping him with the show. Lanlik must've been very gifted with her magic because the way the dirt moved looked like a performance, like she could get it to do anything she liked.

When it settled in the air around him, calming from the show it'd all just put on, Gabriel turned to Lanlik. "What do you usually do with your magic?"

"Normally, my sort of magic is most useful in repairs. It is why I practice my grounded element the most, so when something needs fixing, I can do so. But the winds are also used. In that case, it is normally to speed off danger."

"Are you in danger a lot?"

"No, child. Luckily, we are not." Her magic continued to move the dirt around them, but Gabriel was solely focused on her. "But if we were, I need to be well-honed. I need to be able to protect those I love."

His eyes widened. "Does loving someone mean you have to be in danger?"

Her lips tipped up, warm and inviting. "It sounds bad, but I promise you it is not. When you love someone, you do not mind being in danger lest they're kept safe."

"Are you in love then?"

Her smile turned down. "No. Not yet. But I believe wholly in it, my child. And until I find him, I do not want another."

His brows furrowed. "Why would you have another if you are not in love?"

"I love the innocence of children, Gabriel. You are the reason I have so much hope for this world, for my future."

Gabriel's brows only furrowed. That did not make any sense. If a person wasn't in love, why would they want to be with anyone? From what he'd seen in all of their travels, only those in love looked the happiest. The others looked to be missing something in life.

"Will you tell me how you fix things with your magic?"

Her grin turned bright once more but her eyes still looked a little sad. He felt awful for doing that to her. But she began her demonstration before he could ask her what he could do to make her feel better.

# ASHTYN

Her hands over his body, feeling every muscle and nerve within him, told her he was okay, that he wasn't hurt but only passed out. It made her sigh out in relief, but it also provoked that part of her that wanted the opportunity to get her frustration out on him by smacking him awake.

She wasn't actually planning on doing it, but the adrenaline from fearing for his life was pumping so wildly within her that Ashtyn didn't realize her hand was flying until she heard the sound reverberating off of Gabriel's cheek, and he sprung awake.

His gaze was wide and wild until it landed on Ashtyn and calmed. "Did you just slap me?"

"You needed to wake up," she grumbled as she rose to her feet, leaving him lying on the ground.

He scoffed, but a glance in his direction proved he wasn't angry. "Sure, beautiful. I'll allow that to be your reasoning. But only because it proves that you feared for my life. I think you're already showing how much you care for me. To think, we could've been married two days already had you not been stubborn."

She grimaced, storming off for the inn, to the rooms they'd been given. "I should've left you for the animals." And yet, her shoulders relaxed knowing he wasn't angry with her any longer. In the night they'd spent so close yet so far apart, in the letter he'd left her bidding her a goodnight, in the time away all day, Ashtyn had come to realize she'd been a fucking moron to do that to him. If she didn't want to be like past her, she couldn't act like it. It was her job to make sure she didn't turn back into that woman, and that started with not hurting Gabriel with such insinuations.

He laughed as his arm fell over her shoulders, bringing her in to kiss her crown. "How did you know I was out here anyway?"

She pushed away. "One of the guards saw you and came for us. You're lucky I'd already started the healing process for all those in that home when he got to us."

"Are you done healing then?"

"No. I need to check on them in the morning to make sure their bodies are taking well to it, but until then, there're others here who also need my help. I'm going to clean this muck you got on me, then I'm going back to them."

Gabriel glanced down and noticed for the first time that both of them, but mostly him, were covered in mud. "Are you offering a shared bath, beautiful?"

She narrowed her eyes. "You're lucky I offered your life after what you just did."

"What I did! The ground exploded. How was that my doing?"

She huffed. "What happened? If there're random explosions, then the people here aren't safe."

"They'll be fine."

"How do you know?"

He didn't answer right away since they'd reached their rooms. Instead, he got the water started for her shower then began stripping right out in the open for her to see. Ashtyn, for her part, hid behind the screens left for maidens and stripped out of her mucked clothes.

Finally, Gabriel answered, "I recognized what happened. I'd witnessed moments like this when I was living in the South before the palace. Plus it was empty. I think the townsfolk know not to go there. There were men watching me go like I was crazy. If anything, we'll just be sure to remind them."

Her eyes widened at any prospect of him in a similar station before neck snapping to view him after she'd wrapped herself in a towel. She couldn't fight that there was pure curiosity within her eyes, but she didn't question him any further as she moved for the shower and hung her towel to block his view before getting in. The showers were some of the very good that came of King Edmund. He'd gotten this form of advanced technology for every single one of his towns and villages in the North, no matter how small or poor. Every single one had running showers and baths rather than the olden ways of having to heat the water and pour it into a tub. She remembered doing so as a child and was glad that had been quickly remedied all over the lands.

Gabriel didn't join her—thankfully—but he also didn't hide away from her views. Behind the towel that barred her body from his viewing, she still saw glimpses of him. He watched her with an unwavering stare. His cock grew heavy with the need to fill her, and though a foreign part of her desperately wanted him to listen to it, she was glad he ignored it. She was still angry with him even though she knew none of what happened was his fault. The simple fact that he could've died proved Ashtyn's original point—he shouldn't have come with her. *She* was the danger. Bad things happened to those who got close to her.

She didn't want to get out from beneath the beating water when she was cleaned but was forced to do so when Gabriel began forward as if readying to join her in the shower. Her body begged her to remain by his side, but she ignored it to listen to her head instead. She had a very smart head, after all.

She scurried away with the towel before he could get any view of her, and dried herself slowly as her body and mind fought over which was in control of the situation. She had that little war with herself with her back facing Gabriel, so she didn't get lost watching his hands move over his body, but it didn't seem to help all that much when she had such an active imagination and now knew exactly what his cock looked like... throbbing and ready for her.

Ashtyn busied herself behind the screen once more, pulling out a plain dress to wear and took her time getting dressed. By the time she was fully clothed, the shower was off, and Gabriel was drying himself with a towel as he reached her side.

He quickly threw on a pair of trousers, then grabbed her arm when she tried to make it for the door. "Stop. Your hair."

She touched it subconsciously. "What about it?"

"Let me brush it, Ash."

She searched his eyes. They were so genuine, she couldn't deny him. "Okay," she said softly, her heart winning this battle. He needed to stop that control he had over her.

He left her for the chair by the window. The curtains were mostly closed but a bit of sunlight still showed through. He dropped a pillow on the ground, then took a seat on the chair.

Ashtyn subconsciously licked her lips as her gaze dropped to the pillow between his legs. His gaze latching onto her mouth told her it sent the wrong message.

She dropped immediately, facing away from him so her hair was in his hands, and hugged her legs to her chest.

He was gentle with her as he took her long strands into his lap and began to softly detangle and brush them. "You don't know about my time before the palace, do you?"

He knew she didn't, but she wouldn't reprimand him at the moment for such a ludicrous question. Not when she felt so heavenly with her hair being nurtured. "I don't know much about it at the palace. Obviously I wouldn't know of it before."

He chuckled. "My feisty little healer."

She rolled her eyes before they fell closed with a sigh because of the delicate way he brushed her hair. "I'm guessing you were in the South for a while? Is that how you know of magicians?"

"My smart little healer."

"Your annoyed little healer," she mumbled.

He laughed loudly as he leaned down to kiss her forehead. His lips remained skimming that patch of skin, making her relax deeper into him. "At least you're mine, Ash."

She rolled her eyes and pulled away.

He remained hovering over her, his breath at her ear when he said, "We don't have to talk about it if you don't want to."

Ashtyn froze with that statement. She'd assumed he'd force their relationship's growth almost like he'd forced his way onto this journey—no matter he had the excuse of his magician's knowledge that the Posse was using. Ashtyn wasn't fool enough to think he wouldn't have found a way otherwise. In this moment, she hadn't thought he'd allow her the chance not to learn more about him. He was giving her an out, the same way he'd given her an out with their marriage, allowing her to set the speed.

But... she didn't want the out. Not right now.

She opened her eyes and caught his. Their faces were close together when she whispered, "I'd like to know."

He kissed her forehead once more before lifting back to continue brushing her hair. As he did so, he began talking, "I don't remember having parents. My earliest memory is from an orphanage and even they weren't entirely sure about my past. All they knew was I'd come from a couple from the neighboring village, one who'd passed not long after I was born. They told it to me like a romance—that my mother died in childbirth and my father of a broken heart. They used to tell me how in love the two were, but as an adult, I know they were making that part up, that they had no idea about what my parents relationship had been like. But I choose to believe that story."

"That's not surprising."

"How's that?"

"You're a hot twenty-four-year-old virgin. The only way that would be possible is if you had an unbreakable belief in love, of there being only one person for everyone."

"And you don't believe it."

"Not that I don't believe it. I want to, but..."

He kissed her hair quickly before saying, "I'll show you, beautiful."

She cleared her throat. "So how'd you end up in the South?"

"The orphanage did what they could, but it wasn't very well kept. A group of us, the oldest being fifteen at the time, ended up leaving to 'travel the lands and find our home' when I was seven. We ended up in the South. That's where I met Lanlik. She was twenty-five at the time and a magician. She took me under her wing when she found out I didn't have a family, almost raising me like a mother. She knew I wanted to live up here though, so she knew our time would come to an end at some point. But she was lovely. When I got there, all I'd known about magic was that the North didn't allow it. But that house, it was... extraordinary. It was a lot, a lot of things and color and people, but it felt like a home. Lanlik spoke to her sisterhood, and they allowed me to remain with them. That's how I know so much about magic—they showed me. Lanlik is the reason I know so much about elemental magic. That explosion back by the lake, that's something she could do with her magic. She never did, obviously, but she had the power to, the same way Evony would now. What she used her power for was the opposite—it was to repair damages that came from things like that."

"Did she know why things like that happened to begin?"

"You told me, back when you were healing Papa Ignatius when he'd been stabbed, you told me how you heal. That you can go into bodies and almost speak to our insides. Almost like magic."

She nodded. It had to be magic. She was convinced it was a small element of magic, but it didn't feel like magic. She didn't get that same feeling she did when Evony's magic filled a space.

"That's what Lanlik did too. She spoke to the elements. She found that there were disturbances that caused things like that. Things that couldn't be seen by us but was felt by the lands. It can help evidence one of our hypotheses—this plague could be coming from some natural cause."

"So we need an elemental magician to be able to find it?"

"I don't know," he whispered. "I don't know where this plague is coming from. I'm only hypothesizing. But... I'd been around two explosions during my time in the South. They were both like that. They both called to the elements the way it had at the beach. Like I wasn't meant to be hurt, but there was a force that needed to come alive. It is difficult to explain, but I was thrown back simply because I didn't move. Any sane person would've moved, especially these villagers."

She nodded slowly. "I understand."

He huffed, still brushing. "Do you?"

He didn't believe her. "Not in actuality. But sometimes... I have dreams."

"Dreams?"

Ashtyn sighed. "They do not come often, but sometimes, I feel that the elements are guiding me too. Like I'm meant to be lost and they're trying to take me home. I do not understand it normally. And I never stay asleep long enough to find out where I'm meant to go. But I always feel safe, like I'm not meant to be hurt." She hadn't properly thought of those dreams in quite some time.

"Maybe you do understand then."

She was lost in thoughts of all those memories brought up in her. Memories? They weren't memories but they felt like it. Were dreams so strong as to feel like real events?

Ashtyn shook herself out of such heavy thoughts and instead focused on what was happening outside of this room. She needed to get back out there, find the other three people who were sick and help them with what was left in the day. But she didn't want to move. She wasn't selfish often, not anymore, but in the wake of those memories—dreams— Ashtyn didn't fight it as she so often did.

She allowed her body to settle and her eyes to shut, attempting to be kind with herself, to allow this time with Gabriel, at least for a little while longer before she got back to her job. "Was Lanlik your favorite magician?"

She couldn't see him, but the joy that escaped his voice told her he'd broken out into a large grin. "My favorite magician, yes. My favorite type of magician, no. She was my favorite person because she essentially raised me for three years then brought me here to Papa Ignatius. But my favorite type of magician were definitely the ones who worked with animals. Animal whisperers, I guess."

She chuckled softly. "Of course."

He set the brush aside and took the time to slowly play with her hair, pulling it together and running through the strands with his fingers. "One of the sisterhood was an animal whisperer. Her name was Mina. She was thirty-two when we met and unfortunately the first to get married after I arrived." When Ashtyn snort-laughed, he corrected himself. "I mean, it's amazing she found love, but she was my favorite type of magician and she'd moved out so we couldn't work her magic every day together like we had before. But I visited often, then met another animal whisperer, Hansel, and spent time with both of them in my three years living down south. They're the reason I'm so good with the horses."

She scoffed for real this time. "I don't think you can be that good with animals and not have it innately in you, horse boy."

He laughed, pulling on her hair a little hard to snap her head back so their eyes met. "I did have it in me, but they definitely helped." He softened his hold and allowed her head to fall forward once more. "I learned about other animals with them too. I couldn't speak with the animals since I'm no magician, but they got into the animals minds and interpreted for me. It felt surreal to experience it. It's what I miss most."

She tugged on her hair so he'd release it and turned in her spot to look up at him, hands resting on his lap. "You're friends with Sapphire now. And she's the Master, so I'm sure she can probably do the same thing if she tried. Ask her."

He gave a warm smile. "Maybe I will. Although Sparrow won't allow it until after she's given birth."

She giggled. "Yes, you will definitely have to wait. I'm a great healer, but if the Master Assassin kills you, I don't think I can do much about that."

His hand ran into her hair as he grabbed the back of her head and held her in place, stared into her eyes like he was reading his future. He leaned in slowly and brushed his lips with hers. "I'm glad to know you care so much about me, wife."

"I'm not your wife."

He smirked. "Soon-to-be wife."

Her eyes narrowed, but before she could argue, he kissed her.

He'd done so before. Soft and chaste. This kiss was soft, but it was so different from before. This was a true kiss, one filled with passion, one that might burn down nations to keep his lips on hers.

This was the kiss her friends—if she could call them that—spoke of. One that cleared all worries and escaped into paradise.

His tongue slipping into her mouth made her gasp. His exploration almost made her moan. Her need to reciprocate this fevered passion sent her heart racing.

She could no longer fight herself when he made her moan by sucking on the tip of her tongue.

Ashtyn pulled away to regain some control of her senses but didn't push him back. She lost herself in his eyes and for once in her life, she allowed herself this pleasure she'd never known possible.

THE DAYS PASSED IN A BLUR. One moment she was sitting before Gabriel as he brushed her hair and the next, she'd healed seven more people and checked on all of them.

She'd only been at work for three full days and gotten to ten people. It wasn't a great number, but as she learned how to home in her skill for this particular problem, she got faster at detecting the help needed in every patient's body.

But her entourage wanted to get back to the palace to discuss matters with the Posse, so they were headed back. They passed by one village with two sick—one with the plague, the other with the common flu—so Ashtyn insisted they stop and she would heal them and was glad when no one protested. It extended the trip a whole day as she also needed to check on them to make sure the sickness was gone, but she was glad to do so, even though none of it would matter if she didn't stop the source from continuing to spread it, from spreading it back to those she healed.

They were on one of their final breaks before making it to the palace, this time having stopped by a small village where her entourage could interact with the village folk. She wasn't in the socializing spirit.

But Gabriel was.

Gabriel always was.

He was by the small set of stables this place had and smiled at a group of children as they all circled him wanting to learn all they could. They looked to range from ages five to ten and all desperately wanted his attention.

From Ashtyn's perch on a branch midway up a tree, she could perfectly watch him interact with said kids while the rest of their little entourage did their own things—the warrior duo getting out of sight and hearing distance from the children while the guards relaxed. Three of them were quite social as well, speaking more with the adults, but they didn't demand attention the way Gabriel's presence did.

Even the adults looked to cling to every word out of Gabriel's mouth from where they stood yards away, probably unable to hear beyond the squeals of the children.

But they still watched him, admired him.

Especially the women.

Ashtyn didn't focus on that matter. As much as she didn't like it, she was used to women panting over him. They did so at the palace all the time.

Instead, Ashtyn went back to watching him with the children as she thought back to what he'd told her of his past over the last few days. After originally learning of his time in the South, Gabriel had sat her before him to brush and play with her hair as he told her more and more every night without her having to ask for it. And each time, Ashtyn found herself... softening to him.

Like when he told her he'd been the test subject to magical practices—from being levitated across the yards to making him 'fall in love' with another then back out with the use of a special magic only one magician he knew had to simply help with the required materials.

Or when he told her of the others he'd known, those who weren't magicians. Of the woodworkers, leatherworkers, and butchers he spent much of his time with, absorbing as much as he could like the children around him were now doing.

Or the time he climbed down the cliff they lived by because he wanted to see what was in the cave by the oceans and lost track of time, and by the time he got back to the magicians three days later, they were in a fit.

Every single one had the same effect. She wanted him, but she could keep that information to herself. He already had a wide enough ego where it came to her feelings.

But from this distance, Ashtyn smiled down at him. He was so good with children. So patient and kind and accepting. He gave every single one of them the same amount of attention and had a way of making each one feel special. Even from a distance, Ashtyn could tell as much. The way those children stared up at him, said as much.

It said so much.

It showed just how great of a father he was going to be.

Ashtyn snapped out of her thoughts. She never lied to herself about Gabriel. Well, almost never.

But she absolutely never allowed herself to think of any future Gabriel. That had nothing to do with her, and she could not allow herself to become distracted in the fantasy.

So Ashtyn looked away, needing to distract herself.

In the distance, she could see the peaks of the palace. It was so far out still that Ashtyn was sure she was probably envisioning something that could not truly be seen yet, but still, she thought of the palace. Of going back to Atiana's rooms and seeing that dress again, hoping it was ready. She didn't have anywhere to wear it, but she also never had visitors to her suit so she could prance around in it all night long with no one the wiser.

Ashtyn smiled to herself at the thought. She didn't know why she'd commissioned this dress to begin. She'd wanted one, yes, and Atiana had been all too happy to oblige, but why? She could've just altered a ready-made gown, yet she'd envisioned this specific ivory mermaid style one, and Atiana had outdone herself.

She was so close to being able to try on that beauty once again yet so far away.

Lost in thoughts of possibly another gown she could commission since Ashtyn had no other real uses for her coin, Ashtyn didn't realize how much time had passed. It could have been mere minutes or a whole hour.

What finally got her attention back to those down in the village was the feeling of eyes on her, as if beckoning for her to turn back around. She met charming brown ones when she did. They held a sparkle that felt specially put in place for her.

She ignored her pinking cheeks and scrambled off the tree, needing to be out of his sights.

# CHAPTER 13
# ASHTYN

The palace had a calming feeling about it, almost like she was coming home.

It was an odd sensation, one she'd felt more than once this past year. Was it because she hadn't left the confines of the palace grounds since showing up to it, so when she'd gone after Sapphire, then Emerald, she'd been able to truly experience how she felt for the palace? That it had become home?

Was that it? Or was it because it was only a few weeks before going after Evony that she'd spoken with Gabriel for the first time? Was it that she knew she was coming back to the grounds Gabriel lived, even though he had been with her on both of those journeys the way he'd been with her this time?

Either way, they were back, and Ashtyn was at peace.

As her gaze longed for the cottage at the end of the grounds rather than her cold rooms, her chest ached a bit.

Maybe she wasn't entirely home.

Not that it mattered. She wasn't headed for her rooms. Not quite yet.

First, she needed to see the Posse, her entourage of eight around her.

Gabriel's hand, ever consistent, landed on the small of her back as he continued his conversation with two of the guards, the three back to discussing a bet they'd made while in the last village about a young couple. Ashtyn wasn't listening. She was simply glad for the support as they all followed Tristan and Norya, now in excited conversation with Miels, to the King's meeting room.

It'd been hours since they'd been back, given the time to shower, eat, and relax, they were now back to business. Ashtyn could lie to them all that she didn't want to be surrounded by them but deep down, she couldn't help how much she enjoyed this. Being part of this group, helping the people of the lands, being part of the King's confidants.

Yes, she would never admit to such a thing aloud.

Inside, King Edmund was already sitting at the end with his Assassin to his left. The Magician sat in her husband's lap, looking to be taking a nap as he smoothed one hand gently up and down her back while the other lay on her rounded stomach. He was in a heated debate with the King, and though they hardly showed it, Ashtyn knew they were aware of the new group who'd joined them.

Beside them sat James with his pregnant wife also in his lap. She wasn't napping since the pregnancy hadn't hit her as hard as it had Evony, but she snuggled into her husband anyway, whispering into his ear and distracting him from joining Edmund and Sparrow's conversation. Not that he looked bothered by it.

And beside them—the barbarian, and to Ashtyn's surprise, Princess Rosaelia in his lap. The girl was bright red which eased some of Ashtyn's shock, proving it was Killian who had pulled his wife into his lap as Emerald would've been too conscious of all the bodies in the room to do so on her own. Either way, she looked content as she silently watched the others while her husband tracked the new group entering the room. Norya was like a sister to him yet he still seemed on edge, like he didn't want anyone around his wife, like he'd do anything to protect her.

And though Sparrow was by far stronger because of his Masterhood, Killian was far more feared within the palace. He was an Island barbarian with scars marring his face. People feared walking around him, he definitely didn't have to worry about anyone touching his wife.

Gabriel followed Tristan as the man sat beside Killian to the King's right, taking Norya into his lap. Norya leaned in to whisper in his ear as they waited for this meeting to start, and Ashtyn was taken aback by how... soft the moment was. The two were so big and powerful for so long that she forgot sometimes how soft they went for one another. How Tristan giggled with her. Was that the right word? Giggling wasn't masculine and he definitely looked masculine doing so, but... nope, for sure giggling with her.

Ashtyn wasn't even aware she'd been staring until Gabriel's whisper in her ear snapped her out of it, "What do you think they're so giddy about?"

Her cheeks flushed. "Maybe they're happy to be back in their suite so they're not tormenting us with how loud they are."

Gabriel snorted. "Absolutely not. Probably planning on how to make it worse when we head back out."

Ashtyn couldn't hold in her laugh. "Yeah, you're probably right."

Then Gabriel's hand, so warm and large on her back, pushed softly to lead her once again, and she realized while they'd been standing there whispering, the guards had taken their seats. There was only one remaining seat left.

Ashtyn wanted to throw a tantrum. They'd known exactly how many people would be showing up. Yes, the three couples had taken to sitting in laps, so they expected the same of the warrior duo, but she and Gabriel were *not* together.

Gabriel took the remaining seat between the warrior duo and Noah anyway. He looked at her expectantly, his legs spread wide as he waited for her.

She wanted to be stubborn and remain standing until she got a seat of her own. Or until Gabriel chose to give his up and be the one standing. But the shine in his eyes said he wouldn't be doing that.

She narrowed her own and glanced at the five guards. As if noticing her attention, all of them stiffened and scooted into the table.

Gabriel's smirk was large as she met his gaze again. *I own you*, he mouthed.

*I hate you*, she mouthed back.

As if realizing everyone was ready—well, just about everyone—the King and Assassin ended their conversation, and while Sparrow gave his wife loving kisses to rouse her from sleep, Ashtyn met the King's eyes.

There was mirth there.

Ashtyn crossed her arms before her chest. "You're not going to get me a chair? Really?"

"It's right there." He eyed Gabriel.

Ashtyn scoffed. "Seriously?"

His eyes were shimmering. Teasing. Was this the man the Posse got to see constantly. He was sexy.

Ashtyn was back to wanting to be stubborn, but...

But a single glance around the table showed how comfortable all the women were in their men's laps, and though

Ashtyn knew it was stupid to give the stable hand such hopes, she couldn't deny she wanted to feel that at ease. Especially with any conversations that were bound to take place.

She finally huffed out and made her way to him.

He was grinning from ear to ear when she settled into his lap, his arms wrapping around her waist to hold him to her, and she couldn't lie—this was the most comfortable she'd ever been.

She didn't turn to him as she grimaced. "Don't get the wrong idea, horse boy."

"And what idea is that, wife?" he whispered.

"I still don't like you. And I'm not your wife."

"Yet." He kissed the spot below her ear, and shivers raced down her spine, her entire body really.

Ashtyn ignored him while the others began talking. Frankly, she wasn't entirely sure why she was there. The men did all the talking—telling the others about the sick they'd found, how she'd healed and checked in on them, how she felt after each one as if they could know such a thing.

When she scoffed, she felt Gabriel's grin on her cheek but didn't turn to him as he said, "She still thinks I don't know everything about her. Trust me, I can tell how tired she gets and when she needs the breaks. The amount she's been doing has gotten her tired, but she doesn't need to be forced to stop yet."

Ashtyn rolled her eyes. She didn't care if what he was saying was true.

Then the men continued—telling the others about what they'd found, which was mostly nothing, about those they'd spoken to in the villages while she'd been busy healing, and about the explosion that Gabriel explained would be best to have magicians go around the lands and stabilize it. He explained how it was done every few years in the South and having gone nearly four decades without it, the North was in desperate need, and it probably wouldn't be long before more began happening.

Ashtyn didn't allow herself to look at him, but fuck if her core didn't tighten at his confidence, his expertise.

"Good," the King nodded, his glances jumping from Gabriel to the guards to Sparrow as if asking him a question.

Sparrow finally nodded, holding his wife who'd gone back to sleep—or at least, she'd closed her eyes but was probably still listening, ready to butt in when she didn't like something —and said, "They're good."

He was referring to the guards. Had they been getting tested for something? Either way, they'd passed.

They all sat up, waiting to hear what that comment meant.

And Edmund didn't make them wait to hear it. Thankfully, she was just as curious as them. "You boys knew to go out to protect our healer but also to scour for the source of such a problem, and possibly other problems. What you didn't know was that Gabriel wasn't only allowed to go because of his obsession with the healer"—snickers came from all around the table, even rumbling from the body beneath her—"but also because he lived in the South, with magicians. Other than these three"—he pointed to Evony, Gemma, and James— "who couldn't go because of their situations, he's our best source. Part of his job was also to find anything that may require magicians. I'm glad he found something that doesn't have to do with the sickness. Something that truly requires them because... Because I will be reversing the laws against magicians in the North." None of the guards looked shocked or angry. "I have meetings specifically for this cause often. I have a man out now researching to see the North's accep-tance. But any way we can show our people that magicians are here to help is a benefit for us." He finally turned back to

Ashtyn. "Which leads to my next point. The South has called for you."

She stiffened. "Already?"

He shrugged. "Word gets around. Even when you think it is secretive. Especially for something so important as healing. And the council has their snitches."

She snorted. "As if you don't."

He winked. "Most importantly, though, is the fact that you may be the Healer. They have been on the search for a Master Healer for some time. They were convinced that Master would be Southern. I do not think they are overjoyed that I may have another. You will be going. Soon. I know you wish to continue healing but this will get them off our backs sooner, and it will give Gabriel the opportunity to check in for magicians. I cannot put everything on pause until you have healed and possibly found the source. I need to move as many projects along as I can."

"I understand but I..." *I'm scared.*

As if he heard her, the King responded, "There's no need to be scared. The others will be with you."

"I—"

Edmund could pick up her worry, and the way his eyes shined, he was sorry for it, but his voice was strong as he concluded, very sure of himself, "Gabriel will always be with you."

Ashtyn finally turned to meet his gaze, and there was so much emotion there, she nearly choked on her own spit.

"You've got me, beautiful," he whispered against her lips so they were in their own world, her blonde locks blocking the rest of the room. "I'm going to be with you, protect you, for the rest of our lives."

Ashtyn held his dark eyes for long minutes. So long, she was sure the others around her had gone back to their discussion but she didn't care enough to check. All she knew was this —Gabriel in her little bubble her hair afforded them. And in his eyes, there was nothing but...

She swallowed, then whispered, "You're aggravating."

His lips tipped up. "You're so smart."

"You're insufferable."

"You're warm-hearted."

"You're a pushover."

"You're powerful."

"Stop being so nice."

"Stop being so perfect."

"I hate you."

"I love you."

"I hate you, Gabriel."

He seemed to love that even more. "Lucky me, there's a thin line between love and hate. I have much less work to do to push you over."

She shook her head and was very conscious of the fact their noses rubbed together, brushing. "Insufferable," she breathed against his lips.

His eyes sparked and his hand slipped from her back to the nape of her neck and brought her down for a kiss he knew she'd pull away from.

Her cheeks pinked because it'd taken a few moments longer than it should've to do so.

THE FOLDABLE WALLS that made up her office were gone. Her desk, which she only recognized because of the carvings on the side, was still there, pushed up against that window she loved, but her chair was gone. And stacked on it were piles of files, without a doubt the ones she'd refused to organize.

Ashtyn's good mood from earlier immediately evaporated as she paused at the entrance to the infirmary and snapped around to find the rest of the place the same as before. All of the infirmary beds with their curtains that had been there before were there, all the chairs they had lining the sides, all the stools and mini tables.

She forced herself to take a breath in, remembering that bubble she'd had with Gabriel only an hour ago to settle herself down, then marched for Arba's office. She didn't give the woman the respect of knocking, which until this point, she'd always done even though Ashtyn hated her. This time, she merely barged in.

Arba was in the middle of a conversation with a servant which was a normal occurrence as the servants liked coming in for regular checks. Ashtyn didn't want to do this in front of the poor woman, but she was too aggravated.

"Where the hell is my office?"

Arba rose, keeping poised as if she wasn't the poison of this place. "Ashtyn. Would you please wait until I am free? I am with a patient."

"And I want to know where my space is before I go to the King and require I take this office instead!"

Arba's eyes widened, fury brewing within them. She calmly looked over to the servant and gave a fake smile. "Tamor. How about you come back in an hour. We will finish then."

Tamor didn't seem to need any convincing as she fled the room.

Arba took only a moment for Tamor to be out of the vicinity before turning dark eyes on Ashtyn. "Who in the hell do you think you are, girl, speaking to me in that manner?"

"And who do you think you are getting rid of my office?"

"Your office was a menace to the space. It only caused more trouble."

"Then you should've given me a real office to begin with."

"What does it matter anyhow? You're gone now." She smacked her hands together as if wiping off dirt. "No harm."

"My ass!" Ashtyn barked. "I am not gone. I am still a healer at this palace. I may not be a studied medic in the same way as the rest of you, but I know how to heal my patients and I've read the same books you have for the things that weren't innate. I am not finished with this profession."

"Then where have you been? Frolicking with that stable boy because you're to be married now?" she remarked, but the derogatory tone she took when speaking of Gabriel felt harsher than when she spoke of Ashtyn. As if being a stable hand put him beneath them.

"I've been on a trip for the King, healing those sick with the plague. *For the King*. You do remember that, right? That we work for the King? That I am the King's healer?" She stepped closer. "Because I think you have a tendency to forget and I've been kind enough to let it go, but I promise you, Arba, that will finish."

"Excuse me, young woman."

"Touch my things again and I'll report it, and I think we both know the Assassin will be on my side. And what he says will go. Now, I want my office back." She could ask for another office. A real office. Arba probably thought her a fool to not be doing so, but Ashtyn didn't want that. She'd become accustomed to her space in her time at the palace, and she didn't want to give up her view out that particular window.

Arba stepped around her desk and didn't stop until she was inches from Ashtyn. "You will not threaten me in my own ward, little charlatan."

"It's not a threat, Arba. I do not make threats. I am

informing you of the consequences if you play with me again." She began to turn when she remembered one more thing. "Oh, and if you speak of Gabriel like that again, I'll report you simply because I can. I will ruin you in the palace, Arba."

Arba scoffed. "I see the possibility of marriage has done you no favors."

"I see life's done *you* no favors."

Arba ground her jaw. "You may return your office to its original character. We are through here."

Ashtyn laughed. "I won't be doing anything. You and your cronies took it apart, you'll put it back together. And I mean it better be back together when I'm finished working."

She didn't wait for Arba's rebuttals. Back in the main space of the infirmary, Ashtyn found the first bed and smiled at the patient within. "Cabol, you're back."

Cabol was an older servant who only worked because she didn't like to sit about. She had a mean rash on her arms and tended to require coming in often. Taking care of her didn't require any of Ashtyn's use of feeling because the rash was an external problem that didn't take well to that form of healing. It meant salves and cleaning were the best course of action. Something, she liked to remind herself when Arba was being especially harsh, she did as well, if not better than, the other medics. Schooling was a load of crap when all that was truly required was the studies of the medicinal books and a passion. Ashtyn had those, the latter of which to a greater degree than any of the other medics here.

Still, looking over Cabol's arm, Ashtyn especially appreciated these patients because she got to prove to herself and the others she wasn't only a healer because she had that unique, almost magical, ability to heal.

She made herself heal the 'normal' way often simply to

keep up with the skill in case her ability ever faded, but cases like these where she was forced to were especially nice.

# CHAPTER 14
# ASHTYN

They were both Northern, so it wasn't a shock to anyone that they'd have a Northern wedding.

What was a shock to Ashtyn was that everyone was going along with Gabriel as he told them to prepare for it this time around. Apparently the stable hand no longer cared that Ashtyn was refusing. Apparently he thought she wouldn't hide again this time around. Or he thought he'd find her.

Honestly, he likely would. She didn't exactly have many hiding spots.

The greens beside Gabriel's cottage—as outdoor or intimate room weddings were the Northern custom—were being decorated with garlands. It was stunning, the little flowers on the garlands a beautiful baby pink color whispering through the winds.

There were no seats put in place which didn't surprise Ashtyn as Gabriel had been informing everyone he wished for an intimate occasion. Not that it would be happening to begin with, but if it were, she knew everyone would be looking on from a distance anyway.

The Posse, though, were allowed to be there alongside some of his stable friends. Ashtyn rolled her eyes as she turned back from the window in her office. She was tired of this showcase he'd made of her life. The idiot didn't understand the word no.

Ashtyn huffed as she moved back to her desk. There were light snickerings all around the infirmary and because her office didn't have any real walls, she could hear it all—gossip about her coming nuptials. Apparently the other medics no longer cared to be on Arba's side about hating her when it came to such juicy gossip.

She growled beneath her breath. All she had to do was wait for the setting of the sun. Once that passed, the Northern custom will have been broken and they'd have to wait until the next day. She'd do the same thing the next day, then they'd be back on their mission—one that was looking more and more exciting the more she heard about this wedding.

The gossips shrieked causing Ashtyn to grimace. "Ugh, the lot of you need a life," she muttered beneath her breath.

Then the reason behind such horrid sounds presented itself from behind the curtains to her office.

Gabriel closed her makeshift door as if that would keep the others from trying to eavesdrop on them, then moved for her. His smile only seemed to broaden at her narrowing stare. "Hello, beautiful."

Giggles came from beyond her office, and Ashtyn knew they were listening in.

"That sound"—she pointed to her walls as her shoulders stiffened—"is your fault."

He leaned over her desk until their faces were a mere five inches apart. "They're excited for our wedding. Weddings are always exciting."

"Oh?" She feigned naiveté. "Is someone getting married?"

He laughed, loud and proud. Beautiful. The sound was delicious. Ashtyn wanted to drink it up, make it her elixir for life.

Then he moved around her desk until he was right beside her, pulled on her to stand, then led her to the window with the perfect view of his cottage. The garlands were now fully up creating the perfect altar, and more flowers had been dropped around the grass for where guests would stand, the spot for bride and groom left unmarred. Though the winds continued to blow, it all surprisingly remained in place.

"I hate that you don't have a real office, but I've always liked that you have a clear view of our place from here."

"Gabriel, we're not getti—"

She tried to pull her hand from his, but he held tighter and turned from the window to face her. The sunlight streaming in cast him in a beautiful light. If only she were an artist capable of capturing such perfection.

"You're right."

His lips tipped up at her widening eyes, and disappointment settled in the pit of Ashtyn's stomach. She'd been the insistent one, but she hadn't expected he'd fall in line so quickly, not after everything he'd put her through that year. She should be elated he was finally understanding, but...

"I didn't do this the right way, Ash. We're both Northern. We know how a proposal works, and I didn't do it right. So until that is done, there will be no wedding."

She tried to pull her hands away once more. "You should tell them that. They might kill you for all the time they wasted decorating your cottage yards."

"Ashtyn Lilibet Dubois." He took both her hands softly and met her brown orbs.

Her breath hitched. "What are you doing?" a whisper left her.

Northern custom dictated a proposal happened with the male softly taking the female's hands and asking her. Simple, intimate.

But he wouldn't. They weren't really...

"We know I have been yours all this time, and as much as you like to be difficult, we also know you've been mine. We don't need anything else to prove our feelings to one another, but as you love to point out, unfortunately, there're others in this world. Tie yourself to me and let everyone know—from the tip of the Island to the bottom of the South. Let them all know you're mine. Marry me."

She was struck. His voice was so soft, so soothing. He was so gentle, so completely the opposite of her. He deserved so much better. It's what she'd been telling him all these months he'd been trying with her—he deserved better.

But in this moment, she couldn't be selfless any longer. She wanted him. And though she knew his infatuation would fade out and he may resent her in the future for agreeing, she whispered, "Yes."

His soft smile almost made her melt. "Truly? No arguments?"

She shook her head, unable to form any more words.

He placed her hands on his chest. "The sun sets in a couple hours. But until then, before you need to go get prepared, I want one thing."

*One more?* she thought but somehow refrained from saying aloud, from ruining this beautiful moment.

When she didn't say anything, he stepped closer, hands slithering from hers on his chest, down her forearms, then up past her shoulders until he was cradling her face. Every inch he passed sent shivers running through her. He had such a strong hold on her.

"Before we're in front of our friends, can I have a piece of you now?"

Her brows furrowed.

He leaned in until their foreheads touched. "I'd like to have my marital kiss in private, cherish this moment with you."

Her breath shivered out. She often forgot that he was as romantic as they came—maybe because she wanted him so badly, knew other women did as well. Knew for most men, resisting so much temptation would be nearly impossible.

It wasn't impossible for a romantic though. Gabriel had proved as much.

"Then kiss me, Gabriel." She shouldn't be saying that.

He leaned in until his lips brushed hers. "I love when you say my name."

She smiled as she pushed up on her toes, taking his mouth with hers. It was tentative at first, but after a second, Gabriel took over. He was almost harsh in taking her, but soft as he nibbled on her lips.

The kiss was unlike any she'd had in her years past. Those had been... disturbing. Uninspiring. Forgetful.

Her kisses with Gabriel, all of them, were... exhilarating. Passionate.

Short.

At the inn, he'd taken his time kissing her, though even that hadn't felt long enough. And now, he pulled away and forced her gaze to meet his, both of their lips plump with evidence of what'd just happened. "I'll have more of you later."

There was a spark in his eyes that said he knew her spout of compliance wouldn't last long, and he was looking forward to all the trouble she'd cause, almost as if he couldn't wait to battle her for the rest of their lives.

As his touch left her, a chill settled at the loss of warmth. As he took her hands from his chest and brought them up to kiss, a new sort of warmth settled into her down south.

South,

south,

south.

His lips quirked into a smirk like he knew the effect he was having.

"Do you not plan on kissing me when we wed then?"

His brows furrowed. "Of course I do."

"Then why have the marital kiss now?"

He smirked. "You're still growing accustomed to us. A chaste kiss when we marry will do. I don't want you overthinking, overanalyzing a kiss simply because we're in front of others."

She fought her smile. Thoughtful, romantic. Gabriel.

He kissed her knuckles a final time, winked, then stepped back and without a word, left her office.

It gave her a moment to properly breathe.

And that's when she realized she was wet between her legs. In all her life, she'd never felt like this. In any encounters with men in the past, men she'd slept with, she'd never felt like this. This... needy?

She swallowed to give herself the moment to calm down, then moved for Atiana's rooms. She'd fool-heartedly accepted his proposal, so she needed to get that dress.

She couldn't help but laugh—though she hid her face in his shoulder so no one else saw—as he followed Northern custom and carried her through the door to his cottage.

The wedding had gone beautifully.

She'd worn that gorgeous gown that made her feel other-worldly. He wore his finest trouser and jacket set.

As per Northern customs, they met at the altar at the setting of the sun and said the phrase that made them one—the female going first which Gabriel's twinkling eyes told her he loved—and proudly kissed her in front of everyone. That soft, chaste kiss he'd promised. One that wasn't too much to be done in front of others. And because they were in the North, there was no celebration afterward like there would be in the Island Nation, rather they were simply let off to consummate the event.

Ashtyn tried to fight him when he lifted her to his arms, but he only narrowed his eyes—though they twinkled under the setting sun—and reminded her it was a wedding custom.

When he placed her inside and they were finally alone, Ashtyn felt her body ease in a way she couldn't remember doing in years. She tried to enjoy it as much as possible because there was still a final part to this night—consummating the marriage.

Ashtyn moved without speaking for the room she knew was his. She'd been in this cottage only twice before and each of those times, she'd berated herself but still memorized everything about it. Like the fact that his bedroom was the door on the right, only about a dozen steps from the fireplace he always had going.

She stopped before the bed, enjoying the warmth of the space because of the flames lit in the fireplace across from the bed. In such a small cottage, Ashtyn was surprised to find a second one, but she smiled still. This felt like Gabriel. Like warmth. She turned for him and was shocked by the heat that spread through her at the sight of him leaning against the doorjamb.

"The final custom," she stated. The only one all three lands shared in its entirety.

His lips tipped up as he slowly pushed off the wall and stripped out of his jacket. The shirt beneath was loose but somehow still left little to the imagination.

He dropped the thing on the chair in the corner, then prowled to where she stood.

She shouldn't have been the nervous one. *She'd* done this before. *She* was the experienced one.

And still, her nerves were a bundled mess as she turned so he had access to the ties to her dress. As his hands slipped over the ties, loosening them, her breath fastened with anticipation.

"You're stunning in this gown." His breath hovered over the skin at the back of her neck. "But I cannot imagine anything better than you naked for me."

Her breaths weren't stable as she grew wet with anticipation. This was... was this how women normally felt? Was this why they loved sex so much?

With the gown loosened, his touch left her as he held the gown open for her to step out of. While she calmed herself, she heard him settling the dress on the chair in the corner, so it wasn't left forgotten on the floor.

Then she turned to face him completely bare.

It wasn't her first time naked in front of a man, but it felt like it.

He eyed her from that corner and though he didn't look nervous, he swallowed at the sight of her. "Beautiful, Ash."

His lips tipped up as her gaze tracked his soft lips to the shirt that still covered him. Like he caught on, he stripped out of it and settled it on the chair with his jacket and her dress.

Then he moved for her again.

He didn't touch her as he nodded for the bed, an unvoiced

demand to get on it. And like never before, Ashtyn wanted to listen. She wanted to do anything to please him.

Settled on the soft comforter, she waited for him.

"Spread your legs," he demanded.

She was nervous. Why was she so nervous? He needed to stop this whole confidence charade to make her feel better!

Instead of demanding he do just that, Ashtyn swallowed as her legs opened, giving him his first glimpse of her cunt.

A small smile lifted as he asked, "Do you ever think of me when you touch yourself?"

"No." Her voice was small with anticipation.

His jaw gritted, but his voice was still soft as he asked, "What do you think of?"

"I don't." Her hands fisted into the comforter as she waited for him, gaze latched onto his chest. "Touch myself. I don't think those pleasures are for me." None of her past experiences had been what she'd wanted and never had she been able to lose herself in her mind enough to give it to herself. She finally met his eyes. "I told you not to tie yourself to me."

His dark brows went from bewildered disbelief to something physical. Then, he smirked. "Oh, they're absolutely for you, healer."

"Are you going to prove it, horse boy?"

"No." He smirked as he met her astonished look. "You are. I won't be touching you now or anytime soon."

"What?" She sat up, legs still spread for him.

"You need to learn that pleasure exists, and I want you to know it, to experience it, without the need for my touch. Though we both know I will always have a part of your pleasures. You've had a part of mine since we met."

"Gabriel, what are you saying?"

His hands landed on the beams at the top of the four-poster bed. "I'm saying you're going to lie back and enjoy your own touch tonight. And I'm going to watch."

Her legs flew back together. "What?"

"Spread your legs, healer," he ordered with an amused grin.

"Stop enjoying this!"

"Oh, I'm going to be enjoying this more than you can imagine." He leaned forward, arms gripping the banister making the muscles in his arms bulge. "Now spread your legs and lean back."

She was breathing hard.

She couldn't do this.

But he wanted her to.

She leaned back on the propped pillow, eyes never breaking form Gabriel's, and spread her legs. Her skin was on fire from his attention and nearness, and there was a wetness between her legs she still wasn't accustomed to.

"Show me how you touch yourself."

"I told you." She glared. "I don't!"

The idiot needed to wipe that stupid grin off his face before she smacked him.

"Let your fingers glide over your skin. Travel for your nipples."

Hearing those words made her want to close her legs again, but this time, it wasn't out of nervousness, it was simply in order to get some type of friction. But she remained spread and followed his instruction.

Her skin was sensitive, nipples peaked before she reached them, and her back arched at the small touches she made. His attention on her breasts as she took them in hand almost had her begging for his tongue.

How very off. She'd never begged anyone for a sexual favor, yet she felt the need now, when he hadn't so much as kissed her since the altar.

"Play with your nipples, Ashtyn." When she didn't do any more than continue fondling them because she wasn't entirely sure how to please herself, he instructed, "Show me what you want my mouth to do to them."

She gasped as the unexpected image assaulted her immediately, and she tweaked her nipples, aching off the bed and moaning involuntarily. She had a clear image of Gabriel sucking on her nipples, of his eyes staring at her through those long lashes. Of the way his teeth would bite on them, teasing the pain out as her nipple popped out of his mouth.

"Good job, healer. You're a quick study."

"You're a jackass," she grumbled as a moan left her and her legs snapped shut for some friction.

He was still smiling, wide and proud, as he demanded, "Open your legs, love. Send one of those beautiful hands between them."

She obeyed and spread her fingers through her arousal, cunt sensitive to the air, better yet her touch.

She was hypnotized by the way his grip tightened on the banister as he watched. As his muscles flexed and his eyes got impossibly dark. Her fingers moved without thought, doing what felt natural as she took him in from head to the tent in his trousers. Her fingers slipped between her folds, over her clit, then inside.

She gasped with the sensation as he spoke to her. "That's right, beautiful. Finger yourself but keep playing with your nipples. I want to suck them so bad right now."

Her moans came out without permission as she took him in. The way he watched her looked like a starved man seeing food for the first time, like the heat of a fire on a freezing night, like the adrenaline that spiked in a dangerous situation.

"Damn, Ashtyn, you're torturing me," he moaned. "Let your palm hit your clit while you finger yourself. Imagine it's my pelvis hitting it while I thrust into you. Yeah. Like that, beautiful."

With one hand tweaking her nipples and the other rubbing her clit and fingering herself, she was feeling too much pleasure. Her hand was completely wet now but she was too focused on the sound of his moans. They had her head snapping back and eyes screwing shut as sensations grew inside her. She didn't know what to do with them.

She needed to stop thi—

"Don't you dare stop, healer!" he growled. "My lords, you're so sexy. I want you on my tongue, Ashtyn. I want to taste you until you pass out."

She didn't know anything in this world but the feel of her hands and the sound of his voice, the heat of his stare that her body recognized even with her eyes closed.

"You're doing so good. Imagine I'm inside you. Are you clamping down on my cock?"

She needed to sto—

"Don't you dare!" he growled again.

At the demand, her moans reverberated through the room as she hit the crescendo.

Her world ended, and all she felt was pleasure. Pleasure that felt like it lasted an eternity before she was down from the high, fingers slowing on her body.

When she opened her eyes, Gabriel looked to barely be restraining himself, the tent in his trousers unbearably large, but he still gave her a wide, proud grin. "Becoming your husband is the single best thing to ever happen to me."

She smiled, still fazed in the aftershocks of pleasure, as she took him in. And it was only then that she realized she'd heard his name while she'd been coming.

Her eyes snapped wide. "Was I screaming your..."

His grin was shit eating now. "Name? Like it was the only word you knew."

She glared. "That never happened."

He finally released the banister and fell onto the bed, crawling between her legs until he reached her face, and their lips were mere inches away. "Nothing in this world could make me forget it."

Her eyes narrowed. "You're already making me regret it."

He laughed as he gave her a chaste kiss and fell to the side.

"What're you going?" Her legs were still spread, expecting him to strip from his trousers and take her.

"Going to bed."

"What?"

He closed his eyes, amusement clear on his features. "I told you I won't be touching you tonight."

She growled but didn't argue as she turned to face him. "Don't you want to change, get more comfortable?"

He chuckled, eyes never opening. "If I take these off, there's no way I'll last the night a virgin."

She huffed in frustration and turned to her other side, not needing to look at him any longer.

His laughs made her want to turn back and punch him.

Even more so when his hand slipped around her waist and pulled her into him so her ass rubbed against his very hard—and very much still clothed—cock.

"I hate you," she muttered to the light chuckle in the room.

# CHAPTER 15
# GABRIEL

Watching her sleep was therapeutic. Not only because she was finally his but because there was a softness to her she never allowed others to see. Gabriel was sure part of this ease came from the orgasm she'd just given herself, her first one, but he hoped it was also because he was there.

Without needing to worry about her wellbeing anymore given she would be by his side every night, Gabriel allowed his mind to drift off to this predicament they'd found themselves in. They were looking for the source. Everyone thought it must be man-made to some degree. Gabriel hadn't been sure but now, he couldn't fight the reminder of those pretty eyes, laced a soft hue that watched him as he walked toward the lake that would end up exploding. Had those men been part of the explosion? He'd been told that getting to them had been an impenetrable force which made Gabriel think they could have a magician on their side.

He scoffed to himself. To think, while they were trying to

bring magicians back to the North, one—or more—could be working to kill Northerners. Their motive made sense—wanting to come back to the North. But their victims didn't. Why go after those in villages and towns, especially the ones higher up in the Northern Lands. The palace would've been the prime location to strike, but that was farther down south, closer to the Southern Lands border.

It could be a practice round.

That could've been why those men were watching Gabriel so intently. They realized that he was there with the crown—how could they not, he was there with the guards—and wanted to test their destruction. Was that part of the plan then? Get people sick, then get the lands themselves to turn on civilization. In which case a magician would be needed to right it. If this magician wanted more than coming back to the Northern Lands, if she wanted power of the Northern Lands, it was ingenious. The population would practically beg her to lead, and she would have their help to get rid of King Edmund and his line so she could take it.

Made sense she would think it so simple. She didn't know the Master Magician was in that line, and she would be able to stop such destruction, even while pregnant—though not ideal.

Even still, man-made, whether magician or sorcerer, or worse, both unified, would cause a world of trouble. Gabriel planned on keeping his thoughts to himself for the time being because he knew Ashtyn would worry too much about people's safety, and she already had enough to stress over, but he'd look into it. Everywhere they went, he'd find out which magician or sorcerer was behind this.

His heart grew heavy with the thought which didn't sit well with him. This was one of the best nights of his life. The last thing he needed was such darkness to enter it.

Gabriel shook himself from those thoughts, and smiled

instead as he softly took Ashtyn's hand so as not to wake her. His thumb ran over the top as his smile grew. She'd had this hand in her cunt only an hour ago. He knew the moment he brought his own hand up to his nose, he'd be able to smell her on her fingers.

He swallowed, watching her instead. He hadn't shown it, but he'd been a bit nervous tonight as well. Showing it was the last thing he'd do because Ashtyn had been nervous enough as it was, but that twinge of doubt had been in him. He'd known from the moment he'd met her that he'd need to get into deeper conversations with the men in his life about sexual experiences so when the time came, he'd be able to execute, and he was more glad than ever that he'd pushed the embarrassment of such questions aside.

Then the nervousness had vanished when he'd guided Ashtyn through her experience and all she'd felt was pleasure. There were no nerves then. Gabriel was the embodiment of confidence. He knew what he did to her, what the simple sound of his voice did to her. He couldn't find it in himself to feel any more nerves for anything else they did in the future. With all the knowledge of every possible experience Gabriel had learned thanks to the conversations he'd had with the guys—though they'd teased him relentlessly through the process—Gabriel knew he could give Ashtyn the experiences she needed. He'd definitely be jacking off before she touched him though because though he wasn't a child who would blow their load with a simple touch, he wasn't sure how much he'd be able to restrain himself when she touched him. He'd been practicing, holding himself from coming, but he knew it'd be a different experience altogether when it was her hands, mouth, and cunt.

"Gabriel," a breathy whisper came from her lips, and Gabriel smiled.

He leaned in close to kiss her shoulder and whispered back, "I'm right here, beautiful. Sleep. I've got you."

Her lips tipped up a little as if she'd heard him but she was still sound asleep. Relaxed.

And he would make sure she stayed that way.

# CHAPTER 16
# ASHTYN

She woke up sexually invigorated for the first time in her twenty-four years.

Which quickly turned into sexual frustration when she turned to realize Gabriel was already out of bed. When she found him in the living space, he was dressed for the day and checking the contents of his bags.

"Where're you going?" She stayed by the bedroom door.

"Making sure everything we need is prepared. I want to make sure everything we need will be ready for whenever we need to ride out again." He shuffled through some more things, then closed the bag. "I need to grab a couple of more things, but otherwise, we should be prepared."

He turned for her and instantly took her in from head to toe. She wore a silk robe she'd found hanging on the door, but the thing was loose to give him a glimpse of everything he could taste.

"If we're not leaving today then we still have time to ourselves?"

He gave that charming grin, eyes shimmering with pleasure. "Not yet, wife."

She grumbled, stomping her foot like a child, and turned back for the room. In the corner opposite the one that held her beautiful gown sat a small bag with a change of clothes. She put the simple dress on quickly so she could be away from the handsomely frustrating stable hand immediately.

Ashtyn had no idea what was going on with her. She normally didn't care for any sexual acts. What had he done to her?

She glared at him as she left the cottage while he enjoyed eating at the small table. To her horror, Tristan and Norya, the two Posse companions who rode with them for their journeys, were outside, near enough to the cottage to see her storming out.

"Aren't you supposed to be less grumpy after your wedding night?" Tristan's eyebrows wiggled.

"One would think," she ground out.

"Oh no." Norya joined her teasing man. "You look worse now. There's no way *he* couldn't please you. He looks like he could please a woman without touching her."

*He could.*

"Couldn't or wouldn't?" She gritted as she passed them, tired of talking about this. She needed to get a few things if they could leave at any moment.

There were a lot of curious eyes from those in the palace, from senior members to servants. Apparently everyone had the same thought—she should be more lively. Considering she'd stated before to a few of them that she didn't enjoy sex, they probably shouldn't have been so surprised. But maybe they had Norya's mentality too—the one Ashtyn now had after last night—and figured there was no way *Gabriel* couldn't please her. They probably didn't know he was a virgin. Lords, she didn't even think that would deter their thoughts. Gabriel was that desired. People instantly assumed any moment with him would be amazing.

Ashtyn did too. She knew when he decided to touch her, she'd be writhing beneath him.

But what the annoying gossips didn't realize was unlike every other newlywed ever, her new husband hadn't consummated their marriage. Apparently that was off the table, and for the first time in her life, Ashtyn wasn't happy about it.

She forwent going to her rooms, not needing anything specific from there, and headed to the infirmary. Though it was far less private than her rooms, her makeshift office was the space she felt most herself.

Well, was the place she felt most herself. Now the memory of Gabriel's cottage, of the warmth of the fire before the bed and the second one in the common space, of the comfort of the furnishings and the solitude from the rest of the palace was all she could imagine.

But because she'd been most comfortable in her office, Ashtyn spent much more of her time there. Which was why her journal was always kept locked up in the drawer at the top of her desk. It held thoughts on everyone she'd healed written within. She'd need to add those from the journeys now too.

In the infirmary, she was met with more odd looks. This time, along with the confusion on her unpleasant mood, they all wore one look—what the hell was she doing back so soon?

She ignored them all as she enclosed herself in her space and sat at her desk, finally able to take a full breath. She pulled the key she'd slipped into the pocket of this dress and opened the drawer that held her one prized possession.

She opened the journal to a page she'd read nearly every night for a year—to one of the only entries written in red in.

*He's a stable hand. Charming and always smiling.*

*I wonder what could possibly keep him smiling all the time. Is it a woman who's constantly on his mind? Is it his love for the horses? Is it the men he spends his days with? I don't know about the first, but I know he loves his horses and his companions. He must love women too. All the women at the palace love him...*

*I've been here a week. I don't understand this attention—since when do men capture my attention so fully? It doesn't matter, he's for another woman, not me. That makes my heart hurt. Is that possible? For a heart to hurt? Or is it pure dramatics? I think it's dramatics. Must be. Apparently his charm works from a distance too to make my heart act out like that.*

*Why am I writing about him? This is my healing journal.*

*Anyway, Gabriel, since I'll never speak to you, I'll tell you here —if I were to choose a mate, I think you would be it.*

She'd written that after noticing Gabriel from beyond her window a little over a year ago when she'd first gotten to the palace.

When Papa Ignatius was stabbed and Gabriel brought him to the infirmary for her care earlier in the year, she'd spoken to him for the first time leading to a single entry in red ink. She flipped to it now.

*His voice is rough, but soft. How is that possible?*

Then Gabriel's attentions had been on her, and all of that affection she'd thought she felt shriveled up inside her. He claimed to have fallen for her, but she knew now as she had then, he was infatuated with the woman who healed the father figure in his life.

Ashtyn closed the journal and brought it close to her heart. She sighed, then picked up her quill to drop into red ink and opened it to the latest page to add the date and a new entry.

*I married him last night.*

S℈HE DIDN'T KNOW why she was spending any time in the stables.

Maybe it was because Gabriel wasn't there, so she felt that she could. When he was around, she was normally too consumed in his activities to pay proper attention to these beautiful creatures.

Ashtyn was currently softly brushing Bella's side with her fingers, silently thanking the animal for all the rides they'd taken thus far and all they would take in the future, for being her companion in these healings.

Though this time was given to her and Bella, Ashtyn couldn't help the way her eyes caught the glint of the ring on her finger with each stroke. It was a plain band, nothing like that of either Princess's, but somehow, it still caused feelings to bubble up within her.

She was so lost in looking at the thing as her hand continued brushing the horse with her fingers that she didn't realize anyone was beside her until a hand landed beside hers, brushing the horse as well. His matching ring glinting under the sunlight told her who it was.

Not that she needed the hint. Her body knew.

And she was now married. No other man would try to come so close to her. Not that any had tried in her recent past. Thankfully.

Her brows furrowed. Barely any had come up on the trips either. It would change now that gossip was slowly rising, and especially so when it's gone around that she's been to the council in the South, but...

But that hadn't even been a thought when accepting Gabriel's proposal.

"What do you want?" She didn't turn for him, didn't fully trust herself to.

"You." His breath hit her ear.

He was standing so close, her shoulder brushed his chest with every inhalation.

"Too bad. You missed your chance last night and this morning."

He chuckled. "You're my wife, Ashtyn. I have my whole life."

Her brows furrowed. She hadn't exactly put that together. They had married, he continued to call her his wife, she knew she would now be mercifully left alone as a married woman, but somehow, her mind hadn't let her connect that to the future. The one where she had a husband and a forever.

Her heart dropped.

How could she have done this to Gabriel? Her moment of weakness yesterday by agreeing to the wedding now bound him to her. He'd be stuck for the rest of his life.

"You freaking out about us yet?"

"What?" She snapped from her thoughts.

"It's been quite fast since the proposal. You said yes, prepared, and we got married. We... had fun last night and busied ourselves with preparations for the trip this morning. You're no longer as busy as you have been, you've had time to think. To overthink. You're back to freaking out about us, right?"

She forced sarcasm into her tone. "You think you know me so well."

"I do know you, healer. And I'm excited for the rest of our lives where I can learn everything there is to know about you and to prove to you, once and for all, that I *am* in love with you."

Such pretty, pretty words.

"And that *you* are in love with me."

She planned on ignoring him after that declaration, but she couldn't bypass the insinuation that she had any strong feelings for him. "You've got to be kidding me."

He laughed, his free hand slipping around her waist to pull her into him. "Don't worry, wife, I won't tell anyone. And we can stop discussing it for now. How about we have a small horse lesson now? You did say you wanted to learn more about them for this trip."

*Yes, for this trip. But also because your eyes light up when you're around them.* The little voice Ashtyn forced to the back of her mind yelled.

"Stop calling me that."

"What? Wife?"

When she nodded, he released her and moved to stand beside her. Shockingly, he wasn't offended. "Why would I do that? You're my wife."

"It sounds..." *Dreamy.* "Weird."

He kissed her cheek. "You'll get used to it. Wife."

As she rolled her eyes, he turned for the horse. "Don't roll your eyes at your instructor, healer."

Ashtyn bit the inside of her cheek to stop from laughing, but she couldn't hide the amusement in her eyes as she shook her head. "I'm regretting this already."

He winked as he began to speak.

And speak.

And speak.

It was near nightfall when he finally stopped behind her, hands massaging her shoulders. "How much of that did you pick up?"

"Is none of it a sufficient answer?" *I was too distracted by you.*

He chuckled, his lips brushing the side of her neck. "I tend to get carried away."

*It's quite sexy.* "Tell me about it."

"We must eat. Then to bed less we need to be on the move tomorrow."

She nodded, her heart sinking. She lived in a suite that was cold and dark, a place she never looked forward to heading to. But he was right. She needed to get to the kitchens for a quick meal, then she needed rest.

Before she could make it more than two steps toward the palace, her hand was tugged back, and she slammed into Gabriel's chest. "Where're you going?"

"To my rooms."

He quirked an amused brow. "Wrong direction."

"What're you talking about? My suite, and the kitchen, are that way."

His nostrils flared and a flash of anger overtook the lightness of his eyes for only a second before he clarified, "That isn't your suite anymore. It's now an abandoned room to go along with all the other abandoned rooms in the palace."

"What—"

"Ashtyn." He pulled her closer, fingers running gentle soothing circles over her back. "You are my wife. You'll be sleeping by my side. Forever."

"So it's not bad enough you made me tie myself to you, now I have to leave my rooms?" She didn't know what she was arguing for. She preferred his cottage far more than her suite. She simply couldn't stop the words from spewing out.

Gabriel only rolled his eyes and turned for his cottage with a vise grip on her hand. "You hate that suite, wife. It was the one way Arba could truly ruin your stay here with—that and the sad excuse for an office you got. Let's not forget that I was obsessed with you before you became mine. I know that simple fact about you."

She huffed and pulled on her hand as she was dragged through the greens. "Just because you were a stalker doesn't mean I want to live in your cottage."

He stopped abruptly, turning for her. "You don't like the cottage? Where would you rather live?" His brown orbs were so soft, searching for the answer that would please her most. So pure.

She finally sighed as the whisper left her, "I love your cottage."

"Stop doing that."

She quirked a brow, and as she waited for what he meant by that, she appreciated how handsome he looked in this moment.

"Calling it mine. You're my wife. It's ours."

He turned again, and this time, Ashtyn allowed him to drag her to the home. "You call me your wife too much."

His delicious chuckle heated her body. "You don't call me your husband nearly enough."

"I don't call you my husband at all."

His grip on her hand tightened. "I know," he gritted, then threw her a striking grin. "But you'll start. Soon enough."

She rolled her eyes. "The kitchens are still the other way."

"I have food, beautiful."

When they reached the cottage, but before Gabriel could open the door to let them in, Ashtyn tugged on his hand. He gave her the attention she required.

"Before we go in there, we need to be on the same page—we married to keep the men away from me on this trip. You did it because of your annoying insistence that I'm yours and I did it because I don't plan on being with anyone else in the future anyway, so it didn't really matter. Either way, it wasn't a love match. It was a business transaction. So when we're on this trip, we will be the couple who shares a suite and are unavailable to suitors, but here, you don't need to taint your space. You can continue living alone."

He watched her intently as she spoke, so intense. After her spiel, he shockingly looked even more sure of himself. "Done?"

Her shoulders slumped. "Yes."

"Good." He stepped closer and took her face in his hands. "Now it's your turn to listen. Because *get one thing straight,* healer—I am your husband in every form of the word and it is nothing but an honor to share my home with you, to make it ours. I just need you to loosen up and allow me to reverse our roles. Allow me to heal that part of you that's afraid this won't work. Just stop resisting me. Please."

She wanted to argue even though that was a reasonable request, and he seemed to know it because his eyes sparkled as he leaned in to kiss her before she could taint the moment. "Lords, you're going to make life exciting, aren't you, beautiful?"

He pulled her inside when she did nothing but narrow her eyes. Inside, he winked and a sexy little smirk told her he knew she was going to ask for sex like she had before, and he had no plans of seeing the request out.

She requested it anyway. "Can your healing begin with my body?"

His head fell back as he laughed. "I'm still not touching you, Ash. But you're more than welcome to touch yourself. I'd do anything to watch that again."

"If you can't do this simple thing for me, then what reason do I have to loosen up and stop resisting?"

"You know you keep insisting I touch you. I think I should let you know that you have free rein over my body. If you want me that badly, you can have your tastes." His glittering eyes gave away both how badly he wanted her, but also how exciting it was for him to know she wanted him in return.

It was still a new concept to Ashtyn—this desire for another.

So she narrowed her eyes at him. The thought of starting their moments frightened her but she'd rather jump into the Rivorbant Waters—the dirtiest part of the world at the northern tip of the Island Nation—than admit it. It was nonsensical considering she'd had sex before, but they'd never been moments she'd enjoyed or necessarily had to do anything other than lay there. She didn't want that with Gabriel. This need was new to her, and she wanted to do all sorts of things to him, things she wasn't sure how to initiate.

She didn't respond for a long while, letting her dark look be answer enough to his ridiculous plans. Then finally said, "So I have no reason then."

He gave her a once over, biting his bottom lip to stifle that large grin. "You're telling me the only way to get you to be a decent person is to finger you?"

Her body flushed with excitement. "I think your tongue will be just as fun. But, ultimately, of course, in order to consummate this 'marriage,' I will need your cock."

He stepped closer and flicked her chin. "I like this side of you, Ash."

Her brow rose. "The horny side?"

His responding laugh didn't help with her confidence in this new side she was learning about herself.

"No. This desperate side."

"Oh, please, you want my body as much as I want yours."

He shrugged. "Maybe. More even. But I think I'll hold out a little bit longer. I want you begging me, Ash."

"Not gonna happen!" she seethed.

He moved for his food stores before she finished that statement, still amused as he stripped out of his shirt and threw it at her, giving her a view of his muscled back.

Ashtyn snagged the shirt off her face, inhaling his scent and experiencing the whole-body shiver that racked her as her center grew hot, wet. She took a large inhalation of his scent as he busied himself preparing their meal, then muttered under her breath, "Fuck."

# CHAPTER 17
# GABRIEL

She was finally in his bed. Their bed.

Gabriel had been going to sleep thinking of her since they met earlier in the year. Thinking of what she could be dreaming of, if she was comfortable in her cold suite, if she was ever lonely. Those moments he was glad that as unpleasant as she was with him, she was worse with the others at the palace, so he knew she didn't have any company. That ease had also made it possible for Gabriel to think of how sexy she was when she was telling him off instead of wanting to be sick that another was touching her, that she was allowing another to touch her. He wasn't a violent person but the thought of her with another sent a deathly cool through him. It was part of the reason he was glad those other men she'd been with were nowhere to be found, were nobody's in her life now.

With her beside him now, he didn't have to think of the negatives of what could be any longer. He was able to focus solely on her, on her beauty, both inside and out. It'd led to the easiest sleeps of his life.

Dreams of Ashtyn's hair blowing in the wind while she

rode a horse, Gabriel chasing after her plagued him. Dreams of her laughs as they ran through the greens, as they tackled one another to the ground, as they got dirty everywhere. Dreams of them washing that dirt off one another. Dreams of them finishing work at the palace daily, feeling accomplished and proud, then meeting before the hearth in their living space to speak of everything and nothing at all while they prepared their meals. They were the most peaceful pictures his mind could conjure, and all a life Gabriel was working them toward.

He'd only woken because the specific dream of washing one another had been too much and his body had needed the release. He hadn't allowed it for himself when he awoke, but watching her sleep took over his time until he could fall back asleep.

That was, until a hand smacked into his chest and unease filled the room. Then Ashtyn tossed around, eyes fluttering uncontrollably as she called out incomprehensible words that were clearly upsetting.

"Ash." He shook her shoulder softly so as not to frighten her.

When her head tossed around once more and she squealed like she was afraid of whatever she was seeing, Gabriel became forceful with his efforts. "Ashtyn, love, wake up. Wake up."

Her eyes popped open, but they were glazed over.

"It's me, beautiful. It's Gabriel. I'm not going to hurt you." Her body sank into the sheets as her eyes closed once more before finding his. "I'd never hurt you."

"I know," she whispered, voice hoarse from sleep.

He hovered over her, wanting to remain the thing she focused on as she came completely out of her nightmare. "You want to talk about it?"

Her head barely moved, but it was answer enough.

"Do you have nightmares often?"

She shrugged.

"Is it always the same thing?"

She swallowed and bit her lip like she was contemplating something, then turned to face him. She looked smaller than her usual 'rage in your face' anger. It made him want to wrap her in his arms and never let go again.

"It's not necessarily always the same. They tend to be around the same themes, I guess. They used to be more about..." She licked her lips and started again, "These past few months they've been more about..."

He stroked her hair. "You don't have to tell me, Ash. If it's too hard—"

"Sapphire tells me that's what the men in our lives are for —dropping our baggage on them. It's why women are so pretty and graceful—their husbands carry their hardships, so they have nothing weighing them down."

Gabriel chuckled. "I'm sure Sparrow would love to carry all of Evony's baggage if it were possible." He stroked her hair, growing serious. "You want to unload yourself on me? Accept that I am your husband in all matters?"

Ashtyn gave a soft smile. "I... you want me to loosen up. I want to please you. You gave up the rest of your life for me, the least I can do i—"

"You please me by breathing. I want you to do things because you want to, not because you think I want them. That is how you'll please me."

She bit that delicious bottom lip. "If Sapphire is even a little right it would be a waste not to put you to use. After all, your job is to carry the hardships."

*Oh, my amusing little healer. I'd carry the world on my shoulders for you.* "Always."

She turned toward him, cocooning herself in the safety of his arms, their faces only inches apart. "When Sparrow found me, I wasn't in great shape. Mentally, I mean. I'd overworked myself and instead of figuring out a balance that would make me feel productive and give me a chance to live, I worked even more. It just helped me out when I came across this village that needed a healer. It was the best distraction I could've ever asked for. I was so exhausted when he found me. I figured if I could help people, I might feel better. That they might... I don't even know what I wanted. Maybe that's why no one could ever give it to me. I... the reason I'm not a virgin isn't because I desired those men so much. It was because I'd heard of how amazing sex was and I wanted that. When they turned out underwhelming, I thought something must've been wrong with me. I threw myself deeper into work, then I... I started to resent everything even more. I've always cared for people's wellbeing, but when Sparrow found me, I was sad.

"The nightmares had never been of anything horrible that happened to me per say. I'm lucky to never have encountered anything so bad. The nightmares are more flashbacks I guess. Or reminders of what life would've continued being like had the Assassin not brought me here."

"And these past few months?" Gabriel's thumb stroked her cheek to keep her grounded in this moment rather than flying back to those years of her life. The last thing he wanted was for any of this to send her back to the emptiness her life had held before.

"Usually the dreams were of everything that happened before the palace, but these few months, they've been more focused on the men I'd been with."

Gabriel's jaw ground. "Oh?"

*They were nightmares. They were dreams she hated. They weren't moments she wanted to relive.* He reminded himself.

Then something he hadn't considered before sprung to his

thoughts. *Was she forced? Did she ever beg for help? Were those memories the ones she wanted to erase with his touch?*

"They were never forced, Gabriel."

His glazed-over eyes found hers and searched the softness her eyes rarely held.

"I know that is what you're imagining. But that's not what happened. I may not have enjoyed the times, but they were consensual. The three I'd been with, I guess I wanted them. Or I thought I did."

The pain in his chest eased, but not by much. "You guess?"

"Well, I never had the same type of feeling around them that I do with you." She wouldn't meet his eyes, but considering how vulnerable she was making herself, something so unusual for her, he wouldn't force her to do so. "This heat and wetness between my legs, this feeling that I might combust."

His smirk was completely involuntary, and he didn't even realize he was doing it until she glanced up and narrowed her eyes at his mouth. He couldn't help it, but still, he tried to ease her hesitations. "You should know, I have the same feelings for you."

She scoffed. "Could've fooled me."

He chuckled softly as he forced her to meet his eyes. "I refuse to touch you, Ash, because I need you to learn things about your body before I come along. I need you to accept these things happening. You've refused it for so long, I need you to know it's normal."

"Doesn't mean I have to like it."

He kissed her temple. "Wanna tell me about your dreams?"
*Translation: Wanna tell me about the men you've been with?*

"The first one wasn't great but that could be because it was my first time, and he wasn't the best at foreplay. None of them were actually and I didn't know any better. We did it twice and both times were okay, I guess. He was a nice guy, a tough guy, I thought I really liked that. The second guy was the toughest of the three. Similar to Sparrow in his strength and scariness. I thought I liked him the most, and to be fair, he was the best out of the three. I started to believe I simply couldn't reach that climax everyone was chasing. The final guy was more powerful than tough. He had a lot of control and power over others. He... showed me that men were only after their own pleasure." She played with the hairs on his chest to get out this final part. "I was called pretty a lot back then. That last guy only called me 'pretty girl.' I hate that word."

"I know." Gabriel wanted to kill all of them, but more so, he wanted to envelope Ashtyn in his safety.

Her gaze shot to his. "How?"

"You recoiled the first time I called you it. That was the last time I ever used it for you."

Her lips tipped up. "Is that a skill you picked up in your stalking?"

"That's a skill that only works with you. I only care about things that have to do with you."

She went back to avoiding his attention. "Whatever."

Gabriel took this moment to take her in without all the walls she normally erected around herself. She was a lot softer than she allowed people to believe. Knowing that softness had been there at one point and was erased because she could never find what she was looking for struck Gabriel square in the chest.

"And the dreams? What happens there?" He wanted her speaking again, to listen to that beautiful voice, and he figured there wouldn't be much time to get this vulnerability from her, so as much as he hated how much pain she held, he needed her to speak them out, to allow him to carry that hurt.

"I need you to know they never forced me." When Gabriel's brows furrowed, anger overtaking, she swallowed. "They didn't. But in these dreams, I'm tied to them. One of the three, the fun is finding out which one in each dream." She grimaced. "We're married and I'm forced then. I'm crying internally but no one can save me. I'm stuck and a fear I've never realized exists within me."

That look in her eyes said she was done talking, so Gabriel leaned in and kissed her. "I promise you, wife, those dreams will disappear. I'll do anything in my power to make that happen."

"You know sex would really help with that."

A laugh burst through his lips. "I thought you preached sex wasn't great."

"That was before the orgasm caused by imagining your hands and tongue on me, the one that came from your stares alone. After that, sex has to be great. It has to be. So... if you wanna help..."

He was smiling wildly. "You know what'll also help? Learning to please yourself. Those dreams aren't going to disappear simply because we're married making them impossible from coming true. They'll disappear as you learn to enjoy yourself, your strengths, believing you wouldn't allow that for yourself. *I'm* not going to be the thing that ends them. You are."

"I thought you said you'd do anything to make them disappear."

"I will." He kissed her slowly. "I'll do everything to make you love yourself, to make you please yourself. When you start to trust yourself, those dreams will fade away and you'll finally know, without those doubts, that we're perfect for each other."

"Then you'll fuck me?"

He couldn't stop laughing with her. How had he not known what a comedian she was? "Oh, then you're not ready for the things I want to do to you, Ashtyn."

She couldn't be. His boyish stable hand charm hid that animal that lurked beneath, wanting to eat her up, and he couldn't wait to let that side out when she was ready.

She smiled then, sweet and playful, gone was the darkness the dreams had caused within her.

"What?" He gave her a nervous smile.

"I don't think I've ever heard you truly curse."

"That's because I don't curse."

Her brows furrowed. "Say fuck."

"No."

Her mouth dropped into the sexiest little pout. "Say fuck, Gabriel."

Gabriel threw his arm around her waist and pulled her closer. He kissed her exposed neck as her face fell into the crook of his shoulder. "Sleep, beautiful. We have much to do come morning."

# CHAPTER 18

# ASHTYN

It was their second day on the road. Down, down, down to the southern point of the Southern Lands where the council building sat. The one that would inform her of whether or not she was a Master.

They'd stopped at a town for the night, the horses already being taken care of in the stables and each of them already given their rooms and bathed. And still, all nine of them found their way back outside.

The back of this inn had fire areas where logs sat around a large fire in three groups. One set was taken by a few people already. From the looks of it, there were maybe three sets of strangers getting to know one another. They passed around a pitcher of wine since alcohol was more a part of the South.

No one sat at the fire in the middle, and the last one off to the side closer to the woods held her group. Everyone but her.

Tristan sat on a log with a stick to poke at the fire while Norya sat on the ground between his legs. His other hand played with her hair as they laughed with the group about something.

Colt, Noah, and Wells also sat on logs around the fire while Gian and Ares took to the ground with their backs against the logs. Gabriel was also leaned against a log as he joked with the group. They each had a hot cup of cider in their hands like the one Ashtyn currently carried, and there sat a large plate of pastries beside them.

They were more than a group traveling together for the palace. They were friends.

Ashtyn's heart ached. It'd been a long time since she had friends. She'd been selfish with her last group though. The friendships hadn't broken apart because of what the others had done but because of her. She'd craved attention too much. So much, she'd pushed everyone away, then convinced herself she didn't want friends.

As she watched those eight, she knew that was a lie.

She'd known it was a lie for a long time now, but never had it pierced her as sharply as when Sapphire and Gemma had waltzed into her office and demanded they were friends. Never so sharply as being invited to a girl's night with those two, Princess Rosaelia, Atiana, Norya, and Etel. She'd convinced herself she was only there to appease the princesses, but that'd been a lie. She'd been there because she'd wanted their friendship. She'd merely been too scared to think that lest they forgot about it, decided to drop her.

They hadn't. That group was persistent.

This group she watched made her remember how much she wanted friends. In the time away from the girls, Ashtyn had let herself resort back to lying to herself.

Not anymore.

Not while she watched everyone by the fire, and her heart tugged for her to join them.

So she listened.

She'd been listening to her heart a lot more recently and had yet to be disappointed with the results.

She got a few smiles as she joined them but otherwise, they continued their conversation. No overt attention, and unlike the her from years back, this felt good. No, fucking great.

She sat on the log Gabriel leaned on, her leg touching his shoulder, and he nonchalantly leaned in to kiss her knee as he continued his loud exclamation with Noah and Wells. They all wore large grins as they fought which made Ashtyn smile.

From the log beside her, Tristan grabbed a pastry and handed it over with a wink, and Ashtyn's heart galloped. Not because of any flirtations but because of how normal this felt. Being friends with these people felt... natural.

The apple strudel was still warm because of its proximity to the fire and paired perfectly with her cider. Ashtyn enjoyed it as she listened to everyone's exaggerated remarks.

"Tell her I'm right!" Gian exclaimed as his eyes met Ashtyn's.

She held her strudel before her open mouth as the attention turned to her. "Excuse me?"

"Tell her women find sword fighting sexier than hand-to-hand."

Norya scoffed. "You're absolutely ridiculous. Why! Why on the lords' green lands would we find sword fighting sexier?"

Gian smirked. "Hand-to-hand has its show of masculinity, I get that. But sword fighting shows that masculinity with grace and control. Women love a man in control."

Ashtyn thought it over. She's witnessed both of course. Living at the palace meant they could watch the guards train, and as she imagined both scenarios, she couldn't believe her answer.

She gasped into her cup, lowering it after a sip. "Shit. He *is* right. When they use the weapons, there's masculinity, brute force, but also grace and intelligence about where and how to strike. There's balance, and that's super sexy."

"Thank you!" Gian exclaimed, and immediately there was a ruckus of everyone joining the argument. Suffice it to say, Gian won.

And Norya's pouting lips as she sat back meant she realized maybe she'd been wrong too. Tristan's attention on her as he massaged her shoulders and whispered in her ear seemed to get her out of it quickly.

Ashtyn wasn't entirely sure what the men were discussing now but she was happy to be there instead of up in her room where she'd contemplated staying even after Gabriel asked her to join them. She'd done it mostly because of how adorable he'd looked when he'd left the room hoping she'd come down too, and now she was more glad than ever.

She didn't want to let herself hope it, but she couldn't help it—by the time this was over, she could possibly have friends.

Real friends.

GABRIEL WAS ALWAYS SMILING. His charm was so endearing, it was more effort to frown than not when around him. It was unnerving, this control he had over her.

She never normally had trouble keeping her emotions in check, which Ashtyn considered a good thing with this trip down to the Southern Lands. It was an experience she'd been avoiding her whole life—going before the council. She'd always known she could possibly be a Master. She'd simply never wanted to find out, to make relationships more difficult to create than they'd already been since she didn't want the falsified interactions that came with any sort of power. It was scarier still considering neither Evony nor Sparrow, who'd both gone through this and been named Masters, could tell her what to expect. Both had the simple tasks to recite their background, then poof, Masters.

Luckily, she didn't need to fear the falsities any longer since any of the people she may like to have in her life had already thrust themselves into it, even with her attempts to make them go away. From Evony and Gemma to Atiana and Etel to Rosaelia and Norya to the nonas from the Island. They were all infuriating in their own ways, but Ashtyn wouldn't lie that she enjoyed their company. Theirs and those of the men who came with them like package deals. Somehow she'd gone from no peers at the beginning of the year to the friendship of the entire Posse—excluding maybe the King himself—now.

Though she was aware that one thing above all else eased her mind the most as she rode to the southern tip of the Southern Lands—Gabriel was already hers. Even if she fought calling this a real marriage—which considering it wasn't yet consummated, it wasn't—the relationship she'd feared losing the most had been Gabriel's. Now, tied together before finding anything out, Ashtyn knew he wanted *her*.

His constant insisting it also helped.

"Thinking of me, wife?" he asked from atop his horse.

"What makes you think that?"

"I can feel you undressing me with your eyes."

She fought her amusement. "Oh, you poor little virgin."

"I can't wait until you do unspeakable things to me, healer." He gave her a cocky side-eye that she hadn't known him capable of. "But please refrain from starting anything now. Atop a horse is not the best time for a man to become aroused."

She snorted. "I think this the best time, actually."

"Horrible, mean woman."

*Sexy, charming man.*

Ashtyn smiled but didn't continue the conversation because she was capable of being a decent person from time to time. They weren't long from their destination, so she spent the rest of the ride thinking of getting Gabriel naked without looking over at him. Let him think her too preoccupied with the worries of the South. She didn't need him to know just how much his presence eased her.

When they reached the large council building, the heads both Masters had told her about were waiting for her little entourage.

Gabriel was every way the gentleman as he hopped off his horse and held out a hand to help Ashtyn down as well. Her entire body ached from the entire ride down, wanting to be off of horse for at least a week even though she knew that wouldn't be possible in the near future. His hand slipped to the small of her back as the group of them moved for the Southerners.

There were a total of six council members, four of whom were women and two men. They would be among the group that would be in the meeting for her naming. Any other Master and a few trusted personnel of the council would also have the option of attending. Otherwise, it was a closed event. Which, considering all they did was learn of the person's background, seemed overkill. Well, at least, based on the accounts of the two Masters she knew, that's all they did.

Technically, Ashtyn wasn't sure if she could take in this many companions, but she'd insist they all join, even the guards. They'd journeyed all this way and were trusted by the Posse. They deserved at least that much.

And she was sure it would bother the council members which was only a positive.

"Hello, Miss Dubois." The woman in the middle, one with

dark skin and long dark hair spoke. Her voice was heavenly, calming.

Surely a trap.

"It's Fournier," Gabriel corrected. "Ashtyn Fournier."

Ashtyn's breath caught in her throat. He'd called her his wife plenty of times since their wedding, but this was the first time she'd heard her name paired with his. It sounded right.

The woman's eyes sparked as they jumped between the two of them before landing on Ashtyn once more. "My apologies, *Mrs.* Fournier. I see you've brought your husband. Would you like him to join us?"

Ashtyn hadn't been expecting the question. She figured being married meant he had an automatic pass to come in, to anything that regarded her. It wasn't that the Island and North were forceful in their cultures, but it'd been such a custom for the husband to have every right to his wife—and in turn for the wife to have all access to her husband—that Ashtyn hadn't considered an alternative where she could keep him away. It was unnecessary, but she appreciated it all the same.

"Yes. My friends have all joined me on this journey therefore I expect *all* of them in there." It meant they'd all learn of her history but oh well.

All of the Southerner's eyes sparked like they wanted to argue but thought better of it when the woman in front gave a soft nod. "Very well. I am Nida. The members"—she pointed to her left and went down the row—"Alerik, Samone, Senine, Jodiah, and Abeta."

When Ashtyn didn't say anything, Gabriel gave a polite nod. "Nice to meet you all."

It wasn't actually.

"We've been told you desire to be gone soon?" Senine asked. She was a tall beauty, her skin the darkest in the group and her hair the shortest of the women. Almost as short as those of the men. "I must confess, with the exception of the Assassin, the Sorcerer, and the Magician, the other Masters required more than a single visit."

"If it were up to me, I wouldn't have wasted my time here at all," Ashtyn snickered.

To her surprise, Jodiah and Abeta's lips twitched up rather than the stoic look of their friends. It was nice to see at least two of them had a sense of humor, even though Ashtyn hadn't been joking.

"Then let us not waste your time," Nida stated. "Follow us."

All six members turned and moved into the council building. Ashtyn took the moment to look around, meeting Tristan's green orbs for reassurance that she had the Northern Posse on her side, then began after the council.

The others came with her, and Ashtyn tried to ground herself in the feel of Gabriel's hand on her back.

They moved through the large expanse of the building, the corridors as grand as those at the palace with more of a marble sheen rather than the stoniness of the Northern palace. There weren't any doors along the sides and surprisingly, no one else littered the floors. They must've been brought through an entrance that only led to the meeting room because there was no way there were no other rooms in this whole council building.

Or maybe there were secret doors up and down these halls.

The large double doors reminded Ashtyn of the Posse's dining hall but when they opened, the space was nothing like the Northern one. This room had a large table sitting in the middle with chairs spaced three feet apart from one another and a single chair at the other end of the table, for their highest member she assumed.

She was shocked to find there were already people within

the room, six of the chairs filled and the walls lined with more. She didn't recognize any of them, but she could tell some of them were Northern, though far fewer than the Southerners.

The council members took their seats as Nida guided her to the end of the table where she pointed out the chair. Ashtyn only blinked looking at it. "You want me to sit there? Isn't that for your superior? You, I guess."

"We do not have superiors. All council members hold equal vote. That spot is for you." Nida glanced around her. "Your husband may join you at the table."

Translation: We are allowing them all in so you don't cause a problem, but you better not try to take them all up there with you.

Ashtyn smirked, ready to comment, when Gabriel interrupted, "Thank you."

Their group settled back against the walls while Ashtyn took her spot at the large chair. It was technically large enough for both her and Gabriel to fit, but he allowed her to sit alone while he balanced on the arm of the chair. It almost seemed more powerful, the fact that he was sitting there. Ashtyn didn't mind it at all.

Rather, she was utterly turned on by it. Gabriel had promised he'd always protect her, and this—sitting up there where his large body could block part of her—felt exactly like he was upholding his promise. Even the way his position demanded attention felt like protection. Like he knew she didn't want so much attention on herself so he was taking as much as he could. Ashtyn knew if she asked him to move, he would. If she asked him to sit on her chair so she could take his lap, he would. If she asked him of anything, he would do it.

Her shoulders deflated. She was not alone. He would always make sure of that for her.

Nida sat across from her, but it was Alerik beside her who

started. "While you have come from the Northern crown, you know the proceedings from the Assassin, so we will not spend any idle time. You are no child to require such."

"Highly appreciated," Ashtyn remarked sarcastically, even though she was a jumble of nerves on the inside. The only thing keeping her steady was her fingers twitching with Gabriel's trousers underneath the table. Anything to be closer to him, to be touching him.

Gabriel's hand traveled up her back, settling around the back of her neck and his thumb pressed into her as if reprimanding her for the comment, but she knew even a part of him was amused. The others in their group had been. She caught the way they, namely Tristan and Norya, fought their amusement.

Senine inhaled slowly. "Depending on what you tell us, we will more than likely need more. Most aren't as easy as the Assassin, Magician, and Sorcerer."

Ashtyn only gave a single nod.

Then Nida stated, "Begin, healer. From the beginning. When did you realize your skill?"

She'd been twelve when she first noticed it. Fifteen when she first realized the full scope. Eighteen when she began using it in its entirety.

# CHAPTER 19
# ASHTYN

"I was playing with a group of kids when we got hurt. We were twelve. Well, I was twelve." Ashtyn hadn't thought about those moments in a long time, and she didn't realize a smile had graced her lips as she spoke of them now. "I have no real recollection of my first decade or so. Medics thought I suffered a major concussion before they got to me. I was alone, no parents, nothing. I remembered a few things any kid would I guess. My birthday, my favorite colors, my favorite snacks. Nothing significant to point to where I'd come from and from whom. So I mean, technically, I don't know if it showed up for the first time at twelve but the first time I remember it was when I was playing with those kids.

"It took a while for the medics to heal me. Well, actually no. I felt fine pretty quickly, but they thought that outrageous, so they kept me for a while. I suppose for any other ten-year-old it would've been outrageous but my healing ability was working itself without my realizing it. When I was better, two of the older medics allowed me to stay with them so long as I was of help. I did all the busy work—getting them materials, filing, organizing. And in my free time, I played with the other kids in town. Fast forward nearly two years, we were playing a game of chase and one of the kids tripped over a twig and fell over a steep ledge in the forests. While we waited for a couple of the faster kids to run to get help, the rest of us went down to him. His name was Bobi. He was such a sweet kid, always laughing. Even then, with his body broken, he was smiling so that us crying ones would feel better. I didn't even realize I was doing anything, but my hands were on his chest and all I could think is 'You have to get better. Your body is strong, it will heal itself.' Something happened then. I hadn't realized it back then but the pain in his eyes subsided a bit. I was lost in thought though. I remember thinking 'You've got to heal. You're too good. Help yourself heal.' And it was like his body listened to me because his body started to slowly heal. To stop bleeding. I couldn't do anything about the bones because they needed to be put back, but his other injuries... they started healing.

"Obviously, I didn't know that was because of me. We just thought it a miracle that his bleeding was slowing. He still needed the help and stitches from medics, but I'd helped his body begin the process."

"And did anything happen in that moment that you can remember?" A member around the table asked, reminding Ashtyn that she was before the Masters council. "A shift in the air?"

"Honestly, I don't know. I was so heartbroken for Bobi. I think we all were. I don't think any of us could tell."

A single nod from Nida. "You may continue."

"Nothing more happened for a while. I grew up, became the typical girl, giggling with her friends and basking in the attention of boys. Then at fifteen, I..." She swallowed. There was a reason she didn't like to remember certain things. "When I was fifteen, there was this girl I thought was a good friend. We were both pretty"—Gabriel's thumb brushed her skin as she shivered with the use of that word—"both of us got attention, but I had that of the boy she wanted. You know, typical teenage girl drama. But... she really wanted him. She pushed me while we were on a walk in the forest, and I broke my leg with the fall. Then she left instead of helping me, knowing we were too far out for my yelling for help to do me any good, and on a trail most didn't frequent. She left me for dead. She knew, come nightfall, it'd be me against the animals until the possibility of someone coming by there again. If I could survive that long. So yeah, for dead.

"I think I was in more pain for what she did to me than anything. It took about an hour before I got myself to focus on the real problem—if I couldn't walk, I wasn't getting out of that forest alive. So I focused on my leg. I don't know how I knew what to do, but it felt innate. I said to myself, to the healthy bits in my right leg to go to my left, and within a few hours, I was fine."

"I thought you couldn't do anything about broken bones?" someone asked.

"Well, not with limited time. When I was with Bobi, he had more serious injuries and I knew help was on the way. Plus, it takes a lot more of my energy to heal bones. In the forest on my own, I had all the time and energy in the world. Well, the pain kinda took away some of that energy, but you get the point.

"When I got back to town, it was nearly nightfall, and Lia was shocked, of course. I didn't look good either—sweaty, dirty, just all-around bad. When that boy, Alan, ran for me, she didn't like that. When more attention came to me because of my state, she really didn't like that. I basked in it. But I was still mad. By the end of the week, I knew she wasn't going to give up. She... shocked me though. Dragged me out in the middle of the night with the help of Luke by promising him sex. They got me to the woods. She had a knife this time. Luke got scared when he saw it and ran, but Lia attacked. I didn't try to fight back, per se. I was just dodging and somehow the knife got pointed around and into her stomach.

"I knew enough by growing up with the medics to not pull it out, but she was stupid enough not to listen, and she started immediately gushing out. That's when I remembered my leg, Bobi. I figured maybe it had been me all along. At least with my leg, it must've been. And..." Ashtyn squeezed Gabriel's thigh where she was holding him under the table. "I thought about not even trying. She'd tried to kill me. Twice. I actually got up and stepped away, but I couldn't turn my back. When she started choking out blood, I fell to my knees and placed my hands over her stomach and tried the same thing I'd done with my leg. I got the help from her legs too because I knew they weren't injured. Well, actually it was because I assumed that was the only way to do it.

"When she was healed, I ran back. I couldn't do anything about being in the middle of the forest, plus I was sure Luke would've already told someone. So I just ran back for a bath to clean her blood off. When they found her and brought her back, she was healed. No one believed it. They all looked at me like I was a goddess or something." Ashtyn scoffed to herself. "Her plans backfired because I got more attention then than I ever had before. I basked in it."

"You began using it to help your town?" Senine asked.

She shook her head. "I didn't know how to control it then. The ability came when I was panicked. Now I can control it always, but I wasn't practiced, and I didn't put the focus on practicing so I just helped the medics the same I always had with maybe a bit more basic medical healing. Nothing with my abilities." That's when she'd begun slowly studying medical books and putting her practical skills to use.

"And how did you begin using your abilities?" Alerik asked.

Ashtyn looked around the room, past all the unknown faces to those of her entourage off to the side. None of them gave much away, but there was pride in the warrior duos' faces that Ashtyn didn't entirely understand, but she appreciated. And something akin to awe in the guards' faces. When she finally glanced up at Gabriel, there was only...

She didn't want to think of that emotion.

So she focused on his hand still massaging the nape of her neck and the way her hands fidgeted on his thigh as she lost herself in memory once more. "As I got older, I moved away. I wanted more, even if I didn't know what that more was. I still loved that attention, dated a few guys." Three, to be exact. The three she'd told Gabriel about. "Then one day, I was nineteen, I couldn't do it anymore. I... didn't want any of it anymore because it wasn't fulfilling. I stopped wanting the attention of all those boys, basically stopped focusing on them and completely on myself. It was nearly three years before the Assassin found me. The first year was the hardest as I taught myself how to control it, but it didn't take as long as I thought it would for it to work. The next two, I just moved from place to place healing, and I got better. Then the Assassin found me, heard about the way I heal from those I was healing, then saw me in action. He figured I must be a Master or something close to it. I've been at the palace since."

Nida's eyes narrowed. "If he suspected that nearly two years ago, why are we just hearing of it now?"

"I didn't want to come," Ashtyn bit back.

Someone scoffed from the side. "Since when does the Assassin care about that? The man looks out for himself and the crown alone."

"*Do not* talk about him like that," Ashtyn growled. Sparrow was a lot of scary things, but he'd always been loyal to her. She wouldn't allow them to bash him.

Alerik cleared his throat as if he could sense a fight coming and he wanted to dispel it. "Like we said before. Some are easier. The Assassin, we just needed to hear his story and it was clear. But usually, as in your case, we will need to see you in action as well."

Ashtyn nodded. She'd suspected this might come up as well.

"Lucky for us too that you're here." Abeta smiled. "Two came into our infirmary after getting trampled by frightened horses. They could use the help."

Ashtyn's heart sputtered like it always did when someone was in need of her help. She needed to get to their side.

She nodded and stood. "Let's go then."

IT HAD BEEN A LONG DAY, and it felt like a waste.

To be there the entire day, to spend the time riding down to this point of the South and the extra time they would need to ride back up to the northern points of the Northern Lands. It all felt like a waste of time, considering her answer had come out to neither a yes nor a no. She could've spent this time healing people of the plague, though she knew everyone was glad for the break since she was more likely to drain herself than stop if given the opportunity.

They'd said only the Assassin, Sorcerer, and Magician had

been named instantly, which made sense given those specific skill sets, but Ashtyn still felt frustrated with the outcome of this journey. At least she'd been able to heal those two who'd needed her. And yet, still, the council needed more time.

They were in a spacious inn now, much nicer than any she'd been to in the North, and she had a feeling it was because the warm weather here meant the upkeep could be made more frequently.

The room she had with Gabriel was intimate with a dark rug and matching curtains decorating the space. The window was large, and Ashtyn knew come morning, the sunlight would be beaming in beautifully. There was a large bed in the middle and a fireplace off to the side. It wasn't very chilly down at this point of the South, but Gabriel still had their fire burning because he knew she liked it, both the feeling and the sounds.

She knew he liked it too even if it made him sweat more than it did her. It was why he preferred the chillier North where he could have the fire going and be fine.

They'd both taken their baths, and it was now time again for bed. It was both her most favored and most hated time of the day. The easing feeling of him beside her didn't take away from the knowledge of having him so close and not being able to enjoy it. It was cruel.

Ashtyn was just turning from the large window, curtains left wide open to the hills beyond so the sunlight would beam in come dawn, when she saw Gabriel stripping out of his sleeping trousers. He *always* kept those on. It was their one barrier.

With his back to her, she took in the definition of all his muscles before her gaze dropped to his ass. It was defined and plump, and she wanted nothing more than to bite it. "What're you doing?"

His head turned, and a small smirk rose on his lips. "Another lesson."

Ashtyn rolled her eyes, crossing her arms before her chest. "How was the first a lesson? All you did was stand there and watch me touch myself."

He turned fully now so his front was on display. His eyes shined with mischief witnessing her resist looking any lower. "Today, I won't be watching anything."

"Meaning?"

Gabriel was such a charmer that a cocky smirk almost made him look sinister. "That first time, you needed to learn how to touch yourself—and don't think we won't be doing that again, by the way." He ignored her narrowed gaze as he moved for the bed. "This time, you need to learn to touch *me* without concern. Anything you wish to do to me."

She scoffed. "What makes you think I'm worried about touching you?"

He sat on the bed, back against the headboard as he picked something up from the nightstand. "The fact that you haven't done so yet even though you beg for sex daily."

"Oh you're a real piece of work," she mumbled, gaze now following the lines of his body until she was staring at his cock. She'd sucked a cock once before and hated every second of it, but in this moment, Ashtyn desperately wanted to know what his tasted like.

He held the cloth up, then proceeded to tie it around his eyes. "You've never gotten the chance to do the things you enjoy to a male, and I understand that is because you never truly wanted them, but you want me now, so I don't want you to be nervous about it. I want you to enjoy my body, but I know you will not do so if I am watching, so I'll be blindfolded. You can take your time, touch and taste me however you please, healer."

He sat back then, relaxed and patient.

Ashtyn couldn't move, couldn't lift her jaw up off the ground. He wanted her to have her way with him...

She realized then that her desire to have sex with him could happen tonight but threw the idea out immediately. She wanted him to take her, to look her in the eyes, to consummate the marriage and make it a real one because *he* wanted to. Because though he said it often, his refusal to consummate made this feel like it had an expiration date.

She moved a little closer but remained on the opposite side of the bed. "Are you sure? I'll be your first touch."

He moved the blindfold for a moment so his sincere gaze met hers. "We're married. You're my only."

He dropped the cloth back down and waited.

Ashtyn didn't know what to do. Should she stop him? Call him crazy and simply go to bed? Did she want that?

No. The answer was quite simple.

So how did she start this? Should she strip and join him skin to skin? Should she only touch him? Was she allowed to taste him entirely?

*Anything you wish to do to me.*

It was technically a dangerous proposal because she could end up doing wild things, but he was probably as aware as she was that she wouldn't escalate things that far.

Ashtyn breathed slowly to calm her nerves and finally began to strip. When she stood naked, her skin tingled with anticipation, and she took in this moment of being naked before him. He didn't know it, but still, having both of them bare felt like a step in the right direction.

Naked and only a few feet away, she could consummate this marriage. But that wasn't her decision to make. He'd chosen to not fully tie himself down and she would respect that no matter her desires. She knew what it was for her wants to go unheard, so she wouldn't do that to him.

She swallowed as she moved around the bed until she reached the clothes he'd left on the ground. She took the shirt he'd worn after his bath and put it on. She was still naked underneath and the moment the shirt moved, they'd be skin to skin, but Ashtyn needed this little barrier.

Then she moved for him.

He was calm, but his cock twitched when her fingertips grazed his calf. The hairs stood alert, but he didn't move.

Her fingers shook. She swallowed. She shouldn't be nervous. She'd touched a man before.

But never like this. Never because she wanted to. Never how she wanted to.

She took in a large breath, then traveled her gaze back up his form until she was looking at his face. His beautiful, masked face.

Her lips tipped up softly. In a million years, she wouldn't have known this was something she would ever need, yet he'd been able to read her. This man knew things about her she was still learning. It was astonishing. Exhilarating.

Ashtyn pushed herself to kneel on the bed between his legs, that moment straddling his one leg almost causing her to rub herself on him until she came. She knew Gabriel wouldn't mind. That he'd love being used for her pleasure, but she didn't want to be selfish with him. Tonight would be about his pleasure.

Between his legs, her hands grazed his legs, getting comfortable touching him. After a few minutes, she was fully caressing his legs. All the while, he sat patiently while his cock bobbed, precum dripping out.

She licked her lips. Oh, what a development, indeed. She'd never wanted to taste anything so much in her life.

Ashtyn swallowed, then quickly moved her hands so she wouldn't psych herself out.

They were on his thighs, slowly making their way up until she was leaning over his body, touching his hips. Then higher still. She ignored his begging manhood and instead took her time enjoying his chest, the hairs gliding between her fingers.

"I've thought about the way these hairs would feel against my nipples one too many times," she whispered.

Then gasped, eyes widening. Had she just said that aloud?

His smirk confirmed so. "So have I."

Her hands fidgeted, trying to figure out if she'd just ruined the experience for herself.

Gabriel knew her mind was beginning to take over without needing to look at her because his hands softly took the ones on his chest and held them steadily there. "Don't freak yourself out, beautiful. Pretend this *is* your imagination. Go wild."

She almost scoffed. They knew she wouldn't be doing that.

But she tried to take his advice.

"In my imagination..." she began. "I would want to kiss you."

He gave a genuine smile. "Please do."

Her hands were still on his chest, his having fallen back to his sides when she leaned over him until their lips were brushing, whispering, "I've never initiated a kiss before."

He didn't say anything or move. He wasn't going to give her the out of leaning in. This was for her to do as she liked, and that meant she needed to make the moves.

So Ashtyn kissed him.

He moaned into it immediately, opening his mouth for their tongues to clash, his a little more dominant than the situation he was leading on. She internally smirked at that.

Her hands ran up his chest until she was holding his face, nails digging into his scalp, and she unconsciously moved until she was straddling him. She didn't care if she wasn't wearing anything and his cock was about to touch her wet cunt, she needed to feel the heat of his chest against hers, even if it was through this thin shirt.

She made an involuntary gasp as his cock slid between her folds, and it was as if the sound put him in action because Gabriel's hands finally slipped up her thighs until they gripped them.

He growled into the kiss, and she finally pulled away. Her hips were writhing over him, both on their own and with his guidance, coating his cock in her juices.

Her head fell back at the pleasure.

She would come like this in no time.

Ashtyn's eyes snapped open, and she pushed away until she was between his legs once more. "No."

His hands immediately shot to the side, his breaths coming in uneven as he muttered, "Sorry." He was still blindfolded, but he was no longer quietly sitting there.

"Don't be. That was my fault."

"Did you not enjoy it?"

"I loved it," she whispered.

"Then why stop?"

"I want tonight to be about your pleasure."

His lips tipped into a genuine smile. If only his blindfold was off so she could see his charming, warm eyes too. "Your pleasure is my pleasure, wife."

She shook her head even though he couldn't see her. "I want to taste you."

"Isn't that what you were doing?"

She shook her head again as if he'd be able to see this time. "No."

He swallowed so she knew he understood. "Anything you'd like to do. Enjoy your husband, healer."

Ashtyn bit her bottom lip but didn't allow herself to contemplate anything. She leaned over him immediately and licked his shaft. She glanced up at him as his entire body stiffened from the touch. "Unfortunately, you're coated with my juices now."

"How could that ever be unfortunate?"

"I wanted to taste *you*. Not us."

He smirked. "Next time then. Today, taste us."

She smiled. Why was that such an endearing statement? She didn't know, but she listened to it.

She took him into her mouth and sucked on only the tip while her hands wrapped around the base. His head fell back as his mouth opened in an O. Ashtyn pulled him out slowly, then sucked him back in, a little deeper this time.

She moved slowly, taking her time learning what to do, what he liked, and enjoying the sounds coming from his lips.

After a few more bobs, she found her rhythm, then allowed her hands to stroke and pump as well.

Gabriel groaned. Loud and hard.

Ashtyn's brows furrowed when she glanced up. She pulled him out and sat back on her haunches.

He whimpered but didn't complain. After all, this night was about what she wanted.

She moved until she was straddling him again, but this time, she didn't lean in. This time, her fingers slowly grazed up his arms until they were by the blindfold. Then she slowly pulled the thing off so she was looking into those melting chocolate eyes.

"Hi." She smiled.

He broke into a large grin. "Hi, beautiful."

"I want you to watch."

"You sure?"

She nodded as she moved off his lap until she was between

his legs again, then bent over to take his cock into her mouth again, eyes on him through her lashes.

"Lords, Ash, look at the curve of your back."

She realized then that the position she was in—with her ass in the air—would be a very striking one to a male, especially with her shirt bunched by her breasts, exposing all of her to him. She smirked as she took him in her mouth again.

She moved slowly at first, getting comfortable while learning again what he liked. When she got it, she was hypnotized with watching his reactions. The furrow between his brows, the gasps, the moans, groans, *growls*. The way he'd bare his teeth like an animal's, never taking his eyes off her.

She loved it.

Loved the feel of his body writhing beneath her, the way his hips pumped up like he wanted to fuck her mouth, the way his hands landed in her hair, pulling.

She moaned as his fingers got tighter in her scalp, realizing then that doing this act for him was making her wetter than she'd ever been before. It turned out—*his* pleasure was her pleasure.

That moan must've been magic because he came with a long groan, head thrown back, incoherently calling her name.

He tasted... a bit salty but sweet.

The last and only time she'd done this before, Ashtyn hadn't been wet, and she certainly hadn't allowed him to finish in her mouth. This time...

She couldn't imagine allowing him to finish anywhere else.

Except maybe inside her if he ever consummated their marriage.

When she swallowed his cum, her tongue darted out to catch any strays, then she sat back on her haunches, watching him.

He was breathing hard, but his eyes were on her, bright with... amazement?

She smiled, though she could feel the heat in her cheeks as she mumbled, "That was fun."

He laughed, booming and loud, and reached out to grab her until she was back to being straddled on his lap. "That indeed, wife."

She leaned in to kiss him, thankful he'd given her this opportunity.

# CHAPTER 20
# GABRIEL

anlik had found her husband three weeks before the two of them had taken Gabriel up to the Northern palace. That was over a decade ago.

In all the years, he'd continued sending the odd letter back and forth, so he knew they had children, and they knew he'd found his woman. They'd didn't know, however, that he'd married said girl.

Gabriel had planned on writing to them, but the mention of the possible need for magicians made him antsy that instead of a letter, he might be able to come down and see them. It'd been fourteen years since they left him, but Gabriel wasn't worried as he walked against the winds toward the cottage at the end of the cliffside with Ashtyn and the others falling behind him.

The home was a little farther from the others in town but still close enough to the sisterhood's home and the shop they sold their services out of. Gabriel was half shocked he still remembered the way around the entire town, that he'd been able to find this cottage having never been here before, based solely on the letter Lanlik had sent him back when she first married and they built it.

As he made his way forward, Gabriel tried to clear his mind of the night before. Being blindfolded had added an extra layer of pleasure by wiping away one sense, his others, especially touch, had heightened. Gabriel was beyond thankful he'd made himself come before going to her so he could last longer. He'd spent years preparing himself to last as long as possible when he finally found his woman, and the practice was finally coming in need. Gabriel couldn't stop glazing over with thoughts of their night. It was an addicting feeling and one that made continuing to resist Ashtyn nearly impossible.

So much so that he was glad to have this other mission while they were in the South. His need to find magicians who could help them, who they could trust, was just barely enough to get him to concentrate on something other than his wife.

"Are you very anxious?" Ashtyn snapped him out of his thoughts.

He glanced over to her, then back toward their destination. If he paid too much attention to her, he'd get sucked back into the night before. "Not at all."

"Then why are you walking so fast? You look as if you wish to get this over with."

He slowed his pace. "I hadn't realized."

"It is okay to be nervous, you know. It has been a long while since you've seen them." She'd been learning everything about his time here as a child, that he hadn't had a chance to come back in all the time that had passed. It was enough to shake anyone with apprehension and excitement.

"I know." He took her hand. "I'm not nervous about seeing them. I was only absorbed within my thoughts." He kissed her knuckles. "The memory of last night has become quite the distraction."

Her cheeks pinked, and she remained silent on the matter. Gabriel didn't push her as they were nearing the home now.

The door snapped open before he could get to it, and on the other side stood a girl who could only be about seven and who looked exactly like her mother. "Who're you? I can sense you're familiar, but I don't know you."

Gabriel smiled. "Ah, so you're the magician child."

She stood taller, a wide grin about her face. "I am."

"Gamina, who's at the door?" A familiar voice traveled through the winds.

Gabriel's smile broadened, and he realized his grip on Ashtyn's hand had tightened when she ran a soothing hand done his arm to relax him. Maybe he was a bit nervous.

"Gamina, please tell me you at least used your magic to check on the guest? You know your mother doesn't like the odd guest at her house instead of the shop." A moment later, Hansel was standing behind the little girl. When her eyes met Gabriel's, they widened. "Cavalinho?"

He smiled. "I'm a little bigger now, I think."

That was an understatement considering he'd been a small kid and was now six feet tall.

Hansel burst into laughs as she pushed forward and took Gabriel into her arms. She was only ten years older and had always treated Gabriel as a little brother, so being in her embrace felt comforting.

She pulled away only enough to look him in the eyes, tears watering her eye line, before snuggling back in. "Oh, cavalinho, I didn't think I'd be seeing you today!"

Gabriel snuggled into the hug. "I know, Hans. And unfortunately, I cannot stay long. I came to ask for help."

She pulled away abruptly, tears gone and a seriousness clouding her hazel eyes. "What is it?"

"I'm okay," Gabriel emphasized.

She breathed a sigh of relief, then glanced behind him to the eight others who'd come with him. When she met Gabriel's eyes once more, she knew she could trust them, even though they were Northern and Northerners weren't very accepting of magicians. "Come in, then."

Hansel led him in by the hand as Gabriel's other hand reached out for his wife. Ashtyn took it but her hold was so tentative, it was like she was worried about doing so.

The others didn't speak as they followed Hansel through the home to the back where the kitchen was, and all the sound was coming from. They passed by several kids on the way.

"You met Gamina," Hansel explained as they walked. "She's Lanlik's youngest. That there is Hank, my first. And that's Pati, Anvel's second."

When they neared the kitchen, Hansel raised her voice. "Lanlik, I've a surprise for you!"

Turning the corner, Gabriel caught Lanlik's eye roll as she called back, "Dear lord, are you working with Gamina now?"

He allowed a soft chuckle to leave him as they stopped by the entrance. Lanlik's gaze met his and all else froze. "What is this?" she whispered.

Hansel released him and moved to stand by the others in the room, some familiars, others not. "Everyone can now meet my cavalinho!"

Lanlik's eyes widened as she finally accepted what was before her. "Gabriel?"

He nodded as he took a single step forward, Ashtyn's hand leaving his to allow him this moment with the woman who had raised him for three years. "Hi, Lani."

She sputtered as she ran for his arms, her hold that of a parent who thought she'd never see her child again. "Oh, my dear boy," she mumbled time and again into his ear.

When they finally pulled away, Rudo, her husband, came

for Gabriel. They embraced for only a moment before the final three women whom Gabriel knew around the kitchen came for him.

After getting to them all, Lanlik took his arm as her gaze landed behind him. "Gabriel?"

Gabriel turned. "These are friends. Tristan is a spy for the Northern Posse. He and his woman, Norya, who's an Islander and could kick everyone's butts here, are our main protection." Tristan scoffed at the implication that Norya could beat him even though she definitely could, and Norya beamed at it. "Then we have Gian, Noah, Colt, Wells, and Ares. They're trusted guards also here for protection. And this here is Ashtyn." They knew she was a healer from every letter he'd sent about her in the past year. "My wife."

Sputters came from all around. "Wife?"

He turned back for them with a little shrug. "It is new. I hadn't had the opportunity to send a letter about it."

Lanlik's eyes watered. "Oh, how lovely."

Gabriel intertwined his fingers with Ashtyn's and kissed her knuckles enjoying the way she pinked. "Quite."

"Is that why you have come? To present us your wife? But why would you need guards for such a thing?" Lanlik asked.

"Unfortunately no. I love that you get to meet her, but we are here for another purpose," Gabriel grew serious, and the room shifted.

They all settled into the space as he began to tell them of the plague, Ashtyn's healing and her possible Masterhood, and the possible need for magicians to cure this thing.

After his group answered all of their questions, Lanlik stood tall. "I think I know exactly who can help you. And they are not tied down with families so they can certainly travel with you."

He'd expected none of them would wish to come given

their families here, but Gabriel had thought a possible member of the sisterhood he hadn't yet met could join them.

They wasted no time—though Gabriel wanted nothing more than to spend at least a week here—as Lanlik took Gabriel's hand, and she and Rudo led his group toward town to the house the sisterhood still resided in.

When they entered, Gabriel was sent back in time nearly fifteen years. It all looked the same, the sound box still playing off to the side.

"Cousins, we need you," Lanlik called out.

Rudo turned to clarify. "These three came to us about four or five years after you left. Their mothers were sisters and had them all within weeks of one another. Only Belinda's mother was a magician, but they all ended up becoming one as well. Lucky for you too, they all are gifted with a variety of magic. I'd say they're as close to Masters as you could get. Calling to them as 'Cousins' is enough to get all of their attentions."

"As close to?" Tristan questioned, straightening.

Rudo shrugged. "Oh, their magic is nothing compared to the Master's, but they are some of the most powerful magicians we know." Then Rudo met Gabriel's eyes once more. "But they, like another of ours, have more to their lives than this town."

It was as if he could read with a simple glance in Gabriel's direction that these women would be doing more than helping with the plague, that they would be needed to reintroduce magicians to the North.

Whether or not he could tell, Rudo was right. These three, if they agreed, would need to be ready to give a lot more to the world.

As the three women came out of the back room, Gabriel was struck by their beauty.

"Gabriel," Lanlik started. "This is Astreya, Belinda, and

Caetana, some of our best magicians and the closest resemblances to Northerners. Cousins, Gabriel has a request for you."

Their skin tones matched that of Evony's—darker than a common Northerner's but not quite as tanned as most Southerner's. It would help with blending them in, though having Southerners in the North wouldn't be a problem since the nations were friends in all things but the acceptance of magicians. That would soon be changing, but it would help them to blend their magicians in with the rest of the group for the ease of this already complicated mission.

Astreya had long black waves that flowed down her back. Her lashes were long and thick, framing the beauty of her stormy blue eyes. She looked similar to Evony in those matters, but there was a little more exoticism to her looks, her eyes more seductive than Evony's calming.

Belinda had straight black hair that stopped at an angle at her shoulders, the fronts longer than the back. Her eyes, like her cousins, were striking with the long black lashes and alluring grey-green eyes.

Caetana also had long locks, though not as far down her back as Astreya's, but her hair was a dark red. Her lashes were just as beautiful but there was a different type of seduction that came from her darker orbs. They weren't as hypnotizing as her cousins', but something about them made them more so, more dangerous to the heart.

Or maybe that was because Gabriel liked darker eyes.

Gabriel gave a polite smile as they all took him in from head to toe. "Hello."

Astreya's eyes snapped to his, sparkling. "Gabriel," she said softly, causing shivers to run down his spine. "We've heard maybe too much about you."

His cheeks flushed. "Sorry."

She laughed, her beauty shining. "Do not be. You left an impression. Be proud of it."

"I see a ring, Gabriel," Caetana started. "Where is she?"

Gabriel didn't hesitate to turn for Ashtyn who stood a few feet behind him, but he hadn't expected to find her arms crossed and an even darker expression on her face than normal.

His fingers grazed her cheek softly, thumb pausing on her bottom lip, and he couldn't take his eyes off of her as he spoke to the Southerners. "Do not mind her grumpiness. She's much softer on the inside."

Norya scoffed then. "Good luck getting to that inside."

Their entourage laughed alongside the Southerners, and Ashtyn's frown deepened as her gaze traveled over the three cousins.

He dropped his hand to hers, pulling her arms from her chest so he didn't have to stop touching her, then turned back for the magicians. "We do not have much time here in the South, so we can get started on our purpose for being here. If you do not wish to join, we will need to find others."

They all nodded, but the way the three cousins eyed his entourage, he had a feeling they would be joining. That, and something about them, said they weren't afraid of hardship.

HE'D BEEN RIGHT. It'd taken no effort to get the Cousins to agree. Matter of fact, it felt as if they'd agreed to come even before hearing Gabriel's reasoning. They'd eyed his group, and Gabriel hadn't been able to tell whether their gazes had lingered on the guards out of apprehension or desire.

Either way, they were quite the threesome to behold. He

had no fears they could handle themselves, especially around a bunch of Northern men who were raised with a touch more propriety. A touch being so very much more. Lords, the Cousins made his guards blush with mere looks more than any flirtations they could throw at the women.

His group was now preparing to head back to the council building, Ashtyn taking a nap in Lanlik's cottage while Gabriel sat out back, listening to the crash of waves beyond the cliffside as he pulled out the wood carving he'd been working on for the last couple of weeks, and got back to it.

"Glad to see you've still got it. Much better now too, huh?"

Gabriel stiffened, stopping his work. His gaze flew behind him, and his heart stuttered. His carving was placed on the small table with his knife as he took the man into his arms. "Kody!"

"Hey, son!" Kody hugged him tight, still as large as Gabriel remembered him being.

Pulling back, Gabriel looked him over. Older, yes. Roughened around the edges because of his hard labored job, yes. Happier, absolutely.

"How'd you know—"

"You thought you'd come back, and Hansel wouldn't run home to tell me?"

Gabriel's grin grew. "Right. How could I forget the way Hansel would run to you?"

The woman had met Kody through Gabriel. He'd been going to get mentored with his woodworking, and Hansel had insisted on walking him, given his eight-year-old self. She'd immediately blushed and sputtered at the sight of Kody, and Gabriel had been so confused.

After that, Hansel had blushed and scattered away anytime Kody was around until almost a year later when Kody finally cornered her against a tree. Gabriel didn't know what was said between them since he'd been watching from atop another tree at a distance, but he'd seen Hansel as she'd been looking for him. Seen her notice only Kody and turn to run off. Seen Kody run after her, grab her, throw her against a tree, cage her in. Seen them talk for less than a minute before he was kissing her.

After that, Hansel ran to him.

Every.

Single.

Day.

For every. Single. Thing.

And Kody loved it. Loved being needed by her.

He'd explained to Gabriel as much as he might understand at that young age that they were in love with each other, and what that meant for them.

Gabriel was glad to see nothing had changed.

Kody wiggled his eyebrows in response to Gabriel's teasing, then the men went to sit by the small table. Kody took his carving from the table and examined it. "My wife did mention you were married." His gaze snapped from the ring on Gabriel's finger to the carving once again.

"I am."

"That smile looks about as wide as mine when I finally got Han."

"Yes, well, you pined for her for about as long as I did Ash before getting her."

Kody laughed. "I didn't realize becoming your mentor would affect even your love life so much."

Gabriel laughed, pushing at the man's shoulder. "Ash is just stubborn. Han was a shy wreck around you."

Kody's grin was large as he glanced from Gabriel to the carving and back multiple times. "You know, our first meeting, you were right. Just a kid and you were beyond wiser than me."

"About what?"

"Wanting only one woman. I didn't realize it until Han, but you'd been right in questioning why any man would want anyone who isn't their woman."

"I'm glad. For you and me. Ashtyn's my only girl, and I love that."

"Good." Then Kody's teasing eyes met his as he held up the carving. "Good luck. And have lots of fun."

Gabriel pushed him again, getting more move from his large body than before, as he snatched the carving back.

Gabriel loved this, being back in this home, around the most important people of his childhood. He hated that Ashtyn wasn't there with him, but she needed the sleep. Plus, they would be coming back. She could meet Kody then.

# CHAPTER 21
# GABRIEL

Gabriel still didn't understand how Masters were chosen. He thought he'd learn something while in the South, but they kept their decision-making process to themselves.

He stood off by the horses while Ashtyn went off on the heads, telling them she had no intentions of sticking around because "they hadn't decided yet where her power stood." She was so sexy when she was riled up in that manner that Gabriel had to turn away to keep from getting hard. They had a long ride ahead of them, for days still, and the very last thing he wanted was an erection while atop his horse so early in their journey.

Lanlik stopped before him, the blessing he required to get his mind out of the filthy places it was headed. "She's feisty."

"I know," he replied proudly.

She gave a warm smile. "She's territorial too. I do not think she approves of the Cousins joining your journey."

He bit his lip. "Good. She's so closed off about her feelings, I treasure any opportunity for her to show it."

"Are we speaking of your wife?" Astreya stopped beside him.

Lanlik smirked. "I'd be careful, Strey. She might kill you if you get any closer."

Astreya laughed. "I'm sure she would. I love her."

Gabriel's grin broke out with pride as the other Cousins joined them. "Yeah, I love her too."

All of the women scoffed amusedly as Belinda replied, "We can tell. You two can't keep your eyes off each other. She watches you like a hawk when you're not looking. A very turned on, wanton hawk, but a hawk."

Gabriel's head fell back with a roaring laugh. "Wait until I tease her about that."

Caetana gasped. "Are you trying to get my cousin killed?"

Gabriel winked. "I won't mention where I heard it."

They were all smiles before Lanlik took his hand. "What's the plan, my love?"

Gabriel sighed, hating that he had to leave Lanlik and the others so soon after so many years apart, but he'd come back. Now that he had a wife, he'd come back with her. "We will be heading straight up north, not stopping by the palace. Tristan has already sent word of you three, but we will speak with the King and Assassin more about it when we head back to the palace. For now, they're trusting my decision-making."

Caetana quirked her brow. "And what else would they trust? They may be King and Assassin, but you are the one who knows magicians."

Gabriel bit the inside of his cheek to stop from grinning too wide. He was allowed to tell them since they would be playing such an inaugural role in the North so he wasn't nervous of the consequences, but still, it was quite the secret. "They have the most important thing on their side."

All three looked annoyed. "And what could that be?"

Gabriel's smirk won out. "The Assassin's wife."

"His—"

"His pregnant wife."

"What does that—" Belinda questioned this time.

"She's the Master Magician."

All three eyes popped wide open, gasps unhidden. They looked to have a million questions but were excellent at holding them in.

It was Caetana who finally said, "That is why they cannot use her, why you've come for help—her pregnancy?"

He gave a single nod. "Not only is the Assassin protective over her and not allowing her to exert herself too much, but the pregnancy truly has taken its toll on her, though she likes to deny it. She is tired a lot."

The Cousins didn't say much, but it was Astreya who finally gave an awe-struck smile. "We get to meet the Master Magician."

Gabriel's grin grew wide. "And you're going to love her."

ASHTYN COMPLETELY REFUSED to stop by the palace for any matter on their way back up north. They left two guards to pick up any supplies and food stores they would require, but his wife refused to stop because the Southern visit had already been "too much of a waste of time."

Though—and Gabriel knew he'd gotten her in a moment of weakness by bringing her into his arms and pressing her against a wall—she admitted she'd enjoyed the visit for the simple reason that Gabriel had been able to be reacquainted with those he'd left behind so long ago. Then her sexy lips had pouted when he'd mentioned getting lucky with the Cousins, and Gabriel's heart had pounded extra hard at her jealousy. That reminder meant one thing—gone was the soft Ashtyn, and back was the asshole. He wouldn't have had it any other way truly. Especially when this reaction proved her feelings were stronger than she normally tried to let on.

They were riding to the east of the palace, about a day's nonstop ride, heading to the tops of the lands where more were sick. But as they passed, Gabriel's earlier suspicions began rising. They'd had reports of the sicknesses in the northernmost point. There were more there but they weren't this bad. Not this sick. It made him believe that whoever was causing this was a little bit closer than they'd originally thought. It would be ingenious—start it at the top of the lands, make it affect more people there, so everyone thought it was the worst there but in reality, those with the true problems were those closer to the palace. A day's ride was nothing in fact.

As they stopped to give their horses a break, Gabriel taking his time with each one, the others scoured for sick. All of their women were in vests and trousers except his wife. She refused to give up her simple dresses even on horseback. Her stubbornness made Gabriel shake his head with a smile he couldn't fight.

Norya moved with Ashtyn as she started for homes who needed healing. She'd been trying to conserve most of her energy for when they got to the northernmost towns and villages, but his wife wouldn't have been able to stop and not help. He loved that about her.

As the women went off to do that, the four remaining—Tristan, Gian, Colt, and Noah—split up, the first duo to go around to do the talking since Tristan and Gian were the most skilled at that, and the second duo to check the grounds.

Gabriel half watched both groups as he focused on his

horses. He loved them, and he loved even more that he'd seen Ashtyn talking with Bella more and more every day. She was about to love horses as much as him, and he couldn't wait for the life they'd lead, for their kids who would also love these spectacular animals.

He wasn't paying much attention to the others anymore, but Gabriel couldn't help but look up when he noticed Colt and Noah bump into... nothing. A shield of some sort? Gabriel's back immediately stiffened. Was this what they'd been talking about when Mohawk told him he couldn't get through? Was this the same thing?

They slammed their fists into the thing, but it was immovable.

It reminded Gabriel of all the shields he'd seen magicians throw up. His head snapped around. She must be here. He was convinced now that it was a magician leading—or co-leading —this plague. That had to be the only explanation.

"Cousins," Noah called out. "Some help here?"

Belinda moved for them, her hand grazing the shield once before sticking her hands through breaking the shield. "How odd. Why would there be a block here?" She stared at the trees lining it.

Noah shrugged as he and Colt began to step through.

Right as someone came rushing out through the trail it led. A man. A large behemoth of a man. Screaming. Roaring at them. As he lifted his sword straight for Colt's head.

Had it not been for Belinda's quick reflexes, instating a shield over the boys, Colt's head would be lining on the ground five feet from his body.

Belinda's magic removed the shield the moment the boys had their own swords in hand, and the others were already rushing for aid. Tristan and Gian raced for them as six more men the size of giants came rushing out. Roaring.

Just the time for Ares and Wells to have gone back to the palace. They needed them now more than ever.

Seven against four wasn't great odds, but at least the four were actually seven with the three magicians on their side.

But the men were the size of mountains.

The horses scurried with the suddenness, and the villagers scrambled for their homes, screaming. Gabriel focused on his animals. He shepherded them aside, away from the fray so they weren't injured or frightened anymore, thankful he'd decided to tie them to the trees rather than allow them to wander now. Had that happened, they'd probably only have two horses left. Or none.

Gabriel wanted to help, and though he'd trained with King Edmund on horseback, he was definitely no match for those mountain men. He wouldn't be a distraction for his friends or the Cousins, so he stayed behind and climbed a tree instead. He'd grabbed a bag of throwing stars from one of the horse's satchels and hoped he'd be able to hit one of those men, hoped he didn't get any of his own.

The first thing Gabriel did from atop was search for Norya. She was standing by a door, stiff like she wanted to join but knew she couldn't risk leaving Ashtyn's side. On the off-chance this disturbance created a distraction to get to their healer, she needed to stay behind.

Gabriel's heart raced, both thankful to her for doing so and hurting because she had to watch the man she loved fight biceps the size of tree trunks and she could do nothing about it.

Knowing his wife was safe, Gabriel readied a throwing star, hoping he remembered the one time he'd seen James and Miels talking about them as he watched the fight.

Their men were doing a great job, but Gabriel had a feeling a huge thanks was given to the magicians. He remembered learning of the slowing of time to give magicians an advantage at war. He had a feeling the Cousins were doing just that.

And yet those men didn't look to be slowing down, didn't look to be affected by the magic. If that was the case, he couldn't imagine how fast and powerful they would've been had the Cousins not been there.

His heart raced. There was definitely someone helping them.

Gabriel, crouched on the balls of his feet on a branch high in the air, held on to another branch as he leaned forward, trying to get a better look.

They were moving fast so he couldn't tell if those pretty eyes were part of his imaginations or actually there. They must've been because his imagination never would've conjured light veins running around their eyes. The others must be able to see from such close up, so he'd talk to them about it then but Gabriel knew there was magic behind this plague now.

Then his thoughts blanked as he took in the scenes.

Tristan and Gian back-to-back as their swords whipped around, Colt and Noah doing the same. Astreya, Belinda, and Caetana stopped in a half circle around the fight with their arms up and gazes focused.

They were slowing movement, but Gabriel's friends needed more than that. Not only were those fighters huge, but if they were racked up on magic, they'd be a much larger problem to their four men who were going to be getting tired very soon, sweat already in puddles around them.

Gabriel's hand fidgeted with the throwing star in his hand as he prepared himself, then yelled at the Cousins, hoping they'd hear, "Get one of them apart! Get one of them apart!"

He waited a moment.

Then another.

He was about to shout again when one of the mountain men started backing up, resisting the urge. The others still looked the same so Gabriel figured two of the Cousins were focused on slowing them while one moved the behemoth. They worked incredibly together.

Waiting another moment for the man to be backed out enough to make sure he didn't get one of his own, Gabriel readied the throwing star and let it swing from his fingers.

He'd been aiming for the man's forehead.

It hit his neck instead. Just above his collarbone.

The man's eyes widened as a hand slapped it to stop the bleeding, but Gabriel was already focused on another resisting as he was pushed back. Instead of making a killing strike, Gabriel threw the next throwing star at the second man. Again, he aimed for the forehead.

This time, he got the man's chest.

No killing strike. Again.

But his strikes didn't necessarily matter. The hits were distracting enough, piercing deep into skin that his men were able to get an upper hand. As Gabriel threw another throwing star at the second one again, this time getting him somewhere in the abs, Noah was able to break away enough to swipe his sword clean across the first one's neck while Gian's sword slicked through the chest of another.

With two down, a third distracted with two stars in him which he attempted to keep fighting through, another was pushed away from the fight for Gabriel to handle while Tristan's sword swiped and took down the injured one before turning for another. He was magnificent, unsurprisingly so considering his trainings were mostly held with the undefeatable Master Assassin.

Gabriel threw his third star at the next man to be pushed back a second before he processed the events before him. Gian was going toward him. He was going to get hit. And for once, it was going to strike perfect what with Gian being inches shorter than the mountain men.

Gabriel screamed but he didn't hear it.

He wanted to push off the tree and get him out of the way, but there was no time. The star was flying and...

It struck the behemoth man—who Gabriel was positive had pinked veins around his eyes now—in the shoulder a moment before Colt's sword swiped across his neck.

Gabriel blinked to find Gian on the ground, Astreya atop him.

There was no more fighting, nothing to be heard, but Gabriel's focus was on those two. He was still holding his breath. Astreya was on top, but was Gian hurt?

It took a moment past Astreya's frantic hands swiping over him to see Gian's hand move to the side, eyes open and watching her. She could've thrown up a shield, but sometimes innate instincts were faster than magical ones, especially when cold fear was a factor.

Gabriel's breath left him in a rush.

He was okay. Gabriel hadn't wanted to kill anyone, but he'd been okay with doing so to those men because of the threat they presented to his wife. He wouldn't have been able to live with himself if he'd hurt one of his own friends.

Gabriel jumped off the tree just as Norya and Ashtyn came running for them, Ashtyn immediately caught him running from the tree, her shoulders sagging with relief that Gabriel didn't have the time to appreciate before she turned to their friends to look for injuries.

Norya jumped into Tristan's arms, ignoring the cuts on his arms as her relief washed over her, legs clinging around his waist as they embraced. They normally weren't as showy with their relationship—unless they were getting caught having sex somewhere—so Gabriel knew how deep the fear must've gone in them.

As Ashtyn moved for Noah who had a large gash down the side of his entire left arm and the two magicians stepped around to make sure the seven men were down, Gabriel's gaze wandered to the ground. Astreya was still lying atop Gian, his hands possessively holding her to him as they whispered to one another right before Gian turned them so he was atop.

Gabriel averted his gaze and focused instead on the dead men.

He moved to one—the one with the throwing star in the neck—and found wide open eyes. It was a haunting sight, but Gabriel instead focused on the light shades of pink on the outskirts of his eyes. The veins were there, though they looked lighter now, like they were fading. Had Gabriel waited to check another ten minutes, he was sure they would be gone.

This was all the evidence they needed. There was someone controlling these men. A magician. A sorcerer. A common person with dangerous elements on his side. They were all possibilities.

CHAPTER 22

# GABRIEL

Ashtyn was being unreasonable. Of course she was. Why would she allow her husband any rest?

She'd been healing when the fight broke out. She healed their men when it ended. Then went back to healing the sick.

Healing,

healing,

healing.

It was late, and she needed to rest. He didn't care if she'd done hours, even days, longer before, though he doubted that were possible. He was there to make sure she remained healthy at the end of this, and she needed to balance. If she spent too much now, she wouldn't have enough for the hordes of people they were bound to meet up north.

"Gabriel, if you don't get your fucking hands off me—" she yelled as Gabriel gripped her upper arms and pushed her away from the direction of another cottage she'd been headed.

Gabriel ignored her as he pushed her until they were back at the inn their group was staying in. The others were either down for the night already or around the bottom floor of the inn—which consisted of the dining area—having a relaxed night.

Ashtyn fought him harder now that they were at the inn, and she knew her opportunity of getting away was slipping. "Gabriel, stop fucking pushing me. Get your hands off. I'm not done!"

He scoffed. "You're more than done for the night."

"Says who!" She got in his face.

"Says your husband," he demanded back.

Her nostrils flared knowing the moment anyone heard he was her husband, they wouldn't get in the middle of them. He wasn't hurting her, so they'd have no reason to.

Ashtyn's head swung around looking for help she wouldn't find when her gaze narrowed in. She growled at the warrior duo who were tucked into the corner of the dark room, Tristan's hands in Norya's trousers, gripping her ass, as her hands slithered up the inside of his shirt, leaving scratch marks on his chest as they both laughed at the healer.

Gabriel guided his wife away quickly before the warrior duo pissed her off anymore.

In their room, Gabriel threw Ashtyn to the bed before she could fight some more.

"What the hell is the matter with you?" she accused.

Gabriel stripped out of his shirt and kicked off his boots, then moved for her. She sat up on her forearms watching him with a glare as he took one boot, then the other, pulling them off. "You're resting. If I have to keep you down with my body weight, rest assured, wife, you'll be resting."

His knee fell to the mattress as he leaned over her and pulled on the strings of an easy corset at the top of her simple dress. When that was done, he pulled the sleeves down.

"Why, exactly, are you undressing me?"

"It'll take you longer to try to flee if you're naked." Thankfully she was Northern through and through and wouldn't consider going out even half naked.

With her sleeves slipped off, Gabriel lowered the dress until her breasts spilled out, and his mouth watered with how desperately he wanted to suck on them, bite them and bruise them.

He continued pulling down as she grumbled, "And what if I don't want to be naked? You get to keep your trousers."

His fingers delighted in tracking down her skin as he pulled the dress down until it was past her hips, and he was taking her in. She was so beautiful.

As he finished tugging and dropped the dress to the floor, he leaned over her, holding himself on his hands as their lips skimmed. "You promise to be good, and I'll give you my shirt."

Her annoyed expression lightened with his words more than he'd been expecting, more than they would've if he'd promised to put her dress back on.

"Is that what you want, beautiful? My shirt?"

She gave a tentative nod.

His lips twitched up before he leaned in for a chaste kiss. He pulled back and grabbed his shirt and slipped her head through the neck hole. "There you go. Now slip back. You're done for the rest of the night."

She scowled but did as she was told as he settled in beside her. Facing one another, Gabriel traced her cheekbone. "Good girl."

Even in the dark, Gabriel could see her pulse stutter, but he didn't comment on it. His little vixen was angry enough as it was.

"You know I'm no damsel. I've healed far more than this before," she muttered, still annoyed.

"Yeah?" Gabriel entertained her. "And when was that?"

"When Sparrow found me."

Hand still on her cheek, his thumb grazed her bottom lip before settling around her throat and softly holding her there. "Will you tell me about it?"

She eyed him a moment before giving in. "Sparrow tells me he'd been on the hunt for this group. You know how he gets. He goes after groups who hurt and victimize women and children. I cannot even imagine the duo he and the Magician are going to make in the future. She's scarier than him."

Gabriel chuckled. "All the best relationships have that."

She smirked, eyes twinkling, but instead of commenting, focused on her story. "Anyway, he'd been hunting them and stopping them. But this group... in their rush to get away, they caused destruction to a village I happened to be passing. They thought if they could cause enough destruction, the Assassin would stop and help them rather than follow. He didn't.

"When we got to the palace, he told me about it from his end. That the guilt had been eating him alive, leaving all those to die until he finally got to the group until a few men from the village came after him. He was able to hand the women and children to those men to bring back so they'd be out of harms way, but it'd also given him the opportunity to learn there was some spectacular woman who was healing people with her hands, and she'd been doing it for nearly the whole time. I'd gotten there maybe an hour after everything. It was about twenty-four hours at that point. Sparrow said he was both thankful and amazed that anyone would be able to do that. He said at first he thought me a magician, but after some time together, he realized healing was all I was doing, so he figured maybe I was something akin to the Master Healer.

"Anyway, that's his end. On my end... I'd been traveling for somewhere to stop when I happened across them. I didn't have anything, anywhere to go, so I had no reservations about stopping. I wouldn't have anyhow. There was no way I could've seen all those people and not helped. It was a bloody mess, but I'd actually eaten a nice breakfast that morning, so I had a good amount of energy. Most of the day passed in a blur anyway. I was healing quickly, so I could get to as many as possible.

"I was nearly done with the villagers when Sparrow found the men. That's when the taken women and children slowly started getting brought in. I took, I think, another twelve hours there before Sparrow found me. But I'd gotten to everyone." She shook her head. "The way I was healing. It definitely wasn't good for me. I was nearly at my collapse. The only thing keeping me going was adrenaline. I still remember my last patient. She..." She closed her eyes, breathed in, then opened them once more, meeting his. "Her name was Pina. Those fuckers had ripped her baby out of her stomach."

Gabriel's stomach roiled with the image, and his heart pained for his wife, for the memories she was reliving, but he didn't interrupt. Though painful, he could tell that talking of this was relaxing her as if she was finally able to let it off her shoulders.

"Her baby was mercifully okay, but she kept asking for her baby, and honestly, the only thing that kept me from crying was the fact that I was half delusional at that point. When I thought about it later, I cried for nearly two hours."

Gabriel's thumb stroked at her throat, her pulse picking up beneath his fingers.

She shook her head softly. "She was the last one, so I turned to leave, but then a boy came in with a basic wound. It would take me a minute to heal, but I was barely on my feet as it was. Sparrow caught me and took me to bed. He offered me the position when I woke up, and I've been at the palace since."

They were quiet for some time before Gabriel spoke. "Thirty-six hours. You're trying to tell me I should let you keep going for thirty-six hours? I'd rather kill them all myself, Ashtyn." His voice remained calm, but he held so much conviction in his words.

Her lips twitched, but she didn't allow herself to smile. "Not thirty-six, but I can go for more than *twelve*!"

He leaned in and kissed her before softly mumbling, "I don't care if you can go for more. Keep arguing, and we'll drop it to ten."

"You're being ridic—"

He quirked a brow, and she immediately shut up. "Good girl."

Her eyes narrowed, but her pulse picked up.

Gabriel held her close as he whispered, "Now sleep, beautiful. We have a whole day of arguing tomorrow."

She shook her head as she giggled into his chest, but it was only moments later that her breathing slowed, and she was off in dreamland.

# CHAPTER 23
# ASHTYN

Ashtyn snapped out of her dreams. She was breathing hard and so wet between the legs it was almost painful.

She'd been dreaming of Gabriel licking her to orgasm again and again and...

She glanced over to his still sleeping form beside her. He looked so peaceful, and all Ashtyn wanted to do was smack him out of sleep. He wouldn't ease her need though, he'd made that much clear.

She softly cleared her throat so as not to wake him, then looked back up to the ceiling. She focused on her breathing so she didn't psych herself out of doing this, and gently allowed her hand to trace over Gabriel's shirt she had on. She was wearing nothing underneath, so when she reached the inside of her thighs, she felt the moistness there.

She didn't know what having his tongue there would feel like, being none of her past companions had ever thought so far ahead as to please her, but every time she imagined it, her entire body shivered. She imagined his fingers rather than hers as she slipped them between her folds, soaking them completely.

Ashtyn gasped as her fingertips grazed her clit, then as they moved lower to her entrance, palm pressing into that little nub. She moved slowly, her body arching as a single digit entered her and her palm continued rubbing against her clit; as her free hand reached for her nipples over the shirt; as she gasped Gabriel's name like a prayer.

She pumped in and out of her cunt slowly, entering deeper with each stroke, and her eyes fluttered closed wishing it was Gabriel's cock rather than her finger.

She added another finger to fill her a bit more, to make the image of it being Gabriel's cock more real. She winced from the intrusion she hadn't felt in so long, and her breathing grew shallow.

Gabriel's name was barely audible, but she couldn't stop from calling it out, the vision behind her shut eyes all those of him—of how sweaty he got working on the greens, of how quiet he'd been in the Island Nation as he listened to the discussions while carving at his woodwork, of those glimmering teasing looks he gave her when she wanted anything from him.

Her palm continued hitting her clit as her fingers fucked her, her other hand tweaking at her nipples wishing it were Gabriel's mouth, his teeth biting down on them.

That particular image had moans gasping out of her and her cunt clenching around her fingers. She didn't stop the feeling as it built up inside her, remembering the way he'd demanded she not stop the first time, needing to come around Gabriel's cock, even if it was only her fingers taking his place.

Her body shook with the release like it was pushing off any negativity that had been sitting on her.

She breathed slowly as she came down from the feeling,

taking in the moment of seeing Gabriel's own satisfied look behind her closed eyes. That was a memory she could never forget.

"Good job, beautiful," a rough sound came from beside her.

Her eyes snapped open, ice washing over her as she glanced over.

He was watching her with so much lust, he looked about ready to combust. He didn't say anything more as he slowly reached for her arm and brought the hand that'd just been inside her to his mouth. He sucked on her two digits while staring into her eyes, and Ashtyn's back arched again, pussy clenching with the need to have him inside her.

"Gabriel," she pleaded as he finished sucking all the cum off of her fingers.

He smiled as he dropped her hand and cradled her face instead, bringing her close to kiss. While their tongues fought, she tasted herself and only one thing came to mind—what did he think of her taste?

He took her hand once more and guided it down his chest to the erection pressing through his trousers. "I know, wife. I need it too. I feel it as desperately as you do."

She turned so her body faced him and threw her leg over his waist without breaking the kiss. "Please, Gabriel."

His tongue thrust into her mouth, swallowing her. She wanted him to swallow her whole, to make her his completely.

He broke the kiss to lick over to her ear and bite down at her neck. "Call me your husband, Ashtyn."

She gasped as he sucked on her neck, dropping her to her back as he settled above her, his erection pressing right where she wanted him.

He went back to kissing her and mumbled against her lips. "What am I, Ashtyn?"

"Mine," she mumbled, fingers desperately clinging to his

nape and scratching down his back to get him closer. "Mine, Gabriel. You're mine."

His tongue thrust into her mouth at the same moment his erection pressed into her clit, and she came, moaning into his mouth. How was that possible?

"Your what?" He ground into her again, teasing out aftershocks and preparing her for another mind numbing orgasm.

"My husband, Gabriel. My husband. Please!" she moaned.

He chuckled. "Finally."

As his hands moved for his trousers, a loud banging came at their door and Tristan's voice cleared the fog around them. "Get up, healer! We need you! Now!"

"No!" she cried out as Gabriel stopped above her.

They were going to get up. They had to if there was a need, but it was the very last thing she wanted.

"I know, beautiful, I know." Gabriel kissed her softly before peeling away. He adjusted his erection as he began to change.

Ashtyn grumbled as she joined him in quickly getting ready.

When they scurried out to find their entourage, Ashtyn stopped abruptly. She'd been ready to kill the spy if he'd interrupted for something minuscule, but what she saw froze her immediately. "What the hell happened?"

"We don't know, but the magicians we have aren't healers. They're trying their best, but you're the only one we have available as the town's healers were also hit," Tristan started explaining, then turned to face them and stopped, eyeing them from head to toe. "Sorry for... interrupting."

She shook her head as she stepped forward to get a better look. "I cannot do this all on my own. Too many will perish before I can get to them."

"What should we do?" Colt asked beside her.

"How fast can you ride down to the palace?"

"As fast as you need," Noah answered.

"Then go, and come back with Arba, Jain, and Emmet." She may not have liked them, but they were amazing medics and would be required. Thank the lords they were only east of the palace a few hours, nowhere near as far north as they needed to be for the brunt of the plague.

Noah and Colt moved quickly, and Ashtyn knew they'd be coming back with Ares and Wells too. Good. They'd need the provisions the two had been preparing for those in this town.

Then she turned to Gian and Tristan. "Go to the neighboring towns and see if they have medics they can spare."

They, too, moved quickly as Ashtyn breathed out. She needed to get started.

THIS WASN'T THE PLAGUE. The thing they'd been battling didn't do this to its victims. It depleted them from the inside out. What Ashtyn was working with here was an infection.

And it felt more... dangerous.

But, thankfully, this was a cause that could be treated by normal medics and healers as well, not something that required her special attention because if that were the case, she wouldn't be able to help everyone. Hell, it'd be a repeat of all those years ago when Sparrow had found her—draining every ounce of her energy to help those who needed it until she finally passed out.

Except she had Gabriel now, and as much as it would piss her off, he would drag her away and make her stop before she hurt herself. She both loved and hated him for it.

There had to be hundreds of patients, all of whom had gashes on some part of their body as if an infection was eating them from the inside out. The infected area was white on some, turning yellow on others, and on the verge of mucus green for others. Ashtyn could heal this, as any other medic could, but it would take some time. She needed Arba, whose specialties lay in infectious wounds, and any other help from a medic she could get. Healing infections like these were part of medicinal studies, studies Ashtyn had read even if she hadn't been schooled in them specifically.

Ashtyn was working with a child whose arm had turned that disturbing green color, and she wasn't entirely sure if she was imagining it or if the thing was growing, slowly sizzling out wider.

She was lucky this village had some lotions available, but she'd spent the first twenty minutes preparing a little more before she'd gotten to work. It still wouldn't be enough, but she needed more than a few palm-sized tubs if she were going to get through any of these people.

Ashtyn started with a child whose thigh held a small white gash. That'd been easily healed. She massaged the cream into the area, then poured a sizzling three drops of boiled water with honey and lemon mixed in that she had Norya and Tristan—once he was back—making on the side. Gabriel held the child as the wound stung, then Ashtyn added another layer of the cream and wrapped it with a small strip of gauze.

She'd then moved on to a second child, one whose infection was yellowed and did the same thing.

Gabriel watched intently the entire time. "Is that something we can do, beautiful?" His wide eyes were on all those thrashing around them.

She shook her head softly, working the second layer of cream before the thin layer of gauze went on as they didn't have enough for her to wrap the wounds as she'd like. "Infections like these require a very specific amount of ratio between the cream and water. If you mess it up, you can make it worse."

Gabriel's nostrils flared.

Ashtyn turned soft eyes up at him. "You're helping more than you know. This combination stings. They need to be held down. Especially children who don't understand better."

He gave her a small smile and nodded as they left the second child for the third—the one with the green infected arm.

She'd purposefully chosen three with different colorings to tell the difference, and was able to pick it out. Normally the green would indicate the infection had gotten to the worst stage, but as Ashtyn worked on this third child, she found it the opposite. Green was the least infected, yellow the most.

Yet another reason she couldn't send her companions to help. If she'd simply told them the order went white, yellow, green, they'd be dealing with a much bigger problem.

Working with each took anywhere from three to ten minutes, depending on the size of the wound, and by the time help from another village came, Ashtyn had gotten through thirteen children. After the first three, she'd begun organizing. Those with yellow went first, then white, then green. Then they were ordered in size of infection. Children first.

Then she'd work on the women.

Then the men.

She took only five minutes away from helping to get the two medics from neighboring towns up to date before the three of them started working once more.

It was nearly another two hours before more help arrived. Ashtyn was sweating and Gabriel insisted she needed to take a break, even one as short as ten minutes, but Ashtyn felt guilty doing so.

The second she saw their horses pulling in, her shoulders sagged as she finished with this latest child.

"What is happening?" Arba's worried tone shocked Ashtyn for a moment as she went to meet with her original entourage of guards who were all back now along with the three medics she'd requested from the palace and Miels and Etel. She was thankful they'd had the foresight to come. They could work on concoctions for those in added pain or needing sleep.

"I've been working with the children, so I haven't gotten any answers yet. Now with you lot here, I can set Tristan and Gian into questioning while the rest of us work." She quickly went over the way this infection was taking place, then sent them off to work.

Thankfully all three listened intently then scurried away. Arba went immediately for the women as the children already had Ashtyn and the two neighboring medics, Lo and Noura, helping. Emmet followed after Arba to the women while Jain turned toward the men. Ashtyn was thankful to have a split now. She didn't want the women getting worse because then who would look after the children, and she didn't want the men getting worse because then there'd be no protecting these families. And she was extra thankful that Jain had gone to the men. She had an easy air about her, slightly flirtatious so as to ease the men while soft and thorough with her work. She always did best with the ultra-masculine men at the palace.

Lo and Noura were already finishing up the last of the children and had already decided to split up their work. Lo would help with the women and Noura would go to the men.

Ashtyn was thankful for the help because now she could take those ten minutes Gabriel was harassing her about as she looked out.

Miels and Etel sat in the apothecary, already putting out vials that had been pre-made as they prepared to make more.

They would be focusing on pain then drought drinks. Belinda and Astreya worked with them, taking the vials already made to the children who were grimacing first.

Caetana was helping Norya with making the required sizzling water now that they had plenty of the materials thanks to the magic the Cousins had used to boil so much water and drag in more lemons and honey from the surrounding fields.

Colt, Wells, Ares, and Noah were each partnered with a different medic as they held down the infected so the medics could do their jobs. Only Jain didn't require anyone by her side as her flirtations were enough to ease the men to sit still and take whatever came at them.

And Tristan and Gian walked the crowds the entire time speaking with those healed.

When she finally turned back to Gabriel, he had a steaming cup of lemon water with honey. "I believe this is good for you when ingested as well."

Ashtyn gave a soft smile. "Thank you. For everything. Seriously."

Gabriel leaned in to kiss her forehead, and for a moment, all was right in Ashtyn's world.

Then they got back to work where hours later during another break, she'd been relieved to find the cause of this mess.

They'd had a celebration three days prior. The fish had come from smugglers. They'd thought themselves lucky to have such an exquisite set of fish to eat for such a reasonable price that they'd bought it all. It'd been the best fish they'd tasted. Until the next morning when some had started feeling unwell.

But Ashtyn's group was lucky. This wasn't a contagion but rather bad fish from smugglers. Smugglers, who likely grabbed this fish from the Rivorbant Waters or somewhere close to it in order to sell it for so cheap.

Ashtyn was only glad they'd been there when the infections had sprung. It made her lean into Gabriel and smile to herself. Though exhausted and needing still to check in on her patients, moments like these reminded Ashtyn of her purpose in life.

# CHAPTER 24

# GABRIEL

It was a beautiful day after all they'd gone through with the infected. Gabriel had helped Ashtyn, the healers, and the remedy couple with Tristan, Norya, and the guards until the very last person with that infection had been taken care of. They'd all slumped into bed immediately, then stayed a couple days longer in order to make sure all was well.

That sudden infection was now another item on the list of problems. It was nothing like the problems that came with the plague. Smugglers were always something to be wary of. But knowing this case hadn't been connected to their problems had been exemplary. It gave them the moments to relax in the town, something they hardly afforded themselves.

Gabriel took that time still trying to figure out who was behind this.

And he was beginning to seriously consider the possibility of a magician and sorcerer working together given it was those two groups who weren't allowed in the North. A magician would be able to put up the shields and cause the veins he'd seen before, but an infection like this, he wasn't entirely sure. He figured a sorcerer would have a better way of it.

But for now, the lot of them were back at the palace, replenishing and readying for the next trip out. King Edmund had the medics from the infirmary on rotation to head out and check on that town along with checking the area. For now, their little entourage could focus on their main goal, one they kept getting sidetracked from—this plague.

Ashtyn was currently with the Cousins allowing them to help her recovery. Gabriel smiled to himself remembering how he'd convinced her with a few breathless kisses to be nice to the Cousins. She'd been a blushing mess when she'd left him, and he wanted to do that to her again.

The sun was out, and even though there was a chill in the air because of the nearness of winter, the sunlight hitting skin brought people out for at least short periods of time. This was the peace Gabriel needed after such horrendous days. He could not wait until this mess was over, and he had Ashtyn to himself.

Around Gabriel were Tristan and Miels with their women, the men watching their wives train with a bow and arrow—something Norya had begun teaching Etel a few weeks ago.

Surprisingly, Princess Rosaelia was also out as opposed to in the library, especially in the chillier weather. It was clearly because of her Islander husband who was used to much colder days than these.

The most surprising part regarding the Posse, though, was that the Masters weren't out there. Both the Assassin and the Magician loved the outdoors, though Gabriel figured there were only two reasons they might've refrained—either Sparrow was being overbearing with the pregnancy or, which Gabriel thought the more likely case, they were taking the time they knew the Posse wouldn't be bothering them to fool around somewhere in the palace. He'd heard pregnancy could increase sexual needs. Considering the Magician's best friends were also missing and expecting, he figured they were all definitely doing the latter.

As Gabriel soaked in this beautiful day talking to Papa Iskan and King Edmund—now more comfortable with the King than before—about Southern agricultural benefits Iskan could teach them in the palace, he missed his wife.

They'd fought before and she was still angry with him when they'd come back to the palace, but secretly, he knew she enjoyed how much he cared for her. She was just too much of a prideful asshole to admit it.

"Are you sure you want to help, Gabriel?" King Edmund asked. "You already have a lot on your plate with the horses, the three magicians, and your wife."

*And your wife.*

The comment made Gabriel smile. Not only because he loved the reference of Ashtyn as his wife but also because he understood completely what was meant by it—even the King of the Northern Lands thought she was a pain.

"I'm sure. I can trust Dale to take extra care with Papa Ignatius and the other stable hands and keep watch over the horses in my absence. The magicians... have each found a guard to their liking, so they are not my problem to watch over. And most importantly, I can handle my wife plenty fine."

King Edmund quirked an amused brow. "Really? Does she not give you the same attitude she did before you were married?"

*Because we haven't consummated, and my poor wife is horny.*

Gabriel's smile turned sinister at the thought. "She behaves herself when she needs to."

"I don't want to know," the King muttered as Dale's hand slapped down on Gabriel's shoulder.

"I do." He joined with a large grin. "The kinkier, the better."

Gabriel punched the man's arm but didn't try to fight his amusement. Even the King was laughing with them before he turned serious, his eyes widening as his hand smacked into his neck.

Gabriel stood alert at the sudden change. "What's happened?"

"Bee…" He coughed up before the racks took over him, and he fell to his knees.

Bee? There were hardly any bees out in the colder months. And especially not ones that might affect him. Edmund wasn't allergic to the average bee.

"Edmund?" one of the blond spies yelled out.

"Father?" Rosaelia screamed as they came running.

Gabriel, Dale, and Papa Iskan were shoved out of the way as the Princess, the spies, and their spouses stopped around him. Over by the palace, two servants were already running, and Gabriel knew it was to get Ashtyn.

"He's allergic to Alomora bee stings," Miels exclaimed, holding the man who had raised him as a son while the King's airways began closing up.

The effect was happening quickly telling Gabriel he was deathly allergic. Unsurprisingly. Half the population was allergic to Alomora bee stings. He himself was, though not to this sudden degree.

Which was why they did everything in their power to kill them. Gabriel hadn't even known any were still alive anywhere in the Northern Lands.

"I have the poultice," Etel stated as she ran away. The girl was small, but she was fast.

Gabriel doubted the way Ashtyn's abilities worked would help in this manner, but she would be needed to check on him while Etel's poultice did its work. With her help, the poultice's job, which normally took about two days, would be expedited. He'd seen her do it for the kids around the palace and their allergies to other things.

Even as scared for the King as Gabriel was at the moment, his heart pounded with pride for his wife.

Then Ashtyn was running for them, her blonde hair flying behind her. Her gaze was on him, traveling his body as if searching for injury before they dropped to the bodies on the ground hovering around the King.

Gabriel's heart shot out of his chest.

She was checking on him, worried for him. She never had to say it for Gabriel to be able to read it in her gorgeous orbs.

When she skidded beside them, everyone jumped out of the way and allowed her to work.

"I won't be able to stop it. We need the poultice," she informed them. "All I can do now is keep his airways from closing up. When he has the poultice, I can send it around faster, but we'll need it."

She worked like magic as her hands stopped above the King's chest.

That's what it felt like watching her—magic. The way she worked wasn't normal, shouldn't have been possible in any way but magic but she wasn't a magician. Gabriel had a feeling, though, that she held a small bit of magician's blood in her, and it was manifesting itself in the form of healing. Though even that didn't explain her proficiency in the matter since even healing magicians didn't hold quite her kind of ability.

When the King stopped coughing, Ashtyn kept her hands

on him but made space for the others. "I need to continue contact, but we can take him inside."

"No," the King croaked. When they all ignored the King's reluctance to be carried—which would be amusing if he wasn't in danger of dying—he tried again. "Put... me... down."

"Shut it," Ashtyn snapped.

Gabriel wanted to follow after her but only the Posse would be allowed into the King's suite, and though he realized he was a trusted friend to them now, he didn't want to distract his wife.

"Everyone else okay?" He turned for those around him.

When they all nodded, he turned back to the palace where he knew his healer was now bossing the Posse—the group of some of the most powerful beings in the lands—around. He realized then how big of a risk the King was going to in allowing Ashtyn to be off for long stretches of time for this plague because if something happened to her, the expediency of healing he'd become accustomed to would end. The medics in the infirmary would still be able to take care of him, but there were certain matters where Ashtyn was the most efficient choice.

He turned in his spot, gaze focused as he looked for any more Alomora bees. He certainly couldn't get stung and considering half the population was also allergic, they needed to make sure this was taken care of.

Papa Iskan stood tall, reading the decision in Gabriel's eyes. "I am not allergic. I will gather the guards who also aren't, and we scour the grounds with the sprays."

"Thank you," Gabriel breathed.

Standing alone on the palace greens, Gabriel thought back to Ashtyn. Hopefully she wasn't allergic. There was still so much he had to learn about her.

But as memories of her assaulted him, Gabriel smiled. Even

in these serious moments, he knew as his heart beat steadily that he hadn't ever known what love was before. Because what he felt for Ashtyn was...

Surreal.

IT'D ONLY BEEN an hour since they'd taken the King inside, but Gabriel's leg jittered like it'd been days. He wanted to get to Ashtyn, take her home and love her. He acted as if she were the hurt one, but he couldn't help but need to be touching her in times of duress.

With the horses taken care of, Gabriel didn't have much to distract himself with. Any talks of agriculture were put on hold until the King was better again, and he didn't have the patience and stability to be doing any woodwork at the moment.

"You are eager." A voice filled the space behind him.

He was in the stables detangling an already untangled bit of rope as he jumped from one leg to the other.

He turned abruptly at the intrusion to his thoughts and found all three magicians in his company. "Ladies. Did you need something?"

Astreya took him in entirely. "Unfortunately, you're taken."

Even though he knew she was joking considering her forming relationship with their guard, his cheeks still pinked at the attention.

"They talk a lot about you in the sisterhood, Gabriel," Caetana began.

"I've already apologized for that."

They all giggled as Caetana continued. "Why are you jumpy? Are you allergic too? Afraid?"

"No. I mean, yes." He dropped the rope and faced them. "Yes, I'm allergic too. No, I'm not afraid. I just miss my wife."

They all three smiled as Belinda said, "We were just working with those not allergic. Nothing else on the grounds. I have no idea how that would've gotten through. And so perfectly have gotten to the King."

Gabriel grit his teeth, looking anywhere but at the Cousins.

"What is it, Gabriel?" Astreya's hand landed on his forearm, jumping him out of his thoughts right as a growl came from behind her.

The magician didn't turn around, but Gabriel glanced up to find a scarier than usual Gian with his arms crossed, leaning against the far end of the stables. His stare burned into the spot Astreya touched Gabriel.

Gabriel pulled his arm away. "I..." He huffed. "I've been wondering if all this could possibly have something to do with a magician. Or a sorcerer. Ones working together? With the shields, the plague, the power that was put into those brutes we fought off, and now getting a bee that's basically extinct to go after the one person holding the highest position in the North?"

All three nodded.

Then Caetana said, "I've been monitoring the space around us but haven't felt anything in particular. I'll continue the checks though. If I know I'm looking for something caused by a magician, I may be able to spot it out."

Gabriel nodded, thankful to have the Cousins with them.

"Have you told the Posse?" Astreya asked.

He shook his head. "I didn't want Ashtyn to find out. She has too much to think about. I'll talk to the men though. If that could be the cause, they need to know to protect their king and heirs."

They all nodded, and Gabriel was surprised to find they

weren't arguing about keeping it from the women. Well, from Ashtyn in particular. Gabriel didn't necessarily care if the others knew.

"I agree," Caetana said. "It's more important for Ashtyn to focus on the others. We don't need her trying to figure out how else she could help. She overworks herself enough as is."

Belinda shook her head. "If she's trying to be a mean one, she should know constantly trying to help *everyone* makes her quite the opposite."

"Yeah." Gabriel smiled. "She's my little softy."

They all chuckled as Caetana smirked. "Don't let her hear that, Gabriel, or you'll be sleeping outdoors."

He winked. "I'll convince her to let me back in."

"Yeah? You should go do that then. But don't forget to call her a softy first," Astreya teased, then gave him a softer smile. "She's done."

Gabriel's entire being deflated, grateful she'd been using her magic to check on Ashtyn without his asking. "Thank you," he whispered, preparing to move for the palace.

Gian was still leaning at the other end of the stables, arms crossed before his chest and a hard look about him. He didn't necessarily look to be glaring at Gabriel—his clear obsession with Ashtyn meaning no man ever needed to be jealous of their woman around him—but the look wasn't exactly friendly either. Though the hard edge in his eyes could be for the woman he was after rather than him.

Gabriel nodded behind the girls. "Someone's watching very intently."

They all turned, and it was clear which one's he was—though Gabriel had already known—when Astreya's whole body stiffened. She swallowed but didn't move.

Gabriel caught Caetana and Belinda glancing before the two of them before meeting his eyes. They each took his arm, and the three left the stables, passing by Gian who pushed off the building and moved forward.

Gabriel snuck a glance back with the two magicians on his arms, and the three of them caught a glance of Gian pushing Astreya into a far back wall before they were out of sight.

# CHAPTER 25

# GABRIEL

Ashtyn looked shocked to see him in the King's wing when she stepped out of Edmund's rooms with the rest of the Posse. "Have you been waiting here the whole time?"

He gave a single shake of his head as the group who'd come out at the same time each headed for their own rooms. "Astreya let me know you were done."

Her lips downturned. "What were you doing with her?"

He fought from allowing his approval at her jealousy show on his features as he stopped beside her, hand landing at the small of her back. "I was talking with all three cousins. They're nice. I like them."

She scoffed as she muttered under her breath just loud enough for him to catch, "Yeah, they like you too."

He started pushing her for their cottage. "I like this reaction from you, wife, but you know my interests only ever lie with you. Besides, you have nothing to worry about on their account."

"Oh." She quirked a disbelieving brow. "And why's that, horse boy?"

He smirked. "Our guards have caught their attention."

She rolled her eyes. "Oh lords."

Gabriel laughed. "I'm serious. Astreya and Gian seem to have something quite serious with the way he was watching her out there."

She didn't look impressed, but she couldn't hide her body's reaction from him as she relaxed into his hand at her back.

"How's the King?" He changed the subject only because Ashtyn wasn't a fan of delving into her feelings, and he wanted to give her the reprieve for the moment.

Her lips tipped up. "I think much better now."

His brows furrowed, but Gabriel didn't ask for an explanation. He'd find out later what that mischievous look, which she normally didn't wear, meant. Right now, he only cared about her, about them, about loving this thing between them.

When they stepped out of the palace, he brought her closer to his side to fight off the chill. It was darker out because of the shorter days, but not so bad that they couldn't make their way to the cottage with the moonlight hitting the greens. It was romantic. Something Gabriel couldn't imagine bringing up lest his grouchy wife begin to laugh at him. And though he loved making her laugh, even if it was at his expense, tonight, he wanted something deeper between them.

Her shivers cleared his thoughts. "Are you tired? You want a bath first?"

"Yes, please," she whispered.

She sounded so delicate in that moment, Gabriel was caught off guard with the amount of trust she was putting in him to allow this vulnerability to show.

When they reached the cottage, he moved immediately for the bathing chamber and started the water the scalding hot she liked, then turned to find she'd followed him into the room.

"May I undress you?"

"Please," she whispered once again, her gaze slowly roaming from his eyes to his lips to his chest and back up.

Gabriel moved with purpose, his hands soft as they tugged on the corset at the front of her dress. It wasn't one of those tight ones on intricate dresses, but a simple one made to hold the dress up. It only took one tug to get the strings loosened before he was pulling them out.

His fingertips took their time grazing her skin as he reached for her shoulders to help lower the dress. This was to be the first time he'd truly get to touch her body, and he wanted to cherish it entirely.

He got to his knees, slowly pushing her dress down, and inhaled deeply as he breathed in the scent of her arousal right by his mouth. No matter how desperately he wanted to, he didn't taste her while the dress fell to her ankles.

He stared up at her as her hands fell into his hair, playing with it before her hands cradled his face. "Will you wash me too?"

"It would be my greatest honor."

Her lips tipped up, but she didn't mock his softness.

When he rose to his feet once more, he took note of all the shivers running across her body. He didn't say anything as he turned away from her and shut off the water, only filling the bath with salts to ease her muscles. They'd done a lot of riding the past couple of weeks, something she wasn't used to, and they'd be doing more soon, so he wanted to help her body adjust.

Turning back to her, Gabriel caught Ashtyn's fingers jittering at her sides as she patiently and quietly waited. He stuck out his hand for her to take and led her to the bath, careful as he aided her into the tub of steam.

As she slowly settled into it, Gabriel took the moment to step back and take this scene in entirely. His mouth tipped up as he slowly shrugged out of his shirt and stopped by the edge of the tub, getting back onto his knees.

Ashtyn met his gaze and there was so much vulnerability in her brown orbs that he wanted to pull her out and rock her in his lap. Instead, his thumb brushed her bottom lip, and he leaned in for a chaste kiss. Then he grabbed the rag on the side and wet it to prepare for the liquid soap specifically for muscle soreness Etel had made for all of the palace.

Before he could place the soap on the rag, Ashtyn's hand stopped him. His gaze jumped immediately to hers, then she said, "With your hands. Please."

That brief pause before the 'please' nearly exploded that beating organ inside his chest.

Gabriel dropped the rag to the side and lathered his hands with the soap.

He started with her hands, her tools for healing all those people. He took his time with them, not only because they were her tools, but because there was something to say about the soft touch of hands that he loved. He wanted to cherish this moment where their hands fell into one another, knowing the other was their safe haven.

# CHAPTER 26
# ASHTYN

He was so gentle with her.

So soft and thorough as he moved from her hands to her arms, taking his time there before moving to her shoulders. He got behind her in the tub and rubbed out the soreness from them before having her hunch forward to do the same with her back.

His attention to everything she needed, to making sure her body was feeling better rather than simply washing her, made tears stroll down her eyes.

She'd never been taken care of like this. Not that she could remember. Maybe in her first decade where she assumed she had parents, and she liked to believe they'd loved her, but it'd been a long time since that loss. In all the memories Ashtyn could muster, never once did she feel so safe and taken care of.

Finished with her back and shoulders, he moved back to sit beside her and lathered his hands again before starting at her chest this time. His eyes were on hers instead of watching as his hands got closer to her breasts. He wasn't here to grope her. He was taking care of her.

"Why are you crying?" he whispered, calloused hands from all his work outdoors soft as ever as they stroked her skin.

"You make me feel... whole."

His hands were on her breasts, stroking and kneading them, thumbs grazing over her hardened nipples, but neither of them were focused there. His attention was on her face, and she felt the need to open up to him like never before.

"I've always been pretty, Gabriel. Boys have always wanted me. But I've never felt more so than with a simple look from you. And you're not even trying to have sex with me right now."

His hands moved lower, over her stomach, then onto her thighs. His arms, both plunged into the tub, were soaked, but his attention still focused on her as he kneaded her thighs, cleaning and massaging her. "I told you I'd always protect you, Ashtyn. That means not only keeping you safe but also making sure you know it. I am yours. To have and to use in any and every way. I love you, wife."

Her lips tipped up slightly. "And you never let me forget it, husband."

His hands moved over her calves, massaging them before getting to her feet where she had to stifle a moan from the pleasure that shot through her.

"And I'll never let you forget it," he stated as he moved back up her thighs to her core, softly cleaning her but not teasing her.

Staring into his perfect eyes, she could see he was proving he wanted more than just sex from her.

But as she held that stare, she couldn't help but keep going without it, without having him fully.

"Gabriel..."

"How's your body feeling? Better?"

"Yes," she whispered.

He stood, her body instantly missing his touch, and raised a towel as he held out a hand to help her up. "Good. Now let's get you dried and to bed."

Ashtyn took it, but pushed the towel aside as she stepped completely out of the tub. "I don't want to sleep, Gabriel."

They were close, so she felt his words brush her naked skin as he asked, "What do you want, Ashtyn?"

"You."

His swallow was the only reaction that showed he was affected by her words as he eyed her stoically. "You're sure?"

"I've never been more sure of anything. Except maybe how right it was to have accepted your proposal."

He instantly stepped forward, his chest grazing hers as his hands softly moved for her face, one falling into her hair as the other held her still, lips brushing with how close they were. "I don't know if I'll have the control to pull out."

"I don't want you to."

He kissed her then, tongue harsh as it plunged instantly into her mouth. His hand in her hair tightened as it angled her the way he wanted while the other held her jaw in place.

This wasn't what she'd expected. She thought he'd be gentle with her like he always was.

But this was exactly what she wanted.

She moaned into his mouth as his hands traveled down her body and harshly gripped her thighs, lifting her to straddle his hips.

He moved without breaking the kiss, not needing to see to know the layout of his home as he took them to the bedroom.

Gabriel dropped her to the bed and stood between her spread legs. The fire was on and the flickers illuminated the room, illuminated Gabriel's profile, while the sounds of the flames mixed with those of the howling winds outside.

Gabriel's fingers slithered up the insides of her thighs. "I've only tasted you once, and that was off your fingers."

She remembered. Fuck did she remember.

"I want you on my tongue, Ashtyn."

"Me too. I've thought about it too much."

He chuckled, and fuck, the sound was so sexy. "I don't think there could ever be too much."

Then he dropped to his knees before her, and his fingers spread her folds right before his tongue slithered up, licking her from opening to clit.

Ashtyn's back arched off the bed. She'd thought about this a lot. Dreamed of it.

But never in a million years would she have been able to imagine the feel of his tongue on her.

He licked her a few times, testing what she liked. This was his first time, everything they did was his first time, yet it felt as if he knew what he was doing. He hadn't been shy to tell her he'd asked other men about everything in order to know exactly how to please her, but still, this was...

He took slow strokes up her cunt, and she mewled with each one. She wanted more but she didn't know what that was. No man's mouth had ever been between her legs.

"Gabriel, please," she moaned.

He delivered by licking up her cunt and sucking on the nub on top causing her entire body to roll so hard, his forearm on her hips was the only thing keeping her in place.

Then he surprised her by sliding a finger along her slit, then into her opening.

Ashtyn cried out as her hips tried grinding against his face.

And all the while, Gabriel watched her.

His finger rolled inside her, and Ashtyn shot off the bed for a moment, her hand falling into his hair, tugging, while the other gripped the sheets.

He continued licking and sucking her as that finger moved inside her, hitting that spot that made her walls clench every time.

Then to her surprise, as he sucked on her clit, he inserted a second finger, and she was stretched to such glorious lengths that she couldn't control her mewls and cries as she came.

This was nothing like the orgasms she'd given herself. This was so much more intense.

And though his forearm kept her from moving too much, Ashtyn could not stop thrashing as she came all over his face.

And he didn't let up. His tongue and fingers continued their ministrations even after her orgasm until the aftershocks subsided.

She was spent in the most unbelievable way.

And yet, she still wasn't fully satisfied.

"You taste like the sweetest honey, wife."

"I need you, Gabriel," she cried. "Please."

His fingers were still in her, moving slowly and opening her up. "What was that? I don't think you had the right term."

"Husband!" she growled. "Husband, for fucks sake. I need you inside me, husband!"

His laugh was deep and long as he traveled up her body, laying kisses along the way as his fingers continued moving. When he reached her lips, he gave her a chaste kiss before smirking down at her. "We need to clean up your language, wife."

Her walls clenched around his fingers inside her. "Gabriel!"

He bit her bottom lip. "What is it, my love?"

"Gabriel, please!"

He chuckled down into her ear causing her walls to clench impossibly tight. "I told you before, wife. I love this desperate, begging side."

"And you have it. Please, Gabriel, please fuck me!"

As he chuckled some more, making Ashtyn want to punch him across the face, his fingers slipped out of her causing her to whimper, then he gripped her waist and moved her higher on the bed.

"Anything my wife wishes for," he finally said as his lips dropped to her collarbones, then kissed down to her chest, taking a nipple into his mouth and making her arch into him. "Wow, Ash. How have I survived so long without tasting you?"

Her hands fell into his hair, gripping for dear life as he sucked and bit one nipple, then moved to the other.

"Gabriel!" she cried again, *needing* him.

With her entire breast in his mouth, he glanced up at her with that twinkle in his eyes. He slowly popped her out of his mouth, teeth biting down on her nipple before finally releasing her making her rub herself against him even more desperately.

He moved so his cock sat at her opening, then kissed her. His tongue fought with hers, and all she could do was cling to him hoping her nails marked him as much as his mouth had marked her breasts.

He wasn't soft about it.

One moment she was yearning for him while his tongue pumped into her mouth, and the next, both tongue and cock were inside her.

Ashtyn's nails dug into him. She may not have been a virgin, but it'd been years.

Aside from the slight pain that shot through her from being ripped into, sex had never felt like this. She'd never been so wet and wanton.

Gabriel didn't stop kissing her, licking down her jaw, and taking her ear between his teeth as he began thrusting, hard and rough like his control had finally snapped and there was no bringing it back.

"Lords, Ashtyn, you're so beautiful," he whispered into her

ear. "So beautiful while you take my cock." He groaned into her ear, and she nearly came from the sound alone. "So perfect. My cock was made for you, wife. Like your pussy was made for me." His hand moved between their bodies, and he played with her clit. "Look at me, Ashtyn," he growled.

Her eyes instantly snapped open, meeting his, and her cunt clenched, unable to hold back. "Gabriel, I'm going to..."

"No!" he demanded. "Hold it."

Her eyes widened. "Gabriel," she moaned as her hips moved with his. "I can't."

"Yes you can." He pumped harder into her, reaching his own climax. "Hold it, wife."

"Gabriel!" She threw her head back, nails digging into his back as she held on.

"Eyes on me. Hold it," he bit out, hand still rubbing her clit as his cock hit that spot inside her. His other hand tugged at her hair to angle her face to his so she could look him in the eyes shot some pain through her that made it even harder to hold back her climax.

"Gab—" Her stomach hollowed in, and she knew there was no point, she couldn't—

"Another moment, Ashtyn. Hold it!" He rammed into her, holding her gaze, sweat dripping down his body.

"I can't—" She was nearly crying.

"Hold—" he grit out.

Holding his gaze, Ashtyn did everything in her power, but then his hand worked her clit just right and—

"Now, Ashtyn. Come for me. Now."

Her body instantly released her orgasm, and it was earth shattering. He was coming above her too, straining and growling, filling her, but she was so far gone with her never-ending orgasm that she could hardly focus on how sexy he looked.

She came and came, his hand still working her clit as he

slowly pumped his seed into her and sucked on her nipples, and Ashtyn couldn't tell if it this was the longest orgasm known to man or multiple stacked on top of one another.

When wave after wave finally settled and the aftershocks calmed, Ashtyn could finally feel Gabriel softly kissing her chest, neck, jaw, lips.

Over her lips, he played with her bottom lip before mumbling, "You're such a good girl, wife."

Her cunt clenched at the words, his semi-hard cock still inside her.

He smirked, feeling her reaction, as he leaned in, hips softly moving again. "My good, good girl."

She moaned, back arching as her hips moved with him.

"My needy, good girl."

"Yours, Gabriel. Always."

He angled her face to meet his. "Always." Then continued thrusting into her as he kissed her.

# CHAPTER 27
# ASHTYN

On the one hand, finding out she was a Master could help explain a lot of things. She'd always felt... unsure of herself because she didn't know where her power came from. If she was decided a Master, it would all make sense. It would be an inherent gift that wouldn't need explanation the same way Sparrow's inhumane strength and speed didn't.

On the other hand, Ashtyn wanted, more than anything, to keep the attention off of herself. She wanted to be normal, like any of the other servants. It wasn't possible given her status as the King's healer, but it would become even worse if she was named a Master. People would treat her like she was part of the Posse.

Ashtyn didn't want to be part of the Posse. She just wanted to be a healer, married to the horse boy, living in their cottage.

Her lips tipped up at the thought of their cottage. Their bedroom. Their bed. Where he'd taken her again and again and again the night before as if making up for all of their lost time since the wedding. Ashtyn bit her bottom lip to stifle the grin as she walked through the palace on the way to the meeting room Sparrow had invited her to.

When she arrived, he was seated at a small sofa off to the side with his wife's head on his lap as he played with her hair. Evony was asleep, and Ashtyn's heart went out to her. She couldn't imagine what the pregnancy was doing to her if Evony herself was admitting too tired to do much else. It made Ashtyn realize though that Sparrow's protectiveness from the beginning hadn't been overbearing. The bigger the Magician got, the more tired she became, and there was no way they would've been able to use her abilities then. Sparrow was a lot to deal with sometimes, but he was always a good husband.

Ashtyn's heart warmed knowing she had that now too. Gabriel allowed her to heal until he didn't. It was annoying and overbearing when he argued with her to stop and take breaks, but all along, Ashtyn had been secretly grateful. She'd never felt so cared for before, and she knew Evony felt the same way.

Sparrow glanced up at her arrival, lips tipping into a small smile as he started to slowly move his wife's head to meet her at the table.

Evony mumbled at the loss of contact, making Sparrow kneel beside her, kissing her softly and whispering words Ashtyn could not hear. It didn't matter though—the big scary Assassin had his weakness, and he took pride in her. The same way Miels did his Remedies Expert and Tristan his barbar- ianette. The same way the ever-blooming red Princess Rosaelia showed off her savage husband with the scars running down his face. They prided in their other halves the way Gabriel had always prided in her.

Ashtyn moved to seat herself before her knees grew too weak and she fell to the floor. She couldn't remember the last time she'd allowed herself to be emotional, and it was like every emotion was now hitting her at once.

Sparrow met her at the table a moment later, wordlessly turning a missive for her to read. It was from the South and asked for her to journey back down as soon as possible for they believed they knew what she was.

Ashtyn scoffed. "They cannot be serious. They know what I am doing here, and they wish to pull me away to let me know whether I am a Master or not? Do they value themselves too godly to write it in the missive?"

Sparrow smirked. "I knew you would feel that way, so I already have this missive written and ready to send out once you okay it."

Ashtyn took the second paper to find a short response asking for the news in writing as Ashtyn would not be heading back South until it was time for her honeymoon.

Her brows popped up as she glanced at the Assassin once more. "My honeymoon?"

"I suspect that is where you would wish to go with your husband."

It was, but how would he know that?"

His eyes shimmered. "I took Evony to my childhood home for our honeymoon. I suspected Gabriel would want to take you back to his for yours. Or at least somewhere around his since people still live where he grew up."

Ashtyn's cheeks pinked at the memory of all those people who loved Gabriel. Returning to them to celebrate her nuptials would put a lot of attention on them, but Ashtyn couldn't help but feel giddy about it. The attention wouldn't be on her, it would be on them and how they felt for one another.

Then she remembered the sounds she'd made the night before, the sounds they'd both made and her blush deepened at the prospect of Lanlik hearing them.

Sparrow's smirk seemed to widen. "I take it by the look that you and Gabriel are doing well?"

Ashtyn tried to fight off the blush still burning as she narrowed her eyes at the Assassin. "Don't tease me. You're turning into your wife."

He gave a small grin, then eyed the missive still in her hands. "Is the letter okay to send back?"

Ashtyn glanced at it again, then thought of the Posse finding out about her status before her. If she found out alone —though Gabriel would always be at her side, but as man and wife, they would always be one—then she could always hide the results for a short time to process them on her own, whether Master or not. If the Posse found out first, they may have next steps put in place right away, and though they'd taken Ashtyn's opinions into consideration this entire time, she wasn't sure about it then.

But what was there really to consider? If she were named a Master, it would be probably a month before the nations knew there was another Master among them. That would only give Ashtyn the time traveling back to the palace to truly acclimate to her new title before having to tell the Posse for they would need to have preparations in place before the announcements.

If she wasn't named a Master, not much would change with her life except...

Except that part of her that had always wondered wouldn't beat any longer, for she would know she was not. She wasn't so naive as to think that maybe she did want to be a Master and the answer of no would pain her. Finding out before everyone else would give her time to grieve it before their looks came.

Ashtyn swallowed and glanced up at the Assassin. He'd been named a Master before he even hit double digits in age. He'd been so young with no control over what happened in his life. The King protected him as best as he could, but he'd had to take everything that came with the title as a child. Ashtyn could not imagine the whispers that had followed him growing up before he learned to completely block them out.

Then she glanced at Evony. She'd been hidden with her naming and remained hidden to this day. But she'd always been alone. She had Gemma and James before the naming but she'd grown up alone. Evony never expected time to process anything, her entire life had been lived from moment to moment. Ashtyn knew she'd been lonely before coming to the palace. She'd had her best friends but the two were in love with one another, so there was a connection they shared that Evony never could. She'd had to endure her Masterhood in private from the rest of the world, and though she'd had the support of her best friends, it wasn't the support she needed.

Ashtyn's eyes hovered to the ring on her finger.

She had that support. Her husband loved her, was obsessed with her, was ready to throw his life down for her, protect her. She had the one thing neither Master in this room had when they'd been named—their other half to support them.

Ashtyn met Sparrow's eyes once more. "Yes. Send this. I trust you to know what to do with whatever the response may be."

Sparrow's smile was soft, reassuring.

Ashtyn reciprocated it as she glanced between the two Masters before her, Sparrow in the chair and Evony sprawled out on the sofa. They'd soon be expanding their family, and Ashtyn was just as curious as the rest of the Posse on whether their child would end up a Master. Though nearly impossible to find Masters having Master children, Sparrow was the child of another Master. Ashtyn could see the two of them bringing on more, especially considering it was equally as unforeseen for two Masters to fall in love with one another.

Ashtyn smiled softly to herself as she glanced back to her hand, playing with the ring on her finger. Oh, to fall in love. Worlds changed for such an act.

Gabriel was carving out his woodworking at the table in their cottage when Ashtyn returned to it. They could be heading back out soon, and this time, unlikely to return before all was done, and Ashtyn was struck frozen before the open door, taking him in. This was her husband in their cottage.

Worlds truly changed, and hers was on its head in the most incredible way possible.

Gabriel glanced up, a question about why she was standing before the open door on such a cold night in his eyes.

Ashtyn slowly closed the door and leaned against it.

Gabriel carved a few more times before his gaze completely settled on her, and he put everything onto the table, grabbing a rag from the side to clean his hands. "Is something the matter?"

Ashtyn didn't speak. Was something the matter? How could it be when they were together and safe?

"Beautiful?" Gabriel stiffened in his seat.

Ashtyn sighed. She loved when he called her that, even more so after finding out he did so because he'd been able to catch early on that she didn't like being called "pretty."

Gabriel slowly rose. "Ashtyn, you're worrying me."

She took in his large form. He wasn't nearly as big as the men in the Posse, but he was still tall, and all the work he put in outdoors defined his body in a way that made her salivate. His brown floppy hair was pushed back out of his face so it didn't get in the way of his work, and Ashtyn could imagine how adorable it would look on a five-year-old Gabriel. His eyes gleamed as if the browns were frozen that way after a lifetime of smiles and teasing from their owner. He was so handsome it almost hurt to look at him.

But he was more than just looks. He was good. So very good.

He cared for his animals, but he also cared for his friends. He helped Dale whenever he could, rushed to Papa Ignatius's side, spoke lovingly of Lanlik and all the others from the South, teased Atiana, and laughed with the members of the Posse. He was a companion with the guards they rode with and a true friend to most every servant in the palace. Everyone smiled when they saw him, not because he could charm his way into anything but because he was so kind, so caring, *so good*. His charm came naturally then.

"Ashtyn, baby, you're scaring me." He took a tentative step from behind the table and toward her.

Ashtyn finally met his eyes without backing away, clinging to the door handle to keep herself upright and the nerves at bay. She wasn't nervous about his response, more so the fact that she'd never spoken such words to anyone. "I think I'm in love with you, husband."

Everything was so still that for a moment, Ashtyn was convinced the magicians had stopped time as she stared into her husband's eyes.

Then his lips tipped up and he took another, much larger, step toward her. "Say that again."

Ashtyn swallowed, pushing off the door to stand on her own, and squared her shoulders. "I'm in love with you, Gabriel."

His breath left him as he rushed her, cradling her face in his, fingers digging into her scalp as he held her still. He angled her face to meet his gaze as he groaned. "Again."

Ashtyn clung to his sides, his shirt scrunched where she held on to him. "I love you." She rose to the tips of her toes. "I've never said that to anyone before." She dipped closer to him. "I love you."

His fingers tangled into her hair as he brought her in for a kiss. It was rough and passionate and filled with everything he felt for her, everything he'd always promised he'd felt for her. Ashtyn finally believed him, trusted him to take her heart in exchange for his.

Gabriel slammed her back into the door, his body grinding into hers as he held her still with his hands in her hair. "I love you, Ashtyn. Always."

She clung to his back. "It's a good thing we're married then."

He chuckled as his lips moved back for hers, his tongue instantly invading her mouth.

Ashtyn sighed into the kiss. She never wanted this night to end.

CHAPTER 28

# GABRIEL

Ashtyn had insisted he behave when he asked her to share his horse and insisted that she would not leave Bella. So Gabriel had gotten off his horse and joined her on Bella. The animal was strong enough to take both of them, and Gabriel would've done anything to make that blush on Ashtyn's cheeks deepen as their entourage watched them.

They were a couple of days' ride out from the palace, and Ashtyn had been hard at work, leaving Gabriel to only see her when he forced her into breaks and at night to sleep, so he was going to enjoy their ride even with the others around.

"It's too bad you insist on sticking to the dresses," Gabriel whispered into her ear as his hand settled on her stomach. "It would've been so easy to stick my hand into your trousers."

Her pulse picked up where his lips hovered, but Ashtyn tried to remain impassive. "Then it's actually quite a great thing that I chose my dresses."

"How about on our next stop, you change. I'm sure the Cousins wouldn't mind you borrowing some."

His lips skimmed her jaw as he took every second to memorize her profile. She was stunning, and apparently his words were amusing.

"I never pegged you as an exhibitionist, horse boy."

"For you, I'd be anything."

She shuffled so he was pushed back a little—though her round behind against his cock wasn't helping matters—then muttered, "Behave yourself."

He chuckled but listened to her demand anyway. His hands settled around her hips as they rode on, but his mind wandered to everything else. He wasn't sure what to think anymore regarding the involvement of a person in regard to this plague. After some thought, it was nearly impossible for this to be the work of a magician unless they were following this entourage and purposefully making people sick. But that wouldn't work because all of Ashtyn's patients had been sick for a while.

That lended back to the sorcerer theory. If so, any sorcerer with a good amount of power would be able to make the concoctions needed.

But then that lended back to the partner theory because a sorcerer would have a much more difficult time passing such a sickness around, so he'd need the help of a magician to pass it through the winds.

Though, again, that left questions—if it were in the winds, any one of them could've gotten it by then.

"If this plague isn't passing through the winds, how else would you assume?" Gabriel asked his wife, still lost in thoughts.

She leaned into him as if she knew he'd behave now that he was thinking of the plague. "I would've guessed food, but that's made me wonder too. If it was food, everyone would be getting sick. Same with anything drank."

"Are there any similarities you've found in your patients before they got sick? In terms of their lives."

She shrugged. "I don't think so. I've had a patient who was a gatherer, a teacher, a medic, and a chef. I've had children who do not work, and I've had elderly who mostly boss people around. I've had men who's priority is to hunt for their community, and I've had men who work on cutting wood. I've had women who sew and women who wash. They've all been normal members of their communities."

"Hm." Gabriel leaned in to smell her hair, something so innocent that seemed to always ground his mind. "What do you think happens if we can't figure out what's causing this?"

She sighed. "I'm too hopeful that with the Cousins, we can get it."

"Really?"

"No. But if I say it out loud, it must come true, right?"

He chuckled into her hair. "I mean, I called you my wife enough times."

"What do you think?"

"I think you're too good. I think you'll want to continue healing until it's too much for your body and mind. I think you'll come to resent me because I'll force you to stop, and everyone will listen to my demands because they know I'm right and I'm your husband. And you'll resent me even more for it."

"I want to say that wouldn't happen, but..."

"But you're a stubborn wife."

She sighed again. "I feel like I'm reverting back to the old me sometimes because I want to be selfish. When I think of us not being able to find the cause of this, I want to forget about all these people hurting and just go back to the palace. Then I hate myself more for only thinking of myself."

"Don't. That only makes you human, beautiful. You think

the rest of us don't want to be selfish, aren't selfish? I want to be selfish with you *right now*."

She laughed, and lords, was it the most beautiful sound in the world. "And of this plague? Do you have any ideas that might help?"

He shrugged. "I've considered magicians and sorcerers and even a common person who somehow smuggled whatever in order to devise this. The only reason why I can think of is for the palace but it would not make sense to make people so far north suffer if they want against the palace. Those people hardly even know what the royals look like."

"I've considered..."

"What?"

She swallowed and looked down, and Gabriel's heart-strings pulled. Ashtyn was a lot of things, but shameful normally wasn't one of them.

"What, beautiful?"

"I've considered the royals themselves," she whispered.

"Why?"

"I don't know. Because I'm cynical."

"Baby..."

She huffed. "Because if they could get these people sick then they could show how great they are by sending their best healer—not that I'm tooting my own horn, but we all know it —and then make it easier to bring in magicians."

Gabriel considered it. "They do have the Master Magician on their side."

"And barbarians who surely know sorcerers powerful enough in the Island to help them."

"Is that still a consideration?"

Her brows furrowed as she stared ahead biting her bottom lip. She was quiet for a couple minutes before saying, "No. It hasn't been for a while. I... It was a thought when I was first recruited to do this. I was trying to come up with what could be the cause and then when I saw my first patients, it felt daunting but then I realized, the palace has all this information. I figured they have so much information and a magician on their side and access to sorcerers so maybe this was all on them. It wasn't like I focused on it constantly, but it was a thought that would pop up every now and then.

"I dropped it when we were headed down south. That night around the fire at the inn. I guess I hadn't really trusted anyone until then, but then I watched you guys together before I joined. Everyone was truly friends and there was a camaraderie that I recognized in you guys that I'd seen tenfold in the Posse, that I'd seen with the women that have forced me to be their friends"—they both chuckled at that—"I knew then that it wasn't the palace. I trusted them fully after that night."

"Have you considered anything since?"

She shrugged. "I've tried to do what I haven't done in a long time and trust you guys. I... actually do believe you all are doing everything in your power to help everyone. I feel connected to you in that way. To find other people who want to help just as much. Lords, it makes me sound like a sap."

Gabriel chuckled and kissed her hair again. "Don't worry, beautiful. We'll figure this out. We'll deal with it. Then I'll take you home and make love to you over and over and over again."

She shook her head with her laughs. "I don't remember being worried about that."

"No?" His hand pressed into her stomach so she was thrust back into him, his cock firmly between her cheeks now. "I think you're desperately worried."

She shook her head some more. "Don't do that, Gabriel. We actually have shit to worry about."

He nipped at her neck, easing her body so she wasn't pressed so tightly against him. "I am worried, beautiful. I'm just trying to make light of it so we don't lose our minds."

She turned with a warm grin that only looked more beautiful under the beaming sunlight. "And that's another reason I love you."

# CHAPTER 29

# ASHTYN

Ashtyn was more than frustrated. She was annoyed. With her husband. This was all his fault.

She'd done such a great job for years pushing people away, not caring for anyone, then he'd bulldozed his way in, and now she was vulnerable. Her chest ached every day that she couldn't figure out what was happening and help.

Ashtyn was standing by the tents her entourage had planted to the side of the village, not wanting to take any more from these people who hardly had any.

As she stood there trying to think of what she could be missing when it came to helping these sick, a sound came to her. It was like a rough clicking.

No one seemed bothered so Ashtyn pushed the thought aside and focused once more on the sick. When she healed them, their blood was a thick black, laughing at her attempts. It coiled in the people's bodies and sucked the life out of them. What could that possibly be from?

The sound came to her again. As she looked around, no one else seemed to notice. Norya was sitting in a tree sharpening her arrows, and Ashtyn's lips twitched. She and Tristan had gotten into an argument twenty minutes prior and now she was sharpening her weapons. Oh, how Ashtyn loved that girl.

But those sounds were distracting her.

She turned again and now she saw it. There were six horses galloping for them without their riders if they ever had any.

As they got closer, Ashtyn's eyes narrowed.

Those weren't domesticated horses. She wasn't even entirely sure if they were horses. They looked... sick? Possessed? Mutilated?

Their coats ran with thick veins, and they were stained with both mud and what looked like blood. But it wasn't any of that that scared Ashtyn to her spot. It was their eyes.

They glowed red with pink pupils and black edges.

And they were charging fast from the other side of the village.

It happened so quickly. One moment she was standing there, the next she had a front-row seat to a rabid animal's mouth opening, and a child who couldn't be more than ten caught between its teeth. The animal shook his head, blood seeping into his mouth where the boy already lay unmoving in its mouth before it flung the child away and kept running.

Aside from Norya, who thankfully already had her bowstring and arrows flying at the animals, Ashtyn was the only one from her group still outside.

She heard screaming, but she wasn't sure where they came from. The villagers as the six rabid horses ransacked their meager living? The victims who were caught either in the mouths of those sharper-than-possible teeth or trampled beneath those larger than life hooves? Her friends as they scurried out of their tents?

Ashtyn's gaze was too focused on the way a hoof landed on

the chest of a woman, immediately seeping through her body. The way the life left her before she could be in too much pain.

She was too focused on the way the eyes of one horse glared at two children as they scurried away while his mouth chewed on the torn leg of someone who must've been lying in the heap of the growing dead.

She was too focused on those left behind the six horses as they came ever closer to her group. On the bodies of men, women, and children lying broken and bloody. There were intestines thrown around and limbs torn apart, and eyes left wide open.

Bile stormed up her mouth, but Ashtyn could not move.

They were coming for her. She felt the stare of those horses as if she were their sole prey. So dark and cold. So similar to the laughing faces she saw in the blood of those she healed with the plague. So conceited and vile. So... disastrous.

She was hypnotized by these animals when she was knocked off her feet, landing on a body before being rolled over.

"What the hell are you doing standing there!" Gabriel yelled.

Ashtyn's eyes were still on the scene beside her. Norya was up in a tree, shooting arrows that were thankfully slowing the animals a little. Colt and Wells were up in trees on the other end, sending throwing stars that slashed into the legs of the animals to stop them.

The Cousins stood off to the side, only Belinda fully dressed as the other two were clad in only men's shirts, as they focused their magic on the animals.

Huh. That must've been what was stopping them. Or maybe it was the combination of the magic and the wounds from the arrows and throwing stars?

The other men were rounding the surviving villagers and

pulling them back as much as possible, all of them shirtless since they'd been thrust out of their tents by the screams.

"Ashtyn!" Gabriel's voice edged into the white noise around her as his hand clasped around her jaw, and he made her face him. "Ashtyn!"

Her glazed eyes finally met his. "What?"

"Baby, look at me. Focus on me. You're okay, all right. You need to focus."

Her mind was still cloudy. She swore she saw those balls of pink pollen flying around them as she closed her eyes. This felt like a nice time to nap.

Gabriel's hold on her jaw sharpened, and Ashtyn winced as he forced her to look at him. "Ashtyn!"

His eyes held a lot, but the main thing she saw there was... anger? Was he angry with her? What the fuck did she do?

Her mind snapped back. "Gabriel? What the hell happe—" She glanced around them to the horror taking place. The Cousins' work was already slowing the animals, and they were beginning to stumble as they moved.

Ashtyn's stomach roiled as she pushed Gabriel off of her. "Gabriel. I'm going to—"

He scurried to the side right as her stomach let out its contents. Gabriel pushed her hair back as he held her, letting everything leave her body. Her eyes watered both from the sting of the vomit coming up her throat and from what she'd witnessed. She didn't want to turn back around. She couldn't...

Gabriel slowly helped her to her feet, and she trembled in his arms. He held her with her back to everything, and as much as Ashtyn appreciated it, she knew she needed to see what had taken place. These villagers were living the nightmare, the least she could do was witness it.

Still in his arms, allowing him to hold her up against his chest since her knees were too weak to work, Ashtyn turned.

The rabid animals were all on the grounds, breathing slowly as if coming off of a fever. Their coats were stained, but their eyes were turning away from that odd coloring back to the light browns they naturally had been. Their teeth looked normal once more, and they whimpered like they were scared and in pain.

Ashtyn's heart went out for them. Even with all the horror they'd caused, they hadn't been in control, and they were as scared as anyone else. And hurt. They'd taken a lot in order to be stopped.

"The horses, Gabriel..." She clung to his shirt. "They're scared."

He kissed her crown. "I know, beautiful. I'll work with them."

Then Ashtyn's eyes landed once more on the mess around them. The broken and torn bodies, the blood, the gore, the wails of screams. Her stomach roiled again, and she turned into Gabriel's chest, clinging to him and breathing in his scent to steady herself.

## CHAPTER 30
# ASHTYN

Ashtyn's stomach recoiled, fighting her, wanting to throw its contents out.

She fought it. There was no need to put anyone's focus on her when there was so much to take care of.

The others were out dealing with the mess, so she was lucky to have the tent to herself. She slowed her breathing on the cot, and after some time, even the war in her stomach stopped even though the images of what she's seen out there continued.

After another hour, she was able to make herself forget that altogether.

She wasn't dreaming.

She was sitting up in the cot, yet the visions passing by her closed eyes felt like dreams, like the ones that came to her sparingly.

Of the girl chasing pink pollen through beautiful gardens until they reached the forest.

Lost in the memory of that dream, Ashtyn's brows furrowed. She recognized that sighting of forests. It sounded ridiculous. There was so much woodland area, it didn't make sense in the slightest that she'd recognize any of it.

Her memories of those dreams tugged her back.

This time, she saw herself lying in the fields with a large tree blocking the sunlight from her eyes. There were pretty pink flowers everywhere.

She remembered that tree from the one time she'd run through the forests as a child in order to get away from her village. She remembered being so at ease there, like she never felt anywhere. Peaceful in a way only Gabriel was able to bring her now.

She remembered those dreams assaulting her with each of the three men she'd been with years back. Visions that told her to get away, to run into the forests, to follow the pink pollen.

Her brows furrowed some more as the memories focused as Ashtyn realized she hadn't only seen those pink balls of pollen in her dreams. They followed her still.

She scoffed to herself with how delusional that sounded, but her heart knew what her mind tried to push aside. It fought her until the memories of those pink balls sprang to vivid images behind her closed eyes.

The pink dust that had led her down that particular path when she'd left Baron. The ones that had encouraged her to go northeast instead of west. The ones that had led her straight for that town with all the sick. The ones that had put her right where Sparrow would find her, that brought her to the palace.

Those same balls that directed her for the woods when she'd arrived to the palace as if they were trying to lead her somewhere.

Surprisingly, always by the stables, by his cottage. It was those pink balls she saw in the air when looking out her window in her office at the infirmary. It was those balls that called to her, telling her she needed to follow.

Her eyes snapped open.

Those balls, those little specks of dust, pink strings of pollen, were... her good omens.

They were the ones that had directed her away for so long. They were the ones encouraging her feelings for Gabriel in a way they hadn't with any other male. They were the ones she'd seen on countless occasions while out here, sometimes leading her north, other times south.

Her brows furrowed. Did the little balls know where she needed to go? But how?

A throat clearing shocked Ashtyn out of her thoughts.

"I'm sorry, healer." Colt bent his head. "How are you feeling?"

"Much better now. Thank you."

He gave a small, weak smile. "It never gets easier. Especially when the innocent are involved."

"Good," she replied softly. "I hope it doesn't. You don't need to become immune to such atrocities."

His close-lipped smile was small but genuine. He cleared his throat again and stepped into the tent this time, hand out with a paper. "A missive from the palace has arrived for you."

Her brows furrowed. For her?

She took it tentatively but didn't so much as look at it until Colt left the tent.

Tensions rose within her, and she had no idea why.

Glancing down, she peeled the missive open to see Sparrow's handwriting within.

*Healer,*

*News from the South has reached us and not a single one of us knows what to do with it. Even the South is perplexed.*

*Remain on your mission, find and heal the source, but when you are done, and Evony has given birth—for she insists on being a part of this—we will head down to the Southern Lands once more.*

*For now, know they have declared you not a Master at all but a possible magician.*

*They believe since you do not have a memory of your first decade that any proof or teachings were wiped with your memory. And without the teachings continued throughout your life, you would not have ever used "magic," so no one would've been able to suspect your status.*

*They believe your abilities come from the remnant of magic but aren't quite sure if that would grant you Master status as it is only with healing... that we know of. It is why Evony insists on being there. If your healing ability is so powerful, she believes you may be able to test some other aspects of being a magician. Even if not, if your healing magic is powerful enough to make you a Master, then you are linked to Evony in some way as healing is the one ability that drains her. Maybe the link is only in the Fates, but it is something we will look into.*

*I do not know if this knowledge may help you, but lest it does, know it, Ashtyn. You have magic in you.*

*Sparrow*

Ashtyn didn't need to reread the letter. She believed what she'd read. It all made sense. From the very beginning Evony had said her healing wasn't as strong as the rest of her abilities. That could be because nearly three years before she was born, Ashtyn had been. With those particular abilities.

She'd sensed magic in herself, and it was because of that feeling that Ashtyn was certain the little pink balls that always seemed to be watching her from a distance would be what led her to the source of this pain in the Northern Lands.

Ashtyn moved slowly, dropping one foot to the ground then the other. She surprisingly wasn't dreading stepping outside. She should be considering this was the end. She felt it now.

She walked to the flaps of the tent quietly. Hopefully no

one would notice her leaving. She wasn't sure where this was leading to but if it was dangerous, she couldn't bring them all down with her.

Outside, the sunlight beamed down even in the chill of the start of the winter months, and in the distance, she saw the little pink balls of pollen. They were calling for her to follow into the forests.

She didn't follow them immediately.

First, her gaze slithered over to where Gabriel was, helping the others with the sick animals.

Her heart hurt. The very last thing she wanted to do was leave him, hurt him. But if something were to happen, she could not live knowing he'd been hurt because of her.

Her chest banged even harder knowing nothing would hurt him more than losing her, but she ignored it.

She turned back to the balls of pollen, then her head swung in the opposite direction where healthy horses stood off to the side grazing. Her horse was there.

Ashtyn moved quietly to Bella. The horse technically wasn't hers, she was Princess Rosaelia's, but Ashtyn felt more tied to her.

Her hand settled between Bella's eyes, her ring glinting under the sunlight, as Ashtyn whispered to her, "What do you say, girl? Wanna help me end this?"

Bella neighed once, and Ashtyn understood it as the answer it was.

She brushed at Bella's mane a moment before the horse lowered itself to make it easy for Ashtyn to get on.

Atop the animal, Ashtyn hoped the others were too preoc-cupied as she led Bella toward the balls of pollen seeping deeper into the forests, further from her.

They were nearly out of view and ready to begin truly riding when her luck ran out.

"Ashtyn, what are you doing?" Gabriel's booming voice hit her.

She wanted to turn to him, let the look in her eyes be apology enough, but she didn't. She couldn't risk it.

So she kicked Bella, and they rode off, chasing after pink balls.

# CHAPTER 31

# GABRIEL

"Ashtyn!" he screamed again to the distance.

She was gone, without a word or a glance back. As Gabriel watched her retreat, his chest banged, but surprisingly, it wasn't from the pain of losing her. It was of surety.

His brows furrowed as the memory of this part of town came to him from a past he would've never remembered before today. The memory showed a clearing at the end of the trail Ashtyn had gone down. One with a tree he remembered blowing to him, calling for him. Now he was flabbergasted by how sure he felt that his wife was headed for that clearing. And even more so at such a memory. It must've been one from before he traveled with the orphans. He didn't know what had prompted him to remember it now, but he felt as sure about this as he had with the decision that Ashtyn was his.

Gabriel ran for his horse and knew the others were following him. He didn't know which of them would come with him and which would remain with the people, but he didn't care. Something had triggered Ashtyn to leave so abruptly, and Gabriel feared it was something that would put her in danger. He needed to be there to protect her if that happened.

Their group rode into the forests and were barely a couple hundred yards in when the path closed up, branches as wide as the horses themselves covering their way, roots and vines from the grounds coming up to entangle the path.

Gabriel had to halt immediately, but he was at a loss. Ashtyn was nowhere around, but Bella stood off to the side grazing at grass as if patiently awaiting her return. Had this path covered itself after her? Gabriel's heart raced with the answer he already knew. If the path was stopping them from getting through, his girl was in more danger than he'd thought.

And he couldn't imagine this was the doing of any other person. They wouldn't go after a healer. They'd go straight for the royal family.

The thought that this could be anything, but another person shot fear spiking through Gabriel. He needed to get to his wife.

Gabriel immediately hopped off his horse and heard the others doing the same, the horses neighing and backing up as if they could sense an odd presence. His animals were smart. They'd known a while back that something in the atmosphere had been the problem, and they knew now. "Someone take the horses back," he ordered to no one in particular. "We don't need them running off on their own."

Turning for the group, he was surprised to find two of the village folk with them. They were the ones to take the horses, seeming more afraid now than before to follow them within. Gabriel was glad they were going. This wasn't their fight. They hadn't agreed, like the rest of them had, to come into this trouble.

"Cousins," Tristan ordered.

The tangle of nature before them was alarming. Like the deepest depths of the darkest forest. Forbidden and frightening. Gabriel's own heart raced with fear and every instinct within him told him to step back, to run away like the horses had.

He swallowed to push back the need to run. Gabriel did take a step back, not because he was allowing the terror to take over but because he needed to give the Cousins space to perform their magic. They weren't as strong as the Master Magician so they needed to combine their magic. They did so by holding hands though Gabriel wasn't sure if that was required. For most magicians, it wouldn't be, but he wasn't sure if being cousins, their blood played a larger role with their abilities.

They came together, and the winds in their little part of the forest shot fast. It was difficult to breathe through it and even more difficult to hold their positions rather than allowing the winds to carry them back.

The forest seemed to truly come alive then.

Vines shot out of the ground, and Gabriel felt lucky they were all able to jump out of the way, though not so much when he noticed Gian jump toward the girls rather than away. Their magic would keep them safe. He would have no such help.

He couldn't blame the man though. Had Ashtyn been here, he would've done the same thing.

Everything uprooted with their magic, leaves and acorns and even small animals, carcasses and alive, shot through the air and slammed into trees and people alike. Colt fell to the ground as a carcass of a medium-sized animal slammed into him, but the man didn't show his pain. Not now. He was a guard, trained to fight past the pain until war was over.

The trees around them seemed to be growing, pushing out

any light that might've helped them make their way through this trail, any light that would aid the magicians in knowing what they were aiming for.

The guards surrounded the Cousins, each trying to fight off flying scraps so they didn't slam into the girls as they worked. Gabriel fought to make his way around the edges of the clearing they were in, trying to figure out which way they'd come from and which they needed to head in. Everything was in such disarray he'd hardly know which was right.

And in the whole of the mess, Tristan and Norya battled around him, protecting him so he could figure out where they needed to go.

Sparks of sunlight shot through the gaps in the growing trees and roots as if pushing back the darkness to allow them to get through. As if the skies were on their side.

The winds were an altogether other story.

They weren't on any side. Surely not. Not with the way they rammed the roots, breaking them from the ground, and not when those broken pieces flew straight for their group. Not when it took all of their energies to stop from flying.

In those sparks shining in by the sun in even this frigid of late autumn days, Gabriel saw the way through. The part that memory seemed to serve correctly and would lead straight through to a clearing. One he hadn't seen in two decades, so he found it astounding he remembered at all.

But to get through, they needed these natural beauties fighting them to stop.

As if reading his mind—or maybe he screamed it through the winds—the Cousins shot their magic toward the roots attempting to enclose that spot.

It strained them. They barely stood upright with guards behind each one to keep them standing, but they did not back down from the fight. Whatever was causing nature to act out like this had to be magical, and it wanted everyone to stay away from Ashtyn.

Whatever it was wanted his wife. That much was clear by Bella being left behind and Ashtyn allowed to pass through.

The Cousins were able to push the roots aside enough for Gabriel to run through, and he heard Tristan and Norya screaming past the winds behind him, but he couldn't make out what they were saying.

When they got through the storm of leaves smacking into them, branches cutting them, and dirt and mud marring them, Gabriel finally heard one thing past all that wind—a terrifying scream.

One heightened by magic.

He turned abruptly to find Astreya in the grasps of the root as if the tree was dangling her high. The screams came from all over—Astreya's from the pain caused by the pressure the root was ensuring, her cousins from the fear of anything happening to her, the others for ways to help their new friends, but most of all, from Gian.

"NOOO!" His scream was so violent Gabriel was sure he felt the grounds shake.

He'd learned long ago while living in the South that mating with a magician, finding that lost soul to come together, could cause the slightest bit of magic to thrum beneath even the most normal of mortals. That's what was happening to Gian. He'd mated with his magician.

As if the ground shaking was all the cause the chaos they were in needed, the root dropped Astreya, and all else went back to place as if not a thing had just taken place. As if they hadn't just been at war with darkness, winds, and nature.

In the deafening silence, Gian's screams beside his crumpled woman was anguish.

"Go." Tristan pushed at his arm. "Go. We need to find the healer. That's what'll help them."

He was right. Not only would Ashtyn be their best bet, but she was his wife, and Gabriel needed to find her more than he needed to help anyone.

It still pained his soul to turn his back on those he'd traveled and laughed with as he ran through the tangle of roots no longer trying to kill them.

# CHAPTER 32
# GABRIEL

Gabriel was breathing hard as he ran with Norya and Tristan on his heels. He couldn't remember how long this trail was, how far he would've gone as a child to reach it.

So he simply ran.

Ran and ran and ran until...

A branch shot out of nowhere, and he smacked into it so hard the wind was knocked entirely out of him as he lay on the ground attempting to clear his vision.

His companions stopped above them, their forms domineering as they eyed every possible threat before Tristan dropped to his side to help him up while Norya continued assessing.

They weren't in another clearing but on the simple trail with a few branches and roots sticking out but nothing ominous.

And yet, the atmosphere felt chilly as if the forest had taken the season they were in and cranked it to feel as if it were far more extreme, as if they were in the depths of an Island winter rather than a Northern autumn.

They all shivered, Norya least of all considering she was used to such harsh weather, as Tristan helped Gabriel up. His vision wasn't completely back yet, and he was still wheezing for breath, but Gabriel focused on the space around them.

Other than the freezing temperatures and that one set of branches that now blocked their route, nothing was different. The branches were thick and placed firmly in place, making it impossible to try to make a way through.

Both warriors beside him took out their weapons and began hacking, though with how cold it was around them, they were shivering as they did so, their hands running cold far quicker than normal. Gabriel himself was damn near frozen given he wasn't exerting energy as they were.

The branches were thick and reminded Gabriel of the ones he'd seen made when Lanlik had purchased illegally smuggled potions from an Islander sorcerer to their garden hidden from the public. She'd used it on some dying branches and within a year, they were so strong, nothing could get passed them. When they needed the plant moved, it'd taken damn near every male muscle to do it with those branches.

"Weapons won't help," Gabriel concluded. Only a sorcerer's potion would be about to break this apart.

Finally, both warriors stopped hacking at the unmoving branches.

Tristan grumbled as he sheathed his sword back into place, rubbing his hands together for warmth, and instead grabbed the edge of a branch and pulled it tight. Somehow, that worked.

Gabriel's eyes widened at the space it was giving. With only one spy pulling at it.

"How the fuck is your strength working and weapons weren't!" Norya exclaimed as she moved to her man's side.

The space Tristan had been holding wasn't very large and popped back into place when he released his hold. His arms had been shaking trying to keep the branch back, and he quickly stuck his hands beneath his armpits for warmth.

"There must be some kind of magical element or something," Tristan concluded.

Gabriel shrugged. "I cannot imagine what. Magic would only work if a magician is around to control it. Unless there is someone here somewhere, that can't be it. For something to take place without an actual person, a sorcerer would've needed to be involved."

Norya moved to the other side and tried her luck at pulling at the branches. Her arms shook almost immediately but she was able to do it.

She huffed as she let the thing fall back. "If that's the case, then something could still be holding us back. For some reason, it let the healer through. I don't like any reasoning for that."

"Yeah." Gabriel stared at the way hoping his wife was safe. "Me neither."

Tristan's attention burned Gabriel's profile, and when he finally met the man's gaze, Tristan looked to have made up his mind. "We'll hold it open, Gabe."

"What?"

"Nor and I will hold it open for you. Neither of us can hold it open large enough for a whole person to fit through but together, we can make a gap for you. You need to find her. We'll figure out a way through, but you need to get to her. The sooner, the better."

Gabriel wanted to argue he wouldn't leave them, but the

spy was right, and selfishly, he wanted to get to Ashtyn more than anything. "Thank you."

The two gave a single nod, came together for a quick whispered conversation as they kissed, they stepped back to hold onto each side. They counted down, then pulled with all their might.

For a moment, Gabriel was struck with how strong they were, with how strong Norya was. It was incredible.

He only let the thought distract him for a moment before he ran and flew through the opening they'd made for him. It was just big enough with their shaking arms for him to dive through.

Gabriel grunted as he fell to the ground on the other side, the path ahead clear.

The branches were already back in place given neither warrior could hold it for too long.

"You okay?" Tristan's voice broke through.

"Yup," he yelled back.

"Good. We don't need the healer killing us if something happens to you," Norya joked.

Gabriel chuckled as he got up and started moving forward. "I'm going!"

"We'll see you soon, Gabriel," Tristan's confidence pushed Gabriel forward with some of his own. They would get through this and get back home.

# CHAPTER 33
## ASHTYN

Her heart still hurt leaving Bella out there as she had, but Ashtyn had known when she hit those tangled trees that the rest of the journey would be hers alone. That had been made clear when she so easily slipped through the way toward this clearing with only a tree in the middle.

It was an expansive place of greenery with the most beautiful piece of nature settled in the middle. Large and full of life.

Full of wild baby pink flowers.

The pollen was still all around her, but most of it seemed to take homage in the flowers, like they were finally home.

Ashtyn moved slowly through the flowers on the ground, her gaze latched onto the flowers hanging from the tree. They were a soft pink and got lighter the further up the petal, nearly an ivory inside.

She stopped an arms-length away from the massive piece of life, and her hand shook as she raised it to graze the bark of such an expansive thing with her fingertips.

Her whole body shivered feeling the power within it.

*You've come home, my darling.*

The sound came from everywhere and nowhere.

"Home?"

*We were conceived here that lovely fair day. Planted me and consummated for you. We are but one since that day.*

So this is where her parents had created her. That's why she'd felt such a tug for it. Was it also the reason she had any power at all?

"But wouldn't it take longer than a quarter of a century to grow to such greatness?"

*We wield power. You give yours away to heal. I take mine to grow.*

Take mine. Like taking the life forces of all those sick. Infecting people and taking away their will. All in order to grow stronger here in the middle of the woods.

It made sense though. Ashtyn hadn't been able to see the connection, but if the Tree was infecting people to take from them then the answer would've been in the lands. The ones the hunters ran through and woodcutters cleared; the ones that gatherers took from to give to the chefs, seamstresses, medics; the ones the teachers used to instruct their children. It would've only taken touching the wrong thing, inhaling its pollen too much or too closely.

"If you've been taking life to grow, why start infecting people now? You've had twenty-four years."

*We are nearly a quarter of a century. It will be a powerful time for us.*

The sound came from nowhere, no living object, but somehow, Ashtyn heard the grin in the words. As if putting all those people in danger was something to be proud of.

Her fingertips grazed that dark bark. It was softer than normal trees in the same way the flowers here were prettier than anywhere else. It was all from those left sick in the towns and villages.

"Why had you been calling me?" Because that's what those pink balls in all her dreams, in her daily life, had been—a calling. To come here.

Home?

That didn't sound right. As if this could be home. As if anywhere without Gabriel could be home.

*We are both great, my pretty, but we would be so much more together. You needed to come home.*

Ashtyn stopped herself from grimacing. Instead, she asked the question that'd been nagging at her since she realized it was this tree communicating with her. "How are you possible? What did my parents plant?"

*My seeds come from long ago, back when a Master Grower and a Master Sorcerer came together to create power. They were stopped before they could plant me. My seeds have been kept in the Sacred Garden for years. Too long. Your parents were not aware of what they'd taken from the Gardens. They created me. Us. We are one, Ashtyn.*

It said her name with a hiss as if it would force her to comply if she thought against it.

It shouldn't surprise Ashtyn that the Tree would know she wouldn't want to participate. It'd been in her dreams, it wasn't too far of a stretch to believe it could wiggle into her thoughts.

"And Gabriel?" she asked the other nagging question. "I've seen your pollen around him."

It laughed. The Tree chuckled at her, and it was both deep and haunting.

*That was a match I needed, but you... you are a stubborn child. Impossible to lure.*

"Why would you need anything to happen between us?"

Invisible, yet Ashtyn heard the smirk in its voice. *Why, his parents were the gardeners who gave your parents the seeds. They believed themselves to be celebrating their little boy's birth when they drank too much and gifted the seeds to your parents.*

Ashtyn's breath caught. Their parents—whom neither of them knew—had known one another, if only briefly.

"That doesn't explain why you need him." Ashtyn could handle a lot of things, but not anything happening to Gabriel. It might've been the Tree's plan to get them together, but she knew their feelings were completely their own. It was the only thing in this world she was so sure of now.

*Gabriel takes care of life. I need him to take care of us long into his death, darling.*

"How could you possibly know…"

*His parents were gardeners, it would be innate in him to take care of the living. But I needed him to know magic as well. Why else do you think he joined the group heading to the South? It worked only in my favor that he loved it there long enough to learn all he did, then want to come back to the North which you so stubbornly always refused to leave, though I cannot blame you. The North is where I am.*

She wouldn't let the Tree touch Gabriel, but first, she needed to know what it desired. "What exactly do you want with me? Why lead me here?"

*Join me, darling.*

"Then what of the population?" It was already clear it cared nothing for her relationship with Gabriel, for his broken heart, but what of all the others?

*With your power, I will not need them. Join me.*

Ashtyn internally gasped. The Tree was telling the truth. She could feel it.

But if that were it, then she had to agree. She had to give in to the Tree. She had to give up her life as she knew it for everyone else's safety.

Ashtyn turned to look the way she'd come. Gabriel was after her no doubt. He'd likely seen Bella out there already and was making his way to her.

She scoffed internally. She'd told him not to tie himself down to her. That it wouldn't be worth it. This was proof.

He'd married her, and she had to leave him.

She blinked to stop the tears watering her eyes and stared toward his direction another moment. "I love you, Gabriel. Ardently and annoyingly so."

Ashtyn sighed and turned back to the Tree. "Leave them be. Take me. Don't *ever* mess with Gabriel."

*I knew you'd agree, pretty girl. Now come. Come home.*

Ashtyn had the urge to raise her hand to the Tree. When her fingertips grazed it, her body tingled.

# CHAPTER 34

# GABRIEL

Gabriel's heart hammered. He was close to her, he could feel it even if he had no conscious idea where he was headed or what might lay ahead of him.

Then she was there. His wife but...

She was made of flowers. Pretty, pink flowers that danced around her form. She smiled at him, and a hand made of those same flowers reached up as if asking him to dance.

"Ashtyn?"

She gave a nod, and when she realized he wouldn't be taking her hand, dropped it and moved instead. She danced in slow, playful circles around the trail. It was larger here as if leading to a meadow.

She looked so happy, so content, so... unlike herself.

"Ashtyn, beautiful?"

"Yes?" It was her voice and not her voice coming from the flowery form.

He took a tentative step forward. "What's happened, Ashtyn?"

"We are home!" she exclaimed as she continued her dancing around the trail that was now light and airy.

"My love?"

She ignored him, dancing around the grass. It looked as if it were spring rather than nearing winter. What kind of elements could be in control in this area for it to affect the weather so?

Gabriel held out his hand now. "Ashtyn, beautiful. Take my hand. Let's go home."

"Home! I am home!" She wore a large grin.

It looked like a dream, witnessing his wife in this state, made of flowers and corporeal.

"Ashtyn?"

It took a moment, but she finally turned to face him, looking as if she were in the clouds. "Yes?"

"Ashtyn, you look very pretty today."

Her grin widened. "I do, don't I? I am the prettiest!"

Gabriel's stomach dropped as he shook his head, gaze shifting everywhere but at the flowery woman meant to be his wife. He knew where he'd come from but not where to go.

"What are you looking for? Your pretty girl is here!" She danced in circles again, drawing his attention.

Was this her? The girl Ashtyn used to be? The one who craved attention and was called pretty constantly. Had she loved it back then as she hates it now?

"Yeah? The cottage is waiting for us. The horses need tending to."

"Horses! How lovely. We own horses."

He shook his head. "Work with, Ash. We work with horses."

She kept dancing in circles. "Never! I'm too pretty!"

Gabriel was stuck in his spot. This wasn't his wife. Not anymore. This was the woman Ashtyn had been running from. She'd been so afraid of becoming her again, Ashtyn had gone from the most giggly girl Gabriel was witnessing before him to the grump who hated everyone.

They were so different, yet Gabriel found himself drawn to this Ashtyn as well. "You will not need to work with them. You may remain home and raise our children."

She jumped with joy, and Gabriel knew there was still some of this Ashtyn in his Ashtyn. They were the same girl, though with different priorities now.

This one looked to her left and back, then toward the spot Gabriel had come from. "Then let's go home!"

Gabriel's heart sped up as he nodded. He felt a little saddened to see her go, but as this flowery Ashtyn moved for him, Gabriel ran through her, breaking all the flowers into the winds where they carried around the clearing. It was astonishingly beautiful.

Then he turned toward the one way that Ashtyn hadn't glanced and ran to find his wife.

# CHAPTER 35
# ASHTYN

The winds rustled branches, and flowers flowed in the air. It was all so welcoming, so fresh, so at peace.

The winds picked up, and her branches shuddered, but all calmed. The sunlight beamed down, but no heat hit her. No chill touched her from the winds. She did not feel any of it.

They did not feel any of it.

What was life outside being the Tree? There wasn't one.

A scrambling came from beyond, then a man with floppy brown hair came out, his face and arms covered in cuts, his shirt torn up. *What an oddity. A man in our end of the forest. How did he get through? We do not allow men through.*

*This must be the one here to serve us.*

He stared with wide eyes, almost horrified. There was a change of color in his eyes, too human to know what it could mean.

Their branches shook as they focused only on their servant. "You've come to us."

He jumped, glancing everywhere before landing back on

the Tree. He was staring at their eyes. How nice to have eyes now. Humans adored eyes.

"Ashtyn, my love." He tripped forward, slowly moving for them.

"We are the Tree. Are you here to serve us?"

"Ash... no. You're not the Tree. You're Ashtyn, a healer."

*Healer? Whyever would we heal others when we could take from them? We do not need to take, but we certainly would never give ourselves up for another.*

"It's Gabriel. Gabriel, your husband. The man who refused to give up on you no matter how much you pushed him away. The man so proud that his wife is a healer, that his wife serves everyone in the lands, always helping them."

*We do not serve anyone but ourselves.*

What a ridiculous thought this man was having. To serve others. What was the purpose? He seemed so sure of his words. Were humans all so passionate about such ludicrous words? Words implying worrying about others' wellbeing. Others' wellbeing... others' wellbeing... others'.

Ashtyn's breath caught, seeing her husband standing before her and knowing she could not do anything to help him. But she needed to protect him. She would not allow the Tree to use him. He needed to live.

Her mind banged as if there was a fight for control.

"We... I... We... I need to protect him. "

Gabriel jumped once more, chocolate orbs focused on her eyes now covered by the bark of the Tree. "Ash, baby, I'm here."

Had he heard that? Had she been able to say it articulately enough?

"There is no Ash. We are the Tree." The voice almost hissed.

"Ashtyn." Gabriel rested his hands on either side of where her body was losing itself to the Tree. "You are a Northerner. A healer. The magical healer, I don't care what the South may say to that. You are a healer! You protect people. You're grouchy and an asshole most of the time, but you care about others' wellbeing more than anything. You put yourself at risk in order to protect everyone."

*He is lying. What fantastical stories. We are but a Tree ready to outlive humans.*

Those eyes were shining, and a flash of a memory entered her mind—those eyes staring down at her as words were muttered. *With this ring, I take your soul in exchange for mine.* There were flowers everywhere and a blur of people around them.

"You have friends, Ash. Friends back at the campsite, back at the palace. You have others wanting to see you return home. Friends. Do you remember them? Evony? She's the Master Magician. And Gemma. They were the first people you became friends with. They were raised in the South and entirely inappropriate, but they make you smile. I know you remember them."

*A Master Magician? Our servant is in cahoots with the Master Magician? Oh, what an advantage we have drawn with such a servant.*

Another flash of something passed her eyes—a dark-haired girl leaning over the body of a man in the greens. Another man—this man right before her—hysterical beside him. So much emotion so openly available.

"You remember the Posse. Sparrow, the Master Assassin. He's the one that brought you to the palace. You two are friends as well, even if you do not admit to it. You remember them, Ash. Miels and Etel and Rosaelia and Killian and Norya and Tristan. You remember the guards with us, the magicians. Astreya, Belinda, and Caetana. Astreya was hurt, Ash, trying to get to you. Gian is with her, but she needs you. Remember your life, Ash."

*Life? But we had life in the beauty that was nature around us. We will live long after our servants pass. We are life.*

"Remember me, beautiful."

A sharp flash of those eyes hovering over her as a great pleasure ran over her form, a climax of something exhilarating exploding from her as she held on to those shoulders, around that waist... those eyes. So... perfect.

"You're my wife, beautiful. I'm not giving up on us, remember? I've been quite annoying. You say so every day."

Another sharp flash, one almost too painful for them... her? This time it was one of standing by a window as he took her hands in his and asked for her to be his...

"Wife, beautiful. You are my wife. And I proudly carry the title of your husband every day."

"We are the Tree," hissed throughout the clearing around them.

*We are the Tree.*

The servant's hands ran down their body, his hands shaking as they ran over the bark that covered all but their eyes. *We loved our eyes. We would not conceal our eyes.*

"No, no, no!" His hands shook violently as they caressed the Tree before his eyes snapped back. "Beautiful, listen, please come back to me. Please."

Those hands. So soft as they ran down. He must work with wood.

"How pleasant that you can work with your hands. You will serve us well in clearing our branches when needed."

His eyes snapped up to everything around them.

He sighed as if he was giving up. Good. The best servants were those who had lost their will to fight any longer.

His head fell on them until their eyes were level. So very close. What frightfully beautiful eyes he had.

"I will not touch you," he mumbled.

A flash of a mem— "You will do as we say!"

His lips quirked up on one side. "I will not touch you. You need to learn to love yourself."

*We love us.*

"To heal yourself."

"We are in no need of healing. You will do as we say!"

"You will heal yourself. When I think you deserve it, I'll touch you. You remember that, right, beautiful? How I touched you."

*We could feel his hands on us now. They were lovely, if soft and shaky.* "You are our servant!"

He chuckled now. "You remember how you begged for my touch, beautiful? You'll be begging me again."

"We will do no such thing!"

Gabriel stepped away from them, and such an emptiness entered, it almost felt as if the life was sucked right out from within them.

"NO!"

He smirked. Humans could be cocky? It did nothing to have a cocky servant. "Beg me, wife. But know the rules. I will not touch you until you heal yourself."

"WE ARE IN NO NEED FO—"

His hand snaked up to his lips, rubbing them slowly, and a heat entered her form, bringing Ashtyn out. She wanted to yell out for him but could not.

"We are—"

"Gabriel!" she interrupted the Tree's control over her.

His eyes sparked. "There you are, beautiful. Now come to me. Beg me."

Heat swelled within her, so raging she only felt this way when she'd been healing for hours on end.

Healing... she was a healer.

*No! We are the Tree. We do not heal, we take!*

Gabriel licked his lips, and the memory flashed so hot, Ashtyn burned—that tongue gliding over her lips, down her neck, across her body, sucking and biting down on her nipples, moving farther south until he was licking her, sucking her, loving her.

His eyes flashed like he knew what she was remembering. Impossible.

"Your eyes tell me everything, beautiful. Come back to me, and I will make you come until you pass out. Come on out. I have a future planned for us."

Ashtyn wanted to listen, but another pain shot through her, this one feeling internal.

The Tree.

She was part of the Tree.

And she abandoned it when it needed to be healed.

"We do not need—"

Ashtyn ignored it and sent her abilities within herself, searching for the darkness that always told her what needed mending.

She found it in the soul at the root of the Tree. It was dark and seeping... blood. The Tree was infected, trying to survive on the life forces of others.

Ashtyn ran her power back up, looking for that healthy part of herself, the one clinging to her husband, and spoke to it. *Come with me. Help me heal the Tree. We may not be of one, but we are one, and it is in pain. Help me heal it so we can go home.*

To Gabriel.

Every part of her knew home meant Gabriel.

Gabriel must've still been speaking, but she didn't hear

him. She focused solely on taking that healthy dose of herself to the root of the Tree, healing it for a healthy life far outliving humans.

"No! Don't! We do not want—"

Her power made its way down while her gaze focused on those charming brown ones known as home.

*Don't! No! We are—*

The darkness seeped into the light and wanted to envelop it, but nothing could drag her out of the sunlight that shone in Gabriel, in his eyes beckoning her home.

*We are all-powerful. We do not need... We...*

The darkness seeped through, drinking in the light. There was so much of it, the roots cleared, healed. They took on life like never before.

It could've taken hours or minutes, Gabriel never left her.

*Thank you.* The sound was like a breath of fresh air.

Ashtyn internally smiled, lost was her form. *I'm sorry I did not know to heal you before.*

*It was not known to be needed.*

*May I go home now?*

*Is the servant your home?*

She couldn't help internally laughing. The servant? What a thing to call him when she was cross with him from now on. *He is.*

*Good. He is a good servant. He will do you well.*

Her heart warmed in a way it never had before. *He will.*

Then, like her power was still at work, heat poured around her form and a body emerged from the bark of the Tree, her body.

Gabriel's eyes widened. He was about to smile when she was suddenly thrust out of the Tree and he paled, readying to catch her.

She flew through the air and was lucky to land against his

body when they toppled to the ground, the air leaving him as he smacked against the ground.

"Gabriel," she huffed a whisper, catching her breath. Then louder, "Gabriel! Gabriel?" She scrambled up and took his head in her hands, her power working to heal anything that might've happened to him. "Gabriel," she cried.

"That's not my name," he groaned, eyes still closed.

Ashtyn gasped a sigh of relief as she laughed. "Husband."

"Close," he croaked.

"My husband!"

He opened one eye slowly, closed both, then opened them to meet her gaze. "There ya go, beautiful."

"I hate you," she muttered.

He bit his bottom lip. "Then you are not deserving of my touch."

She straddled his lap, uncaring if it hurt him a little. "You're my husband. I will not be able to survive without your touch."

His hands ran up her thighs, her ass, her back, and pushed her down. "Mm. My wife is horny, I see."

"You promised to touch me."

He chuckled against her lips. "Wives. All they think about is sex."

Ashtyn laughed as he kissed her, his tongue welcoming her home.

# CHAPTER 36
# ASHTYN

*You will be conceiving your future here as well, I see.*

The sound came from everywhere and nowhere. Ashtyn did not get up from Gabriel's lap as she turned to face the Tree.

"As well?" Gabriel asked.

"This is where my parents conceived me," Ashtyn answered, not taking her eyes off the Tree that now looked... bigger? It wasn't, but it stood as if... it was proud.

"Yeah?" Gabriel's hands ran up and down her thighs. "Then I think this is the perfect spot to touch you. There must be something here that guarantees you'll come with child."

Ashtyn snapped from her loving gaze upon the Tree to Gabriel's mischievous eyes. "What? Since when do you want children?"

"I've always wanted children, beautiful."

She huffed. "I meant since when do you want them *now*?"

He smirked. "Since I heard it just now. I want my child in you."

She shook her head. "Husbands. All they think about is pregnancy."

He laughed, head thrown back. So sexy, so inviting, so...

Wet. She was so wet.

Ashtyn leaned back down until her lips hovered over Gabriel's. "I'm so wet, Gabriel."

His laugh stopped immediately, eyes darkening.

"Maybe that's why babies are conceived here because all I want is to ride you until there's no cum left in you." Her hips swayed against his, feeling his hardened cock pressing into her. "I want to—"

"You're okay!"

Ashtyn snapped her head up to find Tristan and Norya tumbled out of the woods. Her nostrils flared. "You always have perfect timing!"

Tristan smirked. "Sorry. You're free to continue."

Ashtyn sat up, Gabriel coming up with her but not letting go where his hands held her waist. "Oh, shut up."

Norya smirked and held the front of her man's shirt, tugging him closer to her. "Come on, healer. You can suck the life out of your husband *after* you've healed those who need you."

"The plague?" She'd been so caught up with the Tree she'd forgotten all about that.

"Astreya, Colt, and Wells."

Ashtyn snapped up to her feet. If they were hurt, it was because they'd been coming after her.

Gabriel slowly rose after her, and she realized he was still hurt too.

"You first. What's wrong?" she snapped at him, annoyed he hadn't said something before.

He smirked, trailing his fingers down her face. "Just sore. I'm fine."

"You have cuts everywhere, Gabriel," she seethed.

He flicked her chin. "Minor things. I'm fine. *They* need you."

She searched his gaze for a moment and knew he wasn't lying. He never lied to her. They became one with marriage, and he always operated under that promise. Surprisingly, she realized staring into those eyes, she'd also never lied to him.

Gabriel's hand fell to the small of her back. "Let's go, wife. You can ravish me after."

She fought her grin and turned to follow the others.

It was a clear trail out. "What got you all looking such a mess?"

All three scoffed as Gabriel answered, "It wasn't this clear when we were coming for you. That Tree didn't want any of us getting near you."

That made sense. It took life, protected itself. It had been too infected to allow anyone else near it. Now the fields were clear around it as if it was welcoming everyone by.

"This walk is so different from before," Norya said. "Now, it's so inviting. Like we could come back anytime."

Tristan pulled at his shirt and rearranged his trousers. "I'm taking you back, Nor. We could have some fun in that field."

Both Gabriel and Ashtyn snorted and got narrowed gazes from the others. "What?" snapped the barbarianette.

Ashtyn smirked. "Didn't realize you two wanted kids already."

"We don't," Tristan muttered. "Not yet."

Gabriel smirked, but it was Ashtyn again who said, "Then be careful. That's the baby-making clearing."

They both rolled their eyes but there was wariness within them.

It sounded ludicrous but with the tension that filled the air around the walk, the need to go back and come over and over was strong.

When they cleared the walk, Ashtyn knew she hadn't been making up that feeling because a lightness entered them. And though she was still wet, she didn't feel the stifling need to jump Gabriel's bones any longer.

Both Tristan and Norya glanced at the path in shock.

Ashtyn smirked, passing them by for the tent she saw her entourage surrounding. "Told you."

They were both still focused on the path when Ashtyn and Gabriel made their way through the tent flaps.

All heads snapped toward them, and a breath of fresh air filled the room. Gian, especially, looked relieved, and Ashtyn knew he would kill her if she didn't go to Astreya first.

"You're back!" Colt, though injured, yelled. He and Wells were slumped back in chairs but didn't look too badly injured. Astreya, on the other hand, had blood seeping out of her mouth.

"We thought..." Belinda started. "Everyone around us began feeling better about two hours ago as if by magic. We thought..."

That something must've happened to her in order to heal them all collectively.

They'd been right, though she doubted anyone could've come up with what had taken place.

Ashtyn moved for Astreya's cot. "Something did happen. I'll tell you all later."

She internally smiled. Telling them felt like the natural thing to do, like one would their closest family and friends. It was astonishing that not only did Ashtyn find them to be confidants, but she hadn't thought about it for a moment. They were her friends. She had true friends.

She sat beside the injured magician, Caetana at her other side while Gian took the spot above Astreya's head, pushing her hair back. Astreya's hands were above her body, holding on to the guard as if his presence alone could heal her.

Caetana quickly brought her to date, "Belinda and I have done what we can but none of us hold strong healing power."

Ashtyn slowly nodded as her hands found the spot above Astreya's chest to look for the source of the problem.

She found it in the darkness and blood that was slowly filling the girl's lung from a puncture from a rib. Ashtyn slowly moved through the magician's body, taking the warmth from the girl's heart—no doubt so strong because of the man above her and her cousins around her—and brought it down, encouraging it to heal the source of the pain.

Warmth filled her, and Ashtyn was glad the magician was so filled with love. It made this so much easier to complete. The woman would be sore for a few days, but she'd be alive.

It must've taken ten minutes, maybe more, but Ashtyn never wavered, slowly encouraging the wound to heal. It breathed a sigh of thanks to her when it was completed, and her lips tipped up into a small grin. She'd always taken for granted these conversations only she could have with life. No longer.

"There." Ashtyn sat back.

Astreya coughed and no blood came. Her color was already coming back as Caetana wiped a wet rag over her face to get rid of the blood.

Ashtyn moved to Colt and Wells's side as she watched the magician. She slowly got up on the cot and turned to her guard.

Gian's hands shook as they held her face. "You're okay."

She moved until she was in his lap and nodded.

"Promise?"

"I promise. You've got me."

Gian breathed a sigh of relief and brought her in for a tight embrace, eyes snapped tight before he blinked them open with water lining them. He met Ashtyn's gaze and there was nothing but thanks there.

Ashtyn nodded. She never needed their thanks. This was what life was about.

She turned for the men and caught Gabriel's gaze. He stood off to the side, allowing her to work, and there was such pride in his look. So much love, it almost knocked the wind out of her.

Ashtyn squatted beside the men, starting with Wells since he looked to be in more pain. "You guys tell me what happened first."

THE RIDE back to the palace was filled with laughter and love, and for once, Ashtyn felt that she belonged, that she deserved all that surrounded her.

They stopped at every village and town they passed in order to check on the sick, but every one of them was getting better by the day. Ashtyn smiled to herself knowing it was because the Tree was no longer hurting. The poor thing. She would go see it again, and not only because she wanted to keep her little promise of riding her husband until—

"Sparrow, my love, this pregnancy must have affected my sight for that cannot be a smile on our healer's face, can it?" Evony's teasing remark made Ashtyn turn from Bella.

The other members of the Posse were there, likely to welcome Tristan and Norya back while eager to find out all that had happened.

Sparrow held his wife from behind, his large hands on her rounded belly. "Gabriel, did you drug her?"

Everyone laughed, Ashtyn alongside them.

Then James smirked, holding Gemma the way the Assassin held the Magician, his hands wrapped around her larger belly. "I can wager a guess as to what the drug was. Let me see. Is it a whitish liquid, possibly coming from a shaft attached to a stable ha—"

Gemma's giggling as she elbowed him made him start biting down her neck.

Ashtyn felt more than just her cheeks turn bright red at the insinuation which Norya did not make better as she scoffed. "Based on what we heard from their room after everything was taken care of, I'd say you're on the right track. Lots and lots of drugs."

Luckily, Ashtyn wasn't the only pink one there. Though the conversation was about her, Etel and Emerald also turned a bright pink, their husband's eyes twinkling like they were about to turn the teasing on them.

Ashtyn cleared her throat. "If you don't mind, I'd like to check on something in the infirmary before meeting with you. Enjoy your conversation on... drugs."

Everyone laughed as Ashtyn walked away, but as she passed Astreya, she couldn't help hearing her turn to Gian with a pout. "Can you give me lots and lots of drugs, please?"

Ashtyn quickened her pace. She wasn't normally one to shy away from sexual conversation much, but she couldn't handle it all revolving around her. All of that attention. And on her sex life! She was a Northerner, after all.

She had no real business in the infirmary. She'd merely missed the space.

Stepping into the large room, everything looked the same.

The beds and small tables and supplies were all in the same spots. Even her makeshift office was left alone.

Ashtyn smiled brightly, taking a deep breath of the antiseptic and clean materials. The fresh, cold air outside was obviously much better for her, but this was her work—healing people. Though the other medics were a pain, she'd missed being in this room daily.

As Ashtyn slowly walked to her office and looked out the window, everything settled for her. She was in her office in the infirmary where she worked to help those who needed her, and out of this window, she could see her cottage.

She was busy with thoughts of what Gabriel would do to her in their cottage that night as she stared out the window when a voice said, "I don't think I've ever seen you smile."

Ashtyn turned to find Old Lady Arba standing at the curtains that made a makeshift door to her office. "That's because I never really had reason to before."

Arba awkwardly looked around the room, gaze jumping from the desk to the single bed to the window Ashtyn looked out of before settling on the healer. "You have been here nearly two years."

"I have."

"And in those two years, I never saw you work as you had in that village."

Sadness filled Ashtyn's chest. "You have. You just ignored it because it wasn't to such a large extent."

Arba nodded. "Maybe you're right. I'd been... harsh because of my fears. I should've trusted our Assassin would only bring someone worthy to take such a position."

Trusted in the Assassin and not in Ashtyn's shown ability. It was something to scoff over, but Ashtyn understood. Arba had a negative past with unschooled medics and a positive past with Sparrow's decision-making.

So Ashtyn only nodded.

"Beautiful?" The call came from the front of the infirmary.

Arba's eyes twinkled as a slight smile Ashtyn had never seen directed at her rose on her lips. "I believe your husband is here."

She walked away as Gabriel came to view, his brows shot up as he pushed the curtain mostly closed. "Was Arba being kind? It's far too early for her to already be angry with you."

Ashtyn chuckled. "Kind enough, yes. Hopefully she'll be better now. I don't need a friend in her, but respect."

Gabriel stopped before her, cradling her face with one hand as his thumb grazed her cheek. "I think so. You were extraordinary, and she saw it."

Ashtyn turned to kiss his palm softly. "Was there something you needed?"

He tsked. "Just to be around you."

"Are the others still speaking of drugs?"

Gabriel smirked. "Most of them went off to get *drugs* for themselves."

Ashtyn's cheeks pinked as her forehead fell into his chest. "Why am I turning pink? This is ridiculous."

He laughed, hand falling into her hair and tugging her to look up. "You're Northern." He leaned down to kiss her, then stepped back. "I made you something."

Her brows shot up. "Oh?"

He presented her with the piece of wood she'd seen him carving throughout their journey. "This has been for me?"

He nodded slowly, analyzing her.

It was a hare made of pine tree, so detailed and beautiful as it rested in her hands. It looks to be stretched out, eyes half closed as if in blissful dreams.

Ashtyn was still looking it over when Arba came back and swung the curtain open. "By the way, Ashtyn. No frolicking in the office. These walls will hide *nothing*." As she spoke, her eyes fell onto the piece in her hands.

"Wasn't planning on it. I realize the state of my walls."

Arba's brow flicked up, a glimmer with her eyes, as she glanced at the woodworking, then between them. "Sure."

She left, closing the curtain completely.

Ashtyn's brows furrowed, glancing back at her husband. "Gabriel?"

"Yes, beautiful?" He was leaning on her desk, hands in his pockets, and sexy as ever with that small smirk on his features.

"What does this symbolize?"

"What makes you think it symbolizes anything?"

"Gabriel!"

He chuckled, gripping the sides of her dress and bringing her between his legs. "Pine trees are a relic of fertility. As is the hare."

Her eyes widened. "Fertility! Gabriel, you said you didn't want kids immediately?"

"I hadn't."

"Then why start carving this long before the clearing at the Tree?"

He shrugged, eyes still alight with mirth. "So it was ready for us."

"Gabriel, even had you not given it to me. Being in our home would've put its energies to use."

He smirked, bringing her in closer. "Then it's a good thing we want kids, huh?"

She shook her head, falling deeper into him. "I still hate you most of the time."

He kissed her chastely. "I love that you said our home."

She scoffed. "Depending on how well this works, we may need a bigger one."

His head fell back with a laugh. "I can add to our cottage, beautiful."

"Good." She played with his hair as their eyes met. "Because I love our cottage."

"And I love you."

He kissed her again as if holding a promise between them.

# CHAPTER 37

# GABRIEL

A small celebration was in order. They had so much to celebrate. The winter solstice. All the marriages that happened in the year. The babies coming soon. The quelled rebellion. The movement for magicians to be allowed back into the Northern Lands. The possibility of a future with the Island Nation because of the barbarians now in the Posse. The end of this plague. But especially—the King's betrothal.

Out of all there was, that was the shocking one. The whole of the palace would've expected every and anything to happen before King Edmund ever married again, especially for love.

This gathering was an intimate one, only for those close to the Posse, but the next night, they would hold a palace-wide celebration.

Today, they all adorned beautiful wear as they slowly gathered in the dining hall where more seating had been added for those not normally dining with the Posse—including himself and his wife, Papa Ignatius, Papa Iskan, and Mama Beni. The nonas too, who only dined with the Posse when they wanted to, were to join them.

Most of them were already in the grand hall, standing about softly speaking with one another as gazes continued falling on the King in his chair at the end of the table with his future queen on his lap.

Gabriel smirked to himself, and Ashtyn's fingers swiped at his lips. "What?"

"Like father, like daughter." He nodded for the table. "Evony always moves for Sparrow's lap, and it seems Atiana is not allowed to get off of the King's lap."

Ashtyn giggled. "I'm sure they have a ton in common that they haven't figured out yet themselves."

Gabriel leaned in to kiss his wife as the doors opened, and a red-faced Princess Rosaelia walked in with her husband smirking behind her.

Evony, who unsurprisingly was seated in her husband's lap, smirked. "Who did you walk in on doing it now?"

The Princess took her seat without lifting her eyes off the ground. Killian grinned wide now. "The guard and the magician."

"Gian and Astreya?" Norya asked.

Killian gave a single nod, and everyone laughed as Rosaelia turned a brighter shade of red.

"My, my, twin. You just cannot help yourself, can you?"

Rosaelia's head snapped up. "I do not do it on purpose!"

Killian's hand caressed his wife's hair as he smirked at her, then rolled his eyes to the others. "They weren't screaming, but they weren't exactly quiet either."

"And you allowed her to walk in?" Edmund glared.

Killian smirked. "Who am I to deter my wife?"

Rosaelia smacked his arm, face still burning. He only laughed and brought her into his side to hold while kissing her crown. "Don't worry. I'll stop you when you make your way to walk in on your father and his queen."

Everyone laughed as Rosaelia sank into her husband's side, burying her face in his shirt. Edmund was a shade of pink and Atiana blushed with all that attention on her sex life, but they enjoyed the jabs at the Princess with the rest of them.

Gabriel had never had a family before the South and hadn't truly had one since leaving Lanlik and the others, but this felt like a family. This was a room filled with people who loved one another and were able to show it through the teases they threw about. It was only a matter of time before one of the Posse turned to say something about Gabriel's own wife, which undoubtedly would come at his expense.

"Everyone sit already," Tristan called. "I'm starved."

Scoffs came from all around, but it was Miels who voiced what everyone was thinking. "With the way you two go at it, I'm surprised you're able to survive with only a few meals a day."

Tristan smirked as his hand fell into Norya's lap, but he didn't say anything as everyone joined the table. The Posse had their seats, but there were chairs thrown in between for the rest of them. Gabriel pulled Ashtyn's seat across from Etel and placed himself across Miels.

Gabriel's gaze fell to the hand the King had on Atiana's stomach. He wasn't sure what came over him because he normally didn't speak so bluntly with the Posse, and especially this many of them around, but his eyes shot to meet Atiana's as he asked, "Already pregnant?"

Her cheeks turned a bright pink, trailing down the rest of her exposed skin as every set of eyes turned to them. "No." She pushed his hand away as if that would divert attention.

Edmund chuckled, deep and in love, as he pulled her in tighter, hand finding its way back, as he bit the side of her neck. "Soon."

The whole of the table chuckled at her burning skin, and

Gabriel was pulled from the table's jokes when a hand settled over his forearm. When he turned for his wife, her eyes were shimmering.

"If you ever embarrass me like that, I'll kill you."

Gabriel chuckled, leaning in to kiss her plump lips. "When I get you pregnant, I'm going to do everything in my power to turn you that shade of red."

Her brows furrowed. "I'll kill you."

"And leave our child without a father?"

Her nostrils flared, and it was the most adorable thing Gabriel had ever seen. When he leaned in to kiss her, he heard her mutter, "Thank the lords I'm not pregnant yet."

He kissed her cheek. "No. Not yet, beautiful. I just got you. I want to be selfish with you for a while before we bring more of us into the world."

She did blush now, light and lovely. "I want to be selfish with you too, Gabriel. Though your little woodworking gift may not allow that."

Gabriel's lips skimmed hers. "I've already hidden that out of our cottage. I'll bring it back in a couple of months."

Her eyes narrowed. "I don't think that takes away from its power."

He quirked a brow. "Then its power would've already worked on us. I had it in my bags while we were together all over the North."

"Fuck. Then let's hope it really will hold its power until we put it in our cottage."

Gabriel chuckled as he cradled her face, completely erasing everyone around them. "You know, wife, I think you still owe me. For those horse lessons. I think I can come up with a few things I wish for."

Her eyes sparked, and Gabriel knew he'd never grow tired of his beautiful little asshole.

# EPILOGUE

## ASHTYN

She'd been the one to insist on honeymooning in the Southern Lands. Gabriel lived too much of his life trying to please her, and she'd known the one thing she could do for him was to take him back to the only other family he'd ever known.

They were to be away from the palace for three weeks, so the Posse had agreed to be extra careful with themselves as Ashtyn would not be around for the quick heals. Though now they had the Cousins to help in any magical ways that "were too much" for Sparrow to allow Evony to do, not that any of them were any good at healing.

They'd made quick work of the journey down and would do the same thing on the way back, so they could spend as much of those three weeks with Lanlik and her family as possible.

And still, in the few days it took for them to make it down, Gabriel took care of her in every way possible. He teased her and brushed her hair, listened to her and taught her how to hold the knife for his woodworkings, held her and fucked her.

She wasn't entirely happy about having to share him while they were down here.

Gabriel got down from the horse they'd been sharing—solely so they could fondle one another during the day—and held out his hand for her to join him.

"What're we doing?" she asked as she hopped down.

"Resting for the night."

Ashtyn narrowed her eyes, the sunlight of the day still beaming down at them. "We're only a few more miles out, Gabriel."

"I know, beautiful." He stepped closer, cradling her face in both of his hands and blocking the winds from assaulting her. "But this is our honeymoon, and I want to be selfish with you one more day before we're surrounded."

She smirked. "How naughty, horse boy."

He bit his bottom lip, and Ashtyn nearly came just watching him doing it. "Well, when you refuse to wear trousers so I can stick my hand in them while we ride, I must resort."

She snorted. "Animal."

He winked, pulling her with him as he stopped to speak with the stables, then with the innkeeper. Ashtyn didn't pay attention to the conversations. How could she be when he'd taken his thick winter jacket off, and she could see the strains of his muscles through his white shirt.

She didn't realize everything was all set until Gabriel dropped her hand to take their bags from the stable hand who'd brought them in. He guided her with a hand to the back to a room at the top of the inn where there sat a bathtub at the corner of the room. No screens, no hiding. Everything they did here, they'd be able to watch one another.

As Gabriel closed the door and dropped their bags before it, Ashtyn turned excitedly. "Can I watch you pleasure yourself?"

His brows quirked up. "Excuse me?"

"You've seen me do it. Multiple times. I want to watch you!"

He smirked. "Do I get to watch you in turn?"

She thought about it. She wanted to say no, but she already knew she'd grow too wet with what she saw and start doing so anyway. "If you put on a good show. Then maybe I'll let you fuck me too."

He snorted as he kicked off his shoes and thrust off his shirt. "Beautiful, I plan on being inside you the majority of this night."

Ashtyn bit her bottom lip to stop the wide grin and pulled at her dress. In no time, she was naked and relaxed back on the bed.

"Why do you get the bed?" Gabriel smirked as his hands smoothed over his chest.

The movement made her eyes follow them, her mouth watering as she said, "Because you're a gentleman." She followed his hands to the tops of his trousers where they skimmed before finally peeling them off.

"And you're meant to be a lady?"

"Of course."

His trousers fell and his hand gripped the base of his shaft. "Beautiful, ladies don't ogle at cocks."

Her eyes snapped up. "I was not ogling."

"You're drooling."

Her hand snapped up as her eyes narrowed at his glimmering look, but she was shocked to find he hadn't been joking. She *was* drooling. Fuck, she couldn't help it. His cock tasted too good to have to stay away from.

As he slowly pumped his cock, tightening at the tip with a flick of his wrist that made him grunt that beautiful sound that took her to the edge, Ashtyn decided to play with him too.

She took the drool from her chin and used it to play with her nipples. "Maybe I am. But my nipples need some saliva and since you're all"—she tweaked her nipples—"the way"—she spread her legs—"over"—slipped one hand slowly down her stomach—"there"—she spread her lips for him—"apparently I have to do it."

He growled but didn't step closer. "Yes, beautiful. Do it. Play with yourself. Make me come. Come on, baby. Be a good girl and make me come."

Her head fell back at the praise as she started circling her clit, her eyes glued to his cock the whole time.

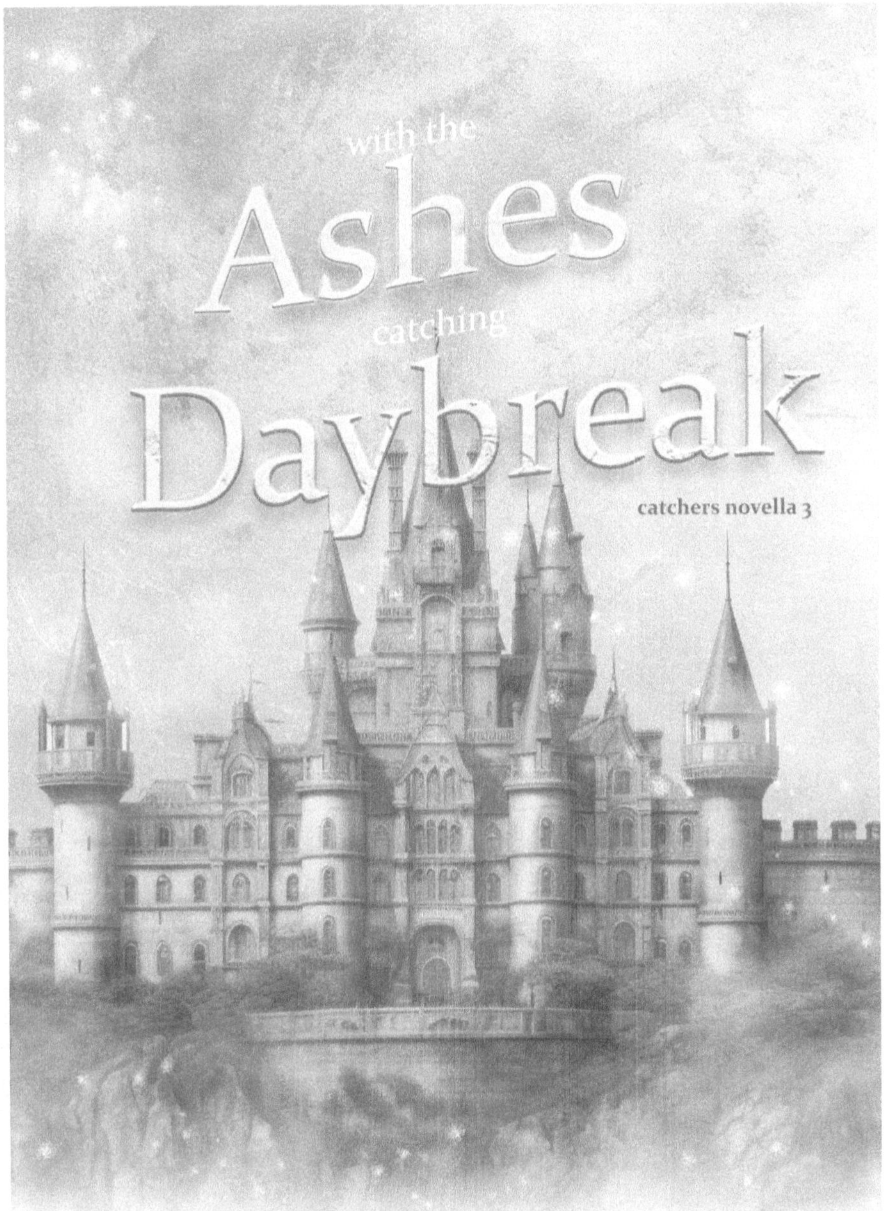

with the
Ashes
catching
Daybreak
catchers novella 3
NELLY ALIKYAN

# WITH THE ASHES CATCHING DAYBREAK

## ATIANA

The audacity of that man. Sure, he ran the nation, but to think he would obligate Ashtyn, who was frankly doing him a favor by healing people from this plague, to marry.

King Edmund was a fair man, one who understood and took accountability for his past mistakes, now trying to right them. He looked over all the members of the Posse like they were all his children and never threatened any of the servants when they inevitably did part of their job incorrectly. If at times he seemed cruel, it was simply to keep things in line, never because he wanted to hurt another. He was just.

But to think he would force her to marry!

Atiana's eyes narrowed to such slits. All she saw was Edmund on his horse, flashes of his sword swiping in. Nothing else. Not Gabriel on the other horse, the trees in the background, or the beauty of Absko as he worked with the King to win their duel.

Then Edmund stumbled and his head shot to her. His eyes were wide after landing on her like he couldn't fathom what he'd done wrong. The look almost shocked Atiana out of her anger—why would the King care if she was angry with him? Though a just man, he never paid particular interest to the petty problems the servants may have with him.

His brows furrowed, then he shook himself back into the training with Gabriel.

Atiana shook her head. If only she had the courage his daughters—which she'd just learned was the case when Princess Rosaelia said she trusted Atiana too much to keep Evony's blood from her—had to be so bold as to confront him about it.

"No." Ashtyn broke her out of her thoughts, reminding Atiana that they'd been speaking of her. "Not at all. They simply let me know that it will be the easier course to keep the men away. Everything, even showing my abilities to help with the plague, has been left to my decision."

Atiana sighed, her gaze softening on the man. That was the man she knew Edmund to be. "Well, we all know you will help them, so the question is—will you choose a husband?"

"I cannot imagine marrying anyone."

Atiana barely stopped herself from scoffing, wanting to show the serenity that allowed her friends to feel comfortable speaking to her about things they didn't tell others. So she quirked a brow instead. "No?"

"What's the supposed to mean? I just said no."

When was the poor girl going to stop fighting her attraction? "Ashtyn, be true to yourself."

"Wha—"

"Gabriel," Atiana interrupted.

It wasn't surprising to get an eye roll from the healer. "Do not worry about any relationship with Gabriel. We are... cordial. You are free to pursue him as you wish."

Atiana's eyes bugged out of her face as she coughed the

shock away. "Are you out of your mind?" What could have possibly sent her to such ludicrous conclusions?

"Excuse m—"

"Why would I ever want Gabriel?"

"You are the one watching him. I've seen you two together."

Sadness passed through her. "Trust me. I have no interest in Gabriel. To me, he truly is a friend. To you, however, things are quite different. Everyone here knows you two are spoken for. Why else do you think none of the men have come for you, other than because of your charming personality?"

"Then why are you—" Ashtyn cut herself off as her gaze landed back on the men.

Atiana fought off her blush. What did it matter if the healer realized her outrageous feelings for the King? The girl hated everyone at the palace. She surely wasn't going to add to the gossip mills. Not that Atiana much cared if she were added to the mills.

Then Ashtyn rolled her eyes in Atiana's direction. "Oh, you're so cliché."

"Me?" Atiana exclaimed. "Gabriel is the charming, sweet stablehand. It doesn't get more cliché than falling for him."

"It doesn't get more cliché than falling for the King? Really? That's your argument?"

Atiana's cheeks pinked now, then even more so as she realized the men were coming off their horses and approaching them. "Shut up," she hissed.

"Atiana," Gabriel called right on time to stop his healer from saying anything more. "Do not be angry with me. The big thing passing off as a horse ripped the shirt, I didn't!"

Atiana laughed as her gaze traveled from Gabriel over Edmund to Absko. The King's horse was her favorite, and she felt a little thrill when the horse nayed in her direction. "Hey! Don't be mean to Absko. He's a sweetheart."

Gabriel scoffed. "You only say that because he likes you. You and Ed. That's it."

As Atiana's cheeks pinked a little more at hearing anything between her and *Ed*, Ashtyn muttered under her breath, "Yeah because he knows who his owners are."

Atiana slammed her elbow into the healer before she said anything more, anything louder. "I think he can tell you have singled him out of all the horses as the one you do not like. You cannot treat poor Absko like that!"

She looked back at the horse, wanting to step up to him and pet his mane, but refraining because of the King's proximity. Then her gaze subconsciously landed on said King.

He was so handsome, even with the hard look he wore around her. It was affirming enough to know he didn't treat any of the help particularly friendly, but it stung to constantly get such a cold stare when all she'd wanted for nearly seven years was one of those stunning smiles he kept exclusively for his Posse.

"I have not singled anyone out," Gabriel exclaimed, thankfully breaking Atiana's stare. "He singled himself out by being mean to everyone but you two."

When Atiana's gaze landed on him, his smile was so infectious, she couldn't help but return it.

"I'm sure he'll treat you well enough when you're feeding him too many treats," the King finally said, his voice brooding, sending shivers straight down Atiana's spine. "I should be heading inside."

He passed the reins to Gabriel right as Ashtyn exclaimed, "Perfect!" Then as the King walked toward them to get to the palace, Ashtyn quickly placed Atiana's hand in the crook of his elbow. "Atiana was just saying she needed to get back to work. Why don't you walk her to her suite?"

Atiana swallowed, frozen in the moment. She was touching him. Yes, it was over his finely-sourced jacket that Odolf had made, but she'd never touched him.

It only took a couple seconds to snap herself out of the shock as her gaze jumped up to me, the cold dark orbs of the King, and she began to pull her hand away. She wasn't a violent woman, but Ashtyn might be made the exception.

Then the unexpected happened, and the King tucked his arm into his side so her hand was stuck there. "Very well."

His voice was soothing and tempting all at once, almost like he was making a promise with his words. Or maybe breaking a promise.

Atiana didn't get the chance to respond as Edmund turned them for the palace. Her free hand at her side jittered. It was the only source of release for all the nerves racing through her body.

She felt the gazes of everyone as they moved through the greens, into the palace, and toward the tailor's wing where her suite was. She didn't care. They could talk all they'd like. Those would be true rumors for the gossip mills, ones that held no merit as the King hadn't spoken a word to her the entire time. Those rumors would be based on no facts. Though even if rumors based on fact spread, she wouldn't care as long as they were reciprocated ones.

Her hand was at the crook of his elbow but she felt the muscle of his bicep still. It was solid. His side, where her hand was tucked into, was also solid. She imagined all of him was solid. Unsurprisingly considering he trained with his men daily.

Her periphery took in his profile. He didn't wear his emotions on his sleeve, a positive for a king, but obstructive to her goals of reading him a little. From what she could tell though, he looked angry. His eyes were as cold as ever, and she swore there was a grimace about his lips.

She swallowed the shot of rejection that rushed through her limbs and blinked rapidly to lose any wateriness that presented itself. There was no reason to assume his disapproval was to do with her, but she couldn't help remembering any moment between them, all of the small rejections of her. How his lips would thin every time she offered to do his tailoring.

They were nearly at her suite, the corridors in the tailor's wing empty as most were off doing other things at this hour. Atiana made herself keep her focus on her door only a few yards out, knowing this was close to ending. She didn't want it to, it was her only chance to ever touch him, but she needed to be away from him before the sting of his disgust with her stung any deeper.

They stopped in front of her door and as she tugged on her hand, he didn't release it. His arm was tucked so tightly into his body, she couldn't move.

"Your Highness," she whispered as that was all the energy she could put into the words and tugged on her hand once more, her other hand on the handle to her door.

His dark orbs caught hers and he held her stare, almost like he was challenging her. When her brows furrowed, he finally released her.

She swallowed as she slowly removed her hand from his arm and turned her back on him. When she entered her room, door safely closed, she rested her back on it. Her eyes watered, but she didn't have tears. It was difficult to have tears because tears meant a hope was broken. She'd never had any hope of his feelings for her being favorable.

She took a large breath in, and as she pushed off her door, a hard knock slammed into it.

Her brows furrowed as she opened it to find the King on the other side. "Your Highness?"

He rushed inside, slamming the door behind him as his hands cradled her face, breath hitting her face. "Don't call me that, Atiana. Please."

His lips crashed into hers before she could make out what was happening.

***Continue the story in
With the Ashes Catching Daybreak...***

# DON'T FORGET TO REVIEW!

Thank you so much for finishing your read! Don't forget to leave a review or rating on all platforms as it helps me as an author more than you can ever imagine!

Amazon and Goodreads ratings help the most but feel free to talk about it everywhere else too—including social medias, blogs, Youtube reviews, and most importantly—word of mouth, and more.

# FOLLOW NELLY'S SOCIAL MEDIA

Follow Nelly's social media to get the scoop as it's happening!

- tiktok.com/authornellyalikyan
- instagram.com/authornellyalikyan
- youtube.com/NellyAlikyan
- amazon.com/author/nellyalikyan
- goodreads.com/nellyalikyan
- facebook.com/authornellyalikyan
- pinterest.com/insinpublishing

# JOIN NELLY'S NEWSLETTER

Sign up for Nelly Alikyan's newsletter to be the first to know about new releases and cover reveals, receive exclusive content —like a special scene or two—and be up to date about any other exciting news, i.e. events, signed copies, etc.

www.nellyalikyan.com

# ACKNOWLEDGMENTS

We're coming to the end of the Catchers world. This story is a softer one based around healing within more than any sword and sorcery type fighting. I think this is one of those books where people find therapy in a way because it is about finding oneself, both on your own and with a partner, a single loving monogamous couple.

I always thank everyone in my life, from my family to all those who give these books a chance. And especially to those ready, I hope you enjoyed!

It's kinda sad to be coming to the end, but we do still have one more novella left with all these guys before we put this world away. I hope the stories helped make your days better!

# MEET THE AUTHOR

Nelly Alikyan is a girl from the Los Angeles Valley who's constantly on the move—from Boston to London to wherever she chooses next. She's the only reader in her family—not her only cause as the black sheep—and has dreamt of being a writer for as long as she can remember.

For more books and updates:
www.nellyalikyan.com